PRAISE FOR BARBARA DELINSKY . . .

"Delinsky is a first-rate storyteller who creates believable, sympathetic characters who seem as familiar as your neighbors." —*Boston Globe*

"Delinsky combines her understanding of human nature with absorbing, unpredictable storytelling—a winning combination." —*Publishers Weekly* (starred review)

"Delinsky has a knack for exploring the battlefields of contemporary life." —*Kirkus Reviews*

"Delinsky does a wonderful and realistic job portraying family dynamics." —*Library Journal*

"A writer who continues to earn her bestseller status." —Bookreporter.com

"Delinsky never fails to entertain." —*RT Book Reviews*

. . . AND HER BESTSELLING NOVELS

ESCAPE

"Great summer read." —*People*

"Delinsky nails it in her trademark latest, a captivating and moving story about a woman who's had enough of her life and wants a fresh start. . . . [She] keeps the story moving with some nice twists on a familiar plot, rich characterizations, and real-feeling dilemmas that will keep readers hooked." —*Publishers Weekly*

"Another appealing page-turner." —Bookreporter.com

NOT MY DAUGHTER

"A topical tale that resonates with timeless emotion."
—*People*, 3½ stars

"Delinsky proves once again why she's a perennial bestseller with this thought-provoking tale . . . Timely, fresh, and true-to-life." —*Publishers Weekly*

"Emotionally intelligent . . . Mother-daughter bonding, knitting, and a ripped-from-the-headlines plot from Delinsky offer her fans what they want—high drama and realism." —*Kirkus Reviews*

WHILE MY SISTER SLEEPS

"Graced by characters readers will come to care about, this is that rare book that deserves to have the phrase 'impossible to put down' attached to it. Delinsky does a wonderful and realistic job portraying family dynamics; the relationship between Molly and Robin, in particular, is spot-on. This touching and heartbreaking novel is highly recommended." —*Library Journal*

THE SECRET BETWEEN US

"Barbara Delinsky can be counted on to deliver straight-forwardly written, insightful stories about family relation-ships. Her new novel, *The Secret Between Us*, is one of her best." —*Boston Globe*

"Relationships are brought to the limit in Delinsky's splendid latest exploration of family dynamics."
—*Publishers Weekly* (starred review)

"[A] page-turner . . . In addition to being immensely readable, Delinsky's latest is thought-provoking; readers will inevitably pause to consider what they would do . . . Highly recommended."
—*Library Journal*

"A polished drama . . . Delinsky does a fine job creating sympathetic characters with personal problems . . . Well-crafted and satisfying."
—*Kirkus Reviews*

FAMILY TREE

"In frank, unencumbered prose, Delinsky's sixth novel raises intriguing questions . . . making for engrossing reading."
—*People*

"An illuminating view of one family's search for the truth when their world turns upside down. The characters are vividly drawn with masterful detail in this one-of-a-kind book. As the author delves deep into a controversial and timely social issue, she exposes the societal hypocrisy and the ramifications of events that hit too close to home."
—*RT Book Reviews* (Top Pick)

AN ACCIDENTAL WOMAN

"Warm and charming . . . The multiple layers of interlocking characters and plotlines add up to one transfixing and thoroughly satisfying story."
—*RT Book Reviews*

Also by
Barbara Delinsky

love
songs

barbara delinsky

St. Martin's Paperbacks

This is a work of fiction. All of the characters, organizations, and events portrayed in this book are either products of the author's imagination or are used fictitiously.

Previously published separately as *Knightly Love* and *Sweet Serenity*.

LOVE SONGS

Copyright © 1982, 1983 by Barbara Delinsky.
Excerpt from *Sweet Salt Air* copyright © 2013 by Barbara Delinsky.

For information address St. Martin's Press, 175 Fifth Avenue, New York, NY 10010.

ISBN: 978-1-250-02532-6

Printed in the United States of America

St. Martin's Paperbacks edition / February 2013

St. Martin's Paperbacks are published by St. Martin's Press, 175 Fifth Avenue, New York, NY 10010.

10 9 8 7 6 5 4 3 2 1

Dear Reader,

I'm a woman with a past—namely, a group of novels that have been lost for nearly twenty years. I wrote them under pseudonyms at the start of my career, at which time they were published as romances. In the years since, my writing has changed, and these novels went into storage, but here they are now, and I'm thrilled. I loved reading romance; I loved *writing* romance. Rereading these books now, I see the germs of my current work in character development and plot. Being romances, they're also very steamy.

Initially, I had planned to edit each to align them with my current writing style, but a funny thing happened on the way to *that* goal. Totally engrossed, I read through each one, red pencil in hand, without making a mark! As a result, what you have here in this dual volume are the originals in their sweet, fun, sexy entirety.

The first of the two, *Up All Night,* takes place largely in a sleep clinic. Ever had insomnia? I haven't, though there are certainly times during the writing of a book when I toss and turn trying to decide what comes next. I wrote *Up All Night* in 1982, yet the problems of insomnia are paramount today. Rarely does a week pass without some mention of sleep problems in the paper or online. And sleep apnea? As disorders go, it's come into its own. A whole raft of studies are showing the positive effect a good night's sleep can have on the heart, the brain, and the spirit. Reflecting this, modern sleep clinics are very different from the one depicted in *Up All Night,* as are the treatments for sleep disorders. But . . . love? It's just the same, as sweet as ever.

Speaking of sweet, the second book in *Love Songs* is *Sweet Serenity*. Originally published in 1983, it was inspired by a candy store in my hometown. When I first walked into the store to buy gifts for my kids' teachers, I had never seen such unusual candies and went from bin to bin, intrigued. Before long, my imagination took over. After I showed the owner copies of several of my books, she graciously agreed to share her trade secrets; though, truth be told, I think she was as eager to be part of my project as she was terrified that I was a spy, planning to steal her ideas for a candy store of my own.

The store in my book is called, well, *Sweet Serenity*, and the heroine is serene indeed until she finds herself face to face with the reporter who ruined her family years before. Does the heroine recapture the happiness for which she'd fought so long and hard? Does a white chocolate Pretzel Joy melt in your mouth?

In *Up All Night* and *Sweet Serenity* you'll find two distinct love stories, one involving a nemesis from the past, the other a new acquaintance, but both involving women who are strong, resourceful, and desperately wanting the happily ever after that comes with true love.

Enjoy!

Barbara

up all night

1

The fiery embers of sunset blazed their reflection across the glass-fronted structure, joining Alanna Evans' own slender reflection as she crossed the parking lot of the medical center's newest wing and entered its lobby. Her honeyed head held high with confidence, she approached the elevator, pushed the up button, and waited.

After a day of nonstop business, she welcomed the moment's pause and breathed deeply to savor it. All sound was subdued in the quiet lobby. A faint hum of conversation trickled from the lounge to her right, the intermittent beeping of the hospital paging system echoed from the reception desk to her left, and the muted rustle of a passing white-garbed practitioner served to emphasize the stark immobility of the shiny doors before her.

She dropped her gaze to look through the lighter bottom of her tinted glasses to the deep blue carpet, against which her gray pumps looked properly subtle. Absently, she straightened the soft pleats of her skirt, adjusted its matching jacket, then shifted her overnight bag to rest the strap more comfortably on her shoulder. As the purr of the elevator signaled its approach, a man joined her silently, standing perfectly still. Her peripheral vision absorbed no more than his remarkably tall, dark-suited form before a gentle chime heralded the elevator's arrival. Seconds later, the door slid open.

Moving simultaneously, both prospective passengers stepped forward. Then each paused to let the other pass. When a chivalrous hand gestured her forward, Alana smoothly entered, pressed the button for her floor, then turned to stand with her back to the wall. The man followed, glancing briefly at the single number already lit on the command panel before stationing himself opposite her in a stance both casual and alert.

With a soft thud the door closed and they were alone. Drawn by an enigmatic impulse, Alana looked across to meet his gaze head-on. His back rested lightly against the wall, his hands thrust in the pants pockets of his finely tailored suit. He seemed a study in contrasts—white shirt against dark gray wool, brown hair flecked with gleaming gold highlights, broad shoulders tapering to lean and narrow hips. And he continued to stare at her.

While Alanna was an unusually attractive woman, well used to the admiring glances sent her way by men and women alike, this particular glance was different. Even the subtly defiant tilt of her chin could not discourage it. Charcoal eyes, deep and intense, studied her closely, evaluating her much as she had done him and remaining uncomfortably persistent. With a cool determination born of practice she broke the contact, raising her eyes to the horizontal panel above the doors. Two. Three. Four.

The elevator glided to a gentle stop. As soon as the doors rolled open she straightened her shoulders and stepped forward. Again his movement paralleled her own. Again she halted, but this time it was Alanna who gestured, with an indulgent dip of her head, for the man to precede her. With an imperceptible nod, he stepped ahead, but not before she noted the distinct twitch of amusement at his lips. Her eye followed his broad back as he disembarked, turned and disappeared through a set of swinging doors to be swallowed up by the long hospital corridor beyond. Only then did she breathe deeply once more, bolstering her composure to approach the nearby nurses' station.

She stood patiently for a moment, respectful of the urgent nature of hospital business and slightly disconcerted by her own upcoming role here. The white-capped head before her was downcast, lost in the deciphering of scrawled doctor's orders. Finally, as if with the sudden realization of Alanna's presence, the nurse looked up.

"May I help you?"

"Yes, please. I'm Alanna Evans. I'll be participating in the IAT study. I believe Dr. Henderson is expecting me?"

Recognition lit up the nurse's face, her broad smile mirroring the white of her uniform as she stood and extended a warm hand, which Alanna clasped readily. "Ms. Evans, welcome! I'm Sylvia Frazier, the night nurse heading the unit. We weren't quite sure just when you would arrive."

Reassured by the woman's friendliness, Alanna relaxed. "I wasn't quite sure myself. It's been a hectic day. Fortunately, I was able to escape from the office at seven." She glanced at the clock and noticed that it was barely seven-thirty; she had made good time.

"Then you haven't eaten?"

Alanna smiled ruefully. "No. But that's nothing new. I'd half hoped to be able to grab something in the cafeteria here, either before or after I spoke with Dr. Henderson. Is she free now?"

"I don't think so, dear." The older woman shook her head, then frowned. "I believe she may be with one of the other participants. Let me check."

Alanna's inner tension was betrayed only by the white

knuckles gripping the strap of her overnight bag. Determinedly, she relaxed her fingers. Looking slowly around,
she shuddered, for a fleeting moment recalling her past
hospital experience, the long, painful vigil at her mother's
bedside so many years ago. Mercifully, she herself had
never been sick, truly sick, a day in her life. Her present
problem was an annoyance more than anything else. A
grave annoyance. As a woman who prided herself on
self-command, she was frustrated.

Her attention snapped back to the present as Sylvia
Frazier returned. "It's as I suspected. She'll be tied up for
a little while. It's slow going at the start. Why don't you
go down and have a good supper?" Her eye skimmed the
slim figure before her with kind, almost maternal concern. "You could use several pounds, I'll warrant. But,"
she shrugged with a guilty grin, "perhaps that's just the
envy in me speaking. I've been at the other end of that
'ideal weight' chart for too long. Run along now. I've told
the doctor where you'll be. You can leave your bag here.
And enjoy your dinner." She emphasized the words, smiling knowingly.

Given the circumstances, and the fact that they would
be seeing quite a bit of each other, it was nice to know that
Sylvia Frazier had a sense of humor. Alanna laughed.
"That bad, eh?"

"Oh, not too bad . . . for institution fare. But it *is* institution fare."

"Any recommendations?" She arched a blond brow
mischievously.

The nurse's choice was instant and from the heart.
"Apple pie, à la mode." Then, catching herself, she
feigned sternness. "After a healthy helping of chicken or
fish, of course. Now, go!" Her gentle order was reinforced
by the shooing motion of her hands. Alanna went.

Five minutes later, seated alone at a corner table in the

sparsely filled cafeteria, she cast a plaintive glance at the junior sirloin before her. Had she really wanted it, or the fries and salad accompanying it? Or was she merely hoping for sustenance to help her through the night ahead?

Only after she took several perfunctory bites did she realize how hungry she was. When had lunch been? An eon ago. Or, to be precise, an executive board meeting, three separate conferences, two endless proposal forms and a dozen phone calls ago.

Slowly, as the meal before her disappeared, she began to unwind. It might have been a trying day, but it had been a good one. Hard work was an integral part of her approach to life. Alanna thrived on it. Her penetration into the elitist ranks of the male-dominated executive level at WallMar Enterprises had been—contrary to recent rumor—the result of long hours, persistence, innate ability and sheer hard work. Realism held taut rein over bitterness in her musings; despite all recent advances against sexism, a woman still had to work *twice* as hard to achieve a niche comparable to her male counterparts in the corporate structure. But, it was worth it. As Vice-President of Development her days were challenging and rewarding, petty aggravations and innuendo notwithstanding. Why, then, her present dilemma?

Insomnia. Millions of Americans suffered from it, yet that fact held small solace when, in the middle of the night, she awoke to find sleep an elusive quality. The pattern was always the same. For no apparent reason her sound sleep would be shattered at one, perhaps two, in the morning. Tossing in bed, she would think, wonder, brood, awaiting the imminent slumber that grew less imminent with each passing moment. For the longer the wakefulness persisted—and it frequently lasted for two or three hours—the more annoyed she became, keying herself up in a way that denied sleep even further.

It was a self-perpetuating nuisance. And Alanna Evans was not one to suffer nuisances willingly, particularly one that rendered her groggy and irritable at seven o'clock each morning, when her alarm rang. Granted, her good nature was usually in order by the time WallMar saw her at eight-thirty, but as the day wore on it became harder and harder to maintain. A steady year of tension and exhaustion was enough; she had finally taken the offensive. Hence the IAT study.

Recalling her immediate purpose, Alanna sat back in her seat, nibbling on a thick steak fry as her eye skimmed the room. There was a scattering of hospital personnel in small clusters here and there and a fair share of visitors. There was also—her teeth clamped down into the soft potato and held—a man walking directly toward her, his dark suit, exquisite physique and daring height identifying him instantly. Had they not, his charcoal eyes would certainly have done so, for they captured her gaze with the same glittering depth and intensity she had fallen victim to in the elevator, and they held unwaveringly as he moved with animal grace through the maze of tables to her corner.

Who was he? Alanna felt a twinge of familiarity, yet she couldn't quite make the identification. Nor did she have time to ponder it for, too soon, the man reached her side. In his hands he held two cups of a steaming brew she half suspected to be his own secret potion. Without even sipping it, she felt under an inexplicable spell.

"I see you haven't had coffee. Will you join me?" His voice was as smooth as the rest of him. Alanna was entranced by his aura of command, so much so that she hadn't moved a muscle since she'd first seen him approaching. Now, snapping back to life, she bit through the steak fry and chewed slowly, pensively, as she regained her poise. What was it about this man that was so compelling? Almost from instinct, with years of training behind her, she steeled herself against his charm.

"I'm sorry," she answered calmly, rising to his subtle challenge, "but I don't drink coffee in the evening. It disturbs my sleep." When she would have looked away in dismissal she found herself challenged anew. For the smugness of her refusal brought an equally cocky smile to the face across from her.

"Then I'm glad I ordered it decaffeinated. Cream? Sugar?" Her headshake was meant as a refusal of his company, but he chose to make a different interpretation and the black coffee was beside her plate before she could protest. Deftly, the man eased his long frame into the chair opposite hers. "It seems we share the problem. How was your dinner?"

With this stranger now firmly ensconced at her table it occurred to Alanna that she'd been given absolutely no say in the matter. "Not bad," she spoke evenly, eyeing the man through her tinted lenses. "I was enjoying the solitude. Time to oneself is a precious thing nowadays."

"And I've shattered it . . . ?" Silvery sparks of humor glittered in his eyes.

"Let's just say you . . . intruded on it." This man needed no ego reinforcement; that he could easily shatter the peace of mind of many a woman was a given. "Are you always this aggressive?"

"Not usually. Actually, I surprised myself right now. I, too, usually enjoy being alone when I have the chance . . . which isn't very often. Aggressive?" He frowned, seeming to consider the word. "Only when I want something badly enough."

"You want something?" she asked innocently. She looked around in a mocking search. "I don't see much that's available. Am I missing something?" Underlying her tone was a streak of amusement. Alanna relished good verbal sparring; this man had the potential to be a worthy opponent. Not to mention the fact that his voice was deep and resonant . . . and very pleasing. . . .

"I believe you are," he countered, "but it's not your fault. You had no reason to be on the lookout for it in as improbable a setting as this. In time you'll understand."

Alanna took refuge behind the rim of her coffee cup, sipping slowly as she studied the stranger. By all rights she should ask him to leave. In fact, it surprised her that she hadn't. She sensed something different in him—something she had felt in the elevator that was even more pronounced now. There was an arrogance about him—but a depth as well. He challenged her.

"What *do* you see?" he asked, surviving her scrutiny unscathed.

Alanna put down her cup, shifted in her seat, and cocked her head in contemplation. "I see a man, perhaps thirty-seven or thirty-eight—"

"Thirty-nine."

"Thank you. Thirty-nine." She stifled a grin. "Tall—oh, say six-three or so?"

"Close enough." He nodded, smiling faintly.

"Weight . . . I won't even make a guess, since I'm no expert at that and since it's quite unimportant." She narrowed her gaze, fully involved in the game. "Athletic build, however. I'd guess you either work out regularly or play tennis—"

"Handball."

"That'll do." She smiled sweetly, feeling immune to his charm as long as she could describe him dispassionately. "Classic features—no, more rugged than classic. Brown hair with sandy highlights," she continued, glancing at the overhead light responsible for the last, "a nose that has been broken at least once, firm lips that express a distinct stubbornness," she grinned as the items in question twitched, "and eyes of charcoal gray that can be even more eloquent than that very glib tongue."

"No offense intended, of course?"

"Of course," she agreed drily, taking another sip of her coffee.

"Go on." Truly enjoying himself, he sat back in his chair, the fabric of his shirt stretching enticingly across his chest.

Alanna ignored the latter with a shrug. "What more is there to say?" She wasn't about to sum him up as perhaps the most handsome man she had seen in years, though it was the truth.

"Use your imagination," came his soft command. "I'm curious to see how the female mind sizes up its adversary."

"Adversary," she echoed. "Very good." So, he knew how she saw him, did he? Well then, she decided, she would let her imagination roam free. "All right." She cleared her throat. "I see a man used to giving orders without having them questioned."

"Would you question them?"

"You bet your life I would!" she flashed back with more vehemence than she had intended. Quickly she caught herself, steadying her voice. "I like giving an order or two myself on occasion. But that's beside the point," she added, reluctant to offer much about herself. "And speaking of that shirt, it *and* your suit are of very high quality—private tailor, perhaps?"

"Europe."

Alanna nodded, as though it were the most normal thing in the world. "Europe. I'm sorry I questioned that." A slender finger pushed her oversized glasses higher on the bridge of her nose. "Then, of course, you must be quite successful at what you do . . . to be able to shop in Europe. . . ."

He nodded, more modest than she would have expected. "I've been fortunate."

On the subconscious level, his vague familiarity got to her. Tilting her blond head, she frowned. "Do I know you from somewhere?"

"You're great!" he laughed softly, sparring still. "Isn't that supposed to be *my* line?"

"Tradition, my dear sir," she replied unfazed, "is irrelevant in this day and age. Well . . . ?"

"Well what?"

"Look." She sat forward with a sigh of impatience. "I really don't make a habit of talking to strange men."

Any discomfort she felt was totally her own. This strange man was quite pleased. "I'm glad to hear that. One less thing for us to argue about."

Alanna leaned down to retrieve her purse. She had begun to feel her control of the situation slipping and she was disquieted. "Please, either identify yourself or I'll be on my way." She paused. "Actually, I do have an appointment in another few minutes. Every game has to come to an end and this one is beginning to wear thin." She paused, her cocoa gaze narrowing. "You walk around as though you own this place and everyone in it. It's a very subtle air—but very much present. Well, you don't own *me*. And I think you owe me the courtesy of an introduction."

His deep, charcoal eyes grew suddenly more serious, remaining as intense as ever. Formally extending his hand across the table, he introduced himself. "I'm Alexander Knight. Alex."

Alanna hesitated, yet somehow her slim hand found its way into his larger, stronger one, warmth spreading through her. Only after several moments did his identity sink in. And with the realization came a heightened flush of pink to her cream-soft cheeks. Her smile crept out unbidden. "So you *do* own the place—or practically. I understand that the new wing—the Knight Center—was your doing." Her hand remained in his. She was aware of the strength he exuded and found it strangely comforting.

"Only in part. My family made the original gift. The rest was the work of other donors and members of the hospital staff. They deserve most of the credit."

"Ah, such modesty," she chided, though her teasing was gentle, her voice soft. His smile was quite disarming—as was his touch. He continued to hold her hand, even faintly caress her fingers. Clearing her throat, she smiled. "My hand, please?"

He released it reluctantly, his eye falling to its partner with curiosity, even a certain tension. "No rings?"

"No."

"Husband?"

"No."

"Fiancé?"

"No." Her gaze now held his with confidence.

"Special guy?"

"No."

She didn't actually hear his sigh of relief when he paused, yet he chose his words with care. "Any particular reason? I mean, you *are* striking enough . . ."

She overlooked his compliment in the urgency of expressing her deepest feeling. "I'm unattached because I choose to be so. It's as simple as that . . . and as irrevocable." The last was added in warning; it had always been quite effective in the past. Now, however, it merely elicited a broad white grin from amid his tanned features.

"I'll enjoy seeing you eat those words one day."

"I doubt it." She was equally as calm and composed. "But," her pause was punctuated with a frown, "I'm curious as to why you seem so sure of that. You don't know anything about me."

"Well, then, we'll just have to do something about that, particularly since you're going to be my wife one day. . . ."

If he had expected an outburst of disbelief or indignation, even fury, he did, indeed, have much to learn about Alanna Evans. She was given to neither, particularly on a subject about which she felt so sure of herself. Her laugh was light and airy, as though it had flitted off the wings of a butterfly on a warm spring day.

"I may have a name for the face, now, Alex," she said melodiously, "but you're still *strange!* Whatever would put such a bizarre thought in your mind?"

"There's nothing at all bizarre about it," he returned, equally as good-humored, yet oddly sober. "You *will* marry me."

Again she laughed. "I've never heard anything so improbable! I don't know you, nor you me. You've never laid eyes on me before now. Besides, you happen to be talking to a confirmed bachelor-ess!"

"Even the most confirmed of bachelors can change." His dark gaze broke through her veneer of humor with its raw intensity. "I have."

"On a moment's notice?" Incredulity replaced amusement, covering up a more significant emotional spark.

"Not just a moment's notice." He spoke with a velvet tongue and frightening conviction. "I've had years to ponder who and what I want. I've never even caught sight of it . . . until now. And now that it's finally appeared I have no intention of letting it slip through my fingers."

"*It?* You sound as though you're referring to a business deal. If that's the case, this is one business that's not on the market."

"Perhaps not on the *open* market," he persisted softly, "but available, to say the least. It may just take you awhile to acknowledge it."

"You're incredible!" Her eyes widened. "You don't even know my name!"

"Ah-ah," he chided, "never underestimate the opposition. Your name is Alanna Evans . . . soon to be Knight."

For the first time Alanna felt threatened. If he had seemed less sure of himself, less arrogant, she might have taken it all as a joke. But this man was no crank if his reputation, or his family's, was worth anything. She was usually able to keep on top of things, yet the fact of hearing her name from Alex Knight's tongue was upsetting. Or, she wondered fleetingly, was it in the warm inflection that his tongue gave to it . . . ?

"How did you know that?" she asked, fighting for composure.

"Sylvia Frazier is a friend. And there aren't too many blond-haired beauties with owl-eyes who drop by the clinic at this hour." He paused, savoring the brief unsureness in her expression before directing his attention to her face. "Do you always hide behind them?"

Alanna frowned in puzzlement. "Behind what?"

"Those glasses. They're very large and, there at the top, the part through which you're glaring at me now, very dark. They must be convenient for hiding your emotions from the world. Are you frightened of what the world might see?"

To her chagrin, dark lenses notwithstanding, Alanna realized that she was glaring. Quickly she forced a smile. It was part of the game, she mused, meeting the challenge with a steady hand that reached up, slowly, toward the tortoiseshell frames. Smiling now in gentle defiance, she removed the glasses to reveal large eyes of a deep, soft brown.

"I wear these glasses for one basic reason," she explained carefully, playing on his sense of expectance. Her pause was deliberate and drama-filled.

"And what might that be?"

"I'm nearsighted." The words flowed forth in a provocative drawl. Alanna grinned, then rose to the challenge as the man across from her presented several straightened fingers for her to count. "Three," she proclaimed proudly. "I'm not *that* bad, though I hope I'm not disappointing you. I *do* manage to live quite well with the weakness."

A mocking eyebrow rose. "I never doubted it for a minute. I'm just surprised you haven't tried contact lenses. Most women prefer—"

"I'm not most women. My glasses and I get along just fine." The object under discussion lay, temporarily forgotten, on the table.

"You have lovely eyes." His teasing tone was gone and Alanna's mouth felt suddenly dry. Though she sipped the last of her now-cooled coffee, she refused to let his relentless gaze intimidate her. Then, with the twinkle of an eye, his humor made a comeback. "It's actually gratifying to know that, while the world sees only your specs, I'll get to see the gems beneath."

"You presume quite a bit."

"Not without good reason."

He could match her, word for word, argument for argument. Though there was an undercurrent of teasing now, there was something else—something that gave Alanna pause.

"You *are* serious, aren't you?" she asked, puzzled, blunt.

Her bluntness was matched by his response. "Dead serious. I intend to marry you." Everything in his expression—from the deep set of those charcoal eyes to the matter-of-fact angle of his head to the firm slant of his lips, which monopolized her gaze for a hypnotic moment— reinforced his earnestness.

Exasperated, she shook her head. "Please, Mr. Knight—"

"Alex!"

"Alex . . . you may be serious, but please believe that I am, too. I have no intention of marrying you or anyone else. My life is just fine the way it is."

"Is it?" He sat forward, challenging her afresh. "Is that why you're here? Is that why you can't sleep at night?"

Alanna stiffened. "I thought dealings with doctors were supposed to be confidential. Whoever is feeding you your information is out of line." The indignance in her tone was unmistakable. "And if you have any power at all in this hospital you should see that the breach is sealed."

"Perhaps," he drawled deeply, "it's precisely my power that caused the breach to begin with."

"Then it's that much less excusable!"

To her dismay Alex smiled, enjoying her unease. The warmth of his gaze melted her resentment, even against her will. "You really have nothing to worry about, Alanna. That's all I know—your name and your reason for being here. And there was no breach of confidence by any doctor; Sylvia spilled the last, as well. Anything further, I guess I'll have to ferret out of you. Believe it or not, this hospital *is* closemouthed."

"That remains to be seen," Alanna commented wryly. Looking away, she caught the glint of the overhead light as it cast its tawny highlight on the fine hairs on the back of his hand. It was an image she thrust from her mind as being far too sensual, far too appealing. Grasping for an escape, she brightened. "Tell me . . . what can *you* learn from surface information? Since you don't know me, whatever makes you think you'd want me as a wife?"

"For starters," he began without hesitation, "I know that you're part of the IAT study—that was what Sylvia told me. It says a lot."

"Such as . . . ?"

"Such as that you're a working woman—a business-woman—at the executive level." At her look of surprise, he explained. "The IAT study—this phase, at least—deals with a very specific group. Executives. Under pressure. Between the ages of thirty and forty-five. I'd say," his gaze raked her form with astounding thoroughness, pausing longer on her lips before returning to the anticipation in her eyes, "that you are at the bare bottom of that scale."

"You're right. I just turned thirty-one."

"And *that* says a lot more."

"My age?"

"The fact that you offer it so freely. Some women are very sensitive—"

"I'm not *some* women."

"Which tells me even more. You're a nonconformist. You're self-confident, intelligent to have gotten where you are, and at least moderately aggressive."

"Moderately?" she asked, amused by his evaluation.

"Actually, with regard to the factor of aggression you're still an unknown factor. You may be very aggressive in the office; in . . . ah . . . other fields you may not have been put to the test yet." The dark gleam which flickered in his eye spoke clearly of the fields he had in mind. Alanna's reaction was instant.

"Do you really think that you'll be the one to test me?"

"Perhaps."

"Don't hold your breath," she warned softly. "I've fought my way from the bottom up, parrying similar threats all too often. Fighting you would be no different than fighting those others who've tried before you."

Even as the words hit the air she wondered at their truth. From that first visual exchange in the elevator she had sensed something different in this man. A fight with him would push her to her limits, of that she was certain. Would it come to that? Despite his claims and her renunciation of them, would she be seeing him again?

"And that's another thing I like about you," he went on, totally ignoring her declaration. "You've got spunk. That's good."

"You're nuts! Do you know that?"

He chuckled. "I've been told so on occasion—but I've usually gone on to prove myself totally sane. Are you interested in putting me to the test?"

"What test—proving you sane?" When he shook his head with deliberate slowness she amended her guess, once again with disbelief. "Marrying you?"

"Ummm." His gaze began to move over her face in a visual caress that was utterly sensual. Beginning with her flaxen-sheened hair, pulled sedately back, his eye-touch stroked the creamy richness of her skin, the delicate symmetry of her nose, the sudden vulnerability of her lips. Awareness coursed through her in echoing ripples.

"I told you," she argued defensively, her stiff tone belying the helpless cocoa of her eyes, "that I'm not the marrying type. Marriage has nothing to offer me that I don't already have."

"Which brings me to my original question. Why do you have insomnia?"

"Insomnia has nothing to do with marriage," she asserted boldly.

"No, but if your life is as perfect as you seem to feel, you shouldn't have insomnia. What causes it?"

Exasperated once more, Alanna sighed. "If I knew the answer to that I wouldn't be here right now. In fact, I'm not quite sure why I *am* sitting here listening to you!"

"You're listening to me," Alex informed her without a second's pause, "because I challenge you. Because I don't 'yes' you all over the place, as I'm sure most of the men you're used to dealing with do. Because I dare to question you. Because I interest you."

He was right. She could simply have stood and excused herself when he arrived at her table, and certainly immediately after he popped his half-baked notion that she would one day be his wife. Yet he *did* interest her . . . and he was obviously interested *in* her. With a quivering in her limbs that she would have liked to attribute to fatigue but could not, Alanna knew she had to leave. Standing quickly, she shouldered her purse and reached for her glasses, slipping them deftly onto her face.

"I really must go, Alex. I have an appointment." She glanced at her watch and saw, to her horror, that she'd been a full forty-five minutes in the cafeteria. "Oh, no, she'll be waiting."

"She'll find something to keep her busy," Alex drawled. He, too, had risen and made to escort her. "I presume you *are* talking about Ellen Henderson?"

Alanna was too aware of Alex's closeness to react naturally to this knowledge of her. Quickening her step, she nodded. "That's right."

"Then I'm very happy that Ellen is a *she*. I'm not sure I'd enjoy having you pour your heart out to a *him*. Unless it was me, of course. I tend to be the jealous type."

As they reached the door of the cafeteria Alanna turned to face him. "Alex, it was nice meeting you, but I really have no time to continue the game. My life is filled to bursting as it is. I hope that you can simply put this weird compulsion of yours out of your mind. We'd both be healthier."

"Would we?" Taking her arm, he guided her in the direction of the elevator, holding her gently but firmly until the car arrived, entering with her and pushing the button for the proper floor. As fate would have it there were, again, no other passengers. After the door blocked out the rest of the world he looked down at her. "I think you're wrong. This is the healthiest thing *I've* done in years."

Without a further word he drew her to him, his hands grasping her arms, his head lowering. She hadn't expected such suddenness. Stunned, she had no time to muster a protest before his lips touched hers. They were warm and gentle, as teasing as his nature. She stood perfectly still, refusing to yield to the pressure as it increased, yet unable to pull away. When teasing turned to seduction she struggled harder to remain indifferent. For, as with everything else about this man, his kiss, too, was different. His lips were vibrant, smoothly awakening her long-dormant senses. The warmth that began in her toes inched slowly upward, slowly and with growing heat as it made its way through her limbs. Her fingers itched to touch, her lips to respond. But his arrogance stayed her; she would no more give in to his cocksure demand than she would agree to his absurd marriage declaration. In the next instant, however, he slyly altered the ground rules.

"Bet you can't do it," he drawled softly against her lips.

"Do what?" she whispered, tipping her head back to study him.

"Kiss me with everything you've got . . . then turn and walk away."

Alanna felt abruptly light-headed. She loved a challenge and this was the perfect out. She could maintain her dignity and meet his dare, all the while giving in to the very tempting lure of his male-strong lips. While a small, private voice within asked if *she* was the crazy one for what she was about to do, that more husky public voice accepted. "You've got yourself a bet."

As though squaring off for a wrestling bout, Alex dropped his arms to his sides. Beaming indulgently down on her, he waited. Alanna's hands found their way to his shoulders, then around to his back, exploring his strength as she brought her lips tentatively to his. With a mixture of curiosity and growing boldness she pressed sensuously against him—then caught her breath and pulled back in reaction to both the heady jolt of excitement that coursed through her veins and the opening of the elevator door.

Mercifully, there was no one on the other side to witness her momentary loss as she grappled for the poise that had been suddenly shattered. "Oops," she gasped. "It looks like . . . we've been . . . thwarted. . . ."

"Saved by the bell is more like it," he countered with a knowingly wicked smile. "Come on." A strong arm about her shoulder pulled her from the elevator.

"Where . . . ?" Numbly, she kept pace; she literally had no choice. They moved a few yards to the fire door, then through it, to the stairwell. "Alex, what are you doing?"

"I don't think I can stand the suspense. You have a point to prove, I believe." He moved her gently against the wall, satisfactorily placing the breadth of his back as a shield against any unwanted intrusion. "Now," he cleared his throat, "that kiss . . . ?"

"But . . . I *did* kiss you."

"Ah-ah. That was no kiss," he teased, his tone seductive in itself. "That was a taste . . . a peck. Now I want the real thing. The bet wasn't for a half-kiss; it was for a whole-kiss."

Alanna was caught up in more than one game, for to their verbal sparring had been added the factor of raw physical need. Tingles deep within her attested to it. "There's a difference?" she floundered, buying time, hiding her growing turmoil in mock innocence. If that had been a half-kiss, she mused with alarm, she'd never have a chance in the world of winning the bet. This man had a touch, no doubt about it. She'd never been so affected before. Even now, as her hesitant gaze met his, she felt the draw. In her knees. Her chest. The deepest nooks and crannies of her body. All seemed suddenly aroused.

Alex moved closer, a long forefinger stroking her cheek, "Oh, there's a difference, owl-eyes," he murmured, seemingly entranced by her lips. "Let me demonstrate."

If only she had pulled away then, *before* his demonstration, she might have saved herself. But she was mesmerized, held immobile by his hands, drugged by the manly scent that encompassed him as surely as his aura of command, and lost in, yes, a web of sheer desire.

Alanna Evans was not an inexperienced woman. Yet Alex's touch was new, his kiss exciting, his nearness an intoxicant she had never before known. Now, as his lips gently sampled hers, slanting tentatively across them, coaxing them apart with subtle promises, she had no wish to resist. Rather, her nascent response was an invitation to a depth of passion she could only imagine. A shudder ran through her at the touch of his tongue exploring the curve of her lips and the softness within. If her knees grew weak, it was of no import. For his arms circled her, drawing her from the wall and against the long, hard-muscled support of his body.

The moment was isolated in eternity in Alanna's wheeling mind. She felt overwhelmingly alive and fresh, electrically charged, drawn from dormancy to heaven. Her arms stole beneath his to his back, her hands reveling in the corded strength there.

Then her pulse hammered loudly as he leaned back. His smoky gray eyes studied her indolently, savoring the flush on her cheeks. "Now it's your turn," he whispered, a deeply crooned challenge. Holding his face just so far from hers, he demanded that she take the initiative to steal another kiss.

Alanna was powerless against the drive stirring within

her. Her usual manner was neither coy nor hesitant. She
had always been honest with herself. When she wanted
something, she went after it. And, at that moment, she
wanted to kiss Alex Knight, to push that budding passion
even further. Eagerly she leaned closer, her slender body
as pliant against his manly lines as layers of raw silk
draped across a bronze statue. Her lips parted in search of
his, reaching, playing only until she felt his ragged gasp,
then, forgetting play, moving in nearer, deeper, harder.

Neither Alex nor Alanna was aware of the door open-
ing not far from them. A throat cleared. "Excuse me. . . ."
A forced cough. "Ah . . . Mr. Knight . . . excuse me . . .
Ms. Evans . . ."

Alanna wasn't quite sure when she finally recognized
the presence of a third person. Alex, however, recov-
ered sooner. Though his arms held her still, he raised
his head.

"Yes, Sylvia?" he asked thickly.

Sylvia Frazier cleared her throat once more before
speaking in a stage whisper which carried a hint of chiding. "Dr. Henderson is waiting to see Ms. Evans. I saw
you two get off the elevator. I really think—"

"Thank you for the reminder, Sylvia." Alex didn't turn.
His gray eyes glittered into Alanna's with a pointed message and, slowly, she grasped reality. She felt the rapid
rise and fall of her chest, the pounding of blood through
her veins, the eerie weakness in her legs. But there was,
still, that last part of the bet. . . .

Straightening, she took a deep breath. "I'm coming
now, Ms. Frazier. Please tell Dr. Henderson that I'll be
right along." As Alanna gently extricated herself from
Alex's arms the nurse diplomatically disappeared, her job
done. But Alex's strong hand stayed Alanna before she,
too, could return to the floor.

"You lose, you know," he grinned mischievously. "If

Sylvia hadn't come along just then you wouldn't have left." He paused, his nearness continuing to affect her. As she looked up at him his gaze grew enigmatic. "Would you?"

A smile tugged at the corners of her lips as she lifted her golden head a bit higher. While she refused to admit defeat, she could not lie. "We'll never know, will we?"

But the sureness of Alex's answer made a mockery of her smugness. "Oh, *we'll* know. And *you* can bet on *that!*"

With a hard swallow, Alanna turned and left.

2

Ellen Henderson was the antithesis of the ivory-tower psychologist. She was young, perhaps a year or two older than Alanna. She was attractive, tall and dark-haired, and dressed in a casual wool shirt-dress and high-heeled pumps. She was warm, compassionate and extremely goal-oriented. Alanna felt an instant rapport with her.

"I'm thrilled that you've agreed to be part of the study." She welcomed Alanna with a sincere smile, as the latter took the chair offered by her desk.

Alanna spoke honestly. "*I'm* glad that you may be able to help me. It's a frustrating problem."

"Of course it is! Hopefully, through your participation in the study, we'll *all* sleep better. It's just a beginning . . . as is so much of work done in sleep labs such as this."

"Can you tell me something, in general, about the study?" Alanna asked, recalling that Alex Knight knew that much more than she did.

Ellen grinned her understanding. "Sure. Let me explain, first off, that there are many different types of sleep problems. The three major ones affecting adults are narcolepsy, sleep apnea and insomnia. The narcoleptic may sleep well at night but falls into helpless sleep-stupors at odd points during the day, often in the midst of crucial activities. A victim of sleep apnea actually stops breathing up to four hundred times in the course of the night; only his body reflexes jolt him back to life. Needless to say, his sleep is constantly disturbed. Sudden Infant Death Syndrome is an early form of this. Then," she paused for a breath, her expression softening, "there's insomnia—the inability either to fall asleep at all or to fall back to sleep once awoken. Of the fifty million Americans afflicted with sleep troubles, thirty million have insomnia."

"Of which I am one."

"Unfortunately, yes."

"What causes it?"

Ellen sighed. "There may be any number of causes. A few are physical—but the physical exam Dr. Ramirez, our neurologist, gave you when you came in two weeks ago ruled out any gross physical problem. You're in excellent health." Her eyes fell to the folder opened on her desk. "You don't smoke?"

"No."

"Drink?"

"Other than the occasional cocktail or glass of wine, no."

"Take any medication to help you sleep?"

"No." She spoke softly, almost apologetically. "I hate to take pills, period. I like to think that I have enough internal discipline to overcome any minor headaches." Her smile held regret. "Unfortunately, I don't have the discipline to control *this* problem."

"You will," Ellen assured her confidently. "That's what we'll be working on here."

Now they were down to the immediate situation. "What *will* I be doing?"

"Well, we have two weeks to work with. Fourteen nights. You *are* free of other obligations for that stretch, aren't you?"

Alanna answered easily. "I had several engagements, but after Dr. Ramirez called I was able to reschedule them."

"Good." The psychologist nodded. "Since we'll be concentrating on behavior modification, it's important to have the time. But," she paused, "let me backtrack a bit before I explain the specifics. The IAT—Insomnia Analysis and Treatment—study is a far-reaching one. We've identified many different types of people with insomnia. Your group, with its own specific characteristics, is only one."

Alanna couldn't help but quote what she'd learned earlier. "Executives. Under pressure. Between the ages of thirty and forty-five."

"Ah, you've been prompted?" Ellen grinned, not at all bothered.

"I met a fellow named Alex Knight in the cafeteria."

Ellen's grin broadened. "Yes, Alex. His family has been wonderful to us."

"So I gather." She also wondered whether Alex Knight had been wonderful to Ellen Henderson, then chided herself for her cattiness. She held her tongue as Ellen continued.

"He does know his facts. Those are the basic qualifications. The theory is that you people—we have four of you here at a time—suffer from insomnia as a result of the pressures you face relating to your careers. All of you are single, which rules out marital tension. All of you live alone, which rules out a bedmate who may disturb your sleep with snoring, restlessness, nightmares—that sort of thing."

Alanna ingested it all, yet her mind rushed on. "Why is the study being done *here?* Why the necessity of sleeping at the hospital?"

"It's a good question, and one I've had to answer repeatedly. What with hospital costs, you'd think this to be extravagant. I admit that it may be unorthodox, but if the field is to make significant advances, this type of study is a must. You see," she went on, "we'll be trying to control your environment, to keep that much more accurate an eye on your surroundings and sleep habits than we might be able to do if you were at home."

Alanna's thoughts shifted to the conversation she'd had with the neurologist and she felt a twinge of unease. "Dr. Ramirez mentioned some very complicated-sounding monitoring devices. Am I in for something awful?"

"No!" Ellen's appreciative laughter was instantly reassuring. "Tonight will be the only night you'll be wired up—"

"Wired up?"

"Nothing to worry about." Again the psychologist soothed her. "We'll be monitoring your brain waves, your heart rate and your body temperature."

Alanna's brow furrowed. "I'm not sure I understand. If you've ruled out any physical problem—"

"We have. These measurements are all related to sleep patterns. We'd like to establish, at the start, that you do go through the normal four stages of the sleep cycle. I'm sure you're familiar with the term. For the average adult the sleep cycle repeats itself many times throughout the night. Once we've plotted your sleep pattern I'll be able to show you a graphic illustration."

Alanna's lips twitched in humor. "I'd like to see that. With the number of finance and production charts I read in a day I often wonder whether I can see things any other way."

"Then you'll appreciate the illustration." Ellen smiled. "I don't actually anticipate seeing anything unusual, but it's necessary to find out if we're going to the effort of controlling so many other factors *and* taking two weeks' worth of your nights."

"Of course. I understand." Feeling slightly more comfortable about the monitoring, Alanna was curious again. "What then? What about the other thirteen nights?"

"OK." Ellen sat forward. "Now we get to the nitty-gritty of the project. We ask you to come in every night at roughly the same time, preferably no later than nine. Early curfew," she quipped, successfully coaxing Alanna into mirroring her smile. "We have a lounge in the unit and a small kitchen. Both are well appointed, very pleasant. You will have your own bedroom and a private bath—nothing fancy, but, again, pleasant. It will be dark and quiet. There will be no disturbances. Please sleep in whatever nightwear you're accustomed to. Above all, I want you to be comfortable. You may spend your evening until you fall asleep either in the lounge or in your room. Follow your usual routine. If you usually shower before bed, do it. When—and only when—you're sleepy, you'll go to bed. You will be woken at the same time every morning, regardless of that bedtime, and you will be expected to follow a fixed routine immediately after waking up—preferably some form of exercise, then breakfast." She paused, again consulting the papers on her desk. "I understand you swim?"

Alanna nodded. "I coach a swim team on Saturdays. Ten- to twelve-year-olds. Girls." At the thought, she brightened. "They're great kids!"

"Do you swim much on your own?"

"When I have the chance."

"Well," the psychologist drew out her words with feigned sternness, "I want you to *make* the chance. There's a pool just down the street which we have access to. If you'd like, you can swim every morning before breakfast."

Alanna knew only too clearly her prebreakfast moods.

"I don't know, Ellen," she hesitated. "My early mornings are pretty bad. . . ."

"Then this will be one way of letting out all that pent-up aggression."

Aggression. That word again. Alanna couldn't help but remember when she'd heard it last. Then it had been on taunting male lips, firm and enticing. . . . Ellen snapped her from the memory.

"Will you try it? You may notice a huge improvement—both in your temperament *and* in your sleep habits."

The last did it. Though skeptical, Alanna was game. "I'll try."

"Great!"

"Ah . . . what else am I going to have to do?" Her good-natured, but wary, question was enough to lighten Ellen's expression even more.

"Nothing painful." She laughed. "We'd like to eliminate stress from the bedroom. That means no heavy reading or television while in bed. Staying in bed *only* while you're sleepy. Getting up and leaving the bedroom whenever you're unable to fall asleep—or go back to sleep—quickly."

Alanna mulled over the suggestions. "Sounds fair."

"You don't nap during the day, do you?"

"If only I had time!" Her eyes widened in surprise.

"Well, don't!" the other woman rejoined just as quickly. "Never nap during the day—even on weekends. And no coffee or liquor after, say, three in the afternoon. OK?"

"Fine." She'd been doing as much already.

"One other thing, though I'll speak more about it tomorrow night when you come in. This is a self-help program. We'll be teaching you techniques of self-relaxation. You know, deep breathing, muscle-relaxing, mind-clearing."

"Interesting. . . ." It had never occurred to Alanna to do that.

"It will be, and it should help. I'll be on duty every night, should you want to talk. And there will be the other participants. You'll meet them tomorrow as well."

"But . . . what will I have to do with them?" This was a totally new thought.

Again Ellen was well prepared for the question. "I like to see this as a kind of halfway house. You may have *no* cause to talk with the others. But they're here with a problem similar to yours. The therapeutic value of talking with others can often be greater than talking with me."

"I see." She pondered the possibility. As a loner, she was hesitant. "Are they all from the greater Baltimore area, too?"

"Uh-huh. There are two men and two women. I dare say you may find you're already acquainted with one or two." If she knew something Alanna didn't, there was no time for guessing. "You may even develop legitimate friendships." The doctor glanced at her watch. "Which reminds me, I still have to brief two more. Let me explain what else I want you to do."

"There's more?" Alanna had begun to feel saturated.

"Just a little." Ellen opened a drawer and withdrew an official-looking notebook with several blank charts in front. "I want you to keep a running log of your thoughts and activities from the time you arrive here at night until the time you leave in the morning. There is also a place to summarize your feelings about each day. I'm interested in general problems, aggravations. At night I want you to enter your periods of sleep *and* wakefulness. For the latter, concentrate on your thoughts upon awakening. If you leave the log here during the day I can go over it to keep pace with your progress." She paused, then grinned sheepishly. "Sound awesome?"

Alanna grinned wryly. "I suppose I've faced greater challenges." *Challenges.* Where had she heard *that* word before? Her grin faded quickly.

"I'm sure you have. And, considering your corporate achievements, I'm sure you'll meet this one as well."

It was a compliment that Alanna accepted graciously, if with mild embarrassment. After all, Ellen Henderson must have received her share of accolades to be in the position she now held.

"Any other questions, or would you like me to show you to your room?"

Sorting it all out, Alanna grew apprehensive. "Ah . . . tonight. When I'm all wired up, what happens if I wake up in the middle of the night?"

"If you lie awake for more than ten minutes, ring for Sylvia. She'll unhook everything so you can get up. Walk around. Go into the lounge. Help yourself to some milk in the kitchen. Read a light magazine or a book. Pure escapism. Concentrate on relaxing. Don't go back to bed until you're really sleepy. You could try filling out the log." She patted the notebook with a knowing glance. "That's bound to put you to sleep!"

By the time Alanna had been shown over the lab and then to her room it was nearly ten. Not only was she armed with her log and sleep charts, but Ellen had given her questionnaires to complete, full of in-depth items relating to her childhood, her upbringing, her educational and occupational histories. Settling into the easy chair by the darkened window, she sighed. Exhaustion had its way of creeping up, suffusing weariness through her body. Perhaps she had been more tense about this than she had imagined. Her lips curved into a wry grin. When it came to the office she was in her element, able to face most every problem with aplomb. Something like this—a more personal situation—was another matter.

The pile of forms lay unheeded on her lap as she looked around the room which would be hers for the next two weeks. It was small, but as pleasant as Ellen had said it would be. Painted a pale blue, rather than the traditional hospital white, its simplicity was relaxing. A small table stood to her left, a dresser to her right. Against the far wall was a nightstand, then the bed. In this case, too, white had been usurped by the pale green of both sheets and blankets. The warm glow of the lamp on the nightstand blended with a floor lamp by her chair to bathe the room in a light as gentle as that of dawn. To her surprise, Alanna felt quite comfortable.

Turning to the first of the forms, she searched her purse for a pen, then began. The starting questions were standard. Name: Alanna Lyn Evans. Address: 2201 North Bancroft. Phone: 555–8821. Age: 31. Sex: Female. Marital Status: Single.

A yawn escaped unhampered. Ellen was right; the task was more effective than counting sheep. Mustering her discipline, Alanna returned to it.

Place of birth: Pittsburgh. Parents: Willard and Elizabeth Evans. Siblings: None.

At the second yawn, Alanna put down the pen. The thought of outlining childhood illnesses and traumas, of which there were few, held no excitement. None at all.

Excitement. The word was a trigger, flashing an instant image before her mind's eye of a man, tall and broad-shouldered, arrogant as they come. Alexander Knight. Aside from the puppy love she had felt for Shep Harding, Alanna had never been stirred by a man in quite this way. Even aside from his preposterous mention of marriage, he was a puzzle. What coincidence had brought them together tonight? Had it only been for a few hours that she'd known of his existence?

Strange, she mused, how time could take on altered

dimensions. It was as though she had known him much longer. Indeed, their kiss had borne an intimacy that shocked her. What had happened to her usual defenses?

Alanna kicked off her shoes and stood to explore the room. Her tapered fingers, their nails well shaped and clear, skimmed the curved edge of the tabletop, then the windowsill, bridging the gap to the bed, marking its length and width before falling to her side.

Would she see him again? He knew where to find her. But what did she know of him, save that he was part of *the* Knight family? His dress and manner spoke of dignity, of class; why, then, his ludicrous idea about marriage? He had been serious! Or had he been? Perhaps he was toying with her; maybe the rich and privileged were accustomed to joking that way. Could he have meant it— that he intended to marry her? The remembrance of the touch of his lips on hers came unbidden to mind. An intoxicating spice—a manly mystique—an insidious explosion of warmth within her. Was she that vulnerable, after all she had led herself to believe?

No! With a determined vow she turned to the closet and began to undress. Alex Knight might have been different, but she was not. She was the same Alanna Evans who had walked toward the hospital today with her head held high. She was a professional woman. She'd worked hard to get where she was. There was time for neither romance nor marriage in her life.

Standing before the dresser in her bra and slip, she reached to carefully remove the pins which had anchored her hair sedately through the day. With the removal of each pin a strand of flaxen silk fell over her pale shoulders, one, then another, until a rich mane of honeyed treasure cascaded to midback. She ran her fingers freely through its length, bending to her overnight bag for her brush, then stroking the fall of hair until it was glossy in the pale light. Once again she thought of Alex Knight and her fingertips feather-touched her lips. How delightful he had tasted, she mused, then grimaced. *Anything* might taste good after decaffeinated coffee!

Forcing her thoughts to her immediate plight, she showered, dressed in her nightgown and robe, then returned to her chair and the paperwork awaiting her. Again, instant sedation. Eyelids heavy. Sleep imminent. Within minutes she had pressed the call button and Sylvia Frazier was with her, bearing a cartload of paraphernalia which, under normal circumstances, would have frightened *anyone* out of sleep. But Sylvia, as she insisted Alanna call her, was one step ahead of her apprehension, explaining every gismo, pinpointing every wire's purpose and destination, reassuring Alanna until she felt no alarm at all. Surprisingly, she was barely aware of the monitoring electrodes when, finally, she was alone once more in the darkened room, awaiting sleep. Within minutes she had succumbed to its sweet, if temporary, escape.

It was shortly after two that the familiar internal alarm roused her. Blinking into the darkness, she struggled for several moments to identify her surroundings. With recollection came an ironic relief. What if, after claiming to have insomnia, she had slept like a babe through the night? Would they have thought her a fraud?

Fraud. It was a word that had been used all too often by a few skeptics to spread their ugly gossip. Perhaps it had been inevitable. From her earliest days at WallMar Enterprises she had kept all professional relationships strictly that—except for her friendship with Jake Wallace. A rapport had arisen between them from the start. Alanna found him to be intelligent and open, eager for her input and a far cry from so many of her more ambitious and competitive colleagues. Jake had no need for pettiness. As president of the company, his power was secure. When he promoted Alanna from Administrative Assistant to Director of Management in six short months no one had questioned him—to his face. Alanna had been all too aware of the subtle innuendos, however, the sly looks, even the leering glances. They all pointed to one supposition: that she was daringly sleeping her way to the top of the ladder. Even now, in the darkness of her hospital room, Alanna felt the surge of anger which raced through her every time she brooded on the injustice of the accusation. One colleague, a young and rather rash man, had voiced the sentiment quite succinctly. "I only wish," he had drawled, raking her slender curves lewdly, "that I had the qualifications *you* have."

Alanna's way had been to ignore the taunts and turn the other cheek in an attempt to demonstrate that it had been by merit alone that she had earned her promotion. The charges were absurd. Jake Wallace was a balding man in his late fifties. Yes, she did adore him—and he adored her. She also adored his wife, who was confined to a wheelchair, and had spent many an evening with them both—none of which helped, since no one quite knew what went on inside the old and gracious Victorian mansion that had been in the Wallace family for years. Perhaps they thought of her as the daughter they'd never had. In her professional outlook she was certainly the son they'd never had. And Jake and Elaine were as close to family as *she* now had. Their friendship was mutually gratifying.

Ten minutes. Ellen had told her to get up if she lay awake for longer. It had been fifteen and she was tense and annoyed. Her frustrated summons for Sylvia was met quickly. Soon she was out of bed and, tying her robe securely around her, headed for the lounge and the hope of a diverting magazine. She'd have to remember to bring a book for tomorrow night. Blast! Why did she have to wake in the night to . . . this?

The lounge was quiet and deserted. Alanna had her choice of several easy chairs and finally sank onto the only sofa and stretched out her long legs. Her feet were bare; she'd forgotten to get slippers. She'd have to buy a pair tomorrow. Bare feet were the rule at her own place, where thick carpets always beckoned. Yet it was warm here and she made herself comfortable.

The minutes slowly ticked away as she turned page after page of the magazine. Finally, bored, she put it down, tossing her glasses onto the table beside her. What had Ellen said about self-help and learning to relax? Mustering her imagination, she rested her head on her arm and concentrated her gaze on the beige carpet, determinedly forcing all thoughts from mind. Inhaling deeply, she focussed her attention on this mental void, willing her limbs to languor, her pulse to steadiness. It worked. Like the slow breakup of clouds on a rain-misted morning, a tentative peace seeped through her. With each deep breath her tension eased until she felt, at last, sleepy. Her lids drooped, yet she was reluctant to move.

Aware of the world now only through the thick shade of her blond lashes, she found the intrusion of human flesh almost surreal. Only vaguely did the image register; as she slowly opened her eyes it sharpened. Human flesh—a pair of feet—masculine and tanned—connected to legs that were strong and roughened by light brown hairs. As she struggled to assimilate the presence it lowered itself calmly before her.

"Hi, pretty lady," a voice crooned with a deep resonance she would have recognized even had it not been imprinted on her memory so recently. In shock, she brought herself to full awareness. Her brown eyes widened to encompass the thick head of hair, sleep-mussed as was hers, the deep gray orbs which reflected her own image, the lips that were sensual and alive.

Forgetful of both the time and the surroundings, she cried in astonishment, "Alex!" Any further exclamation was drowned as his lips covered hers in a gentle greeting. She gasped, yet was, once again, powerless against his spell, savoring the sweet story his lips told so briefly. When she could breathe again she simply stared at him in amazement as he continued to kneel before her.

"What are *you* doing here at this hour?"

Amusement flitted dangerously in the gaze that swept her semiprone form. "The same thing you are."

"*You're* part of the study?" Was that possible? Was that why he had been here earlier? Was that the coincidence that had brought them together?

"Is that so hard to believe? I mean," he teased her wickedly, "I know that I may be handsome and witty and utterly irresistible during the day," he counted off the points, "but is it inconceivable that we share this problem as well?"

What else was it he had said they shared—their sense of challenge? It was a reminder that buoyed her through her confusion now. "You have insomnia?"

He nodded.

"No wonder you knew something about the study." Her thoughts were growing more lucid. "I more or less assumed that it was your family's role . . ."

Alex's expression tensed noticeably. "My family's position in this community, any power they may wield, is only incidental to my participation in the study."

It was, ironically, his vehemence that convinced her. Earlier he had been in full command of his charm. Now, in the middle of the night, when they both should have been sleeping like so many of their peers, his shortened fuse was obvious. And she understood the feeling.

"I'm sorry. That came out the wrong way. I'm just so . . . surprised to see you here."

"Didn't I imply that we'd meet again?" He seemed to regain his humor as his gaze held hers steadily.

"You implied a lot more than that! I'd pretty much written you off as a crackpot!"

His grin was slow and enticing. "I do like your humor." He paused. "Couldn't sleep either?"

"Afraid not. I've been up for a while."

"Reading anything good?" His attention shifted momentarily to the now-forgotten magazine by her side.

"Very boring."

Without quite standing, he moved forward. "Move over. You've got the best spot." He took her shoulders to shift her before she could reposition herself. As he slithered into the corner where she had been she looked at him in alarm.

"Now *you've* got it. That wasn't very fair. I was there first."

"But you've got something even better." In graphic explanation he drew her against him, his body giving her far more exciting support than the sofa ever had. His arm curved around her shoulder; before she knew how her own settled across his middle and she rested comfortably against him. His warmth was as much a relaxant as her deep-breathing efforts had been earlier. Surprisingly, she didn't resist the lure.

"Comfortable?" he asked softly.

"Ummm." The scent of him was all male, filling her senses with a creeping euphoria.

Later she was to wonder at her complacency as she lay against Alex, a devastating stranger who had proposed marriage at their first meeting. Now, however, the silence was restorative, filled with a contentment that she savored, regardless of whatever afterthoughts she might have. His breathing was steady, his hands undemanding. At length he spoke with a resonance that flowed soothingly through her.

"I like you this way."

"What way?"

"Undressed."

Alanna tilted her head back, only realizing that he wore a burgundy-colored robe of thick terry as her cheek rubbed against it. "I'm not undressed," she contradicted him staunchly. "I am very properly covered by several layers of fabric."

"But soft. So very soft," he hummed against her hair. "And I like your hair down." His hand moved to gently explore its length. "It's like silk—golden silk."

"One hundred brushings a night and very hard to control at times," she quipped lightly, unable to accept the compliment with the pleasure she felt.

"That's why you wear it knotted back? For control?"

"Among other things."

"What things?"

The faint frown that brought her brows together was hidden as she relaxed her head once more. "It's hard enough projecting an image of efficiency and professionalism at the office without having a loose mop to cloud the issue."

"Ah." He caught her gist instantly. "Your male colleagues. Then I totally agree with you. By all means tie your hair up during the day. As long as you wear it down for me."

"Hmmmm," she chuckled. "No glasses. Long hair. You've got a nearsighted witch."

"A very beguiling one . . ." he drawled, his fingers tilting her chin up so he could study her face. "A very beautiful one . . ."

She was mesmerized, able only to return his gaze,

devouring his good looks with helpless greed. Why was he *so* handsome? Or *was* it all physical? There was that aura again—one that surrounded his entire being with a sensuality she could not deny.

Her lips felt parched, her mouth dry. Every nerve end tingled with awareness. She felt herself sucked into the depths of those dark, charcoal eyes—sucked in and consumed, no longer a separate entity. Was that what life with Alex Knight would be like—the loss of the identity she had worked so hard to establish?

With a flash of fear she tried to pull away. But he held her firmly, refusing her bid to escape. "Don't go. I'm no threat to you." It was as if he read her mind. "If nothing more, indulge me. *You* know how maddening it is when you can't sleep. I'm more relaxed now than I've felt since I woke up."

The last thing she wanted was to leave, yet the strength of his power over her was disconcerting. As to his argument—hadn't Ellen suggested that the participants of the study might help each other? Perhaps, she mused, if there was some distance—*any* distance—between them . . .

"Just let me sit up," she suggested, her voice uncharacteristically wobbly. "I'll stay with you awhile."

His tone was mocking, yet he released her. "Not exactly what I had in mind, but, if I have no other choice . . ."

"You don't." Alanna sat now at arm's length. No part of their bodies touched yet, to her dismay, she was as aware of him as ever. Driven to break the bond of raw attraction that sizzled between them, she spoke quickly. "Tell me about yourself, Alex. I really know nothing about you."

One dark brow rose. "You did pretty well in the cafeteria."

"That was a game. Tell me something concrete. Like . . . like . . ." she grappled with sanity, ". . . like what you do for a living."

"I thought everyone knew." His dry statement puzzled her.

"That's the second reference you've made in the past few minutes to your family's reputation. Is that bitterness I detect?"

Alex thought for a moment, as though he had never been put to this test before. "Not bitterness. Let's just call it . . . resignation. I'm the third generation of my family in this area. It's often difficult to be preceded by someone else's reputation."

"I'm sure you meet the family standards," she offered in encouragement.

His gaze sharpened. "I meet *my* standards, or, at least, I try to. But I like to be judged on my own merits, rather than those of my family. Do *you* come from a large family?"

Alanna was unaware of his deftness in shifting the conversation back to her until well after she'd fallen into the trap. "No. I had no brothers or sisters."

"Are your parents living?"

The painful memory forced her to avert her gaze. "They died years ago—my mother, when I was twenty, my father four years later."

"Then you're alone?"

She smiled thinly. "Alone . . . but not lonely, as the saying goes."

"You have friends?"

"My share. Mostly my work keeps me occupied."

"Tell me about your work."

Enough was enough. "Uh-uh. I asked you first. What do you do—every day?"

He looked at her evenly. "I head the Knight Foundation."

"Which means . . . ?"

"Which means that I have a finger in a lot of pies at any given time."

Alanna grunted. It was like pulling teeth to get the man down to specifics. Was he always this closemouthed? Or simply with her? As though sensing her frustration, he yielded to her silent plea.

"Right now we're in the process of merging one of our electronics firms with two others. By forming a larger corporation we will have access to a nationwide network." The preoccupation of his gaze with her eyes suddenly ended. With slow deliberation he skimmed her neck and shoulders with his eyes, following the soft fabric of her robe to where her breasts swelled. Serious discussion was totally forgotten as Alanna felt the heat within herself begin to rise.

"Do you . . . ah . . . do the actual . . . negotiating . . . ?" She clutched at the conversation, fighting the honeyed currents which flowed around and about her.

His voice was low and at seductive odds with his words. "We have legal counsel for that. But *I* have to be on top of the legal counsel."

Her whispered "I see" fell victim to the web of arousal his gaze spun. His fingers moved to her shoulders, their tips drawing tiny circles on the silken gown.

"You look so pretty," he rasped as those fingers rose to thread through the hair that fell by her cheeks. "Do you always wake up looking like this—or did you do it just for me?"

"I didn't know you would be here!" she cried weakly, her sense of reason suddenly shaky. As his arm moved slowly to draw her closer she grew aware of its sinewed length, bared as it was to the elbow by the robe that barely reached to his knees. It had been bad enough when he had been fully dressed; *this* was sheer madness.

Alex had been right; she *was* different dressed like this. Her proper businesswear had been a shield, perhaps meager, but a shield nonetheless. In it she had known who she was and why she was here. Now she felt exposed—by far more than just the change of attire. Suddenly she felt unsure— and that made her angry. Moving quickly from his embrace, she stood.

"I think I'd better go to bed." Without looking back she crossed the floor and headed toward her room. She had not gone far enough, however, to miss his low-murmured "Chicken." It stopped her in her tracks.

Head low, she took a breath. On its own a smile stole to her lips. He knew just how to manipulate her. That challenge . . . She simply could not turn down a challenge. Shaking her head in grudging admiration, she turned slowly to face him.

"What was that?" She cocked an eyebrow pertly.

Alex rose from the sofa and circled it to stand beside her. His eyes were dark with desire; it took every ounce of restraint for her to hold still. "I called you a chicken. You seem to take the easy way out when the going gets . . . hot."

Her hands found her waist. "I'm not taking the easy way out. I'm simply taking the smartest way. As I recall, we're here for a purpose." Her words were spoken in self-reproach as much as to the dark form towering above her. "A love affair in the middle of a hospital lounge is a little . . . tawdry." Miraculously, her voice remained steady, belying the quivering deep within.

"I couldn't agree with you more. Let's go. I'll put you to bed."

Before she could protest that arm was once more about her shoulders, burning through her nightclothes, fusing her to his side. Before she could withdraw they had reached her room. Before she could escape through its door—alone—he guided her in.

Then, before she could begin to argue, he pulled her into the circle of his arms. "This may be the best sedative in the world." And he kissed her.

3

Naked was a mild word for how Alanna felt. It had little to do with her scant covering and everything to do with the raw vulnerability Alex Knight had uncovered. Her senses were stripped of all defense by the powerfully tender persuasion of the lips that covered hers, the hard male body against which his arms molded her.

"Alex, don't . . ." she gasped when he abandoned her lips to rain havoc along the sensitive curve of her neck.

"Alanna, do . . ." he echoed against her ear, nipping its delicate lobe before slowly working his way back to her mouth. "Show me one more time . . . I can't quite remember how it was. . . ."

On the verge of losing control, Alanna had no suitable retort. Instead, she gripped his shoulders for support. "I can't," she whispered, knowing that, once she began to give in to him, she would be helpless.

"Sure you can." He spoke with such gentle conviction that she had to listen. For while one part of her fought the incipient cry of desire that murmured through her body, the other part sought a rationale to permit its full and joyful expression.

His hands framed her face, tilting it up toward his as he spoke, his lips but a breath away. The dim light from the nightstand cast his manly features into bold relief, imbuing them with even greater positive force. "Forget who you are, what you are. Forget who I am, what I am." His tone was near-hypnotic; her eyes were glued to his commanding features. "Forget where you were today, where you are now, where you may be tomorrow. All that matters is this moment. Your woman to my man, my man to your woman. Give in, Alanna. Explore the feeling. It's new and wonderful."

His soft words were headier than any wine, his nearness more potent than any drug. With the tremor that passed through her went all thought of resistance, all will to protest. In its place was the taste of passion he had given her and the yearning to know more. Yet Alex awaited her sign. He wouldn't force her, nor would he allow her to remain passive. Intuition told her that he would demand in return everything he gave. The thought excited her. If she wanted him she would have to challenge him as well.

The thought was made all the more exciting by his hands, which drifted from her face to her shoulders, then lightly down her arms to rest expectantly at her hips. "You can't do it," he goaded softly. "Why? Not woman enough?"

The spell was momentarily broken. Alanna gasped at his taunt and its implication, stunned by the maelstrom of emotions that swirled within her. Indignation blunted anger, to be quelled in turn by desire, which erupted in a sigh of need, raw and ever-building. Freed of all pretense by his dare, she would meet him head-on. *He* would eat *his* words, she vowed, by the time she was done.

Her hands lifted to his face, her fingers tracing the rugged lines of his cheek, his jaw, then running around to the vibrant hair at the nape of his neck. His pulse throbbed beneath her thumbs, her own quickening to keep time.

When she lifted her lips he met them, still holding back, still demanding that she take the initiative. Unspoken, the dare was repeated. And she met it, deepening her kiss, running the tip of her tongue along the firm line of his lips, then venturing further with darting sweetness in a bid to contest his ability to withstand her provocation. His imminent surrender was electrical.

Slowly he raised his arms, his hands tightening around her, lifting her until she was nearly off her feet. She clung to him for support as his lips grew active, demanding. To her starved senses it was a delightful feeling, that of yielding to a power greater than herself, of absorbing that power and gaining strength from it. With that strength she returned his kiss, weaving her hands through the thickness of his hair to hold him closer.

Her feet left the ground as he lifted her, his kiss as strong as ever while he carried her to the bed. The coolness of the sheets against her flaming body, however, was a stark reminder of reality.

"Alex . . . ?" she whispered, only to be stilled by his thumb against her lips.

"Shhh. I said I'd put you to bed. I'm only doing that."

When his hands reached for the tie of her robe she demurred. "Alex!"

"Shhh. You'll wake everyone up."

His lips silenced her further, drugging her anew as his fingers drew the robe apart, then slid within to begin a sensual exploration of the curves that awaited enticingly. He stroked her sides and her midriff with maddening torment until, caught in an explosion of need, she arched toward him. Only then did he touch her breasts, lightly at first and with a tenderness that hit its mark. This gentleness was totally irresistible. Though his touch grew bolder it was exquisitely precise.

Alanna's palms itched to touch as well. Her gaze

followed them as they moved to the vee of his robe, settling against his bronzed chest to allow her fingers access to its hair-roughened warmth. Reveling in this textured landscape, her fingers trailed downward. Muscles rippled beneath her fingertips in a deep tremor of excitement which accompanied his low groan. In the dim light her eyes were bright and alive, her lips moist and open as he reached for them with raw hunger. Then reality entered to shatter their intimacy.

"Are you two at it *again?*"

For a split second they stilled, stunned, tumbling from the heady peak of passion. Alex's subsequent groan was one of frustration as he pushed himself up to rest on stiffened arms.

"Sylvia," he growled huskily, identifying the intruder without even looking around, "you're worse than any chaperone!"

The nurse stepped into the room and closed the door behind her. Mercifully, she didn't approach the bed. Alanna's flush was mirrored on Alex's face, a flush of passion, not embarrassment. Her eyes drank in his color, his hair in disarray, his gaze still dark with desire.

Though stern, Sylvia's voice held an undertone of appreciation. "May I remind you that this is a hospital? We're all here on official business."

It was Alex's discomposure that gave Alanna the strength, despite her lingering exhilaration, to rebound. "That's right, Alex. This is a hospital." She grinned, feeling safer from her own rampant desire with Sylvia in the room. "Official business only. You heard the woman." She felt an odd satisfaction at having the edge on Alex Knight, regardless of how tentative or superficial it might be.

"I hear, I hear," he muttered grudgingly, admitting defeat only for the moment. "You haven't heard the last of me, Ms. Evans." Leaning down, he placed a sober kiss on her cheek in a show of defiance before levering himself off the bed, straightening his robe with dignity and stalking barefooted to the door. "And *you*, Nurse Frazier, had better wipe that smirk off your face. Hmm," he paused, eyeing her closely as Alanna followed the action from her bed, "what happened to the timidity that gave you such tact earlier?"

"That timidity, Mr. Knight," she countered with an utter absence of the quality in question, "vanished with your clothes. As soon as you shed them you became *my* responsibility. As is Ms. Evans. And I will have no hanky-panky in this sleep lab."

Alanna stifled a grin, but Alex was less successful. His head fell back as he chuckled broadly. "Hanky-panky?" He finally caught himself. "This isn't hanky-panky. I plan to marry that woman." One steady hand pointed back toward the bed, then shifted to his hip. "What you interrupted was a lovers' tryst, a meeting of minds and hearts and bodies—"

"Enough, Mr. Knight!" Sylvia threw her hands up in exasperation, then clamped one on Alex's arm and ushered him through the door as though he were a recalcitrant child. "Back to bed."

Though Alanna had been unable to see his face during the exchange she had clearly heard his humor. Annoyed as she was that he should reveal his bizarre whim to a third person, the situation was suddenly funny. Or was it the fact that it was nearly four in the morning and she was strangely light-headed? Or was she light-headed because of Alex's lovemaking? Regardless of the possibilities, the roguish glance he had cast over his shoulder at her just before he disappeared had done nothing to bring her down to earth. Sylvia did, however, returning quickly to—of all things—wire her up again.

"Oh, Sylvia," Alanna opted for sheer honesty, "my mind is humming, my face is flushed, my pulse is racing—and you're really going to record *that* for posterity?"

The nurse was well aware of the predicament, as her knowing mock-glower suggested. "It may be the only way to keep him away from you for the rest of the night." The older woman stopped fussing over her equipment as she reran the earlier conversation in her mind. Her expression was suddenly kind. "Are you two really going to be married?"

Alanna grinned mischievously. "Alex seems to think so. But he's in for a rude awakening. I have no intention of marrying anyone. Not to mention the fact that I only met him for the first time tonight . . . in the cafeteria."

"Oh, dear," Sylvia moaned, "I'm afraid that was my doing. I had no idea he'd make a pest of himself. It's usually the women who pester him!"

Alanna could only muster a pointed "Oh?" before the nurse rushed on. "Of course, it's about time he did settle down. I've known his family for years now. They spend their share of time here in the hospital, what with donating such large amounts of money and all. They keep track of everything that happens here—"

"As though they owned the place?" Alanna couldn't restrain an echo of her earlier statement to Alex, but regretted its sting instantly.

Sylvia, however, didn't seem to mind. "They've been very generous and they happen to be lovely people, every last one of them." Absently she began to reconnect the electrodes.

Alanna saw the opening and she quickly took advantage. "Every last one of them? Just how many Knights are there?" Though the Knight name frequently graced the pages of the local papers Alanna had never followed the family in detail.

The nurse laughed. "You'd sometimes think there are one thousand and one Knights, what with their presence around this hospital. Let me see," she rolled her eyes, "there are the senior Knights, the junior Knights, and five Knights of your Alex's generation, not to mention a handful of grandchildren, most of them born right here in this hospital."

Alanna ignored the reference to *her* Alex, sighing wistfully. "How nice to be part of a large family. Is Alex the oldest? He said that he heads the foundation."

Sylvia completed her wire-work, placing the last two electrodes on her patient's temples. "I believe he has an older sister or two. He *is* the oldest son; that's why he has taken over the company."

"Is his father ill?" It seemed the logical conclusion, for a father to turn over the running of the family business to such a relatively young son.

"No. Ironically, the money they donate to this place rarely benefits them. They are, as families go, very healthy." She stood back, pensive. "No. But the Knight family works in unique ways. The father hands control down to the son early on, the theory being that in order to benefit from the extensive education they give their children, that up-and-coming blood has to have power. Hence, your Alex is now in charge."

"He's not *my* Alex!" Once, she could ignore; a second time, she could not. But curiosity came fast on the heels of reproach. "Are his parents still . . . active?"

"Hah! You wouldn't be asking that if you had seen them at the dedication of this wing a few months ago. Alex may be the official head of the foundation, but his parents are very visible indeed! Now," she changed the subject without a blink, "are you comfortable?"

Alanna glanced at the machines beside her. "I suppose so."

"Then good night. Or rather, good morning. I'll be going off duty at six. The daytime nurse will wake you at seven. Think you'll be able to fall asleep?"

"I certainly hope so," she answered quietly. "Much longer and it will be dawn. Then there will be no point in even trying." Her lips thinned in frustration. "And I have to *work* tomorrow. . . ."

Sylvia sensed her frustration. "There, there. Don't get yourself worked up about it or you'll never be able to sleep. Concentrate on relaxing. Try to clear your mind of worry and annoyance." She grinned slyly. "Think of Alex."

Against her will, that was exactly what Alanna did. She found herself conjuring up images of a face that was bronzed and rugged, a body that was warm and firm, a voice that was deep and resonant. She felt her pulse begin to speed up and determinedly focussed on more steadying topics, only to find her mind drifting back once more to lips that were masterful in the thoroughness of their kiss.

She felt those lips against hers as though they were real—then realized, in a moment of shock, that they were. Her eyes flew open to make out the bare outline of his form in the darkness. It was the world of sensation which was fully illumined for her—the warmth of him, the scent of him, the solidity of him beneath the hand she raised.

"Alex?" She whispered hoarsely. *"What are you doing?"*

"Just kissing you goodnight, love." His breath fanned her cheek, then tickled her ear. "I brought your specs back—you left them in the lounge. They're on the dresser now. Sleep well." He kissed her once more, a firm declaration of possession, then was gone.

He was crazy! That's all there was to it! *Crazy!* Creeping back into her room after Sylvia had so deliberately ousted him! *Crazy!* And his weird persistence on the subject of marriage . . . ! *Absolutely crazy!* Then she caught her breath at the realization that, for all she knew, *she* was crazy, *too!* Why else would her body be tingling and a strange sense of comfort be floating about her? Why else would she be touched, as she was now, at the thought that he had been looking after her, even in this very small way? Why else would she be wondering when she would see him again? In the morning? That night? When? Oh, yes, there was certainly a touch of craziness in her, all inspired by one Alex Knight. On that oddly giddy note she fell asleep.

As Sylvia had promised she was awakened at seven by the new nurse on duty, a young, extremely attractive woman about whom Alanna immediately began to wonder. Had she woken up *all* of the sleep lab patients? Of course, she must have. And that would include Alex. Had *he* appreciated that? He seemed the type, she mused snidely, not even bothering to excuse her waspishness as part of her early morning mood. Perhaps Ellen Henderson was right; at this moment Alanna would have liked nothing better than to stroke out her frustration at the swimming pool down the street. With a sigh she began to dress. That would have to wait until tomorrow when she was equipped with her suit, cap and goggles. For today, she had better concentrate on getting herself in shape to function as usual at WallMar Enterprises. She would stop at home after work today for anything she might need tonight and tomorrow.

Dressing carefully in the clean clothes she had packed yesterday, she struggled at length with her makeup to counter the inner tension she felt. When the nurse returned with the coffee she had requested, she was grateful. Coffee helped. Standing back finally to examine the finished product, she was satisfied. Her plum-hued dress hugged her figure and contrasted with the lightness of her coloring. Her hair was pulled back into its traditional sleek knot, exuding efficiency. Her eyes were highlighted with brown, her cheeks accented with pink, her lips glossed with plum to blend with the dress. Glasses perched upon the bridge of her nose, she hoisted her bag, then her purse, and headed for the door.

There was no sign of anyone in the lounge. Passing by the nurses' station, Alanna handed in her log and the half-completed questionnaires, then headed for the cafeteria and some breakfast. Again there were no familiar faces. It was only when she had retrieved her car from the lot and was headed for work that she admitted a twinge of disappointment. Alex must have left even earlier than she had. What did he look like, fresh in the morning? Or did he awaken with a touch of the bear, as she did? Perhaps it was for the best that their paths hadn't crossed, after all. He needed time to realize the absurdity of his proposal—and she needed time to reinforce the same idea in her own mind. The morning light clearly illumined its folly. Alex was headed for his life, she for hers. This was the way it was destined to be; it *was* for the best.

WallMar Enterprises welcomed her, as it did each day, with a deskful of messages and memoranda. Here was involvement—instant and unavoidable. Within the quarter hour she dealt with three men, all unit directors under her jurisdiction, who entered simultaneously, each bent on testing the strength of her shoulders. There was a small matter regarding personnel concerning one of the men, a more critical issue of funding for a newly instituted project concerning another. It was the third, however, who drew most deeply on her store of patience.

"I tried to get you last night, Alanna." It was Brian Winstead who confronted her insolently. "There was no answer at your apartment. I gave up at about one." His tone lowered in scathing sarcasm. "Is your phone out of order?"

Brian's implication was obvious. Alanna's refusal to stoop to his level was equally so.

"I was out all night," she stared boldly at him, challenging him to deepen his slander to her face. With two onlookers, the standoff was a tense one. Whether it was the chill of her glare or the evenness of her words, or simply the fact that she was his superior in the corporate structure, Alanna did not stop to analyze. When he failed to offer a follow-up she continued smoothly, "What seems to be the problem, Brian?"

Sitting behind her desk, the image of composure, Alanna hid from the world the inner torment that this subtle needling caused. The three men before her stood witness to her utterly professional handling of the problem, a matter of delays in the shipment of several lab supplies, the manufacture of which was a new direction for WallMar, which had earned its reputation as a quality company with a number of paper products. Making notes to herself as Brian spoke, she offered her spontaneous advice, with promises of more specific information later in the day.

After the trio's departure she helped herself to a cup of coffee from the department supply, then returned to her office, shut her door and spent twenty minutes studying the proposal from her next three visitors, who arrived promptly. They were scientists, men with whom she had already met on three separate occasions. The project they presented was risky, but did have the potential, in her eyes, of developing into a lucrative venture for WallMar Enterprises. Alanna eagerly briefed Jake Wallace on the meeting as soon as the scientists had departed.

"It's a fascinating proposition, Jake," she began, taking a seat close by his own desk chair. Her folders were on his desk; as she needed papers from one or the other she reached easily for them. "We've never ventured into this particular field before."

Jake Wallace stroked his clean-shaven jaw. "Umm. Biotechnics. Sounds very complex. Do *you* understand it?"

"Yes. It's really very simple. These men want to be able to apply modern biological techniques to make highly accurate tests for diagnosing various diseases. What interests us, obviously, is that they need our money. The total amount we're talking about is roughly one percent of our assets, so our risk is a reasonable one. With this money they can put together and—with our help— produce and market kits for diagnosis."

Jake nodded, listening intently as he skimmed the page of figures Alanna had placed before him. His ability to listen and read simultaneously always amazed her, yet he did both well. It was as though his mind was able to soak up information much faster than most; Alanna admired and envied the talent.

She sat back silently as he read the rest of the information she had compiled. When he lifted his head he smiled and she knew she had cleared the first hurdle. "Think you have another winner, Alanna?" The twinkle in his eye hinted at a touch of paternal pride.

"I think *we've* got another one, Jake. I haven't steered you too far wrong yet, have I?"

"Since you've joined us, my dear, you've had miraculous success. If it hadn't been for that small matter of desktop computers—"

Alanna grinned, sensing his teasing. "I'll never live that down, will I?"

"Well, blast it, girl, you keep doing everything else right. It's only fair that you make a mistake or two—and that *we* can know that we're not the only ones who make them. You do know," he sobered abruptly as his train of thought shifted, "that the board meeting is coming up next week? I'm proposing you for Executive Vice-President."

"Executive Vice-President?" Alanna's eyes widened in disbelief. "Jake, isn't that a little too much?"

Jake Wallace let loose one of his famous guffaws. "You're the only one in this corporation who would question her own promotion, and there's no one who would deserve it more."

"I don't know. . . ."

"What don't you know? Jim Callahan is retiring and you've already been doing most of his work for the past few months."

"I know. . . ." She stood to walk around the room. It was ironic; when she should be thoroughly pleased she had reservations. Jake was, fortunately, someone to whom she could talk freely. If the promotion did come through she would present a face of total confidence to the company. Now, however, if there were matters to discuss, she could consider both the pro and the con.

"This is awfully close on the heels of my move to Vice-President for Development. Don't *you* think so, Jake?" She turned to face him.

"That was over a year and a half ago," he reasoned gently. "You earned the position then; now you've earned a chance at this new one." He studied her closely. "What is it that worries you?" When she hesitated he helped her. "The men? They're still at it?"

A sheepish smile crossed her face. "Unfortunately, yes. Brian had a good line this morning." She imitated his drawl. "I tried to get you last night, Alanna. . . ."

"And did you explain where you'd been?" Jake, who knew about the IAT study, asked.

"Of course not!" she snapped. "I don't have to explain myself to Brian or anyone else!"

At her vehement defense her mentor grinned. "I agree with you. That's precisely why you should accept this promotion to Executive V.P. without hesitation. You've earned it and you do the work. That's all that matters." He frowned. "By the way, how *did* it go last night? Any great insight as to the cause of the problem or a solution to it?"

Alanna shook her head, leaning comfortably against the edge of Jake's credenza. "No. It's very interesting—everything that Ellen Henderson told me about insomnia. And I am hopeful. As for last night, however, I'm afraid I have to chalk it up to experience."

"What do you mean?"

"It was an introductory night. I was—as they put it—'wired up' to establish my sleep pattern. The real work, if you can call it that, begins tonight." Even as she talked her mind had shifted to another topic. "Jake," she heard herself speak right out, "have you ever heard of Alex Knight?"

"Of course I've heard of him. Only someone who is deaf, dumb and blind could not be aware of the Knight family!"

"I guess I put that poorly." She smiled self-consciously, thereby attracting Jake's even more intense scrutiny. "*What* do you know about the man?"

"Why?"

It was a typical Jake Wallace rejoinder, bringing a broader, more relaxed smile to Alanna's face. "I can always count on you, Jake," she shook her head in acknowledgement, "to get right to the point."

"That's how I got where I am, my dear. You should know that by now."

"Oh, I know it very well! You seem to be able to sift out the important questions from the unimportant ones. How do you do that?"

It wasn't the first time she had asked him the question;

as in other instances, he humored her. "Instinct, Alanna. You've got it, too. And, I'm still waiting—"

"For what?" Her blond brows met just above her glasses.

"For an answer to *my* question. Why do you want to know about Alexander Knight?"

"He asked me to marry him." She dropped the bomb without a blink.

Jake did blink. Several times. "He *what?*"

Alanna stifled her enjoyment of his surprise. Right about now it *did* sound like an uproarious joke. "Actually, he didn't *ask* me. He *told* me. He told me that I was going to be his wife."

"Now just a minute. Is he on the up-and-up?" There was a paternalism about Jake that warmed Alanna to her core. If only her own father had been like this—concerned, excited, protective. But her own father had been in a world of his own—and her relationship with him was a world away.

"He's repeated it several times. He says that he plans to marry me." She shrugged, as though it were the most normal thing in the world to receive a marriage proposition from a man of the apparent social standing of Alex Knight. "Now I need to know what *you* know about him."

"Rumor in corporate circles has it that the man's a whiz. His daddy was one in his day; this one is supposedly new and better. Have you known him long? You never told me—"

"I don't know him! I just met him last night—at the hospital, if you can believe it! He's terribly arrogant."

"And a very good catch!" Jake's quip caught her off guard.

"Jake, you know how I feel about that. Marriage isn't my thing. I'm very happy with my life the way it is. Jake . . ." her tone was warning, "I don't like the way you're smiling."

Jake was, indeed, smiling broadly now. "Sorry, Alanna, but I really think the idea has potential. The man is about the right age; he's well established and respected and you could use—"

"I could not!" Dark brown eyes conveyed her determination. Jake knew it well and opted to take a different tack.

"What was the . . . cause for your meeting, in the first place?"

A few deep breaths settled her somewhat. "He's taking part in the study."

"He has insomnia?"

She chuckled, recalling the moment when she had asked Alex the same question. "Yes. It looks as though we're destined to meet at two in the morning in the lounge. Let me tell you, the nurse there is a terrific watchdog. I really have nothing to be afraid of." Her gay explanation was met by full seriousness on Jake's part.

"We'll just invite the two of you over for dinner one night—"

"No, you won't!" She cringed. "I'm trying to *dis*courage the man, not the reverse. He's persistent enough as it is without a formal word of approval from you and Elaine!"

Jake remained sober. "I think you should at least give him a chance. Get to know him. See whether he's serious."

"Oh, he's serious, all right! But, I have no intention of pandering to his whim. I really don't have the time—"

"Nonsense!" His two meaty hands came down forcefully on the desk as he sat suddenly forward. "You can make time for anything you want, Alanna. I've seen you do incredible things since you've been here. Yet you still manage to coach those little girls at the pool and cart my Elaine to the beauty parlor and take courses at the university in the evenings. If you want a little romance you can easily make time for it!"

Alanna would long since have squelched this discussion with anyone else. But Jake was like family. When he spoke it was from the heart, and she listened. Not that that kept her from arguing. . . . "I *don't* want romance, Jake. You don't seem to understand."

"You're right. I don't. You know, I do respect you women nowadays. You've really come a long way. But you've pushed aside certain things, forgotten about others. What about love? A family? Children?"

Alanna shrugged, then sighed deeply. "I suppose I've chosen other goals."

"Must it be one or the other?"

"Now, how can I be—heaven help me—the Executive Vice-President of WallMar Enterprises and have a husband and children at home?" she asked grudgingly.

"Men do it all the time. Why not a woman?"

Silence filled the air for long moments. Alanna had never thought of it quite that way. As a matter of fact, she had never spent much time thinking about the subject of a husband and children at all. No man had ever interested her enough to even spark the consideration.

"Why are you saying all this to me now, Jake?" she asked plaintively. "You've never mentioned it before. Why now? I thought you approved of my . . . lifestyle."

Jake stood and circled the desk to throw an arm about Alanna's shoulder. "We *care* about you. You know that. I've never mentioned it before because . . . you never have. I felt it would be awkward to bring it up. But now I have to be honest. You have a lot to give, Alanna. Look at what you do for Elaine and me, for those kids, for so many of the people you come in contact with. Don't you see—you've found any number of substitutes for the family you don't have. Well," his voice lowered and softened, "maybe you should consider whether you're ready for the real thing."

Alanna snorted. "If it's children I want, I could always—"

"—I'm talking about a man. A husband. Someone to spend the rest of your life with."

"I'm an independent woman, Jake."

He eyed her strangely. "You've already proven that. Now it may be time to prove some other things."

Disturbed, she pulled gently away from his arm and walked across the room, blond head down, hands clasped in front of her. "Please don't confuse me, Jake. My life is perfect as it is."

Her dear friend sighed. "And that's why you have trouble sleeping at night."

"Honestly!" she exploded, looking toward the heavens for help. "You sound just like *him!*" Suddenly she had had enough. "Look, I've got to get back to work. Can we discuss the biotechnology proposal later?"

Jake's smile was understanding. "Sure thing, Alanna."

"Good." Heading for the door, she kept her eyes downcast. "I'll catch you later."

He caught her arm, staying her for an instant. "Just think," he spoke softly, temptingly, "you could have it all. Executive Vice-President. Alexander Knight. Love. Security. Kids. Think about it."

For a last minute, she stared directly at him. "You, my friend, are as crazy as he is!" And with that she made her most regal exit in total defiance of the doubts that raged within. Jake was both friend and near-family. She respected his opinion and what he had said that morning lingered to haunt her throughout much of the day. By the time the sun had lowered in the sky and she headed for the hospital once more Alanna was in no mood to play games with Alex Knight. Having fixed a light dinner at her apartment, where she picked up clean clothes and the other things she would need for the night and the morning, she went directly to the sleep unit. It was her fondest hope that she would *not* bump horns on this particular evening with that very disturbing man.

At least that was what she told herself as she stepped from the elevator and checked in with Sylvia. And it was what she told herself as she dropped her things off in her room. It was what she still told herself as she sat down for a few moments with Ellen Henderson.

Yet her eye surveyed every room she entered, her pulse raced as she spotted *his* name on Ellen's desk, her skin warmed when she sought refuge in the lounge on the sofa they had shared so very, very early this morning. And, finally, when that deep and now-familiar voice crooned softly by her ear she felt strangely satisfied.

"How're you doing, owl-eyes?"

4

Without turning, she raised her head. Her lips bore a hint of a smile as he leaned toward her to kiss her cheek lightly. It was impossible to deny the physical effect he had on her, the melting of her insides at his nearness, the quickening of her pulse. Yet she steeled herself as best she could and feigned sternness when he circled the sofa to sit beside her.

"I'll have you know, Alexander Knight, that Ellen asked some very pointed questions about my sleep pattern. It seems there were certain irregularities at roughly four this morning . . ."

His "Tell me about it," suggested that she had no need; he already knew.

For the first time Alanna's glance stole to his face, finding an instant reward in the warmth it held. There was an openness about him—an openness free of both craftiness and any ulterior motive. She could almost imagine that he was her most intimate friend and lover— then she caught herself. He was neither. He would be neither. Perhaps it was time he understood that.

"Alex . . ."

"Yeeess . . ." he drawled, his gaze devouring her with frightening ardor.

"Alex, this is absurd! You take this as a joke. What excuse did *you* give to Ellen?"

"I told her," he said simply, "that I planned to marry you. I also told her that, while I intend to continue with this study now that I've begun, I can make no promises to keep my hands off you."

"Alex!" She shook her head in disbelief. "This has to stop! We're here for very serious reasons. I don't know about you, but it took *me* a long time to admit the need for help. Now that I'm here, I want it."

He shrugged. "So what's the problem?"

"The problem," her eyes flashed in reproach, "is the matter of complications. Kisses stolen in the elevator, on the stairs, in the lounge, *in bed* . . . it has to end."

Alex sobered. "I agree with you there."

"Then . . . you'll keep a safe distance . . . ?" Whether her timidity was in part attributable to dismay, even disappointment at such an easy victory, she was too involved to ponder.

"I'll do no such thing." His lips were firm with determination. "*Stealing* kisses has to end. Once you accept my proposal, even agree to wear my ring, we can do it out in the open!"

Alanna was sadly daunted by his persistence. Shaking her head again, she looked away. "What am I going to do with you?" she asked, half to herself.

His voice was deeper, closer. "You can begin by greeting me properly. I haven't seen you since very, very early this morning. I've put in a difficult day at the office—"

"So have I!"

"Then let me show you the kind of comfort *you* need."

Alanna had no time to protest. Strong fingers cupped her chin, tilting it up as his lips descended to meet hers, parting them swiftly, then proceeding to adore them with a sweetness that stole her breath. It was the kind of kiss she would look forward to at the end of a long day, the kind of kiss she would rush home to, the kind of kiss she could return with a similar offer of comfort and ardor. Which she did. Spontaneously. Reflexively. Intuitively. Without a thought in the world beyond the delight of the moment. It was a perfect pairing, an intermeshing of lips and tongues in perfect harmony with each other. When one coaxed, the other responded. When one challenged, the other satisfied. When, at long last, he moved slowly to the side, Alanna felt bereft. Her forehead fell to his shoulder; her breath was ragged. His was no better.

"That was nice," he whispered against her ear, his fingers curving around the back of her neck to gently massage it. At no other point did their bodies touch. "I'd like to come home to that every night," he voiced her own thought. "What do you think?"

Alanna lifted her head, struggling to sort out her thoughts against the powerful distraction of the fingers that had slipped beneath the neckline of her blouse to draw lazy circles on her upper back. "I think," she breathed shallowly, "that there is a definite physical attraction between us. It doesn't necessitate marriage."

His fingers halted their sensual barrage and slowly withdrew. Alex's expression grew suddenly taut, enigmatic emotions sharpening his glare. "It's true, then."

His statement, spoken in a low and somber tone, puzzled her. "What is?"

"Rumor." At her continued confusion, he explained. "Part of my day was spent learning everything I could about Alanna Evans. There was quite a bit, starting with your appointment as Administrative Assistant at Wall-Mar Enterprises seven years ago, covering your promotions to Director of Development, then Vice-President. And I understand that Jim Callahan is about to retire, leaving an even more prime position open . . . should

Jake Wallace be inclined to name you to it. A remarkably fast rise."

It was the kind of discussion Alanna might have expected to have with one of her more ambitious colleagues—not with Alexander Knight. These words, coming from him, carried far greater impact. Defiance stiffened her spine, hurt directed her gaze. "What are you implying?"

"I think you know."

"Oh, I know, all right." She confronted him with a confidence born of innocence. "But I wanted to hear *you* say it. It's precisely the kind of thing I've had to listen to for the past few years. I expected it from them. Somehow I didn't from you—though I'm not sure why."

For a fleeting moment he seemed the slightest bit unsure. "Are you denying it?"

"I have nothing to deny." Her voice was even, her head held with pride. Only her clenched hands—always her hands—suggested her torment. "If you want a denial you'll have to make the claim first."

His lips softened, though his eyes remained wary. "Always on the offensive, eh, Alanna?"

"What's the matter?" she taunted him. "Don't have the guts to say it?" She could feel herself beginning to boil. "Is this too public a place to air the dirty laundry? It's all right to kiss here, but not to clear the air?"

"Keep your voice down," he warned. His gray-eyed gaze didn't stray from hers.

Alanna stood up. Though she wasn't quite ready to admit it, Alex's unspoken implication had hurt her more deeply than this particular rumor had ever hurt her before. If this man planned to push her to her limits the challenge was now one of maintaining a self-control that was on the verge of shattering.

"I'll raise my voice when and where I please. When I'm at work there is a certain standard of behavior that is expected from me and I stick to it faithfully. *Here* is another matter. This whole thing—insomnia, you, your persistent talk of marriage—is entirely emotional. If I want to yell, I will."

Breathing hard, she stood several feet from Alex. When he smirked, she recoiled. "At least you're not quite the automaton you'd like people to believe," he observed. "Temper is a very good thing."

"Temper?" she cried, then did lower her voice as she realized the extent to which she was letting him upset her. "You haven't heard anything yet! For starters, I want you to leave me alone." She was trembling now. "I don't want little kisses here and there. I don't want clandestine visits in the middle of the night. And I don't want your nonsense about me marrying you! What man wants a wife who has no scruples?" As his glance sharpened she repeated herself. "That's right. Isn't that what you didn't have the courage to say just now? *No scruples.* A woman who sleeps her way to the top has *no scruples.* There. That thought should keep you away from me!"

With a last scathing glance she made her escape, fleeing to her room, shutting the door, crossing to the night-dark window and tossing her glasses onto the nearby table to stare into nothingness. She felt as though she had been attacked, assaulted by some unknown force. Why had he said that? Why had he implied what he had? And why had she reacted—overreacted—that way? Yes, it was an emotional issue. In the office she could ignore it. Why couldn't she do so now? If she had wanted a buffer against the lure of Alex Knight this misconception was as good as any. Why, then, did she feel battered? Defeated? Anguished?

"I'm sorry, Alanna." Alex had entered without her knowledge and stood close behind her. When he reached for her she flinched, and he dropped his hand.

"Please leave me alone," she demanded coolly.

"I can't do that. I've hurt you. I won't sleep well until I make up for that hurt."

"Sleep well! Hah! I guess that's the bottom line!"

"Sarcasm doesn't befit you, Alanna."

"Then leave and you won't have to listen to any more."

"Not until we straighten this out."

Alanna wheeled around and started for the call button. "Then I'll just get Sylvia in here—"

"You'll do no such thing," he growled, catching her arms and swinging her around to face him. "This is between you and me. We don't need a referee."

"Are you sure about that?" She scowled at him. "You've just had a taste of my 'temper.' When it really gets going it's an awesome thing!"

He was still for long moments, weighing his alternatives. When his grip loosened she quickly tore her arm away and retreated to the window to stand with her back to him, her arms about herself.

"You know, Alanna, I somehow didn't picture you as having a violent temper. When was the last time you lost it?"

He couldn't have asked a more poignant question. She remembered the moment perfectly. "Roughly ten years ago."

"That's some self-control."

"Not really. I just try to . . . minimize situations where I will be pushed that far."

"Tell me about it."

This time it was a request, and so gently offered that she was helpless to refuse. After long moments she began. "I had been dating this fellow—Shep Harding— through the last two years of college. We were very . . . close. When I decided to go on to graduate school—to get an M.B.A.—he put everything on the line."

Alex's voice came from directly behind her. "Career or him?"

"Exactly."

"So you let him have it?" She heard the smile in his voice and it coaxed her on.

"You could say that. I told him that if it was a warm body he wanted he could pick up another one at the student union. If it was *me* he wanted he'd have to accept me for what I was. I had no desire to be at home all day, waiting for him. I wanted to be out *there*, doing things, using every bit of myself—"

She caught her breath as she realized how he might, if he wanted, interpret her words. As though reading her mind he spoke softly, putting his hands gently on her shoulders. This time she didn't pull away. "I know exactly what you're saying, Alanna. And, believe me, I have no doubts that you've earned everything you've gotten— earned it through work in the office, everything aboveboard."

She cocked her head sideways. "How can you be sure? After all, many women today—"

"You're not *many* women, as you were so quick to tell me more than once last night." The light pressure he exerted was sufficient to turn her. She had to tilt her head back to study his face. Its intensity held her immobile, as his hands slid slowly along her arms. "There may be rumors, Alanna. But you have also built a reputation as being intelligent, on top of every situation, an able negotiator and an honest person. What you told me back there," he cocked his dark head toward the door, "what you showed me in the process, suggests that if you *were* having an affair with Wallace—"

"Jake is married!" she interrupted angrily.

His fingers tightened. "I know that. Let me finish. If you were having an affair with Wallace you would never have been able to keep up that image of coolness in the office." He suddenly grinned. "It seems, love, that you're much more of an emotional creature than your very proper facade would lead one to believe."

Alanna felt the beginnings of that melting sensation, the thawing of her chill beside the hearth of Alex's warm persuasion. "I don't deny being emotional," she offered defensively, "even though I do keep emotions out of the office. I *do* deny ever having used my body to achieve advancement."

"*Corporate* advancement," he corrected softly.

"*Any* kind of advancement."

A dark brow shot up at her insistence. "What *do* you use your body for? Wouldn't you say that pleasure and relaxation and fulfillment are goals worth advancing?"

She eyed him warily. "I don't sleep around. Period."

"Did you sleep with Shep Harding?"

"Yes, I did. I thought I was in love with him. It seemed the most natural thing at the time."

"I'm sure it was. There's only one proper way of expressing that deepest love that two people can feel for each other. I'm not condemning you."

"I should hope not! After all, Alex, are *you* a virgin?"

As he laughed aloud his arms closed about her and pressed her more closely to him. "You know I'm not. And I should think you wouldn't want me to be." His voice lowered dangerously, a sensual quality creeping from it into her body. "I've learned by trial and error. I've made my mistakes on others. Now, for you," he pressed his lips to her brow, "I know just how," then her eyes, "to touch," his hands began an exploration of her back, "and tease," then rose to her shoulders by way of her breasts, "and find every sensitive spot." His thumbs caressed her neck and throat; his lips trailed wildfire across her cheek. Alanna couldn't breathe, his assault was so sensually precise. Her heart thudded loudly, barely muted when covered by his full palm. She could only sigh her content at being touched with such tenderness, could only open her lips to the return of his kiss. Then she realized what she was doing. With the greatest effort she tore her mouth from his and quickly clutched at the first thought to enter her muddled brain.

"Have *you* ever been in love?"

Alex allowed the small distance, studying her indulgently. "Are we still relating this to my virginity, or, uh, lack of it?"

"I wasn't," she continued less shakily, "but since you've raised the issue, it's an interesting one. Did you wait for your first true love?"

Looking ceilingward in supplication, he murmured, "Why do I sense an imminent discussion of double standards . . . ?"

"*Were* you in love?"

"Of course not." His eyes met hers. "I was young and curious. *She* was the one who knew what to do. It was a purely physical thing."

"Have you *ever* been in love?" Alanna persisted.

A gray glimmer heralded his response. "I am now."

"Uh-huh," she humored him. "But *before*. Or, more specifically, why have you never married?"

"I've never been in love before."

This time Alanna's eyes rolled toward the ceiling in a silent plea for patience. "But there must have been a bevy of women over the years. Didn't any tempt you into considering marriage?"

Humor lurked at the corners of Alex's lips. "One or two."

"Oh?" Did she actually feel the tiniest twinge of jealousy? *Impossible*.

"As a matter of fact," he said, deceptively sober, "there were *three* times when I considered it. The first time was with Sharon. She was a childhood friend; our families would have loved it. The second time was with Jill. I was at college then and particularly annoyed at my father about some petty matter. I might have married her just to spite him."

"And the third?" she prodded, curious.

"The third," he sighed, "was a dear friend who found herself in trouble."

"Pregnant?"

"Yes."

Alanna's eyes widened. "Yours?"

"No. I'd never even slept with her."

She was puzzled. "But you would have married her?"

"Yes." Alex answered without hesitation. "I thought enough of her to care that the child had a name, a father and some security."

"What about the biological father?"

He took a breath. "He was in Vietnam . . . never made it back." The sadness in Alex's eyes spoke of his own sense of loss.

Alanna's voice lowered. "I'm sorry." Hesitantly, she sought the end of the story. "And . . . what happened to her?"

Snapping back to the present, he raised strong fingers to lightly caress her face. "She lost the baby. But she's gotten married since. From what I hear she's got four kids now."

Alanna struggled to digest this newly revealed depth of Alex's character as she fought to cope with the resurgence of desire that his restless fingers were creating. Alex sensed her moment of vulnerability and seized on it, kissing her thoroughly, searching out the depths which, at that moment, she was helpless to seal off. He *was* the masterful seducer, having perfected the art over the years. And he had found her weak spot.

His lips devastated her with their exactness, drawing small sighs and a growing response from her own. His kiss held just the right blend of advance and retreat, luring her toward the point of entrapment. And what sweet entrapment it was. Mindlessly she swayed toward it, unable to think of anything but the pleasure of the moment.

Then, from amid the sensual eddy, she discovered another of his consummate skills as he very gently began to undress her. One after the other, with quiet deliberation, he released the buttons of her blouse. In the process his fingers brushed her skin again and again, always departing even before the whispered cry had escaped her passion-swollen lips. She was enthralled and quite happily at his mercy. Finally, with the last button, the silken fabric fell open. His hands slid along her flesh, easily finding the simple catch of her bra.

Alanna's knees trembled. His touch was wonderful, inspiring feelings of femininity she had forced herself to forget for too long. Now, with the force of waters suddenly undammed, these feelings surged forward. Eagerly she met his kiss and arched her body against him. His lips clung to hers as, with both hands, he eased the blouse from her shoulders, discarding it and her bra on the floor. His fingers traveled across her flesh, hungry, insatiable, for long moments. Then, with a moan deep in his throat, he lifted her and put her down on the bed. Taking both her hands in his and pinning them to the sheets by her shoulders, he paused to look at her, his gaze searing its way from her face down her neck to the twin peaks of her breasts, now full and creamy, awaiting his touch. Her breath came in shortened gasps, adding to the temptation of her body.

Alanna thought she would explode. This man had unleashed a flood tide of desire within her; only his possession would salve the growing ache within. But he stilled, almost in awe. His hands released hers, then fell to cup her breasts, holding each as he lowered his head to that soft fullness. One at a time he teased the rosy peaks until each was a tiny pebbled dome quivering for more. When his lips returned to hers she could deny him nothing. Her kiss contained her very soul—for it was there that Alex Knight had found her vulnerability.

"I love you," he whispered, then repeated it louder, more firmly. "I love you."

Her returning whisper was shaky. "You don't love me. You may love my body, or some image of the woman you think you've waited for all these years. But you don't love me. You can't. You don't know me."

Alanna watched as he straightened and reached for his tie, his eyes dark with smoldering passion. "I do love you, Alanna." Hard upon the disposal of his tie went his jacket. She lay still, mesmerized. She knew she should stop him—this was totally improper—yet she wanted to see him as he saw her now. Reaching forward, she set her own fingers to the task of unbuttoning his shirt, gasping as she pushed it aside to reveal his chest, so broad and bronzed and solid. He picked her up then and pulled her against him, their bodies, bare from the waist up, touching with a rapture Alanna could only have imagined. She cried aloud at the beauty of it and clung to him, savoring the strength of him against her breasts, her arms, her torso.

"I love you, Alanna. I need you." He spoke softly and with conviction, his breath wisping the few loose strands of her hair. He held her back and removed each pin in turn, then spread her golden tresses over her shoulders, his fingers going on to trail further over her flesh.

Alanna was caught up in a hurricane of desire. Its winds blew with such force that she couldn't resist it. His words rocked her, yet she couldn't refute them. His hands inflamed her, yet she couldn't pull away. Her senses swirled round and round, faster and faster, each concentric circle bringing her closer to the center of fulfillment.

Nothing was beyond his reach. His lips never left hers for long, drugging her again and again while his hands played against her with the very expertise of which he'd spoken. She was vaguely aware that he had removed her skirt, but it didn't matter; all that was real was the headiness of his touch, the driving need for more of him.

It was Alex's raw whisper that brought her out of her daze for a moment. "Alanna," he growled, "do you know what you're doing?"

Blinking, she followed his gaze to her hands—*her* hands—where they lay at his belt. She knew exactly *what* she was doing; it was the *wisdom* of the move that halted her abruptly.

"Oh, Alex," she moaned in apology. "You do something to my mind! I had completely forgotten where we are—"

He took her hands in his and lifted them to his mouth, kissing her curled fingers. "I think we've both been carried away." His pause was pregnant with meaning, his eyes growing darker by the minute. "Damn it! I can't even say we'll carry on at my place tonight, can I?"

At first Alanna shared his regret. For the first time in years she had wanted a man. Really *wanted* him. Even now her body cried out its need. On second thought, however, she *was* appalled at the setting. This hospital room was no place for lovemaking. And this hospital room would be her home for the next two weeks.

Finally she was relieved. Things had happened much too quickly. To have been carried away by an overwhelming physical craving would have been wrong. She was a woman of calm and careful deliberation, not one to be bowled over by a singularly attractive man. And he was attractive. No, *magnificent*. Her eye skimmed over his physique in appreciation; then she was jarred out of her reverie by his low bark.

"If you continue to look at me that way I won't be responsible for anything I do. So help me," he looked over his shoulder, "I'll make love to you in the bathroom with my back against the door to keep Sylvia out!"

Alanna burst into spontaneous laughter. "That's an amazing picture," she finally gasped, crossing her arms over her chest in a token gesture of propriety. "I don't think Sylvia would appreciate your efforts."

"My efforts, Alanna, are going to be played through in another minute if you don't do something to stem the tide." Standing, he hauled her up beside him, turned her toward the bathroom and gave her a firm but gentle shove. "Take a shower or something. *I* intend to!"

Smiling now from another emotion entirely, she took his advice, seeking haven in the bathroom, stepping out of her slip and panty hose and finally discarding the wisps of silk that were her panties atop the pile. Her thoughts were of Alex as she bent to turn on the water, then stretched to adjust the shower spray. He was, in spite of his arrogance and his one-tracked determination to marry her, an endearing sort. And the effect of his lovemaking on her—that went unchallenged. Standing nude before the mirror, she reached back to wind her hair atop her head when her attention was caught by a movement in the mirror.

"Alex!" She whirled around, then stood stock-still, caught anew in the web of enchantment he cast so well.

His eyes didn't miss an inch of her, yet she stood proud and unwavering before him. When he approached she let her hands fall to his shoulders. His shirt was on but still open. It had taken only his gaze to ignite the sparks of passion, barely banked at best, within her. His nearness now was more than she could bear. If he intended to carry out the threat he'd uttered moments before she wouldn't stop him. Her own need was far too great.

"I love you," he moaned against her lips, kissing her deeply, plunging his tongue into her mouth, tasting every recess before wrenching his lips away. Her fingers were white as they clutched his shoulders, her shudders visible when he bent his head to kiss her neck and tongue her breasts. When he moved lower she could only let her head fall back and sigh her delight. That Alex should take such pleasure in her body was heady enough in itself; that his pleasure should set off such shock waves of ecstasy within her was even headier.

At what point her knees buckled she didn't know. Suddenly she found herself kneeling with him. His hands framed her face; his lips caressed her features. It was only the taste of the moisture on his upper lip that brought a returning glimpse of reality.

"The shower!" she cried, jumping up to fumble with the controls until a deep voice from behind gave a firm order.

"Get in, love. I'll see you later."

She turned in time to see him leave the bathroom and its penetrating cloud of mist.

Hot, hot water punished her body in a steady stream as Alanna tried to understand what had happened. There was Alex—Alex who declared his intent to marry her, Alex who claimed he loved her, Alex who wanted her very much. And there was Alanna—a passionate Alanna she barely recognized. The Alanna she thought she'd known had no need for a man; this one craved Alex desperately. The Alanna she thought she'd known was in full and absolute control of herself; this one had thrown caution to the winds and lost herself in desire. The Alanna she thought she'd known was a professional, with her life neatly mapped out; this one wondered what the future held.

Without doubt she was still opposed to marriage. She had spent the past ten-plus years of her life building defenses against it. Hadn't her mother told her, "Don't succumb, Alanna. You have too much to give. Develop yourself to your full potential. Don't end up *this* way. . . ."

She grasped the shower control and twisted it until the water ran cold and sharp. The frigid battering was just punishment for thoughts of yielding to the autocracy of Alex Knight. If she married him *she* would be a Knight. Her mind conjured up the image of a docile society bride, sweetly accompanying her husband to dinner parties and openings and yachting meets and Labor Day barbecues. What would happen to Alanna Evans? Though poised and polished, she was not of that ilk. She had her own life . . . and liked it that way.

With a muffled groan she turned off the shower. As she dabbed the moisture from her skin her thoughts turned to the phenomenal physical attraction she felt for Alex. It was mutual—and that made it all the more exciting, all the more dangerous. Where would it end?

"Don't be stupid, Alanna," she chided herself aloud. "You know perfectly well where it will end if you don't watch yourself." Her eye moved to the bathroom door. For a moment of reckless imagining she wondered what it would have been like had Alex made love to her here. She pictured his limbs, long and tanned, his hips, narrow and strong. When a tingling erupted in her middle she fought the image, but it persisted. In all the years during which she'd built her career she'd never been attracted to a man this way—and there had been plenty, *plenty*, of men to choose from had she wished. Why Alex? Why now? Why here?

Cautiously, she opened the door, saw that her room was empty and held a towel against herself as she retrieved her nightgown from her bag and slid it over her head. That done she brushed her hair with a fierceness born of frustration, then settled down to tackle the questionnaires and sleep log she had neglected the night before. By eleven-thirty she was asleep.

By two-fifteen, however, she was awake. The room was dark and quiet. She lay on her side, one hand tucked under her pillow, the other comfortably before her on the bed. The pale sliver of light which crept beneath her door was the only source of illumination. It took several moments for her to awaken enough to move, then stretch, then gradually make out shapes in the darkness. She sat up with a gasp.

"It's all right, love." Alex rose in one fluid motion and crossed to her bed from the chair in which he had been sitting. "It's only me."

"How long have you been here?" she whispered, her perceptions still hazy.

"I'd guess for about half an hour."

"If Sylvia knew . . ." All grogginess had vanished.

"Forget Sylvia." He lifted the covers and slid in beside her before she could anticipate him. "I'm tired, but I can't sleep. Just let me lie here for a while."

It was the sound of true fatigue, the innocent need in his voice, that Alanna found most irresistible. With tentative obedience she let him pull her back against him, curving her body to the firm lines of his. His arm fell across her waist, anchoring her in place.

"Don't you think we're playing with fire, Alex?" she whispered.

"I know we are. But we have no choice. It's either this—or freeze."

His analogy was not quite apt, but she let it go without a fuss. In truth, lying here with him like this was a treat! Then, feeling guilty, she thought back on what Ellen had told her, seeking some justification for this late-night rendezvous.

"What were you thinking when you woke up, Alex?"

"I don't know," he snapped in odd annoyance, then calmed quickly. "I just woke up."

"Right *after* you did, what kept you awake? Normal people simply fall back to sleep once they awaken. We don't. Ellen suggested trying to pinpoint what type of thoughts keep us awake."

"Don't ask."

"I *am* asking." When he remained silent she tried a different approach, one that appealed to the sense of challenge they shared. "You said you loved me, Alex. If that's true you should feel free to share your thoughts with me. *Do* you love me—or are those simply three empty words?"

She felt his body tense behind her, then relax once more. "You play a mean game, Alanna."

"What were you thinking?" she persisted. "If I'm supposed to help you and in the process help myself, as Ellen suggested, we have to talk."

He pondered her words, stirring for a moment to draw her even closer. "You really want to know?"

"Yes!"

He inhaled deeply of the scented jasmine in her hair, rubbing his cheek against its silken flow before speaking. "I had a dream. It's the same one, over and over and over again, but I can never remember it after I wake. The feeling is always the same though, the feeling it leaves me with."

"What kind of feeling?"

"Emptiness. A pervading sense of emptiness."

Alanna suppressed a shudder. "Is that what kept you awake when you woke up tonight?"

"No." He seemed to hug her more tightly. "This time, when I woke up I thought of you."

"Alex . . ." she warned in a whisper, but he overrode her objection.

"You asked. You'll listen. I thought of you. I pictured you standing in the bathroom the way you were earlier. Your skin, pale and satiny. Your breasts, ripe and full. Your hips, slim and . . . so very ready for me—"

"Alex! No wonder you can't fall asleep! Why do you torment yourself over something you can't finish?"

Somehow Alex sensed her own torment. His voice was suddenly clearer. "Why do you say that?" When she had no ready answer he prodded, "Come on, Alanna. I may be reading between the lines—"

"You're not." She sighed, realizing that she'd fallen into a trap of her own making, one from which only the truth would free her. "I said that because it was the only thing that allowed *me* to fall asleep earlier. Men aren't the only ones with needs, you know."

"I thought you told me that you could do very well without me."

"I said," she corrected softly, "that I had no need for marriage, to you or anyone else."

"Haven't you *ever* considered it?"

"No."

"You've never fancied yourself in love since Harding?"

"I've learned the difference between 'fancying' and 'being.' No, I've never been . . . either . . . since Shep."

"But you do date."

"Once in a while."

"Who?"

"Who what?"

He tugged her closer in mock punishment. "Who do you date?"

Alanna shifted to peer up into his stern face. "Don't get yourself worked up, Alex. They're all just . . . friends."

"All?"

"There aren't a whole lot. And I rarely date anyone more than once or twice."

"A policy?"

"No, it just turns out that way."

"Would I know any of your men?"

"They're not 'my men' and I doubt it. They're as far away from the business world as possible."

Alex resettled himself in the darkness, sliding one long leg through hers. "No risk of compromise?"

"None."

"Smart girl."

"Only half of me is smart," Alanna quipped, feeling surprisingly at ease. "The other is selfish. I have no desire to spend an evening out discussing business when I deal with it every hour of the day."

"What *do* you like to do?"

"Oh, I enjoy a fine restaurant now and then, the theater, a movie."

"Parties?"

"A quiet one once in a while. Usually not, though. I like my free time to be more private."

"Ahah! A woman after my own mind! Just me and thee—"

"Alex . . ." Her tone held a gentle warning and his facetious singsong faded. In the next instant she almost wished she'd let him go on with his kidding, for he grew less playful, more pensive.

"A minute ago you spoke of needs, Alanna. Were you serious?"

She hesitated, suddenly fearful of the direction his thoughts were taking. But she couldn't lie. "Unfortunately, yes."

"Why 'unfortunately'?"

Her shrug was cushioned by his chest. "I always liked to believe that I had total control. . . ."

"According to what you've said you haven't been with a man for a very long time."

"I haven't."

"Then why would you suddenly have this problem with *needs?* Why the flare of raw physical desire?"

Alanna flinched at his bluntness. "You put that so delicately," she muttered beneath her breath, but he ignored her subtle rebellion.

"Why, love?" he asked softly. "Why now?" He pondered her silence as she asked herself the same question. But Alex came up with the answer she had hitherto refused to acknowledge. "It's *me*, isn't it?" Again he paused and again there was silence. "Answer me, damn it, Alanna. Am I the first one to stir those feelings since—"

"Yes." Though she whispered the word almost grudgingly, he heard it well. A tremor passed through him in response.

"Ahhhhh," he breathed against her hair. "That's the nicest thing I've heard in years. It almost makes insomnia worthwhile."

Alanna didn't know what to say. Her confession was one she would rather not have made. Would he use this information against her? Would he use her weakness to push her toward marriage? Would he take total and merciless advantage of the physical attraction he now knew she shared?

To her astonishment he did nothing but shift more

comfortably behind her. She felt his chest against her back, his thighs against her own. A gentle hand tucked a loose strand of her hair behind an ear, then stroked her cheek lightly.

"Good night, love," he whispered contentedly. Within minutes his slow and steady breathing told of his return to sleep. Alanna had little time to debate the wisdom of his staying, however. Within minutes the warmth of his body and the comfort of his presence put her to sleep as well.

When she awoke the next morning to feel a tentative hand on her shoulder it was that of the day nurse, not Alex. He had, at some prior and unknown point, returned to his room, saving them both a spate of awkward explanations. Indeed, in her morning daze she wondered whether she had imagined the entire episode. It had been lovely and uncomplicated—his crawling into bed to sleep quietly with her. And she could not deny one very notable fact: last night, even given her brief period of wakefulness, she had slept more soundly—and now felt more refreshed—than at any time in recent memory! On that very intriguing note she headed for the swimming pool.

5

When Alanna arrived at the pool, an indoor facility she had had occasion to visit several times with her girls, there were already a dozen early risers swimming laps. She sat on the edge to tuck her hair beneath her cap and position her goggles when something caught her eye. Or rather, someone. A man. He was easily the most proficient of the swimmers. He stroked smoothly from one end of the pool to the other, then flipped underwater to begin the return lap.

Despite her impatience to start her own lap she found her gaze following this man, mesmerized. Powerful arms pulled him forward with every stroke, those same arms glistening beneath the bright lighting as they sliced the air before entering the water again. His motion was unhurried, his breathing steady. His legs scissored only enough to ensure a streamlined stroke.

"Are you going?" The voice of another swimmer waiting for his own turn to enter the water brought her from her trance.

"Thank you, yes." Lowering her goggles, she slid into the pool and smoothly kicked off from the side.

Lap after lap, she tallied them in her mind. If she made her girls swim half miles each week, she should surely be able to do a mile herself each morning. Forty minutes of swimming. One lap blended into the next as she lost count and the clock remained as the only source of reference.

As she stroked her thoughts returned to that man. He was beautiful. Even now, as he passed her in the opposite direction, overtaking her every fifth or sixth lap and surging ahead with that same steadiness she had admired from the deck, she watched him. How like Alex he was built!

As she began a new lap she conjured up a picture of Alex without his shirt, as he had been for such a short but devastating time on her bed last night. His chest had been broad, like this other man's; the muscles of his arms flexed similarly. Perhaps it *was* Alex! Was it such an improbable coincidence? The coloring was the same—an even sheen of bronze, hair made darker by the water. The height and build were identical, even given the distortion of her goggles. Could it be Alex?

Thirty minutes—and she continued to swim, pacing herself to avoid exhaustion. Several other swimmers had left the pool; several newcomers had joined the group. The man—that man—continued to swim, smoothly, easily, exerting so little effort that Alanna found herself envious. She also found herself surprisingly relaxed when finally, at the end of the mile, she pulled herself from the pool and headed for the showers. From there it was a simple matter of dressing, applying makeup, brushing her hair back and securing it firmly at her nape. When she emerged into the sunshine of a new day she felt more eager for work than she had in months. The tall, lean figure, smartly outfitted in a gray three-piece suit who sat perched on the edge of the low concrete wall, however, jolted her out of her sense of calm. It *had been* Alex! He was now freshly shaved; his hair, still damp, was neatly

combed. In his hand was the sport bag that must have
contained his own things. With a convulsive swallow she
took in his striking appearance and, chin tilted in a semblance of composure, approached him.

"Not bad." He checked the wide gold band of a watch
that ringed his wrist. "Most women take—" He mustered
a grin. "Forget I said that. Have you had breakfast?"

"No." Her answer was short and breathy; she hoped he
would attribute it to haste.

"Then let's go. I think we can pass up the hospital
cafeteria this morning in favor of something a little
more . . . elegant."

"I really don't eat much—"

"Don't argue with me in the morning, owl-eyes," he
growled, leading her by the hand toward the sleek gray
Porsche that sat waiting at the curb. "I need time to
wake up."

"Didn't swimming wake you?"

"Physically, yes. Mentally, not quite."

"How far did you go?"

"Two miles."

"You must have been up at dawn!"

He opened the door, then stood back to allow her to
slide in. His darkened gaze spoke the accusatory volumes that his tongue was not yet quite up to. "Almost."

Breakfast was served on white linen tablecloths covered with the finest of china, silver and crystal at a private club where Alex was a member. It was not until after
the first full cup of strong, black coffee had warmed
him that he was able to speak in sentences once more.
In truth, Alanna found his early morning gruffness appealing; she was not usually up to much herself at that
hour.

His compliment came on the heels of fresh grapefruit

and startled her. "You're a very good swimmer. I understand you coach?"

"Uh-huh." She sipped her juice. "You're not bad, yourself. You didn't say that you were a swimmer."

"You didn't ask." The twinkling in his eyes softened his tone.

"Your stroke is beautiful," she burst out spontaneously, then promptly wished she had chosen a different word. This one had a poignant double meaning.

"Felt good, did it?" he drawled softly.

With calm deliberation Alanna spread raspberry jam on her English muffin. "That doesn't even deserve an answer."

"What's on the agenda for today?" He startled her with his abrupt change of subject. His obvious interest, however, soothed her ruffled feathers.

"Oh, a pretty full day. I have to go over the cost sheets on our newest insulation proposal. That should take up most of the morning."

"Is this another of your pet projects?"

She blushed. "So you've heard of them?"

"They're part of your reputation, love. You should be proud of what you've started."

"I am." She spoke softly, taking time out for a bite of bacon. "When I first came to WallMar Enterprises it was strictly a manufacturer of paper goods."

"*High-quality* paper goods," Alex interjected, "and handling the largest volume of any such company on the East Coast."

"Did you learn that yesterday?"

"No. I've known that all along. Business is my field, too. Although the Knight Corporation hasn't had any direct dealings with Wallace we're well aware of his achievements. You, love, have gilded the image."

"You sound as though I've done something single-handedly," she protested modestly.

"Haven't you? Jake Wallace may be a whiz, but most of the men beneath him are far from genius material."

"Hmmm, you can say that again. Ah—strike that! It was very improper of me to bad-mouth my fellow employees."

His voice lowered. "Even though they bad-mouth you?"

Alanna nearly choked on her coffee. She put down the cup with a thud, then silently sought to calm herself. "I try to ignore that."

"Perhaps you shouldn't."

She looked up at him, aghast. "What would you like me to do? Bring them to court for libel? Smear Jake's name and marriage all over the pages of some scandal sheet just to show that I'm innocent of their charges? I'm not even sure I could do that! People will believe what they want. A person may be innocent until proven guilty, but, once heard, a rumor has this nasty way of tainting things, nonetheless."

"What does Wallace say about it?" He sat forward, his eyes alert.

"Jake takes the same view I do. The bottom line is the business. If it thrives and we continue to be effective we try to avoid a confrontation. As a matter of fact, when I told Jake that I doubted whether I should be named Executive Vice-President, precisely because of the rumormongers, who would be bound to have a field day, he disagreed completely. Poor Jake, he *does* see me as one of the family."

"And you?"

Alanna's brown-eyed gaze beamed straight toward Alex. "I love Jake and Elaine as I might have loved my parents. They've been wonderful to me. I only hope that I deserve the faith Jake has shown in me. He gave me carte blanche from the start. From my very first suggestion—the one that led to our entrance into computer software—he's been behind me."

"It was a brilliant move."

"Not brilliant. Simply . . . timely. When I first interviewed with Jake I sensed his willingness to branch out. The projects I head are ventures that risk a small, very small, percentage of our assets. I've had a fair success ratio, thank goodness!"

Alex continued to look at her, his chin resting on one large palm. He seemed content just to sit, moving only slightly when a black-vested waiter refilled their coffee cups. When it occurred to Alanna that she had been doing most of the talking she attempted to remedy the situation.

"How about you, Alex? What are *you* up to today?"

"I've got a meeting in New York at eleven." He sounded totally unconcerned with the matter, despite the fact that time was passing.

"Eleven! And here you're sitting with me! Shouldn't you get going?"

"There's no rush." His eyes beamed lazily. "I'll be flying, anyway. I don't have to be at the airport for a while yet."

Alanna nodded, her gaze clinging to his. Should she ask? Would he be resentful? Wasn't it as good a test as any to see if he really meant to make her a part of his life? "Is it a critical meeting?" She finally opted for indirectness, opening a subject that he could easily close with a "yes" or a "no" should he so desire. To her pleasure, he did neither.

"It's a meeting with the Board of Directors of Inter-Continental Communications. We've been working to establish competitive sources of long-distance communications; they may be our key."

A vague memory stirred. "Did I read something about that not long ago?"

"You may have, if you're up to date with the trade journals. We've been trying our best to keep it under cover. Unfortunately, the noble people of the press— *whatever* press—have ways of sniffing things out." Alanna smiled her understanding. "All done?" he asked politely.

"Yes, thank you. That was good. My breakfasts aren't usually as formal."

He moved to stand behind her to pull out her chair. "See if it helps with the morning. If it does, it may be worth repeating!" His words were low and spoken by her ear; she recalled them often throughout the day.

Indeed, she thought often of Alex throughout the day—far too often for her peace of mind. She thought of how he had been last evening: alarmingly virile. She thought of how he had been in the wee hours of the night: quietly comforting. She thought of how he had looked swimming in the pool: disturbingly masculine. She thought of how he'd been at breakfast: companionable, despite the hour. As the day slowly passed and she went from one meeting to another, from one phone call to another, from one project to another, she wondered what he would be like tonight.

"Alanna!" Jake called from the door of her office, then entered. "Where have you been?"

Her eyes widened. "Right here, Jake. For the past—"

"I know that. I meant your mind. I called your name three times just now before you finally looked up." His gaze was uncomfortably knowing. "Off daydreaming somewhere?"

Alanna couldn't stem the flush of embarrassment that crept upward from her neck. "I guess so."

"How did it go last night?" He honed in on her thoughts.

"Fine. I slept pretty well . . . for an insomniac."

"Do you think the program will help, then?"

She frowned. "I'm not sure." There were now so many complicating factors. "I hope so."

"Have a few minutes to talk about that biotechnics proposal?"

"Sure, Jake." It was a merciful out, a propitious escape. With Jake here and a concrete issue before her it was possible—if only for a short time—to exorcise the ghost of Alexander Knight. No, not a ghost. A ghost implied a relationship from the past. This was more like a glimpse of the future. And that thought disturbed her even more. Her current problem was much like the self-perpetuating wakefulness of the insomniac. The more Alex Knight intruded on her thoughts, the more unsettling he became and the more she found herself engaged in slow brooding on him and on the future.

The day went on much as the one before. As the afternoon passed she grew increasingly apprehensive and Alex bore the brunt of her frustration. By six o'clock she had blamed him for everything from a broken copy machine to a misaligned finance sheet, not to mention the frequent daydreams that took her from her work. As on the evening before, she arrived at the clinic prepared for battle.

It was shortly before nine when she arrived and there was no sign of Alex. The lounge was empty. Ellen Henderson, however, was free and available; they spent some time together reviewing Alanna's sleep charts and discussing her log. Ellen asked general questions relating to Alanna's initial reaction to the program; Alanna answered each as honestly as she could, though she couldn't quite bring herself to mention Alex's name. There were, indeed, several awkward silences during which Alanna suspected that Ellen considered broaching the subject before yielding the initiative to Alanna, who said nothing. For the time being, she was grateful for the reprieve.

By the time she returned to her room it was nine-forty-five and the lounge, which she'd passed through en route, was still empty. Had he come yet? Where was he? Paperback in hand, she returned to the lounge and read—or attempted to read—for another hour. Had something happened to him? Was he all right? The other two members of the study had drifted through; now one approached and sat down. She was a pleasant enough woman, middle-aged and in the upper echelon of an insurance company. She spoke freely of the petty aggravations she'd had to face that day, of the added aggravation she'd have to face when she awoke in the middle of the night, of the doubts she had of the success of this program, and of anything else that came into her head. It was all Alanna could do to sit still.

There had been, still, no sign of Alex. As politely as possible Alanna excused herself and headed for her room. A shower and one hundred brush strokes later she sat propped in her chair, eying her watch. Eleven-thirty. What was keeping him? Had he been held up in New York? Had some evening meeting kept him? Was he— she gasped—on a date?

Eleven-thirty-five. Eleven-forty. Eleven-forty-five. As the time ticked on she pondered her own absurd state. When she'd first arrived at the clinic this evening, a good-sized chip on her shoulder, she had been marginally relieved that he hadn't been there. As the time wore on she had grown upset, then worried. Now her annoyance was directed at herself for her folly. What was the matter with her? Alex Knight was a man whom she'd met barely two days ago. Granted, what they'd shared in the meantime had had its intimate and very personal moments. But the fact remained that they were still free and separate individuals. Alex had no more need to check in with her than she had to report back to him.

On that defiant thought she climbed into bed. Midnight. What had happened to that "early curfew" to which Ellen Henderson had referred? Did it apply to everyone but Alex Knight? Closing her eyes, she willed anger into abeyance and concentrated on nothing. Cool, clear nothing. Nothing . . . disturbed by the dark and handsome image of one Alex Knight. Nothing . . . hampered by worry that something might have happened to him. Nothing . . . marred by the fear that he might, for some unknown reason, have opted out of the IAT study. Despite the turmoil the man engendered within her, she *was* fearful of never seeing him again. Without stopping to consider her feelings more deeply, she hopped out of bed, drew on her robe, opened the door enough to see a clear way to his room and made a beeline for it, pausing on the threshold to still her thudding heart. Her intention was simply to see if he had come in during the past hour. Slowly and stealthily, she opened the door a crack. If he *was* there she would retrace her steps immediately.

The room was dark; no sound came from within. A slice of light from the hall angled across the bed and she opened the door further. There was still no sound. Yet there was a definite human shape on the bed, *in* the bed. Her gaze followed the outline of his body from his feet up, crossing the line where blanket ended and skin began, continuing over his chest to his face.

One long arm was thrown across his eyes, yet his voice was clear. "Aren't you going to come in?"

Caught in the act, Alanna was not sure just what to do. While one part of her wanted simply to excuse herself and run, the other was still curious as to why, given his previous attentiveness, Alex had avoided her tonight. The latter impulse won. Slipping through the doorway, she closed the door behind her and hesitantly approached the bed.

"Well?" He sounded neither pleased nor angry, simply tired.

"I just wondered whether you got in all right. I didn't see you earlier."

"It was late; I arrived a little while ago. I thought you might be asleep and I didn't want to wake you."

"You don't need to explain. . . ." she began, feeling guilty at having disturbed him, still wondering whether she should leave at once. As he had in the past, he read her mind.

"Come sit with me, Alanna," he offered in soft invitation. "I could use the company." His arm lifted from his eyes; his hand patted the bed beside him. Without a second thought she found herself there, concerned at his state of fatigue.

"Was it such a bad day?" she asked in a whisper.

The light from beneath the door was too dim to allow him to make out her features; rather, his fingers traced the lines of her face in greeting. "Everything went well in New York, if that's what you mean."

"What happened afterward?"

"Just a small family matter. You know how that kind of thing can eat at you."

"I don't," she contradicted him gently. "I have no family. You're the one who is privileged . . ."

His fingers touched her lips. "I sometimes wonder." When his other hand met the first to cup her face and bring it down toward his she put a hand on his chest for support and eagerly met his kiss. His lips were gentle, tired yet sweet; he seemed to take his strength from her, gaining vibrancy with each moist taste.

It was as though Alanna had waited for this all day. Any anger she had felt earlier simply dissolved. There was only Alex and his warm, strong body. When his kiss ended with a light touch to her nose she moved on impulse to join him in bed, much as he had done earlier. With feline grace she stretched out beside him, finding a comfortable niche for her head on his shoulder, her legs falling easily by and between his. When her hand slid to his waist and hip, however, she jumped and made to retreat. Only his arm held her still.

Her whisper was hoarse with dismay. "Alex! You've got nothing on!"

"I always sleep this way," he countered with nonchalance.

"But this is a hospital—"

"And Ellen said to sleep in whatever we were accustomed to. I'm doing just that!"

"I don't know." Her wariness persisted. "Maybe I should go back to my own bed."

"Don't you dare. I like you right here," his hand curved to her hip, "by my side."

She was more than by his side. She was practically molded to him; their bodies fit that closely together. Desperate to break the aura of sensuality, Alanna cleared her throat and tipped her head back to study his dimly lit features. "What's the problem in your family? Anything you'd like to discuss?"

Just as this morning she had wondered whether he would freely share information regarding his work, so now she wondered just how much he would trust her with something so personal. As earlier, she was warmed by his open and honest response.

"It's my father. He's having some trouble adjusting to retirement."

"How old is he?"

"Sixty-three. He turned the company over to me four years ago, shortly before his sixtieth birthday."

"What has he been doing since then?"

"He and my mother travel a lot, visiting their various grandchildren. They've also taken several extended trips—the most recent one to China.

"But your father isn't comfortable?"

"He's torn. He firmly believes that I should hold the reins of the foundation, yet he can't quite let go completely. It can be . . . very difficult. . . ."

"In what way?"

"Second-guessing. Backseat driving. Monday morning quarterbacking. Should I go on?"

Alanna smiled against his chest, absently rubbing her cheek against the fine hazing of hair there. "I think I understand. Why don't you put him to work?"

"That's what I've suggested."

"Well . . . what's the problem?"

"The problem, love, is his determination to be retired. It's either all or nothing with him. He can't see things quite as clearly as we do and therefore can't see that he's already got several fingers irrevocably in the pie."

"Can't you give him his own division? Something that really needs *his* expertise and experience behind it?"

Alex was quiet for several moments. "You phrase it very well, Alanna. From me, it sounds like a consolation prize. From you, it's an opportunity that demands skill." Again he was silent, pensive, and she was satisfied merely to listen to the steady thump of his heart. His arm tightened around her before he spoke again. "I'll have to remember that—'his expertise and experience.' That might convince him. Better still," he angled his head down toward her face, "you'll come and have dinner with us one night. You can tell him to his face exactly how much the company needs him."

"Oh, no, I won't, Alex Knight. He's *your* father."

"You'd like him—*and* my mother," he crooned invitingly.

But Alanna was determined to stay clear of that powerful trap and refused to even consider the question with any degree of seriousness. "I'm sure I would," she quipped lightly. "But it would be totally impertinent of me to walk in and tell your father what to do. I'm no Knight—"

"—not yet."

"Alex . . . !" Her protest was silenced by the lips which captured hers in their sensual net. Suddenly protest was nonexistent. In a moment of accumulated desire—desire built up through an evening of worry and brought to a head by their present intimacy—Alanna was transported to a world encompassing only Alexander Knight.

In the delirium of his kiss she *was* a Knight, with every right to the luxuries he offered. His lips drank in her goodness in turn; his tongue set off explosive charges deep within her mouth. His legs moved against hers with electrifying friction, binding her to his body. He was fit and solid beside her, beneath her.

"Alex!" She tried again, gasping against his cheek. "This has to stop!" Even her whisper was hoarse.

"Why?" He smoothed her hair from her face and held it back with both hands.

"It's . . . dangerous. You know where we are. . . ."

A faint flicker of white broke through the darkness when he grinned. "We're in bed."

"We're in a hospital room!" she countered, trying desperately to ignore the span of lean stomach spread beneath her palm. When she tried to push against it and lever herself away Alex held her closer. His hands slid down, one to her back, one to her hips, to press her more fully against him. Her protest was aimed as much at herself as it was at him. "I'd better leave, Alex. This is getting out of hand."

"To the contrary." He squeezed her gently. "It's very well *in* hand."

"Alex! This is absurd—"

"And lovely." He moved ever so slightly against her, sending ripples of excitement tingling through her extremities.

"Oh . . ." she exhaled, feeling herself losing touch with reality. "Why do you do this to me?"

"We're made for each other, love. Don't you see that? Why must you fight it so?" His hands held her and molded her, doing wicked things in utter innocence.

"I don't know," she murmured, closing her eyes as his lips planted light, dreamy kisses all over her face. "I don't know." The pleasure was exquisite. What *was* there to fight?

"Let yourself go. Trust me. Let me pleasure you."

With a soft moan of surrender she turned her mouth to his and welcomed the full force of his kiss as it spread the flame of desire to every last pocket of her resistance. Her immediate future was in his hands, yet he worshipped her as though she held the reins.

Alanna's body was aflame, Alex's was its fuel. Her survival seemingly depended on him and she arched toward him eagerly. The feel of his body intoxicated her. She combed her hands across his chest, exploring its every sinew. Its manly hardness pleasured her fingertips beyond description, luring her palms hungrily over him. At her touch he sucked in the taut muscles of his stomach, offering a lean plane for her hands to glide across.

His deft fingers released the tie of her robe, slipped it from her slender shoulders and pulled it from beneath her. As she lay on her back he hovered over her, balancing himself on one elbow, visually caressing her. She caught her breath when his fingers slid the strap of her night-gown from her shoulder, pulling it down enough to free a swollen breast from its silken confines. Within seconds his mouth had encompassed a rosy nipple, gently sucking, sending passion racing through the warmest depths of her body. She cried aloud at the feeling, then cried again when his tongue and teeth played at her nipple, toying it into a hard, dark peak.

Alanna was swept up in a torrent of desire. She was utterly lost in his kiss and the yearning to return its intensity. In a fleeting moment of recollection she knew where she was, but it no longer mattered. All that mattered was Alex and what he was doing to her, what they were about to do together. It seemed the highest point of her life, that moment for which she had waited long, long years alone, compensating for that aloneness with her work.

Again her hands sought him out. He gasped when she touched him, then pulled her over onto him and reached for her face. He kissed her thoroughly, savoring her mouth, adoring its welcome. His hands moved to her shoulders, skimmed the length of her arms, found her hips and slowly drew the soft fabric of her gown up to her waist.

Consumed from within by a burning need, Alanna strained toward him. She wanted him—oh, how she wanted him. Yet she was frightened. It had been so long since she had opened herself to a man. The heat of Alex's body spoke of his own raging fire. He encouraged her with the proof of her power over him. Her breasts brushed electrically against his chest when she bent forward to seek his strength.

"Alex . . ."

"Shhh." He kissed her again, drugging her to near-mindlessness.

"But Alex . . ." The last shred of reason found timid voice. "Here?"

"I need you, love," he rasped urgently. "I need you now." His hands reached for her, but she resisted for a last, frantic moment.

"I'm frightened," she whispered. "I want to please you. . . ."

Her words brought a deep groan of desire from his throat. In one lithe move he rolled her beneath him, pausing only long enough to slip her gown over her head, then feel her nakedness with his restless palms. "You please me already, Alanna. Be mine. I do love you."

At that heady declaration Alanna released any threads of caution. Words became a thing of the past, yielding to a kiss that worked its way over her body, finding tiny pockets of sensuality and bringing them to life. His fingers worked a magic of their own, tuning her to him until she had no separate identity. He led her high with his touch to a peak of clamoring need.

The moment was imminent. Alanna's breath hung in her throat, to be released in a soft, sweet cry when she was at long last complete. Alex had made her so. He must have felt it, too, for he clasped her to him, crushing her breasts against the warm wall of his chest for a long, still time of quiet pleasure.

Then, between murmured heart-words and avid cries of ecstasy, he made love to her. Slowly, at first, he set the rhythm, drawing her into it faster and with rising hunger. Alanna floated in a world of passion and promise. Her body throbbed with desire in the growing need for fulfillment. Willingly, she let Alex stoke her fires, returning the heat, hotter and hotter until, at last, clutching him, she felt his explosion and knew of her own.

It was a honeyed warmth that spread through her to him and back as they lay, locked tightly together, savoring the last moments of rapture. Alanna felt fulfilled in a way she had never felt before. Her breathlessness echoed his, but gradually slowed as time put its inevitable wedge between glory and reality.

What came over Alanna then, she would never know. With the speed of lightning, her life passed before her, its kaleidoscopic frames suddenly encapsulated in one moment that held more meaning than all the rest.

Helplessly, she began to cry. Tears streamed down her cheeks to dampen his chest as he slid to her side and shifted her in his arms.

"What is it, love?" he whispered, stroking her hair back from her face. "Did I hurt you?"

She could only shake her head against him, choked by the silent sobs that racked her body. Alex's love had released the emotional flood that had been dammed for years, years in which she had neither cried nor sought refuge in arms such as these that now held her so very tenderly.

He let her cry, sensing her need to express feelings so long bottled up. Cradling her gently, he rocked her until the inner storm exhausted itself. Then, his body protectively curved to hers, he pulled the covers over them.

They could have been in their own private bungalow on a deserted stretch of beach in the bright warmth of the Caribbean, honeymooning with abandon, so deep was the relaxation Alanna felt when the silence of the cool northern night enveloped them. In Alex's arms, content and fulfilled, she fell into a deep sleep. Within moments he had followed her. When they awoke it was morning and their bodies were still entwined. To their instant delight was added a note of astonishment: Sated by love and held by each other, they had slept, undisturbed and at peace, through the night.

6

Ellen Henderson was neither delighted nor undisturbed, and peaceful was the last word to describe her expression when she summoned them both to her office early that evening. Alanna took a seat by the desk; Alex perched on the edge of a low file cabinet.

"How *could* you, Alex?" the psychologist burst out as soon as the door was closed. "This is a hospital, for heaven's sake!"

Alanna had already spent most of her day pondering the matter. Neither guilt nor regret had a place among the many emotions she felt. She was confused, perhaps, as to where the future would lead. She was certainly overwhelmed by the effect this one man had on her. She was even a bit frightened of the force of her own response. But she was also pleased and satisfied, strangely at ease with the knowledge of what had occurred so spontaneously last night.

Alex, to whom Ellen seemed content to direct her initial tirade, was likewise free of guilt. He was downright unremorseful. "I'm well aware of what this institution is, Ellen," he answered her smoothly. "But worse things than love have happened at hospitals."

"I'm not talking about *love* and you know it. I'm talking about *lovemaking*. I would have expected a bit more propriety from you, of all people."

Still Alex was totally in control. "Come off it, Ellen. I'm human. I told you I loved her. Don't be a prude."

Ellen bristled. "Tell *that* to the poor little nurse who walked in on you two this morning. *She* was not terribly pleased."

Alanna looked down and pressed a fist against her mouth, yet her soft laugh could not be entirely muffled. Guilty only at finding humor in what so clearly disturbed Ellen, she shot a helpless glance at Alex. His expression mirrored hers, though he managed to refrain from an open show of amusement.

"Poor girl. Did we shock her that much? You know, Ellen, you really should teach your nurses the facts of life."

"Alex . . ." Ellen warned him softly, yet there was an easing of her tension. Now her gaze shifted to include Alanna. "What am I going to do with you?" She threw her hands up in exasperation, then joined Alanna and Alex in spontaneous laughter. "You know, if I weren't a happily married woman myself I'd probably be jealous of you, Alanna."

For the first time Alanna spoke. "I didn't realize you were married. You don't wear a ring—"

"—or use my husband's name or call myself *Mrs.* It may be a modern marriage, but it's worked well for the last seven years, so it's got to have something going for it."

"What does he do—your husband?" Alanna asked, fascinated that a woman with such heavy career demands could successfully manipulate the mechanics of a marriage.

"He's an anesthesiologist here at the hospital. We coordinate our schedules very comfortably."

"How *is* Sandy? I haven't seen him in a long time,"

Alex asked, obviously as familiar with her husband
as he was with Ellen. Alanna turned her attention to his
dark, casually posed figure as he proceeded to chat easily with Ellen for several moments.

Despite her outward attentiveness, Alanna's mind
wandered helplessly. What *had* last night meant? She felt
different, somehow, yet her body was certainly unaltered.
It was all within—this difference. In the process of his
lovemaking Alex had broken down her defenses. He had
breached her emotional guard. She was suddenly unsure
of the future, of what she wanted from her life. And she
was acutely aware of things she'd never known. Only
Alex's presence had made her see her past as one of loneliness. Only his love had rendered all else empty. Where
was she to go now?

"The way I see it," Ellen's evaluation broke into her
thoughts, drawing her startled gaze, "we have two op-
tions, neither of which is totally satisfactory. First, you
could continue as part of the IAT study, with strict promises," she looked sharply from one to the other, "to keep
your hands off one another. Even if you agreed, I'd be
compromising the project by adding a tension that
wasn't there before. The second possibility," she sighed,
"is for you both to drop out. I have others I can put in in
your place."

"What if we got married?" It was Alex's deep voice
that posed a third possibility.

Alanna promptly vetoed it. "No!" The force of her
refusal brought her to her feet. Suddenly distraught, she
looked from Alex to Ellen and back, then walked to the
far side of the office to stand with her back to them, her
arms wrapped protectively about herself. She felt their
eyes on her, sensed when they looked at each other in silent communication. It was Ellen who came to her rescue,

rising from her desk to approach and put a gentle arm about her shoulders.

"Look, I have a suggestion," the psychologist began. "We'll chalk this night up to an unavoidable complication. Why don't you both take the time to talk, to decide things between yourselves? I've listed the possibilities relating to the study. *You* have to list the possibilities relating to your relationship. Take tonight off and tomorrow you can let me know what you've decided—whether you want to stay in the program under my conditions."

In the silence that followed Alanna knew that Ellen Henderson's suggestion was fair. The problem of insomnia had taken a definite backseat to this more immediate matter between Alex and herself. At her nod of agreement, Alex spoke up.

"Thanks, Ellen. You've been more than understanding."

"It's my job," the woman quipped with a smile, turning. "But promise me that you'll follow the guidelines I've given you—no liquor or coffee, try to leave the tension behind when you go to bed—" She caught herself up short and an impish smile lit her face. "As a matter of fact, I understand you two did very well last night. No waking up at all?" Alex grinned broadly as he shook his head. "You know," she went on, "I really should be furious." But she wasn't. "You've proven something that I don't even have the guts to commit to paper for fear they'll close down the sleep lab! It would be an interesting proposition. . . ." Her gaze narrowed in feigned concentration.

"It *is* an interesting proposition," Alex spoke for Alanna's ears alone when, several moments later, they headed for the elevator. She couldn't muster any response, but simply remained silent, caught up in the whirl of emotions that stirred within. Alex snagged her gaze for a long enough moment to read her turmoil, then he turned her gently toward him. "We do have to talk. Let's go to my place. I can drive you back to pick up your car later."

She found encouragement in his seeming patience and nodded. The Porsche was in the lot. With a light hand at her back he guided her toward it, then held the door while she made herself comfortable. It wasn't difficult in a car as elegant as this. Conversation was a far more trying matter, however. Alanna didn't say a word. Her thoughts raced wildly in a desperate bid to escape the crux of the issue: *What did she feel for Alex Knight?*

In his arrogant way he had found a niche under her skin. His presence permeated her life with its aura of specialness. How had she let it happen? *Why* had she let it happen? Could it be that she *needed* him?

Defensively, she concentrated on the Alanna Evans who had existed so successfully, all alone, for the past ten years. Her mind dwelt on the image of that self-sufficiency, of professionalism, and by the time Alex pulled up before a tall, modern apartment building in a newly converted area of downtown Baltimore she felt more composed than she had all evening.

"This is home?" She leaned forward to eye the imposing structure.

"Uh-huh." He switched off the ignition and scanned the entrance for a sign of the doorman. "It's comfortable and convenient. When I want to stretch my legs and breathe deeply of country air I drive down to my parents' house."

"Do they live far?"

"It's not quite a fifty-minute drive."

"Do you see them often?"

"I try to get down there once a week. Occasionally they drive up to join me for dinner."

"And your brothers and sisters—" Her voice broke

when the doorman unexpectedly appeared to open her door, startling her. Conversation resumed in the elevator.

"I have three sisters and a brother. Joey manages the West Coast office. We talk on the phone often, but don't see each other as much as we would like. The girls are scattered; two are married and one is still in graduate school. She's the baby. She's training to be a pediatrician." His pride was unmistakable.

Alanna was instantly appreciative. "Whew! That's quite a goal!" The elevator opened and Alex led her to a door at the far end of a long, ecru-papered and carpeted corridor. "The penthouse?" She cocked a blond brow.

"Not exactly," he humored her. "My apartment may be on the top floor, but it's only one of four." He put the key in the lock and turned it.

"I'm surprised you've been able to avoid condominium conversion. It seems to be the thing lately."

"I don't believe in it." He looked easily down at her. "To have to make that kind of financial investment and buy into responsibilities that many people don't want seems unfair. Many of these tenants are retired. They've had their day in the country. They've owned their own homes and now they want a simpler life."

"You have an understanding owner." Too late, she understood the twinkle in his eye.

"I *am* the owner. It helps." Grinning, he pushed the door open for her to enter.

Alanna was not quite prepared for the world of understated elegance in which she found herself. But then, why not? Wasn't the man himself a prime example of subtle class? Her eye skimmed the open foyer before being quickly drawn toward the large living room. The overall impression was one of cool serenity; the room had been decorated in a quiet blend of brown, navy and cream. There was a central sunken pit bounded by the plush cushions of a sectional sofa. There were side tables and étagères, each bearing exquisite groupings of small sculptures of stone or crystal. There was a long wall unit containing a bar, a stereo and scattered rows of books, and one entire wall was taken up by windows that looked out on the harbor.

"Well . . . what do you think?" His concern for her approval was endearing and impossible to resist.

"It's magnificent, Alex!" She beamed, turning to face him, first with enthusiasm, then mischief. "Now tell me that a lovely raven-haired beauty with whom you happened to be living at the time decorated it for you."

"No." He approached her. "*I* decorated it. I have specific tastes—in furnishings *and* in women."

"My compliments, then, on the furnishings," she quipped. "As for the women, since I haven't kept track of your entourage over the years I must withhold judgment."

"None of them come anywhere near you, Alanna," he vowed, his eyes dark and enticing.

Quickly, she mocked their sensuality. "Your brain must be addled by too *much* sleep—"

"—and I've never had a live-in lady," he interrupted, far more serious than she and determined to make his point.

She tipped her head in skepticism. "Never?"

"Never." He walked to stand before the wall unit and thrust his hands into his trouser pockets. His streamlined stance exaggerated his height. "I've always lived alone and preferred it that way. Until now." His eyes bore steadily into hers.

Ignoring his final words, she probed his feelings. "It must be difficult . . . living alone, taking care of all those things that a woman would normally do."

"Such as?" He was mildly amused.

Alanna shrugged. "You know, the cooking, cleaning, laundry . . ."

To her chagrin Alex's gaze narrowed and he stalked toward her, very definitely on the attack. "*That* was a sexist statement if I've ever heard one. It's amazing. *You're* the only old-fashioned thing in this room!"

Of the many ways she had viewed herself over the years, old-fashioned had never been one. "What do you mean?"

"I mean that you obviously consider those chores as 'woman's work.' Did it ever occur to you that a man can do those things, too?"

"Do *you?*" she asked with a grin, instantly humored at the image of Alexander Knight folding laundry.

"I cook."

It came too freely. "And . . . the others?"

He waffled. "Well . . . I try not to . . . I have someone . . ."

"A woman?" she drove the point home.

Alex waved a hand as if to indicate the irrelevance of the matter. "As it happens, yes. She was all I could find at the time. But—"

"So who's old-fashioned?"

"*You* are!" He refused to back down. "If you decided to marry me it wouldn't mean that you'd be suddenly chained to the house. I'd still hire people to do those chores and that would free us both up for work . . . *and* play. You assume that every traditional responsibility would be yours. I'm saying that it just wouldn't be so."

"I know, Alex. I know." There was a momentary hint of resignation in her tone. Turning quietly, she wandered aimlessly about the room. "Even living by myself, I've had to make compromises to get things done in between work hours. I have help, too. But I somehow thought that men liked their women to do that kind of thing."

"There's where you're silly, love," he gently chided her. "When a man loves a woman he respects her, as well. I would no more force you to be a live-in maid than I would ask you to give up your career. Don't you see," he moved to stand before her, lifting his hands to curve around her neck, his thumbs steadying her chin, "I love you for what you *are*. I could never try to destroy or change that. The first time I saw you—in that elevator—I sensed the spirit in you that appeals so strongly to me. It's your strength, your independence, your intelligence and self-sufficiency—among other things—that I love."

Alanna's brown gaze climbed to meet his. "Perhaps it's the challenge you love, rather than *me*. I do know how you love a dare," she reminded him lightly.

"So do you."

"Uh-huh. But I don't confuse that with true love. The newness, the challenge, are bound to wear off. What happens then? Where does that leave you?"

If Alanna thought to stump Alex she was taken aback by his total preparedness. "It leaves *us* to seek out challenges together, to find new and exciting things together. We share the love of adventure; that's one of the things that binds us together. For the first time in my life I've found a woman who thrives on challenge as much as I do." His arms fell slowly to his sides; his words held their own weight.

Alanna had no proper retort. It stunned her to admit the merit of his argument. She, too, had never enjoyed a man as much as she did Alex—and for many of the same reasons. There was a good explanation for why she never dated a man more than once or twice; boredom encompassed much of it. Instinctively she knew that Alex Knight would never, *never* bore her.

It was hard enough to admit this to herself; she simply couldn't admit it to Alex. In search of diversion, her eye caught on the bookshelf. "Are you a thriller fan?" she asked, excited.

Alex spent a fast moment looking suspiciously from Alanna's brightened face to the books, then back. "Aren't we both? Suspense. Intrigue. Action. Romance. Mystery. Isn't that what life is all about?"

She avoided his question to study the collection before her. "I think you've got all my favorites." A tapered finger traced the spine of one of the volumes. "One thing's for sure." She smiled sheepishly. "Books like this never put me to sleep! Which brings up the immediate problem." Her gaze met his once more. "What are we going to do about the IAT study?"

"That's not really the immediate problem, love. The immediate problem is *us.* What are we going to do about *us?"*

A flicker of pain crossed her face. "That's very simple," she lied. "Nothing."

"Nothing?" he repeated her statement, his furrowed brow hinting at disagreement "What do you mean by that?"

"Exactly what I said. We're adults. I see no reason to get all bothered about things. Is there a rush?"

"What about last night?" he asked, his tone cool.

"What about it?"

"Didn't it mean anything to you?"

Disquieted and unable to lie on this point, she fled to the window. "Of course it did."

He was close on her heels. "What did it mean?" His reflection in the window, framed by the black of night, towered over hers.

Alanna gathered her thoughts, sorting out those she could share from those that, for the present, had to remain her own. "It meant that we are phenomenally attracted to one another. It meant that we shared something very special."

"I'll say it was special!" Alex exploded, grasping her shoulders and forcefully turning her to face him. "I've said I love you time and again. If you were honest you would return the vow. You do love me, Alanna. Last night proved it!"

To her chagrin he had hit on the core of her confusion. When she lashed out it was as much in argument with herself as with him. "That's being naive, Alex! Just because I let you make love to me doesn't mean I love you!"

"That's just it," his voice lowered to a calmer pitch, "you didn't just *let* me make love to you; you made beautiful love right back to me! No," he caught her tighter when she tried to pull away, "don't run this time. Face it. You felt something last night with me. You feel it right now. I can tell. That cool, suave woman I met in the cafeteria just the other night is not quite so cool and suave anymore. She's discovered that the core of passion she's squelched for years is not quite dead."

"Passion," she broke in, trying desperately to exhibit the coolness he accused her of having lost, "is very different from love. Passion is physical—"

"Not at the level we shared last night!" His face was taut. "Say it, Alanna. There was more to last night than just the physical. Say it. You do love me."

"I think I ought to leave."

"Why? Are you that frightened of yourself?"

"No!" She spoke honestly. "I'm frightened that you'll make me say things I simply don't feel."

"Or *think* you feel?"

She sighed in resignation. "Or *think* I feel."

When he released her she wandered to the sofa and let its deep cushions envelop her. Resting her elbow on the sofa's arm, she propped her forehead against her palm.

It was nearly ten-thirty; her fatigue was emotional, rather than physical.

"I wish I could offer you coffee or a nightcap. . . ." Alex's voice was quiet, more controlled.

"I'm fine without."

"Can I get you *any*thing?"

She shook her head quickly, then continued to shake it more slowly. "I don't know what I'm doing here." The words poured forth unbidden. "I had my life perfectly organized. I was so proud of myself because I'd finally gone to the clinic. Insomnia . . . hah! Little did I suspect that I'd meet a crazy man who had an obsession with marriage!"

His large, tanned hands entered her vision as he propped them on the back of the sofa on either side of her. "He's intelligent . . ."

She shrugged faintly. "Perhaps . . ."

"And successful . . ." His voice was lower.

"Perhaps . . ."

"And good-looking . . ."

She grinned, much against her better judgment. ". . . and immodest . . ."

"Perhaps," he drawled in mockery, then dipped his head until his breath fanned her ear. "He also loves you very much."

The words tore at the defenses he'd already battered almost to shreds. She wasn't quite sure whether her moan was one of anger, frustration or pleasure. But when he rounded the sofa and sat down beside her she slid her arms about his waist and crumbled against him. "Why do you say things like that, Alex?"

"Because I mean them."

"But don't you know that I'm not *ready* for that yet?"

"Is that what's bothering you? The rush?"

She hesitated. "In part, yes."

"And the other part?"

"The other part has to do with my life, with everything I've worked for and everything I've built."

Alex's hand stroked her hair. "A relationship with me doesn't mean that you have to give that up."

"When the 'relationship' is marriage," she argued, "things change."

In the silence that followed the only thing she heard was the rapid thump of his heartbeat. It had a pacifying effect that she couldn't deny. Nor could she deny the vehemence in his tone when he did finally speak.

"You know, for a bright woman you're really being dumb! Where have you been, Alanna? It's not simply a matter of choosing between career and marriage. Women today can have both! I would never ask you to give up what you've worked so hard for and what means so much to you."

His words were reminiscent of those Jake Wallace had used in his office several days ago. From the lips of a man it sounded so simple. In the mind of a woman it was anything but.

"What about a family, Alex?" she asked, looking up at him. "Surely you want to have one?"

"Of course. Don't you?"

"I haven't wanted a husband, let alone children." *Until now.* Shock waves raced through her at the realization that, for the first time, she was actually contemplating the possibility with some seriousness "But even if I did, how would I handle it?"

"We could work it out."

"How? I put in ten-hour days as it is. How would a husband and family fit into that?"

Alex's arms released their pressure. "Where there's a will, Alanna, there's a way. Come the day you want a family, you'll find a happy compromise. Anything is possible—if you want it badly enough."

"Touché," she whispered, leaving his arms and leaning back against the sofa, closing her eyes to erase Alex's devastating presence.

"You're tired."

"I'm weary, if there's a difference. I've been thinking, thinking, thinking all day and I still can't see the light."

Gazing through the golden shade of her lashes she saw Alex lean forward and rest his elbows on his knees, one fist fitted snugly within the other palm. "Would you like me to take you home?" he asked, his jaw clenched.

Alanna looked at him, instantly knowing her answer. There was no need for in-depth soul-searching; every fiber of her being wanted to stay with him tonight. Her voice was soft and vulnerable. "No."

If Alex inhaled sharply, he camouflaged the gasp as quickly. "Why not, Alanna?"

She studied her fingers, surprised at their state of relaxation. "I'm not sure." She frowned in puzzlement before adding a soft, "I'd just rather stay here."

"Why?" When she offered nothing more than a mute sidelong glance he persisted. "You're pretty sure about the decision. Why not the reason behind it?"

"Perhaps I'm not as verbal about things as you are."

"Do you know that I've never talked as much to any person as I have to you? Do you know that I've always held things bottled up inside? One of the causes of insomnia is tension. One of the causes of tension is the internalization of thoughts and worries and problems. I've always done that. Yet I open up to you. *You* may know more about me, the *real* me, than any other person alive. Why is that?"

Alanna reflected on his words. "Perhaps I've asked you things that others haven't dared to ask." She stifled a smile.

"You're damned right!" He paused, contemplating the carpet for a moment before shaking his head and laughing. "The other night in the hospital cafeteria—do you remember what you said?" His gray eyes courted hers. "You said that you imagined me as the type who gave orders without having them questioned. I asked you if you'd question them and you assured me that you would. Do you remember?"

How could she forget any part of that conversation? She looked over at his shirt collar. "I seem to recall it, yes. . . ." Her eye wandered to the firm column of his neck until he leaned sharply forward and captured her gaze with his own insistent one.

"Well, I'm the one doing the questioning now. Why *don't* you want me to take you home?"

"I told you that I wanted to stay here. Isn't that enough?"

"No!"

"I'd rather not be alone."

"Why not? From what you've told me you've been alone for a long time and have done just fine."

Her pale brows met. "I have."

"Then what's changed now?" he persisted doggedly.

Alanna's voice rose in growing frustration. "I don't know!" She clearly sensed he sought some form of emotional commitment, but that was still beyond her reach.

It seemed that Alex's patience was waning. He was suddenly on the floor before her, clasping her hands. "Try to tell me, love. It's important. I *need* to know."

"How can I tell you something that I don't know myself?" she asked soulfully. "I do know that I enjoy your company, that for the first time in my life the thought of a quiet apartment sounds lonely and that I'd much rather be here with you. But beyond that, *what can I say?*"

As though temporarily sated by the mild sign of encouragement, he sat back. If she had expected a smile of victory from him, however, she had underestimated his character. "You'll stay the night with me?" he asked warily.

Her answer was a whisper. "Yes."

"In my bed?"

"Yes."

He straightened and stood, looking down at her from what seemed an unreachable height. "You know what to expect if you stay." The dark charcoal of his eyes demanded an answer.

"I think so." Wasn't it what she wanted, too?

"And that doesn't bother you?"

"Should it?" she asked with a newer trepidation. "I've already admitted that we have something good together." Even now, staring up at the raw vision of masculinity before her, she felt a telltale tingle. "Is it wrong for me to give in to that pleasure?"

"You've avoided it all these years."

"Not wholly on principle. It's never seemed worth following through."

"Until now."

"That's right."

"And you feel comfortable about it . . . now?"

Alanna nodded, then repeated her query. "Am I wrong?"

"Not," he emphasized each word, "if you recognize the underlying emotion." His gaze was speculative. But regardless of its force she was unable to give a name to her feelings. She knew it. He knew it. "You won't marry me, yet you would *live* with me?"

She grew more cautious. "I thought the invitation was for one night. As far as *living* with you . . ."

"Would you?"

"I don't know." In truth, she didn't. There was some

strong drive within that urged her to stay the night; a further commitment was something she would need time to consider.

Alex strode to the far side of the room. Alanna would have followed him had she known what to say. She had no explanation to give herself; how could she satisfy him? He turned to face her boldly, embodying every bit of the force she was sure had earned him many a corporate triumph.

"What if I said it was marriage or nothing?"

His words hung in the air like a storm before falling with devastation around her. Alanna was stunned. Had he trapped her? Was that what the intimacy of last night had been all about? Had he built up her awareness of him to a point of screaming need, a point where she would be unable to refuse his proposal of marriage? Was this a kind of emotional blackmail?

Trying a smile, she spoke softly. "I thought that was supposed to be *my* line."

He was fast with a comeback. "It *should* have been. But as you pointed out to me very clearly the first time we met, tradition is meaningless in this day and age. Well, I'm going to tell you something. Tradition may be out; I would never expect, or ask, you to be a *traditional* wife. But *commitment* is still in, in my book at least! That's what frightens you most, Alanna. Commitment. In your very defensive view, one night at a time is fine. Anything more implies a commitment. And that's what you're trying to avoid, isn't it?"

"No. Not the way you put it."

"Then correct me."

Alanna stood to walk aimlessly around the room. Where could she begin? Anything she might say to him would be a spur-of-the-moment voicing of her own thoughts. There was so much she had yet to work out.

Coming to a halt at the back of an armchair, she leaned on it for support, then moved around it to sit down.

"I never really knew my father." She sought the words that might explain. "He was a salesman, always on the road. It was just my mother and me for as long as I can remember." Alex's gaze leveled, then softened as he listened. "My mother was an intelligent woman. She read voraciously—anything she could get her hands on." A smile curved her lips at the memory. "I used to stop at the library twice a week on my way home from school to pick up books and magazines for her. She understood every nuance of politics and the economy—she was brilliant." She paused, anguish now clouding her features.

"When I was eighteen she took sick. I always wondered whether it was the fact that I had finally gone off to college. She had wanted that so badly for me—to get into a good school and leave Pittsburgh behind. Her single objective was to convince me to make something of my life, to be someone, to use my innate resources to the fullest, to move ahead in the world." Alanna cringed. "She thought of her own life as wasted."

Alex sought to disagree. "But how could it be—"

"It was!" she interrupted, displacing her anger from the time long past to him. "It was! She had so much going for her. Her only mistake was in loving my father."

"Alanna, that's an awful thing to say. How can you—"

Again she cut him off forcefully. "I *know* what I'm saying, Alex! I've had years to think about it—"

"—in the middle of the night?"

Understanding his implication, she smiled ruefully. "Yes, often in the middle of the night. There's so much anger and frustration, with no possible outlet." Her gaze fell to her hands, slender and clenched in her lap. She spoke more softly now, more thoughtfully. "I'm not talking ill of my father, merely claiming that he and my mother were grossly mismatched. He insisted that her place was in the home, raising me, waiting for his periodic appearances. She would never have gone against his wishes. So she did sit and wait . . . and wait . . . and wait. It was a waste of her intelligence."

"Was she unhappy?"

Alex stood close by her side now. When she raised her eyes they were clear and honest. "No. At least, I don't think she was *conscious* of being unhappy. She accepted her life because she loved my father. But the dreams she had for me—those had to express some inner feelings of hers. She never did complain, though. Never."

With a deep breath she looked away to continue the tale. "She was sick for three years. *He* stopped by when he happened to be in town, but it was mainly the two of us, as it had always been. I had transferred back to college in Pittsburgh so that I could be with her. She wasn't pleased about it, but she did need me there. But she never once let up on the theme that I should leave as soon as she died. It was as though," her voice wavered, "she purposely let go of life to free me." Dry-eyed, she looked toward the window. Alex's tall frame intercepted her gaze.

"Did you have any kind of relationship with your father after she died?"

Her blond head snapped back, eyes flashing in remembered vehemence. "No! I did what my mother wanted. I left Pittsburgh as soon after the funeral as I could."

"Do you think he suffered?"

"My father? At *my* leaving?"

"At your mother's death," he softly clarified his question.

"Oh, yes," she grimaced. "There was no one to meet him when he returned, to unpack his bags and wash everything, to make his meals and wait on him hand and foot, then pack his bags once more and send him off. I'm *sure* he missed her."

"You're very bitter."

It was precisely Alex's gentleness that emphasized the harshness of Alanna's indictment. Embarrassed, she averted her eyes. "I'm sorry. I didn't mean to sound that way. It's just . . . just . . ."

"What?"

She took a deep breath, voicing something she had never admitted, even to herself. "It's just that *I* needed someone then, too. My mother and I had been very close. Suddenly she was gone. For the first time I actually needed my father. But I was so frightened that I'd find myself in the role of caretaker, as my mother had been, that I never gave it a chance. Perhaps he would have risen to the occasion and been a comfort. I'll never know." Head low, she silently mourned that lost opportunity.

Alex's voice was smooth and low and as close by as she might have wished her father to have been so long ago. "You could give him the benefit of the doubt."

She smiled, sadly. "I suppose I could."

The long silence that followed allowed her to gather her composure and she felt stronger when Alex took her chin and tilted it up for his study. "I'm glad you've shared this with me, Alanna. It helps me to understand why certain things mean so much to you, that powerful professional drive of yours, for one. But I still think you're wrong." He spoke gently, soothing her even as he expressed a differing opinion from hers. "I respect what your mother told you—and her need for telling you—but it's possible that, if she could see you now, today, having achieved what you have, she would tell you that there's more to life than a career. She told you to realize your potential and you have, in the professional sense. But what about your potential for loving? What about your potential for caring, which you showed when you sat by her bedside night after night after spending long days at school? What about the maternal instinct that she must have passed down to you?"

Helpless to twist her head away, Alanna could only hold his gaze. He painted a picture of a different kind of existence and she could no more summarily dismiss it than she could turn her back and walk away from him. Did he have a point? *Was* she missing something? Her eyes, brown and luminous, reflected the inner turmoil which he sought to understand.

"I also see that you're right," he conceded quietly. When her brows furrowed in confusion he explained. "You do need time. This has happened much too quickly." But he would yield only so much ground before he re-asserted his own sentiment. "I'm convinced that you do love me. In time you'll come to see that, too."

"How can you be so sure?" she cried in exasperation.

"Sure that you love me? There are several ways. Right now I can tell from your eyes."

"My eyes?"

He nodded, sending a dashing swath of brown hair lower onto his forehead. "They're dry. You just spoke of your mother and of a very painful time in your life. It had to be difficult to recall it, but you didn't cry."

"I never cry—" She fell quickly into his trap.

"You did last night. If I'm correct that was the first time in years. *Am* I correct?"

He had begun to encroach more deeply on things that had puzzled her all day. Yet she could not deny the truth. "Yes."

To her astonishment a slow smile spread across his face, lighting it magnificently. "I'm glad, Alanna. Don't you see? The fact that you were able to cry out all that hurt and anger and loneliness to *me*, of all people, says something. The fact that you made love to me," he arched one brow, "says something, too."

She couldn't argue.

He paused and slid his arms around her, drawing her up to stand against him. "When you first told me about Harding you said you had loved him."

"I thought I did . . . at the time." Her voice was muffled against the warmth of his shirt and the broad expanse of chest beneath. The sweet nearness of him blinded her to this latest trap.

"Were you disturbed when you broke up?" He spoke softly against her hair, seemingly content to hold her close.

"At first I was. But I got over it very quickly. I think that's when I realized that what I'd felt was not quite love. . . ."

"You didn't rush off to get involved with anyone else. . . ."

"No. I told you, I've never felt strongly enough about anyone . . ." At last, she caught his train of thought and her words drifted off.

Alex smiled, tentatively at first, then more broadly. "You see? That's another sign of your love for me. You let *me* know you."

"You trapped me into that," she pouted, more disturbed than angry.

"But it stands. You aren't a loose woman, Alanna. You wouldn't have stayed with me last night if you hadn't felt something special. And you certainly wouldn't agree to stay with me tonight just for the fun of it!"

"Fun—hah!" She sought refuge in mockery. "All you want to do is lecture me."

"That's not all I want to do and you well know it." The hands that pressed her insinuatingly against him elaborated meaningfully. "I love you, Alanna. I'm not afraid to say it. Nor am I afraid to show it." With that he swept her into his arms and sauntered toward the hallway leading off the living room.

"Alex!" she cried, squirming only until his arms tightened. "Aren't you being a little overdramatic? I mean, I *can* walk."

"Just setting precedent, love. I'm going to enjoy carrying you to bed over the years."

"Alex . . . you agreed not to push. . . ."

Her feet touched the thick pile carpet of his bedroom. "So I did," he drawled quite unrepentantly. "Now don't move!" He moved to adjust the lights until a single recessed fixture cast its gentle illumination around the room. Alanna had time only to absorb the masculine aura of the bold chocolates and whites of walls, rugs and furnishings before he deftly flipped back the dark-patterned bedspread and returned to her. His hands framed her face as he kissed her long and hard, stealing her breath with the force of his emotion. "Now," he crooned deeply, drawing his head back far enough to let him encompass all of her in his gaze, "I intend to show you exactly how much I love you."

"How much you *think* you love me," she returned in a whisper, referring to their earlier argument. At her smile his eyes narrowed, small crinkles of mischief radiating out from their corners.

"That's not even worth an argument, Alanna. But you keep telling yourself that. Maybe it will temper your response. . . ."

There was something challenging in his tone and in the dark charcoal-gray beams that seared into her intensely. "Are you trying to tell me something that I don't already know, Alex?"

"What I'm doing," he rejoined without pause, "is

daring you to keep that upper lip steady. I'll just bet you can't lie before me and be passive. Though if you don't love me it shouldn't be that hard to resist a response."

"Come on," she chided, "you know that the body has a will of its own, Alex."

"But your will is strong, love. If you work hard enough to show me that your feelings for me fall short you should be able to stay still, regardless of what I do."

"You make it sound dangerous," she quipped nervously.

"Are you up to the bet? While I show you how much I do love you, you can show me how much you *don't* love *me*."

"This is foolish."

"Ready to give in already?"

"No way!" She stiffened her spine, driven by frustration to resist him. "You aren't all *that* irresistible, you know." With a deep breath she drew herself up even straighter. Chin tilted at a bold angle, hands fallen loosely by her sides, eyes lit in defiance, she waited, offering herself as a willing opponent. If for no other reason than to take him down a peg or two, she was determined to withstand the sensory onslaught that she knew would follow. Unfortunately she had underestimated the force of his determination.

Alex was the consummate master, speaking volumes with his eyes as he moved to within inches of her, leaving her shaking before he'd even touched her. His hands were gentle as they tipped her face up, his lips sweet in possession. She relaxed instinctively against him, then caught herself up short. His mouth opened wider, consuming her lips with thorough care, seeming to drain them of every bit of the rigidity she tried to instill. When her lips parted limply his tongue plunged within to probe the recesses of her inner warmth. Alanna steeled herself against the tantalizing foray, but darting tongues of desire licked at her nerve ends in a passion now far beyond her control.

Still she resisted. She reminded herself of his challenge and of what was at stake. But Alex's kiss taunted her for her futile attempt at concentration, tugging at her lips one final time as he drew back to look down at her. The pale light gentled his features, imbuing him with an aura of innocence.

"Not bad, owl-eyes." He grinned his compliment to her marginal success. He seemed undaunted and undisturbed, not in the least discouraged. Oh, yes, she mused, Alex Knight thrived in the ring! Reaching up, he removed her glasses and placed them carefully onto the shelf that comprised the headboard of the bed. Alanna watched his lazy motion, sensing in his languor its intended sensuality. His every move was smooth and fluid, athletic prowess in his every step. Helplessly she surveyed his lean frame, appreciating anew his head-to-toe virility, then telling herself of her immunity to it— between traitorous palpitations of her heart.

He took great pains with her hair, removing each pin, gathering them in a cluster in his palm and placing the lot on his dresser before finally combing the spill of blond silk with his fingers. As though enchanted he spread the strands about her shoulders.

"You seem to be operating in slow motion tonight. Are you enjoying yourself?" she asked evenly, dismayed when the indifference she had tried to inject into her voice emerged as impatience.

Alex grinned wickedly. "Every . . . last . . . minute."

Plunging his fingers into the thickness of her hair, he brought her lips to his once more. And this time he kissed her with a passion that left her dizzy. Dizzy and feeling heady. For with the knowledge that she could draw this man out to his fullest came pure delight. In this state of satisfaction Alanna responded reflexively.

"Uh-uh," he chided against her lips. "Giving up already?"

"No. No!" She caught herself up once again. "Just relaxing for a minute. It won't happen again."

"Don't let it," he drawled in warning, "or you'll never make it. You've got to be strong!"

She tried. Oh, how she tried! She tried to ignore the lips that tickled her neck and throat. She tried to ignore the fingers that reached for the zipper of her dress. She tried to ignore the eroticism of his long, drawn-out siege as he slid it slowly down, his fingers feathering along the line of her spine. It was very, very difficult.

He had to feel the wild beat of her heart when his hands slid beneath the fabric of the dress and around her shoulders, coaxing the fabric down, following to hold the fullness of her breasts. This time she gasped aloud.

"So soon, love?" he goaded her mischievously. "This is nothing!"

Nothing? Nothing the faint roughness of his fingertips as they crept under the lace of her bra to tease her nipple to arousal? Nothing the thumbs that then dipped beneath the straps to lower them and allow her taut, round breasts to fall free? Nothing the mouth that trailed down her neck and nibbled at her shoulder blade before taking those hardened tips, first one, then the other, within?

Alanna barely stifled another cry. When Alex drawled a smug accusation she was quick to explain the hands that clutched his shoulders. "I'm not responding," her singsong tone wavered. "I'm only trying to hold myself up."

"No need." Nudging her backward, he followed her easily onto the bed, covering her body with his. As he kissed her again he purposely let her feel the weight of his body. Alanna balled her fists in frustration. She ached to run her palms along the length of him, to feel the swell of his muscles and the texture of his skin against her fingertips. She wanted to kiss his flesh and taste the tang that was his alone. All she could do, however, was to lie in muted agony, breathing in his manly scent, struggling not to give in to the piercing arrows of need. When his lips finally left hers she moaned.

"Throwing in the towel, love?"

"Oh, no," she gasped. "No."

His mouth silenced her as his hands went back to work, dispensing with her bra and her remaining clothes with a haste that hinted at a certain gratifying wear and tear on *his* composure. Dress, slip, panty hose—all fell to the floor in the flurry. Then, his chest heaving slightly, he stood back to savor her.

"Your hands are clenched, Alanna. Is something wrong?"

Alanna was ready to explode from within. "No, no. What could be wrong? What could be more natural—"

"—than to lie naked before your lover?" he finished for her, expressing her unwilling thought precisely. His eyes caressed her beauty, beaming a molten heat along her skin.

Alanna swallowed thickly. She hadn't pictured herself as a sacrifice to the gods, yet here she was, helpless. Infinitely vulnerable and frantically clutching at the last straws of control. Was there, as Alex claimed, more to the attraction than the purely physical?

In a move that was subliminally arousing, Alex deftly shrugged off his suit jacket and draped it casually over a nearby chair. Alanna's throat constricted as she watched lean, male fingers draw off an already loosened tie. Those same fingers moved over the buttons of his shirt, releasing each, pulling the tails from his pants, tossing the shirt aside. His chest was a bold expanse of bronze lightly hazed with brown; his arms were sinewed and strong. She wanted to throw herself at him then; only his relentlessly watchful gaze restrained her.

Her mouth was dry. Absently she moistened her lips with the tip of her tongue. She watched helplessly as his hands moved to his belt, unbuckling it, unfastening his trousers. Within moments he stood before her, as nude as she. And then he approached. Propping himself on flattened palms, he leaned with maddening grace toward her.

"How can you be so cruel?" she rasped hoarsely, nearing the end of her tether.

"Cruel?" He feigned hurt. "It's not every day that I strip for a woman."

"Thank heaven!" she whispered, then waited for him to lower himself further. "Well . . . ?"

His grin was a knowing one. "Well what?"

Pride slipped inexorably through her whitened fingers until she was left with only the agony of wanting him. "Aren't you going to come to me?"

"In time." His answering whisper was low.

"Alex . . ." It was half warning, half pleading, inspired by her awareness of the bronzed perfection looming over her. He was inches away . . . yet too far. At that moment she knew him to be the key—the key to release the lock that barred her from fulfillment. It no longer mattered that, prior to meeting him, she hadn't even known the lock was in place. What mattered was that she needed him now.

With that realization went the last shreds of her tattered control. Reaching for him, she bridged the distance in an instant and stretched against him, coiling her arms tightly around his neck. Her weight, light as it was, brought his body down on top of hers, but not his head. That was tipped back so that he could see her clearly.

"You admit defeat?" He baited her one last time.

And Alanna reveled in that defeat. "I lose, I lose!" she declared with a conviction that was replaced by urgency when she touched him. Her hands hungered and devoured, making up for what seemed a lost eternity. To her further joy her loss of control triggered his. With a deep and soulful groan he made her his. The heat of the union fused them together, binding them as they moved to the age-old rhythm of passion. Forgotten now was the game they had played, its outcome secure from the start.

Alanna responded to Alex with the fullness of her womanhood. She drew on her intuitive resources to drive him to higher and higher peaks of ecstasy. And he had no intention of leaving her behind. She went with him avidly, her damp body clutched tightly to his. When at last the moment of ultimate delight exploded within and between them it cast its love-glow to enhance the climactic beauty they shared.

Their paired breathlessness slowly receded before Alex attempted to speak. His husky whisper was offered against her brow as he rolled onto his side and drew her against him. "You didn't lose after all, did you, love?"

There was no need for an answer. Her satisfied smile said it all.

7

No, she certainly hadn't lost. But what had she won? She had won long moments of shimmering ecstasy, then utter fulfillment. She had won the joy of having satisfied Alex as well, of feeling his body, warm and content, against hers. And she had won another night of deep and uninterrupted sleep. Wrapped in Alex's arms she felt replete and protected. A sweet serenity filled her through those hours, a sense of peace which held her even when he woke her with a kiss the next morning.

"Rise and shine, love. Time to get up." His voice tickled her ear with its early morning huskiness. Lazily, she burrowed closer.

"What time is it?"

"Six-fifteen."

"Six-fifteen?" Her brown eyes widened. "Why so early?"

Alex seemed amused. "We're going swimming. Remember?"

"Oh, no! That's right! Alex, what are we going to do about the IAT study? We didn't settle *anything* last night!"

His drawl was suggestive. "I wouldn't say that. I seem to recall that you lost a certain bet. . . ."

"You're darned right I lost! It just shows you how taken

I am with your body!" She grinned, knowing that she was skirting the issue but shooting for the diversion nonetheless. Alex saw right through her.

"Don't give me that, Alanna. You love me. Say it."

"What's in a word?" She shrugged with feigned nonchalance.

"A lot. Now say it. You love me."

Alanna nestled lower against him, helplessly admiring the soft skin just under his arm. When she touched it with a slim fingertip he squirmed. "You're ticklish!" she exclaimed, pleased to have found another diversion. But again Alex was determined to have his way.

He shifted lithely to capture her hands in one of his and immobilize her against his body with the other. "I'm very ticklish and even more in love." His eyes, gray and keen, repeated the demand he'd already made twice this morning. She knew what he wanted to hear, but couldn't quite say it. It would mean the commitment she had always feared.

"What *is* love?"

His answer was ready. "Love is when you want to do for and give to and put another's welfare ahead of your own. Love is when your life's meaning comes to revolve around that other person."

"And yours has?" She eyed him skeptically.

His grasp loosened, but without granting total release. "I know that you refuse to believe this, but it has. On the surface I have everything most people want—a successful business, an apartment in the city, a home in the country, enough money to satisfy me. In a nutshell, I have every material thing I could want." She sensed what was coming. "But it's not enough. There's that awful emptiness that I've lived with for years. Frankly, I'm tired of it."

"So I'm a stopgap measure?"

"You know you're not, Alanna." He raised himself solemnly on one elbow. "And this is no time for joking. I've already told you some of the things about you that I love. Well, here's another. You've awakened in me a kind of protectiveness, a need to devote myself totally to one woman. I've never felt this way before."

As his eyes blazed their intensity toward her Alanna felt at war with herself. One side of her wanted to still his confession, to capture the thoughts and emotions he had roused and put them into a more easily controllable dimension. But the other side wanted to hear every word and more; this side hungrily savored his evident devotion. The battle raged within as Alex mused on.

"I'm thirty-nine years old, Alanna. I suppose I've been ready for a wife and family for a long time, but it's never appealed to me until now. I want *you* as my wife. I want *you* as the mother of my children. But mostly I want you with me every day, to share the business, this apartment, that house in the country."

The gentleness of his hand as it outlined her features was in contrast to the fire in his eyes. "Do you know what I want to do?" She couldn't tear her gaze away; mutely she shook her head. "I want to bring you breakfast in bed on the weekends and sit here beside you reading the paper. I want to drop you at work in the morning and pick you up at night and spend every possible minute in between making you happy."

"You're crazy," she whispered, but her smile held undeniable affection.

Alex lay down flat once more and pulled her head to his shoulder to continue the dream. "I may be, but it *is* how I feel. I want to buy you things—little extravagances that you'd never buy for yourself—and take you places. I'd like to travel with you to all the exotic spots you've never taken the time to visit."

"I'm not exactly deprived," she argued feebly.

"I know that! No doubt you could easily afford to take those trips yourself. Why haven't you? For one thing, you won't leave that job of yours for long enough because you're afraid that some ambitious man will steal it from you. For another, though you may not be willing to admit it, it's no fun to travel alone."

Alanna couldn't lie. She'd thought often of travel and had vetoed it for just those reasons. "I admit it," she conceded softly.

"Then," he continued more gently, "why won't you admit that, together, we could have a lovely life."

"Because I'm just not sure of that yet."

"Even after last night?"

"Yes. Lovemaking is still a physical act. Love entails more. Don't you see, Alex?" She raised herself on an elbow to look down at him beseechingly. "I've lived my life alone for so long. I've been totally independent. I rely on no one. Love has never been a high priority with me."

His voice was even. "Then you don't love me?"

"I don't know."

In the silence that followed, Alanna acknowledged, for the first time, that she could easily come to love Alex—if she didn't already do so. As she recognized the vulnerability in his face now her only impulse was to soothe it. Yes, in many respects, if Alex's definition was apt, she was in love. She did want to give to him, to share with him, to do for him. Yet there was still that other life. . . .

He sighed deeply, studying her confused expression for a moment longer. Then he smiled, that broad, white-toothed smile that set her heart to beating double-time. "Now we're getting somewhere. An 'I don't know' is far better than an outright 'No'!" He threw back the covers and got out of bed, turning to face her with no thought at all to his nudity. "I'll get to you yet, Alanna. You may think you have it all now, but you'll be thinking differently soon. *I'll* show you."

Alanna half believed him. To her perplexity, she half *wanted* to believe him. He was, in so many ways, not the least of which was the image of bold masculinity he presented to her now, a divine creature. Her gaze luxuriated in his body for a final moment as she lay in bed. Then, without warning, his hands whipped off her covering and curved under her, lifting her from the bed and setting her upright just outside the bathroom. His release was slow; her body slithered sensuously down his in poignant remembrance of the passion they'd shared the previous night. He kissed her deeply, his lips inviting her waiting response.

"We'll never get *anywhere* at this rate," he finally growled against her moist lips. "You go in there; I'll use the other one. We'll meet in the living room in ten minutes. Can you do it?"

"Anything you can do I can—"

"All right, all right! Just *be* there!"

Such playfulness was a rarity in either of their early-morning experiences. Alanna pondered it with pleasure as she dressed quickly, then joined him for the drive to the pool. An hour later, as they sat down to breakfast, they talked of the IAT study. It was Alex who voiced their shared opinion.

"I think that we ought to let Ellen fill our places with two other people. We seem to have temporarily solved our problem." His eyes twinkled with a silver light. "That's two nights in a row . . . the first time in years for me."

"Same here." She couldn't disagree. "But why? Is it," she blushed, continuing against her better judgment, "simply a matter of physical exhaustion?"

Alex reached across the table to take her hand in his.

Her skin seemed pale against his tan, her fingers that much more fragile. "You know better than that. Even the swimming isn't so much for the sake of exhaustion as for letting out pent-up frustration. And our lovemaking takes it one step further."

"To where?" She cornered him, relying on his apparent talent for expression to help her sort out her own jumbled thoughts.

"To the point of satisfying a need. On my part," he looked closely at her, "it's a need to love and have the person I love with me. Do you remember I told you about those feelings I used to wake up to?" When she nodded he went on. "They've been gone completely these last two nights. When I wake up in the morning I feel filled, not empty."

Alanna looked away. His self-analysis came too close to describing the feelings she had experienced herself. It bothered her that he felt so much freer about expressing them, yet she couldn't help herself. As though understanding her dilemma and willing to grant her more time to resolve it, Alex didn't push for a similar confession. Rather, his talk returned to the immediate matter of Ellen Henderson and her study.

"I'll call her this morning and explain things. You do agree that we should drop out, don't you?"

"Yes. For now, at least. She was right; there have been so many new factors introduced since we agreed to participate that it would skew the results anyway. And if we can continue to sleep through the night . . ."

"Which brings up that other issue." He paused to offer her a warm sweet roll from the basket that the waiter had just brought. She accepted and began to butter it as he mirrored her actions. Both knew what this other issue entailed; both were somewhat unsure, each in his own way. Again it was Alex who took the lead.

"You know that I want to marry you, Alanna." He waited for her nod before continuing. "If you agreed we could be married this weekend and then there would be no question about living apart. But you won't agree . . . not yet. Which leaves us with three possibilities."

She put down her roll, suddenly not as hungry as she had been.

"Eat!" Alex's order startled her.

"I'm not hungry."

"You need something to carry you through the day, Alanna. Don't be difficult."

"I've ordered an omelet. It should be here any minute."

His voice lowered. "I know that, but the rolls are good."

Alanna sighed in frustration. "Alex, what's the problem? Why don't you just get on with what you have to say?"

That was it; she saw it the instant she said it. He was, in his way, as apprehensive as she was about making plans, yet they had to do it. Perhaps she could help him.

Her voice was soft, but loud enough to allow him to catch every word. "You're right. We have three possibilities. We either live together—without benefit of marriage, see each other on occasion or go our separate ways."

"Right." The one word was spoken tensely, all his vulnerability evident.

Alanna thought aloud. "I'd like to rule out the last."

Alex was quick to challenge her. "Do you admit that you can't live without me?"

"That's not the point." She kept her voice down and lowered her eyes. He might have been right, but she couldn't even admit it to herself, much less to him. "But if we don't see each other we'll never be able to work *any*-thing out. And if we don't see each other we'll probably both start waking up at night again and therefore ought to stay in the study. . . ."

"All right," he conceded quickly, reluctant to let things get more complicated than they already were. "Strike going our separate ways." His deep breath could as easily have been a sleepy yawn as an expression of relief. "What next?"

Alanna was far from helpless. Systematically she attacked the next possibility. "As far as living together, I doubt that you would stand for that." Her gaze held faint accusation.

"You're very perceptive. And do you know why I wouldn't stand for it?" Without awaiting her guess he went on, lowering his voice only when her eyes flew to the tables surrounding theirs. "Because I think that that would be the easy way out for you and I won't let you take it. When it gets to the point that you want to spend every free minute of your life with me, that you want to sleep with me *every* night and wake up with me *every* morning, you can damn well confess your love and marry me!"

"Shhh! Keep it down, Alex!"

He leaned closer and spoke more softly, but the vehemence was still there. "I don't particularly care *who* hears me! I love you!"

"I know," she sighed. "You've told me so more than once."

And she believed him. Finally. He *did* love her and the sudden realization gnawed at her. She knew instinctively that Alex Knight would do nothing halfheartedly. If he loved her he would love her with everything he possessed. It was a beautiful thought, but one that was also terrifying. For while one part of her wanted very much to return his love, the other part fought it with every bit of the strength that she had had a lifetime to accrue.

"Where does that leave us?" he asked more gently, back in control. "We see each other *on occasion?*" Skepticism was written on his every feature. "Just what does that mean?"

She grinned, relieved that his acute vulnerability seemed to have passed. For it was to that vulnerability that she herself was acutely vulnerable. "It permits you—us— the pleasure of each other's company when the opportunity arises—"

"Such as tonight?" he rebounded. "For dinner?"

"I'd like that." She accepted his invitation softly.

"Then," he sat back more confidently, "I'm to 'woo' you?" A hint of mischief entered his gaze.

"You make it sound so Victorian."

His mouth slanted wryly. "It's not quite what I would have expected from a modern woman. I wouldn't have called your behavior last night, or the night before, for that matter, exactly Victorian."

Alanna chose to ignore his barb, growing suddenly more sober. "I need time, Alex. You said so yourself. I need breathing space. If, as you hope," she verged on sarcasm, "I'm to discover that I simply can't live without you, I'll have to spend time with you *and* time away, won't I?"

Alex hesitated, then agreed reluctantly. "I suppose you will. But remember, I can only be *so* patient. And I do get jealous. I don't want you dating other men."

Without thinking, she bristled; then she thought. Slowly a coy grin spread from ear to ear. He liked a challenge, did he? "What's wrong, Alex? Are you worried that, in comparison to another man, there might be something lacking in your appeal?"

His protest went no further than a quickly indrawn breath. He was sharp; he saw what she was up to in the instant, but their breakfast, hot and fresh from the kitchen, was placed in front of them before he had a chance to answer.

As soon as the waiter had gone he spoke. "If I said no you would think I was arrogant. If I said yes you would think I was insecure. In truth, I'm neither. I'm more concerned with *my* thoughts, knowing that another man's hands might be touching you. But," his gaze enveloped her speculatively, "on second thought, I think I'll take my chances. See whoever you want; it can only help my cause."

Her "Speaking of arrogance . . ." was muffled behind a mouthful of cheese omelet. Beyond that she let the matter ride. She didn't want to see anyone else, anyway. Her objection had been to his command; it was a matter of principle. Once the command had been revoked she had no desire to rebel against it.

Following breakfast Alex dropped her back at the hospital lot to pick up her car with a promise to stop by her apartment at seven-thirty that evening. She went contentedly on to work, breezing through the day with more patience and endurance than she'd felt in months. Jake commented on her improved outlook when he dropped by her office to talk late in the afternoon.

"You're looking chipper today, Alanna. You must be sleeping better."

She smiled sweetly, trying to hold in her secret. "I am."

"How's Alex?" he asked with a nonchalance she knew to be a sham.

"Fine." Again she smiled.

"Still after you?" He settled his slightly rounding frame into a nearby chair.

"Uh-huh."

"Are you still resisting?"

"Now, Jake. That's getting a little more personal than usual, don't you think?"

"Just answer me; are you still fighting him?"

"On the matter of marriage," she chose her words with care, "yes. On the matter of getting acquainted," *what an appallingly inadequate word that was*, she mused, "no."

"Good. You know, he could help you when I move you up into the Executive Vice-President's slot."

"Are you still serious about that, Jake?"

"Very serious. The meeting is Monday. And if I propose you, you're in."

She shook her head, though not a wisp of her neatly coiled blond hair budged. "I don't know, Jake . . . I appreciate the thought, but it could cause more of a problem among the men here than it's worth."

Jake Wallace sat back in his chair and studied her closely. "Don't you want the promotion?"

She shrugged. "I'm doing the work, anyway. . . ."

"Then why shouldn't you get the credit?" he asked sharply.

"It just doesn't seem to matter—the title, I mean. If I have the power now to set into action—and keep in action—the projects I think are promising, what more can I ask?"

"You can ask," Jake went on insistently, "for recognition and respect from those men!"

"Hah! They'll give that to me when and if they feel like it! A promotion will only get their tails up!"

Jake's voice lowered. "That's where Knight comes in."

"What?"

"Alex Knight. Marry him. That will end all speculation about your . . . ah . . . extracurricular activities at my house."

Alanna rolled her eyes skyward, not quite sure she'd heard her mentor correctly. "Jake, you've been happily married now for some thirty-odd years. Would *you* have gotten married for a reason like that?"

He held his breath expectantly, then narrowed his gaze. "Not unless I loved the person I was proposing to marry."

Her sculpted features were momentarily pained;

quickly she turned away from Jake. "That's just the issue. Alex loves me. I . . . I'm not so sure of my own feelings."

Despite the inconclusiveness of her answer, Jake was satisfied. "I can't tell you what you feel, Alanna. But I can tell you this: When I walked in here a few minutes ago you had that very special look about you. No," he halted her protest, "I wasn't imagining it." Then he feigned sternness. "And don't tell me that it was excitement about the biotechnics project. You've been pleased about projects before, but you haven't looked like this."

"You're reading too much—"

"Oh, no." He shook his head stubbornly. "I know you, Alanna. There's been a change."

"I'm sleeping well." Her smile returned; they were back to square one.

"So you told me." He cleared his throat. "Alanna," he stood, "you're nearly as pigheaded as Elaine when she sets her mind to something. In this case, it's 'the works' at the beauty shop on Saturday. She's hoping that you'll join her for lunch afterward. What time do you finish at the pool?"

After some quick mental calculations Alanna relaxed. "If I drop her there at nine, I can pick her up by one. There's a swim meet at ten; it shouldn't last more than two hours."

When Jake shook his head this time it was in admiration. "You're amazing, my girl. And have I told you lately how much I appreciate what you do for Elaine? I could drive her myself, but she seems to think that this is women's business. It's hard enough for her to cope with that wheelchair; she feels so dependent. Somehow you make her feel as though she's no imposition. Frankly, I don't know what we'd *both* do without you."

Alanna gave her hand to Jake as she walked with him to the door. "The feeling's mutual; you know that. It's so important for her to lead as normal a life as possible.

Driving her on Saturday is the least I can do. And, yes, do tell her that I'd love to join her for lunch."

On Saturday Alanna drove Elaine to the beauty shop, then shared a late lunch with her at a nearby restaurant. Over Potage St. Germaine and salads of fresh endives and almonds they talked with the comfort of old friends— of what was happening at the office *and* after hours. Elaine was eager to hear about the swim team's victory over its opponent and Alanna was too pleased with the triumph to deprive her of the details. When the subject of Alexander Knight came up, however, Alanna was caught off guard. Afterward she realized that Jake would have shared such an interesting tidbit with his wife and she felt no actual regret. Her words were measured, though, and Elaine was unable to pass on any more to Jake than he already knew.

It was late afternoon when she finally had her friend safely returned to the Wallace home. Then she stopped at the supermarket, the dry cleaner and the florist for a bunch of fresh daisies to replace those that had withered in the vase atop her table. The pale gold November sun spilled across her champagne carpet when she sat, at last, quiet and by herself in her own home. Only then did her thoughts return to Alex.

In a slow motion replay of the night before she found herself snowed afresh by the devastating charm and virile appeal of the man. When Alex had mentioned dinner she'd assumed they'd be going out. But he'd had something quite different in mind when he had picked her up and returned her to his place. As it happened, even *his* plans were superseded by a spontaneous demonstration of talents other than culinary.

Alanna was still not quite sure what had taken them immediately to bed in each other's arms, their dinner temporarily forgotten. She blushed at the memory of their abandon. Perhaps, from her viewpoint, it had been the way he had looked in casual dress—jeans and a turtleneck sweater, both of which were alarming to her senses in the snug way they fit.

When they finally returned to the kitchen, hand in hand, Alanna wore nothing but Alex's turtleneck; he wore the jeans alone.

Even now the scent of him filled her nostrils—that musky male tang that spiced his bed, his towels, that warm, oversized turtleneck sweater that fell to her thighs. Tingling, she blushed again, then fought the tide of rising sensation. It simply wasn't fair for this man—*any* man—to wield such power! That she should tremble now at the memory of their passion was mind-boggling!

It had, indeed, been a night to remember. There was not only a jointly produced feast of sukiyaki, rice and cucumber salad to devour, there was Beethoven's *Eroica* to soothe them and a bright birch fire to hypnotize them. When they returned to bed it was to a round of lovemaking that, by some miracle, surpassed the others in pure rapture. It was as though Alex read every soft nuance of her body, delighting in each secret dare, each hidden challenge. For Alanna the game was reciprocal. She discovered that his hard man's body had similar soft spots; it was her joy to seek them out.

Once again they slept through the night and once again it was Alex's kiss that awakened her in the morning. The routine, she had mused, could easily become habit-forming.

The jangle of the telephone brought her from her reverie, and back to the early evening quiet of her apartment.

"Hello?"

"Hey, owl-eyes," the deep voice flowed silkily over the wire, "how are you?"

How familiar and good his voice sounded! "I'm fine." She smiled in response, though she knew he couldn't see. "How did everything go today?" Alex had flown south early that morning for a series of emergency meetings in Atlanta.

"Slow, love. That's why I'm calling."

She read fatigue, perhaps even a hint of discouragement, in his voice and was instantly concerned. "What's wrong? Did something happen?"

"No. Everything is going all right. Just slow. Very slow. Making agreements with this nine-member board is like taking a photograph of a thirty-member family and getting everyone to smile."

"They don't like your proposal?" His humor soaring above her, Alanna was stunned. Alex had explained the fundamentals of the project, one that would merge the brains of a think-tank center in Atlanta with the money of the Knight Corporation to study problems of social welfare. It was such a worthwhile cause. . . .

"They seem to like it," Alex explained gently, "but they differ among themselves as to whether one organization— mine—should be the sole affiliate. Several of the board members believe that they should receive funding on a problem-by-problem basis."

"But that would be such a waste of time and effort!"

"I know that," his low voice rejoined, "and you know that, but try telling it to them." He sighed. "But that's what I intend to do tonight, if possible. . . ." Alanna caught his drift immediately.

"Tonight?" He had tentatively suggested that morning that they would spend the evening together when he returned. "Then you'll be staying in Atlanta?"

His voice was guarded, as though he were unsure of her reaction and wary of showing his own feelings. "I've got to. It's got to be taken care of soon or there'll be twice as much work later." He paused, his tone finally softening. "I'm sorry. I was looking forward to being with you."

Alanna was caught in a whirlpool of emotion, anger and hurt and sorrow swirling round and round each other. In the end she could only sigh. "I am, too."

"I'm hoping to get back by tomorrow afternoon. Will I see you then?" Again he was cautious.

"I can't, Alex. I have tickets for the afternoon show at the Players' Theater."

"You're going alone?" She could almost see his angry glare.

"No. I'm going with two friends—"

"*Male* friends?" *Male* sounded positively evil.

"Alex! Did I ask you how many of the board members you're seeing are women?" She took a breath to steady her suddenly shaky pulse. "It happens that we've had these tickets for two months. And I'm going to the *matinée*, not the midnight show."

"Then I'll take you to dinner afterward," he offered, temporarily pacified.

"We're already going to dinner afterward," she explained patiently. "These are good friends, but I don't get to see them as often as I'd like."

"Are they business contacts?"

"Actually, no. I met them several years ago through a literature course I took at the university. Diana is a high school teacher; Maxine has a doctor-husband and two young children at home."

There was no audible sigh of relief; the lightening of Alex's tone alerted Alanna of just how worried he had been. "That sounds nice. Where will you be eating?"

Alanna's suspicions were sparked by the pointedness of the question. "I . . . don't . . . know. . . ." She drew out the words, each pause relaying the idea that she had no intention of spilling *that* information as well.

"OK, love." He sounded cheerful enough, satisfied with winning one out of two. "I've got to run. Will you miss me tonight?"

"I may just lie awake all night and pine for you." Her answering drawl buried truth deep within its good humor.

Alex saw it quickly. "It should be interesting, you know."

"What?"

"Seeing what kind of a night's sleep we have. This will be the first time we've slept apart in—"

"I know, Alex. I know." His words stirred images she felt were best left alone at the moment. "Just remember not to drink liquor or coffee." Her tone playfully mocked Ellen Henderson's directives. "Don't go to bed until you're tired. Don't lie in bed for more than ten minutes without—"

"All right, Alanna! That's enough! You sound like a mother hen! Just remember that those instructions apply to *you*, too! I'll talk with you tomorrow night, then?"

"That sounds fine." She hesitated, reluctant to say good-bye. "Good luck with your meetings." Humor always helped. "I know you'll charm the skirts off them!" She wasn't prepared for Alex's vehement objection.

"They're all *men*, Alanna! And not one is as interesting a person as you, for all their supposed brilliance," he growled. "I wish that you were down here with me. It's the kind of business trip that would be a second—or third or fourth—honeymoon if you were here."

"Alex . . ." Her warning was well taken and he relaxed.

"All right. No pressure." But he couldn't help a barb. "You can tell yourself *that*, tonight. Sleep well, love."

"You too, Alex."

It seemed a foregone conclusion that sleep would be

uneven that night. And, indeed, it was. Alanna spent the evening sorting out the chaos of emotions that Alex's call had brought to the surface. She felt angry that he hadn't made a point of returning to keep their date, then scolded herself for her presumption. She had no right to demand anything from him, did she? But she was hurt—hurt that he had not demanded himself that his meetings be wound up to allow for his evening return. And, yes, she felt above all disappointed that she wouldn't see him until tomorrow, or perhaps the day after.

All in all, it did not bode well for sleep. How did one keep tension from the bedroom when one's body and senses and memory were filled to overflowing with frustration and unfulfilled desire? She lay in bed for ten minutes, trying to clear her mind, then jumped up in defeat. Twenty minutes later, she tried again; again, failure was immediate. When finally she did fall asleep it was well past midnight. She was not surprised, moreover, to find herself awake again at three.

Sitting in the living room with a glass of warm milk, she perversely hoped that Alex was having as much trouble as she was. Her mind's eye painted a picture of him in bed, the sheets thrown across his lean lines, the white linens a strong contrast to the dark sheen of his skin with the soft fur mat that had cushioned her blond tresses so deliciously. Her skin had begun to warm before she doggedly ousted the image.

Breathe deeply. Think of nothing. It was very hard work, this thinking of nothing! At length she returned to bed and, finally, to sleep. The morning, however, found her back to her rise-and-frown crankiness. Following Ellen's suggestion she did go for a swim at the pool. Then came a morning of leisure, reading the newspaper, sipping coffee, lounging in her warm fleece robe as she never had time to do on a work day. It was potentially a pleasant few hours. Why, then, did it drag?

The question was easily answered, though the answer was far from being to Alanna's satisfaction. It was Alex. Alex. Love. Marriage. Children. Forever . . .

Had Alex been right? What would her mother have said had she been able to see her only daughter now? Would she remind her daughter of the love and family that Alanna had sacrificed on the altar of corporate success? What *would* happen if she did agree to marry Alex? Would she be able to have it all—him, her career and a family? He had planted the seeds of doubt in her mind—a doubt that encompassed those ideas around which she had shaped her comings and goings for over ten years. Could she change her way of thinking?

In the end it came down to one basic factor. Love. Did she love Alex? If what she felt for him *was* love, change was worth considering. Though she believed firmly that love alone was not enough, without it there was no hope at all for a relationship with Alex. *He* was so sure, so very sure!

She spent the afternoon with her friends at the theater before moving on to a restaurant later. It was a welcome diversion from her deeply perplexing thoughts. As always she enjoyed their company, sharing the latest news with them, discussing broader issues as they came up. As she walked up to her apartment building shortly before eight she felt remarkably relaxed considering her lack of sleep the night before. But relaxation faded as her thoughts turned in anticipation to Alex's call.

As it happened she didn't have to wait for a call, for standing on her doorstep waiting for her was Alex himself.

8

Without even a "hello" or a "how are you" he moved toward her and a large and powerful pair of arms opened to swallow her up. Alanna melted into them. Though the air was chill it barely touched the warmth within and between them. For Alanna there was a sense of peace and contentment that had been missing in his absence. She felt as though she was, at last, home.

Alex's tan jacket was soft against her cheek, his hands insistently strong through her own dark wool coat. Their embrace seemed endlessly divine, until the intrusion of several of Alanna's fellow tenants broke the spell. Without a word Alex took her hand and led her inside the building to her apartment, silently taking the keys from her, unlocking the door and guiding her gently in. It was only when the door was firmly shut that he took her in his arms again.

There was a hunger in his kiss that was undeniable and matched with equal strength by Alanna. Her pulse raced through veins fast-warming with desire, the same desire that was reflected with such urgency in Alex's smoldering charcoal eyes when he finally pulled back to look at her. His gaze spoke the greeting; hers returned it. Then another message shot between them and Alanna realized

just how much she had missed him. The deep and won-
drous craving sprang from her core, propelling her toward him magnetically. There would be time for talk
later. Now the need was for a more primal form of communication.

Gazes interlocked, they slipped their coats off and
tossed them onto the living room couch. Her hand disappeared into his as he led her to her bedroom, then reappeared to allow her to undress herself. Heart pounding
with growing excitement, she fumbled with buttons and
zippers and stockings, all the while following the progress of the tall man before her.

Was it a mere thirty-six hours' absence that made him
look this devastatingly handsome? Her shimmering brown-
eyed gaze could not see enough of him. She followed as
he wrenched off his tie and hastily disposed of his shirt,
presenting his sturdy chest for her consideration as he
kicked off the rest of his clothes.

By the time they stood revealed to one another her
knees quivered helplessly. Without hesitation she went to
him, unable to suppress a moan of pleasure when her skin
came in contact with his. Her curves fitted against his
lines with the perfection that had always been there, as
though they had been molded specifically for each other.

Alexis hands sent ripples of ecstasy through Alanna's
body. He touched her everywhere, head to toe, as he
nudged her back onto the bed and her own fingertips, then
lips, followed suit with a need that could not be quelled.

Within instants, Alex made her his and Alanna gloried
in his possession. The heat of their passion built quickly
to the boiling point, dampening their bodies in arousal
until, with a simultaneous cry of ecstasy, they gave themselves over to an exaltation that encompassed both mind
and body.

"I missed you," Alanna whispered breathlessly when

finally the spasms of joy had subsided to allow for speech. Alex took a bit longer, his chest heaving as he slid off to lie by her side.

"I was hoping for something more far-reaching," he rasped thickly, his eye glittering his humor, "but I'll settle for that in the meanwhile. I missed you, too, Alanna."

On impulse she reached up to comb back the thick hair that had fallen onto his forehead. Her hand remained at the back of his head as she lay on her side to savor the sight of him.

His brief command took her by surprise. "Say it."

"W-what?"

"Your eyes did just now, but I'd like to hear you say it with your voice, so that you can hear it, too."

"What?"

"That you love me."

"I love you." It was soft and whispered, barely stirring the air around them, but Alanna *did* hear it and was nearly as surprised as Alex, whose dark eyes lit up with an exquisite happiness she could not have described had she tried later to do so.

His arms brought her against him once more as his lips moaned in her ear, "Ahhh. I've wanted to hear that so badly." Then he set her back an inch to study the still-startled expression that masked her features. "And when did you decide this?"

"I don't know." Still a whisper. Still barely audible. Still groping for understanding. "Just now, I guess."

"What finally clinched it? What brought about the great decision?"

She weighed the possibilities with a slow-growing composure. "I guess there had to be *some* explanation for the fact that we spend more time *in* bed than out."

One dark brow rose. "Could be pure lust . . . seems to me you did suggest that at one point."

"I *never* used the word 'lust,'" she chided, feeling in an increasingly good humor.

"Physical attraction, then. What about that?"

She shook her head determinedly. "By itself, not enough. I mean, do you realize that probably three-quarters of the time we've spent together has been in bed?"

"Chance circumstance, love," he offered, playing the devil's advocate. "After all, we did meet under very unusual conditions."

"Alex, why are you arguing with me this way? Aren't you pleased that your own argument finally got through to me? After all, you're the one who kept saying I wasn't a loose woman. Yet look at me. I've been totally wanton."

"You're in love." He grinned, satisfied. "Your body simply saw the truth before your mind was able to accept it. It's been *love* we've made all along."

Her sigh was exaggerated. "That's what I've been trying to tell you."

"Say it again," he ordered softly.

"I love you," she murmured against his chest, punctuating the vow with a kiss on his passion-damp skin. But a strong finger curved beneath her chin and angled her face up.

"Now, look me in the eye and say it."

His word was her command, in this instance, at least. "I love you."

"'I love you' . . . who?" He could have been speaking to a child.

"I love you, Alexander Knight." She indulgently played the game.

"Again!"

"I love you, Alex. I do."

"Ahhh, love. Why didn't you tell me sooner?" His accusation was soft, to be met by Alanna's incredulous rejoinder.

"I didn't *know!* How could I think to tell you?"

His grin of delight now spread from ear to ear. "It just tumbled out, didn't it—refused to remain inside any longer? *There's* the proof of its authenticity! It's the real thing! You love me," he sighed in what could only be termed relief.

Alanna was stunned anew by her confession. Struggling to assimilate its implications—for she did accept it as a fact—she buried her face against the warm solace of his neck, breathing in the manly tang that had so tantalized her in memory last night. Sensing her need for a moment's respite, Alex held her close. He felt neither a sense of triumph nor a desire to gloat at her long-awaited admission, simply the pleasure of knowing that his sentiment was finally returned.

A strange shyness rendered her voice tremulous when finally she spoke. "How did those meetings go last night?" she asked, intentionally glossing over her heart-reaching discovery of moments earlier. Alex, however, would not.

"That's a fine question to ask on the heels of such an earth-shattering declaration!" he chided, snugly fitting his long arm around her back, stretching his lean fingers to hold the gentle swell of her breast.

Tilting her blond head back, she met his gaze. "I've surprised myself with all this, Alex. Give me time to take it all in, OK?"

Her beseeching gaze convinced him. "OK, love." He smiled indulgently, feeling infinitely patient as he proceeded to fill her in on the meetings that had kept him from her yesterday. His bid had been successful; everything had worked out to his satisfaction. As soon as he could he shifted the conversation back to her.

Alanna would never know whether he had read that deep-hidden source of tension of which she, herself, was barely aware. But his question immediately brought it out. With Wednesday morning so close on the horizon there was Jake's board meeting to contend with.

"What's up at work this week?" Alex asked. "Any news on whether you'll be offered that opening?"

"Funny you should ask," she murmured against his chest, a noted absence of humor in her tone. "The board is meeting tomorrow morning. Jake plans to make the proposal then."

"It's definite?" His eyes lit up with an enthusiasm she wouldn't have expected. Most men would have been instantly wary of such a move by a woman. Not Alex. Perhaps that was one of the things she loved about him. . . .

Her headshake was half in response to that last thought as well as to Alex's prodding. "Not definite—until they vote. But if Jake proposes it, it's as good as done."

"Congratulations, love! I'm proud of you!" His lips touched her brow with their warmth; she felt as though she had received his blessing. Yet the matter was far from decided.

"Whoa! I'm not sure I'll accept the position even if it *is* offered to me!"

Alex looked at her as though she had suddenly become possessed by lunacy. "That's ridiculous! Whyever not?"

"Because," she answered firmly, "I can get just as much done from right where I am."

Alex drove to the heart of the matter. "It's the gossip that's discouraging you, isn't it?"

Her first impulse was to deny the allegation; then she admitted its truth to herself. It was the strength of her newfound love, and the faith it gave her, that enabled her to admit it to Alex. "I suppose so." Resting her chin on her hands, which in turn were resting on his chest, she drank in his self-assuredness. "It's not worth the fight."

What had been a softly spoken statement inspired one that was much more forceful. "Not worth it? Alanna, you've spent the past ten years waiting—knowingly or not—for just this type of advancement. You're a fighter. If you have to you'll show them all!" His voice lowered. "Besides, once we're married—"

"I haven't agreed to marry you." Alanna's quiet voice stopped him cold. He looked at her in amazement.

"But you've just admitted that you love me. What more is needed?"

"What's needed," she took a deep breath, "is for me to be able to feel comfortable with the idea of marriage . . . and everything it entails."

For a long time Alex was quiet. His eyes studied her closely, then shifted to contemplate each strand of loose blond silk that had fallen free of its bonds in the frenzy of their lovemaking. His hands were still, though, and for the first time Alanna sensed a limit to his patience. His words confirmed as much.

"I can't wait forever, Alanna. You've dangled the carrot before my nose by just being you. Now, by saying you love me, you've brought it that much closer. I'm not made of stone." His tone was sober. "How long do you think you can toy with my emotions?"

She slid back against the sheets to look at the ceiling. Perhaps he was right. If she wasn't ready for total commitment was it fair to keep him in midair?

"I'm sorry," she whispered, turning on her side to face away from him, not quite mustering the will to leave the bed. "I don't mean to toy with you, Alex. It's just that . . . I didn't plan on this happening."

"Damn it!" he exploded, drawing her back to face him. "That's your problem—or one of them. In your work you can plan everything out to perfection. That's what makes you as efficient as you are. But in the world of human relationships you can't plot out a beginning and an end. You can't outline what's going to happen. You can't plot the whole thing out, then follow your plan to the letter. It just doesn't work that way!"

Alanna saw frustration in the depths of his charcoal gaze. She saw the faint lines of tension by the corners of his mouth. And she wanted desperately, desperately to give in. How simple it would be to agree to marry him! But the thought of marriage and a family sent tremors of apprehension through her. Until those tremors ceased she couldn't, in good faith, accept his proposal.

Sitting up on the bed, oblivious to her own nakedness, she faced him. The soft light from the dresser cast a golden glow on her hair, her shoulders, the gentle fullness of her breasts. It was a picture of innocent supplication she made as she began to talk quietly.

"I feel confused about so many things. What you've said is right. But it's difficult to change one's way of thinking overnight." She averted her eyes. "I never thought I'd say I loved you, but I have. Doesn't that give you hope?" A crooked smiled played at her lips.

Alex sat up to join her. "Hope can only take me so far. I want you for my wife. I won't rest until you're mine." There was a grim set to his lips that vouched for his determination. For an instant Alanna also wondered whether there was a touch of insecurity in this man who presented the image of strength and confidence at all times to the world. Was he afraid of *losing* her? Was that what was, in truth, behind his demand for marriage? Even as the thought of his possessiveness pleased her, she seized upon his words for diversion.

"So that's it, Alex Knight! You're using me!"

His ruggedly etched features formed a full-blown frown. "What on earth are you talking about?" he growled, his unusual lack of perception adding evidence of his vulnerability where Alanna was concerned. Her grin grew more mischievous.

"You can't *sleep* without me! Come on . . . confess! Did you sleep well last night?"

"Of course not!" The hint of a smile softened the straight line of his lips. "Did you?" he made his counter-accusation.

Her laugh was light and brief. "I certainly did," she looked toward the ceiling in recollection, "from roughly midnight till three, then from perhaps five till seven." When her gaze dropped to meet Alex's once more her humor had returned. "But, no, I didn't sleep through the night as I do with you," she confessed softly, meaning-fully.

With a low groan Alex took her in his arms and hugged her tightly. "You will tonight, love. I promise you that!"

She did, as did he. By unspoken consent, they shelved all serious discussion in favor of an evening in bed talking of lighter things. Alex told Alanna of his childhood, of climbing Mt. Washington, of canoeing through the lakes of upstate Minnesota, of sailing on the Atlantic off the coast of Cape Cod. He talked of his college years, of receiving his master's degree, of joining the family business and having to fight for the respect of the men below him. He spoke of his brother and sisters, of his nieces and nephews, never once directly referring to the children of his own that he hoped to have one day.

In return for the wealth of information he freely offered Alanna related more of her own story, a less exciting one in her mind, but one by which Alex seemed fascinated. He encouraged her to talk of her parents, of the occasional good times they had had despite the legacy of bitterness which she had inherited. He coaxed her into telling him of her days at school, her friends, even her bouts of puppy love. And he drew from her a vivid picture of her life as a working woman and the pattern it had fallen into over the years. All the while he held her propped against him, his arms about her, her head against his shoulder.

When the intimacy of the interchange yielded to something more erotic Alanna grew aware once more of the love she felt for Alex. It was this love that emboldened her in her initial response to the masterful male hands that scorched her body. For the first time she was unafraid to face the extent of the arousal which only Alex could evoke in her. She felt free to exert herself as a woman, as a creature of passion. If there was a challenge now it was within her; she had to convince herself of the strength of her love by expressing it in Alex's arms.

The frenzied passion of earlier that evening had taken the edge off the awesome physical need they had for each other. This slow, more studied lovemaking was an exploration into depths they had skimmed but never probed. Soft words of love accompanied the gentle movements of arms and legs, lips and tongues. The heady wine of love drugged them, prolonging the moment of union with languorous strokings and tender caresses.

With his hands tracing the curves of her sides and hips Alanna found herself above Alex. Looking down at him she caught the golden highlights, cast by the lamp, which burnished the rich brown of his hair. Was he angel or devil, to have such magnificent power over her?

It didn't matter. For she gloried in that power, absorbing it in every cell of her being, then exerting it over him in turn. It was this last which astounded her even more, the strength of the force her woman's body could wield over the sturdy, muscled mass of masculinity which now held her weight.

With the grace of a swan she arched toward him. Her breasts touched his broad, hair-roughened chest, teasing electrically as her lips brushed his. The tip of her tongue circled his mouth, then ventured within its moist bounds when he moaned his pleasure. It was as though time itself had slowed to half speed. Haste was nonexistent. There was only the exquisite savoring of a physical arousal that warmed and heated and reached the near-boiling point in a drawn-out eternity of luscious touching and feeling.

When at last Alex groaned his urgent need, then echoed it with the strength of the hands that lifted her, Alanna was just as eager, taking him to her in a moment of mind-sweeping joy.

"I love you," she whispered between deep kisses.

"You've got me," he drawled as softly, letting her take the lead, seeming to revel in the strength she possessed.

Tiny beads of sweat glistened on her body as the heat of passion burst from within. She felt herself the embodiment of all that was desirable. Alex's hands held her breasts as she arched her back in mindless delight. Her rosy nipples flamed at his touch, reacting as much to his faintly roughened fingertips as to the taut pull of the passion they shared.

Again they savored their joy with leisurely delight, their movements deliberate and thoroughly sensed. Alanna had never felt as rich, as filled with contentment, as when she held him and reveled in his virility. Adding to her happiness was the look of pure love that held Alex's gaze enmeshed with hers. He, too, had risen above the simply physical; he, too, understood and shared this spiritual elevation.

It was only the white-hot explosion of bliss that sent them at last to the spiraling heights from which they fell slowly, reluctantly, still wrapped in each other's arms. Alanna could no longer differentiate Alex's thudding heart from her own, his rasping breath from hers. They were one in every sense. As one they fell into the deep, deep sleep that had been denied them when they had been apart. As one they slept, fulfilled and satisfied, through the night and into the morning of the day that Alanna had been dreading.

The news came shortly before noon to Alanna at her desk. Within five minutes she found herself in the board-room being introduced to the board members as the next Executive Vice-President of WallMar Enterprises. These were men whom she would come to know well in the future, as she would frequently be called to sit in on these board meetings. Some of them she knew already; others received her cordially, if guardedly. It was a reaction that would seem mild in comparison to that of some of her fellow workers.

Words were kept to a minimum, the traditional "congratulations" and "good luck"s filtering in throughout the afternoon. But the sidelong glances, the wary looks, the speculative gazes aimed her way said far more potent things. It was, once again, her usual adversary, Brian Winstead, who put it all into words.

"So it paid off, Alanna," he taunted, not quite daring to fully enter her office, but merely propping himself up in the threshold.

Alanna knew just what was coming. Prepared, she presented her most composed veneer. "Hard work always pays off, Brian," she replied with deliberate innocence.

But the leer Brian sent her way contained no innocence. "And it's meant a lot of nights filled with hard work, hasn't it? Boy, I'm really amazed; I never dreamed that Wallace had the stamina."

Had the venom been saved for her alone Alanna might have preserved her patience. Listening to Brian insult Jake Wallace, however, tried her beyond control. Rising from her desk, she held herself with confidence as she approached the door.

"I think you should come in, Brian. We've got something to discuss and I'd rather not have all of WallMar listening."

Surprised, Brian stepped across the threshold and Alanna slammed the door, her only sign of frustration. To all other appearances she was utterly composed, a remarkable feat considering the challenge before her.

"Privacy suits me well." He shrugged, sauntering toward a chair opposite the desk and sinking into it. His smugness irritated her beyond belief. Determined to squelch it, she perched on the edge of the desk to give herself the advantage of height.

Arms crossed before her, she spoke with quiet disdain. "I'm getting very tired of your accusations, Brian. Are you *that* jealous?"

"Of Wallace?"

"Of *me!*" she snapped.

He seemed momentarily startled by her force. He had never seen her so livid. "I'm not jealous of you or anyone else."

"No? Then why the problem each time I receive a promotion?" Her smile was deceptively benign.

"No problem. Just stating the facts."

"And the 'facts,' in your view, are . . . ?"

For the first time he grew defensive. "You know them. There's no need for me to repeat them."

"You've never been hesitant before," she goaded him, her gaze hardening quickly.

"I've never been specific—"

"You're right!" she interrupted, her temper flaring briefly before she forced herself to be calm. "You've always been vague, but very definitely suggestive. Now I'm asking for details. If you have accusations to make, back them up."

For long moments the battle was purely visual. Each

stared at the other, refusing to back down. The stalemate was broken only by Brian's absurd declaration. "Everyone around here knows how you've gotten to this office, Alanna." His gaze fell to the gentle curve of her breasts and it was all she could do to keep from showing the nausea she felt, but she held herself firmly.

"Go on." When his eyes continued to linger she added, "Say it."

Slowly Brian looked up. "It's common knowledge that you're having an affair with the boss."

Alanna's hands balled into fists behind her. "Is it? Common knowledge? Based on what proof?"

"Aw, come on. Look at you, Alanna." *He* did, once more, and she felt positively raped. "You've got all the right curves in the right places. What man in his right mind wouldn't take what's offered?"

Her eyes narrowed angrily. "And how do you know exactly what *has* been offered, Brian?"

He sat back. "You've gotten the promotions, haven't you? That speaks for itself."

"It does not!" she exploded, unable to contain her fury. "Has it ever occurred to you that I've *earned* those promotions through hard work," her forefinger jabbed at the desk, "in this office? No," she shook her head, "that would be too threatening for you, wouldn't it? It would imply that I legitimately earned a promotion over you. A sexist accusation is more your style; that way you can overlook any possible professional failing within yourself!"

Brian spoke evenly. "A psychoanalyst, too?"

"It's common sense, Brian," she spat out. *"Another* thing you seem to be lacking." She paused to steady her breathing and lower her voice. "I've been willing to put up with your sly little hints in the past because they're so absurd that they're not worth bothering about. But when you came out and mentioned Jake Wallace's name just now you went too far."

"If the shoe fits . . ."

In that instant Alanna realized she would never get anywhere with Brian Winstead. Perhaps that was why she'd never said anything before, intuitively sensing the futility of it. Now he was simply an outlet for the tension that had built up over this latest promotion.

Straightening, she slowly rounded the desk, tempering her annoyance to ponder the next step. When she reached her chair she slid fluidly into it, leaned back and feigned utter calm. Through it all Brian sat with a maddeningly impassive expression on his face. He didn't even blink when she began to talk quietly.

"I have three things to say to you." Her gaze was filled with an anger clearly held back at some cost. "First, I don't want to hear anything else from you on this matter unless you plan to produce concrete proof of your accusations. Second, I don't ever again want to hear Jake Wallace's name muddied by your tongue. He's worked too hard, too honestly and too respectably to build WallMar Enterprises. He doesn't deserve your filth." She inhaled sharply. "And finally, if I *do* catch wind of anything further, you can very probably fear for your job. Despite what your ego might lead you to believe, you are *not* irreplaceable."

"Is that a threat?" Brian sat forward for the first time, more indignant than worried.

But Alanna was not about to give him the upper hand. She, too, sat forward, mirroring his movement. "It's a promise!"

"And you'd swing your weight with Wallace to see it through." It was not so much a question as a statement, verging on the very slander which had prompted their present confrontation. Again Alanna marvelled at his gall.

"Let's get this clear, Brian. Regardless of how you be- lieve I got here, I am now the Executive Vice-President of WallMar. I won't need to swing *any* weight to send you packing. Based on job performance alone your position has been questionable at times. It's on the record, entered by hands other than mine. But you are familiar with the com- pany and, when you want to, you can be quite effective. If, however, that effectiveness is hampered by thwarted ambi- tion you might do better to seek employment elsewhere. As it is," she ventured, feeling suddenly drained, "if you continue with these unfounded accusations your co- workers may just begin to realize what a jealous and petty mind you have."

The object of her scathing denunciation slowly un- folded himself from his chair as though determined to be the one to end the audience. He cocked his head arro- gantly. "People *may* just believe me." And with that he walked to the door and left.

Alone, Alanna settled back in her chair, took several deep calming breaths and proceeded to stew. The con- frontation with Brian was but one small aspect of the situ- ation. Now the force of the whole problem came down on her. Should she have accepted the promotion? Why *had* she accepted it, given the very serious reservations she had? Hadn't these past few minutes made real what she had feared?

But Alex's parting words of that morning echoed in her ears, her only source of courage. As he had stood at her door preparing to leave he'd taken her shoulders and held her firmly before him.

"Now, listen, Alanna." His gray eyes had reached her soul. "I want you to take it."

"Take what?" She'd feigned ignorance, preferring to bask in the pleasure she'd found in his arms such a short while earlier.

"The promotion, damn it!" he had growled impatiently. "You're more than capable of doing the work and you owe it to yourself to have the title."

She had shaken her head then, blond tangles falling about her shoulders. "I don't know. . . ."

But his voice had lowered in the tone of challenge she recalled from that very first encounter she'd had with this man she now loved. "Can't stand the heat? Fire too bright? You can always retire, give it all up, become a full-time homemaker. . . ."

His point had been well-taken. Business had been her whole life until Alex had entered it such a short time before. The precise nature of their future as a couple was still an enigma; her future at WallMar Enterprises was more fully sketched out. She realized that it wasn't Alex's dare that had goaded her into accepting the promotion. Rather, it was his underlying message. She had entered the corporate world in large part for the challenge it offered; to shy away from that challenge now, even considering the sordid aspect of one part of the drama, would be to turn her back on everything for which she'd worked so long and hard.

When Jake appeared at her office door at six and insisted on buying her a celebration drink she was more than happy to leave her work for another day and focus on the positive nature of this promotion. Alex had planned to pick her up at her own apartment for dinner at eight, so she had the time to spend with Jake, to whom she owed so much.

"I only wish Elaine could be here," she mused wistfully after Jake had toasted her future with the champagne he'd ordered as they sat together in a lounge not far from the office.

Jake's eyes sparkled with pleasure. "She's waiting for

us at home. Drinks are just the beginning. There's a full-course meal on the agenda!"

Alanna was touched and excited. "How sweet of her, Jake! But she shouldn't have gone to the trouble!" Then she realized that Alex would be waiting, also. How nice it would be to bring him along, to have him meet these two people who had been so wonderful to her over the past few years!

Her face must have told the entire story, for Jake responded, "Alex should be there by the time we arrive."

The soft brown pools of her eyes warmed with pleasure. "But how did you . . . ?"

"Elaine did all the arranging, Alanna." He brushed the details away with the gentle sweep of one pudgy hand. "You'll have to ask her. You *were* planning to see him tonight, weren't you?"

"You know I was." Her answer held her smiling resignation. "You're a pretty sharp fellow, Jake. Have I ever told you that before?"

"Save it for *him*, dear." The older man beamed at her. "He'll need all the bolstering he can get what with the fame you're finding!"

Alanna's blush was unbidden. "Alex Knight isn't about to be threatened by me. You'll see when you meet him."

What Jake and Elaine Wallace saw was a paragon of charm, wit and intelligence. Alex spent some time with Elaine before the others arrived, comfortably assisting her with the last-minute dinner preparations. When Alanna and Jake walked through the front door it was Alex who nonchalantly wheeled a glowing Elaine from the kitchen, Alex who mixed the first round of drinks, Alex who was fully composed and utterly triumphant in his conquest of the Wallaces.

Much later that night Alanna hugged him especially

hard for the genuine and forthright warmth that he had shown her friends. "Thanks, Alex," she murmured, burying her face against the strong column of his neck.

"For what?" His arms curved about her slender body reflexively as they stood in her living room.

Alanna tipped her blond head back to survey the gentleness of the features that seemed so perfectly to depict manliness. "For being so wonderful to them, with them. Elaine is often sensitive with new people, but she seemed totally at ease with you."

Silver sparkles shimmered in his eyes. "*You* should know about my way with women. . . ."

"But you were great with Jake, too!" she quickly went on. "I can't believe how freely he discussed WallMar with you. He's usually more guarded with a potential competitor."

One dark brow arched. "Perhaps he sees me as a future in-law of sorts." His gaze narrowed. "You know, I couldn't help but notice how he looked at you. He does see you as a daughter. And unless I'm way off base, I think he'd like to see you married."

Alanna scoffed at the suggestion though she knew it to be fact. "If that was the case why would he just have had me promoted?"

"Perhaps he agrees with me that you can do the job whether or not you're married."

Sensing that they were on the verge of a discussion she was still unready to tackle, Alanna moved out of Alex's arms and crossed the room to stand by the sofa. Her voice was very soft. "Please don't hassle me, Alex. I've had enough tension today without this. I already have too many second thoughts about taking the job; what I really need is your support." At the instant she said it she knew it to be the truth. Had Alex not been part of her life now she wondered whether she would have had the courage to accept the promotion she knew was so controversial among her co-workers. It had been this time with him that she had looked forward to all day; these moments made everything else worthwhile.

Alex's long strides brought him to her in an instant. His arms were iron bands, surging with strength as he held her. "Have I told you how proud I am of you?" he whispered, the warmth of his breath flowing over the skin of her cheek. "I have to confess, it was very easy to like Jake and Elaine, seeing how much they obviously adore you."

Touched by his words, she could only cling to him. This was the man she loved; his praise meant the world to her. It put things in perspective, made things special. *He* made things special when he was with her. What would she ever do if she lost him?

Her throat constricted around a half gasp as she understood, at last and with a sudden clarity, the full meaning of fear. It had been hard enough to assimilate the fact that she loved him. This new information—that she did, indeed, want him to be part of her life on a permanent basis—shocked her even more. Shocked her, frightened her, disconcerted her . . . and left her at a loss for words.

As it happened there was no need for words at that moment, for Alex's firm lips took possession of her softer ones and expressed his pride in her in a far more sensual way than mere words had been able to do. And, as always, she was helpless against the heady assault, finding herself caught up with lightning speed in the swirl of desire. All thoughts of the future were forgotten in the mind-dazing heat of the moment. For Alanna, this—rather than the promotion she'd received that morning—was what she'd been waiting for. It brought her more spontaneous excitement, more instant gratification, than anything she had ever known. And she gave to it with every atom of her being, offering her own body, burning now with desire, for Alex's adoration. It was an exalted lovemaking they shared, one that was destined to repeat itself at random intervals throughout the night.

Morning brought the unpleasant necessity that Alex had to leave. He was off to the West Coast for three days.

"Must you?" she protested on impulse, well before she realized that she had no right to rebel.

Alex had pulled on his shirt; his tie hung loosely around his neck. He would go home to change, then head for the airport. "I'm afraid I've got to. It's Joey. Several times a year I have to visit the California offices and give him the pat on the back *he* needs."

"This is Tuesday; when will you be back?"

"I've got meetings scheduled through Thursday. There's a bare chance I may make it back by Friday noon, but I doubt it. What say I pick you up from work on Friday?"

Trying to cope with the pervasive sense of loneliness that the prospect of three full days without Alex brought, she nodded. "That sounds fine." There was more she wanted to say, but she bit her lip. Did she have the right to sound possessive? Did she have the right to ask that he call from California?

"I'll call tonight." He read her mind, smiling tenderly down at her. "Keep your chin up at work, OK? Don't let them get to you."

Standing at the door beside him, she let her gaze linger on him, committing each manly feature, each powerful line to memory. "I'll try." With this image in her mind she might, indeed, have a chance.

Alex called that night, at three in the morning, Alanna's time. "Ellen would be very proud of us, you know," Alanna commented. "She said we should use each other to work out our problems. It helps—talking to you like this in the middle of the night."

The deep voice crackled sensuously over the cross-country wire. "I didn't wake you?"

"What do *you* think?"

He cleared his throat. "I was . . . kind of . . . hoping as much. . . ."

"Alex! Do you mean to say that you're *glad* I can't sleep?"

There was no hesitation in his voice, nor a drop of remorse. "Damned right, I am! Honestly, woman, if you could sleep as well without me as with me you wouldn't have *any* need of me at all!"

His words gave her food for thought as she lay awake after they had hung up. It occurred to her that for a man to want a woman who was as independent and self-sufficient as she was he had to truly love her. It was a mind-boggling thing to know that Alex loved her enough to be willing to accept her as an equal partner. Strange, she mused repeatedly, how her image of him had changed. When she had first met him he'd been the embodiment of the arrogant, domineering chauvinist with his impulsive proposal of marriage. Now she saw that her assessment of him had been wrong from the start. What she had interpreted as arrogance had been self-confidence; what she had interpreted as a drive for domination had been strength of character. And as for chauvinism—this man saw her as a modern woman and was willing to welcome her into his life as such.

In the final analysis Alanna realized that she was facing the greatest challenge of her life. Could she be a wife to Alex and mother to his children while still retaining her career? Could she be the complete, modern woman? Could she broaden her previous view of life to include love and family as well as work?

Half on impulse she phoned Ellen Henderson that morning. Though she hadn't been in contact with the medical center or its staff psychologist since she and Alex had been sent home to "work things out," she sensed that Ellen might offer her insight, comfort or both. Their rapport had been good from the start. Even when Alanna and Alex had unintentionally messed up Ellen's study, the latter had been understanding. It was this very understanding on which Alanna now counted.

"How are you, Alanna?" Ellen remembered her instantly.

"Fine. Uh, not so fine. That's why I'm calling." She felt the same swell of helplessness and awkwardness seeking help that she'd felt when she'd first signed up for the IAT study.

"Problems sleeping again?"

"No. . . . Yes. . . . Well, indirectly. But that's not why I'm calling."

"It's Alex."

"And I can hear your smile over the phone." Yes, the rapport was still there.

Ellen chuckled. "He's quite a man! What's he up to now?"

"Right now he's out of town. I . . . I wondered if we could . . . talk."

There was a slight pause. "I sense that this isn't a counselor-client type of talk."

Alanna smiled softly as she twisted the telephone cord around her finger. "Not really. I was hoping for something on the line of friend-friend."

This time Ellen didn't hesitate. "How about lunch tomorrow? Here? That'll give us more time."

Accordingly, the next day at one, Alanna met Ellen at her office and together they made their way to the hospital cafeteria. It was only when they'd settled themselves in a quiet corner that Ellen broached the subject of Alex.

"Now, tell me about him. You're still seeing him, aren't you?"

"Oh, yes." Alanna picked at her chef salad. "We're still going strong. That's part of the trouble."

"How so?" Ellen grinned. "Is he still running on about love and marriage?"

"He's serious!"

"And you?" The psychologist sampled her hamburger as she studied Alanna's frown.

"I'm afraid to say that he's emerged victorious. I'm hooked."

Ellen's enthusiasm was spontaneous. "That's great, Alanna! The two of you couldn't be more perfectly matched! This is a new twist in the phenomenon of the sleep lab! But you said 'afraid.' What's the catch?"

Alanna's expression was close to melancholy. "The catch is . . . marriage."

It was Ellen's turn to frown, but in puzzlement. "He wants it. He told me as much."

"*I* don't."

"Ahhh, that's right. I remember your reaction that day in my office when Alex mentioned the possibility of marriage. But you weren't sure you loved him then. You are now?"

"Yes." It was evident in every fiber of her being.

"Yet you're still against marriage."

"Uh-huh." Alanna gathered her thoughts. "I've tried to explain it all to Alex. He listens and I think he understands. It's *me* who's the most confused. That's why I wanted to talk with you. You see, I've spent my entire adult life building my career." Briefly she sketched the picture of her childhood and parents that she'd painted in far greater color and depth for Alex. "I ruled out the prospect of marriage and family a long time ago," she concluded. "Suddenly I'm wondering if I was right. I can't decide."

Ellen smiled in sympathy. "Whether it would work *and* be compatible with your career?"

"Exactly. How do *you* do it, Ellen? I remember you saying that your husband is a doctor here. How do you manage it all?" She speared a ripe cherry tomato in frustration as she awaited Ellen's answer.

Her companion was cautious. "You have to understand that we have no children yet. That simplifies things for the time being."

"Do you plan to have children?" Alanna asked on impulse, then caught herself. "I'm sorry. That was none of my business."

"No, no. It's a perfectly legitimate question. And timely. We've discussed it at length. You see, Sandy is, in many ways, very traditional."

Alanna couldn't help but be skeptical. "But you said you had a modern marriage—no ring, no name switch, no title."

"We do. Fortunately Sandy is open to change and loves me enough to realize that I need my work. There's still that part of him, though, that would like me at home, raising his brood, waiting for him." She paused. "Sound familiar?"

Alanna nodded ruefully. "My parents. But . . . Sandy *does* accept your career?"

"He does. We compromise. I make a point to do it big at home one day a week—you know, warm fire waiting, fancy dinner, total attention focussed on him. That seems to satisfy his need. And, to be truthful, I really enjoy it because it does mean so much to him. In turn he shares everything with me on the other days. He's very proud of my work."

"He *should* be! Is there . . . jealousy?"

"Between Sandy and me?" Ellen laughed in relief. "Thank goodness, no! We may both work here, but our fields are as different as night and day. And besides, Sandy and I are both relatively self-confident people. As are you and Alex." The last was added more pointedly as Ellen brought the discussion back to Alanna and her immediate problem.

"Yes, I suppose Alex and I *are* fairly secure. I can't imagine there being jealousy between us. But I do worry about being a successful wife and mother."

Ellen nibbled on a pickle. "The role has changed drastically in recent years, Alanna. Actually, the full-time wife at home is, in many cases, a luxury that only the well-to-do can afford. In your case you'd work because you wanted to. I'm sure Alex accepts that."

"He does." Alanna defended him quickly. "It's *me* who can't accept it, I guess. I imagine I'll feel this horrible guilt all the time. I should be doing this or I should be doing that. Do you ever feel guilty while you're at work about all of those other things that aren't getting done?"

"Sure I do." Ellen smiled.

"Doesn't it get you down?"

"Only until I share it with Sandy. He understands me . . . and my needs. We've always been able to reach solutions together." She hesitated, then frowned. "Lately I've been going through that guilt trip about kids. I want them . . . I don't want them. But I'm not getting any younger, as they say."

"What will you do?"

The dark-haired woman raised her eyes speculatively. "I've decided to leave things up to fate, for starters. What will be from here on will be."

"And if you do become pregnant, how will you handle it?"

"As we've worked it out in our minds, I'll work right through the pregnancy, then see my private patients from our place until I feel comfortable returning to the hospital." She shrugged. "For all I know I may even find private practice to my liking."

Alanna's eyes held admiration. "You sound very positive about the whole thing, Ellen. I'm envious."

"Don't give me too much credit yet." Ellen smiled wryly. "To be blunt, I'm terrified. For one thing, our income will be sharply reduced when I stop working. And then, things could backfire. If I do get pregnant I could be too exhausted to work until the last month or the baby could be a toughie and prevent me from getting back to work afterward. I could have trouble getting sitters or find myself without enough patients to cover the cost. The list goes on and on."

"But you're willing to take the risk?"

"I am."

"May I ask why?"

"It's very simple. I *do* want children. Somehow we'll work something out regarding my career. Regarding motherhood, it's either now or never. With any luck it'll be now."

Alanna dropped her gaze to focus absently on the last of her lunch. If she had expected black-and-white directives from Ellen Henderson she had misjudged the situation. There were no absolutes. It was all relative, all a matter of compromise.

"Have I helped you out at all, Alanna?" The psychologist, now her friend, broke into her silent meanderings.

Alanna looked up, startled. "Oh, yes! You have, Ellen! If nothing else you've suggested that I'm not the only one to fear torn loyalties. It's reassuring to know that it's not just my own private paranoia."

"What I'm also saying," Ellen added gently, "is that it's not your problem alone. It's for you and Alex to work out *together*. I'm sure you will."

Alanna was not quite as sure. The only thing she *was*

sure about was how lonely she was without Alex. He was constantly in her thoughts. Perhaps it was fortunate that he should occupy so much of her mind for otherwise she would have surely brooded about the tension at the office. In her most optimistic dreams she had hoped that, once it was definite, the promotion would simply be accepted as fact. Not so among her male associates. Her confrontation with Brian notwithstanding, few words were spoken on the matter. But the strain of the situation grew greater as the week went on. Men who had previously chatted amiably with her now were aloof. Those who worked closely with her on the various projects under her jurisdiction were similarly distant. Cordial . . . but distant. It was as though Brian had been right; people *had* believed him. Alanna had, indeed, taken a step up—up and away from the confidence of the men with whom she would have to work successfully if her career itself was to be successful.

As fate would have it, it was Alex who, appearing in person at her office late Friday afternoon, presented both the best and the worst of her life to date. The best was himself; a sight for love-starved eyes, he was stunningly handsome in his three-piece pin-striped suit, the shadow of a beard on his jaw. The worst, however, was foreshadowed by the look of barely bridled anger in his gaze as he threw down the first edition of the evening paper, opened to the business section and a close-up photo of Jake and herself sharing drinks at the lounge four days before.

"One Woman's Formula for Corporate Success," the headline read, its implication all too clear in conjunction with the picture. Instinct outlined the copy for her; Alex's anger elaborated on it. Tossing her glasses atop the newsprint, she closed her eyes in defeat. No wonder people had been so wary of her all day.

9

"We'll sue!" Alex yelled, pacing the floor of her office as though he personally had been the subject of the slanderous passage Alanna had finally forced herself to read. It occurred to her that she had never seen him so angry.

"We won't sue," she contradicted him softly and distractedly. "It would only make a larger issue out of this entire farce." Her jaw tensed in frustration. "Someone fed this reporter her information. It could have been any one of the men who might have wanted advancement here. But I can't start pointing fingers." She looked up at Alex helplessly. "There are too many possibilities and no proof."

The eyes that speared her were dark and stormy. In the instant Alanna prayed that she might never have to face this man's wrath; it was truly awesome.

"Well, you can't just sit and let this type of thing go unchallenged, Alanna!" he seethed, slapping the newspaper back onto her desk. "There has to be a limit to journalistic freedom. You *do* have a case for libel."

Sighing, she looked down at the article, bristling freshly. "Of course I do. But be practical. If I go to court it will cost a pretty penny. And realistically, if I go to court someone will try to tear apart my character even *more!*"

She was right. Even Alex, pausing in his anger to ponder her claim, had to reluctantly agree. But his mind ran quickly ahead. "Make a counterstatement."

"A *what?*" Her tone of voice was infinitely weary, just barely curious.

"A counterstatement." Alex had calmed down as a sensible course of action formulated itself in his mind. "If it were me," he eyed her with gentle accusation, "I'd call an immediate press conference—"

"It's *not* you—" she interrupted, only to be interrupted in turn.

His smile was meager and rueful. "I know. And since you won't put up with *that* the next best thing would be for you to submit a statement to the paper contradicting this woman's claims and presenting your own viewpoint. It might actually be," he grinned, "good PR for you."

"Alex! Publicity is the *last* thing on my mind. It's not what I need or want!"

"But a low-key statement, love?" he coaxed her, growing steadily more composed.

Alanna was skeptical. "You really think that would be better than simply ignoring the whole thing?"

"You could ignore it." He shrugged. "But somehow I always saw you as a more aggressive type."

There was the challenge once more. Pulling herself up straighter in her chair, she nodded. "A counterstatement it will be, then."

A counterstatement it was, written jointly by Alex and Alanna and submitted to the newspaper only after a meeting with Jake, two of the members of the board of directors and the public relations specialist on Jake's staff. It was a simply worded piece, disclaiming the content of the earlier article as being pure fabrication. It enumerated Alanna's professional qualifications, her achievements at WallMar Enterprises and listed the projects now in the works because of her initiative. When it appeared in the paper there was an atmosphere of dignity about it. Its straightforward presentation of the facts seemed unimpeachable.

Implicit in the statement was a denunciation of the woman's source, most probably one of the men at WallMar, whose being passed over for promotion had prompted such vindictiveness. The subtle force of Alanna's words was silently aimed at Brian Winstead. She considered him the most obvious suspect, though she could openly say nothing to that effect.

The counterstatement, however, did not appear in the paper until Monday morning. In the interim Alex was a godsend. He devoted his entire weekend to Alanna, accompanying her as she did each of her usual chores, buoying her up.

He was a gentle and unobtrusively helpful presence in getting Elaine Wallace to and from the beauty shop. He manned the supermarket cart while Alanna shopped, endearingly tossing an extra ten dollars' worth of his favorite foods into the pile. He even came to the rescue at the swimming pool when one of the girls, a tiny ten-year-old, appeared with a knee-to-toe cast on her leg and an accompanying heartbroken look on her face. Alex took over her care, sitting in the stands beside her, talking steadily, coaxing smile after smile from the child until the meet was over, at which time he led her outside and kept her company until her older sister was dressed and their mother had claimed them.

Sunday was a quieter day. They slept late, brunched out, walked along the waterfront for hours talking and took in an early movie before returning to her apartment.

Through it all, however, despite Alex's encouragement, Alanna was shadowed by thought of the paper and the statement that would be appearing on Monday. Hers was a strong piece, she knew, but, unfortunately, she had been correct in an earlier fear. People would believe what they wanted to believe.

When Monday morning arrived and she dutifully appeared at WallMar with her head held high she met a world of doubting minds and wary eyes. If anything she found an increase in the unease among the men with whom she had to deal. She was deeply discouraged. Perhaps the greatest source of her discomfort lay in the fact that not one of her co-workers made even the slightest reference to the newspaper article—not even in passing. Surely, there would be *some* supportive comment. . . .

The week passed on leaden feet, seeming to be the longest of Alanna's life. Had it not been for the nightly comfort of Alex and the daily support of Jake she might have thrown in the towel right then.

Only subtle glances and strained interchanges gave proof of the feeling that seemed to run high against her within the corporation. To her dismay, even the other female faces on the payroll eyed her distrustfully, apparently choosing to believe the gossip rather than give her the benefit of the doubt.

Brian Winstead, historically her most vocal opponent, said nothing. She finally decided that either her personal "promise" to him had hit its mark or it was he who had spread the gossip to the papers in search of revenge and so was now sated. But as she had told Alex so firmly when the story had first broken, she had no proof. To accuse Brian blindly would be as wrong as his having made such unsubstantiated claims in the first place.

To further disturb her peace of mind was the growing sense of love she felt for Alex. As the days passed she came to depend on him—on his being there with her in the evenings, at night, when she awoke in the morning. They spent nearly every free moment together, primarily at Alex's suggestion, though she would have been distraught had he not done so. It was a tug-of-war, this wanting to be constantly with him yet fighting the urge to depend on him, and it continued unendingly.

For the first time, moreover, the physical was secondary to the emotional in their relationship. The intense attraction was there, as it always had been, as it always would be. But they now found different ways to express their love. There was more talking, more quiet companionship. During this time of tension for Alanna Alex came through with a wealth of understanding and encouragement. He patiently drew from her a retelling of the highs and lows of each day, dealing with both in a thoughtful and caring manner.

Their lovemaking was gentler, with none of the frenzied hunger of earlier encounters. It was as though each sensed the other's depth of feeling and was satisfied by that alone. They spent more than one night simply lying together, talking, savoring the closeness until sleep claimed them. And there was the quiet pleasure of waking together after an undisturbed sleep to greet the new day.

That she loved him Alanna now accepted fully. That she needed him was a different matter. She fought this reality for as long as she could, finally yielding by the end of the week. What she would have done without his strength she did not know. Without her even realizing it, Alex had insinuated himself into her life, had made himself a vital part of it. What he had originally done in the physical realm—building up her need for him until she was clearly addicted—he now did emotionally. He was always there and she grew to depend on him. She needed him. Yet she couldn't quite get herself to tell him that . . . yet.

There was still that matter of long-range commitment. To confess to Alex the true extent of her love for him would only give fodder for his argument in favor of marriage. So far he had kept his word about giving her time, easing the pressure he might otherwise have exerted in that direction. Quite subconsciously she needed to hold something back—a little something of herself, kept in reserve, preventing total surrender. It was a final connection to her past dreams, dreams that, though Alex's intrusion had rendered them inferior to the new pictures he painted of her future, she was not yet ready to give up entirely. She had spent too long building those old dreams; she still needed time to accept their obsolescence.

As she stood at a crossroads in her life she felt herself pulled in all directions at once. On one side were Wall-Mar and the powerful position of Executive Vice-President, but with suspicion and innuendo shadowing her every move. Then there were Alex and her love for him, growing stronger day and night. And there were freedom and independence and self-sufficiency, long fought for and now threatened by the very love which welled within. For she knew that her life would be empty without Alex. Yet how long would he wait? How long would he be content to satisfy her need for love and companionship and comfort without her satisfying his need for a wife?

With the advent of the weekend her thoughts came full circle. Once more she found herself pondering what her mother might have said or done given the present situation. Once more she found herself wondering whether her parents had ever shared the heights of passion which she and Alex scaled night after night. Perhaps her mother's bitterness had been, in part, caused by a deep, deep love that was never quite returned. Perhaps . . . perhaps . . . perhaps . . . but Alanna would never know. Therein lay the greatest frustration.

It was with thoughts of her own past fresh in her mind that Alanna found herself, on Saturday evening, dressed in a soft blue sheath and navy heels, her blond hair brushed to a shine and hanging beyond her shoulders, en route to dinner with Alex's parents.

"But you said we were going out for dinner to a special place, just the two of us!" she protested when Alex informed her of the change of plans.

"Uh-uh," he chided her with half-hidden amusement. "I never said we'd be alone. You must have assumed that. But I do think that my home is a special place. . . ."

"That's not the point! You could have warned me! I'm not psyched up for this. Your *family,* Alex—why didn't you *tell* me?"

The gray Porsche purred smoothly away from the city, headed toward the suburban countryside in which Alex had grown up. "Relax, love. Where's that cool I always admire? That crystal-clear poise? That mirror-smooth composure?" The corners of his firm lips twitched. "If I didn't know you better I'd say you were scared to death!"

"You bet I am!" she agreed readily. She *was* scared and she wasn't quite sure why. Was it her own insecurity showing? Did she actually fear that Alex's parents might not like her? Resorting to humor to quell her nerves, she quipped lightly, "In fact, I'd like nothing better than to be in jeans and a shirt, back at my place. I'd cook you anything your stubborn little heart desired . . ."

His deep voice lilted in gentle harmony. "But you're here, with me, on the way to the country."

She sighed. "Yes."

He cast her a sidelong glance as she slowly gathered

her composure. "And you'll come with me and meet my family."

"Yes." Why she was so pliant to his wishes she wasn't sure, until he filled in the blank himself.

"Because you love me so much."

His deep growl ignited ripples of now-familiar longing within her. When she reached for his hand he offered it. "Yes, I do love you." She smiled, finding it impossible to stay angry at him for long. "But you've got to do something about these seats!"

"What's wrong with the seats? I'll have you know that this Porsche is a collector's item."

Alanna retaliated with a playful scowl. "The collectors can have it! Bucket seats are for the birds!"

The deep and steady surge of the motor was as smooth in its power as the man behind the wheel when he let out a low, long chuckle. "I won't argue with you there. But it may be for the best. If we *ever* hope to get to my parents' house . . ."

Get there they did. The sleek Porsche easily rounded the circular drive, then came to a halt before the tall, white-columned Georgian colonial. Well lit in the darkness, the house offered a warm welcome that served to alleviate the chill of apprehension Alanna felt. How much simpler it had been, she mused, to stand before that board of directors last week. How much simpler it had been even to face the antagonism of those more vehement of her co-workers. Alex was right; where had her cool sophistication suddenly gone? Yet all the self-chiding in the world could not quell the nervousness she felt. Alex's supportive hand as he led her from the car past a wealth of lush landscaping toward the front door helped—as did the warm welcome offered by Alex's father. His stature was grand, though more mature and mellowed than his son's; his features were likewise well aged, as a fine wine coming into its own. Even his hair, rich and full, but sporting dashing shots of gray where Alex's strands of gold were now, spoke of what the son might look like in twenty years' time.

"Alanna," Alex's voice interrupted her analysis, "I'd like you to meet my father, Benjamin Knight. Dad, this is Alanna Evans."

The strong hand that came out to clasp hers and draw her into the house bore the same brand of dignity that had been passed on to Alex. Alanna found herself quickly responsive to the self-confidence and sure manner of her host.

"Alanna," the older man spoke in a voice somewhat lower and a touch more raspy than that of his son, "this is a pleasure. Alexander seems to be quite smitten. At first glance I can see why!"

"Alexander" seemed not in the least embarrassed by his father's blatant reference to the state of his heart. Rather, the grin he showered on her as she looked back at him one final time before being ushered more deeply into the spacious front hall was nearly reckless.

"Alexander," she replied coyly to his father, "seems easily smitten at first glance, as well!" The gentleness of her tone and the softness of her brown-eyed gaze guaranteed her statement the good humor she had intended. Benjamin Knight's appreciative smile accepted it in a like manner.

"Come." He helped her off with her coat, then guided her toward the living room where he deftly and graciously introduced his wife, Adele, and Alex's sister and brother-in-law, Amanda and Paul Winters. Alex's own surprise at the latter couple's presence was genuine enough to spare him Alanna's later wrath. And, in truth, once in the clutches of Benjamin Knight, guardian extraordinaire, she had begun to feel surprisingly comfortable.

Alex's mother was equally warm, if perhaps a bit more guarded at the start, as was his sister. Each in turn echoed the news that Alex had spoken highly of her and congratulated her on her new position at WallMar Enterprises. Ribbons of invisible tension slithered about in Alanna's stomach, only slightly eased by the glass of wine that Alex placed in her hand. Well aware that she was, in a way, on trial, Alanna willed herself to maintain a state of composure.

"It's quite an achievement," Adele Knight complimented her, "for a woman your age to become an Executive Vice-President in an organization such as WallMar Enterprises."

Measuring her words, Alanna responded gently. "I consider myself to have been very, very fortunate. I was at the right place at the right time. When I first became associated with WallMar there was a distinct void where the type of projects I wanted to do should have been. Jake Wallace had an open mind and was willing to loosen the purse strings to give my ideas a chance."

It was Amanda, who appeared to be a year or two older than Alex and was a replica of the mother, who followed up. Her knowledge of the field startled Alanna. "I particularly appreciated WallMar's entrance into educational slide production. Since Paul is an educator we've seen your ideas serving some very practical purposes."

Alanna turned instinctively toward the man who sat propped against the arm of his wife's chair. "You're in education?"

The pleasant-looking man nodded. "When I decided to marry Amanda I had a choice." His hazel eyes twinkled through his wire-rimmed spectacles, foretelling amusement to come. Amanda felt immediately drawn to him, a onetime outsider who now seemed very comfortable amidst the Knights. His voice was as soothing as his manner. "I knew that I could either enter the fold and go into business or steer a course into a different field entirely. I had been a teacher; now I'm a high school principal. I find the work very exciting."

"And his school system uses WallMar's slide kits constantly," Benjamin Knight interjected. "Tell me, Alanna, has your marketing effort extended across the entire country? At last report I heard that you still had the western states to conquer."

"You're right." Alanna grinned, feeling more and more relaxed. "I suppose it gives us something to work toward."

Other questions about her work followed. Though Alex sat beside her on the beautiful French Provincial sofa, one of several such pieces setting the tone of this elegant room, he let her pave her own way, his evident confidence in her unblemished by her moments of hesitancy in the car.

The conversation flowed gently from business to theater; then Adele Knight disappeared, only to return moments later with a large platter of hot hors d'oeuvres from the kitchen.

"Mother's favorite recipe." Amanda coaxed Alanna to try the delicate zucchini tarts which, surrounded by a variety of other choices, were indeed delicious. But her compliments had to be put off until later; they fell victim to the avid discussion that had erupted between the men regarding the quality of present-day live theater in light of the moving picture industry. Within moments the women, as well, had expressed their opinions. To her astonishment Alanna found herself joining in quite unselfconsciously.

It was a harbinger of what was to come, an evening of stimulating conversation, fine food and wine. At one point Alanna looked down into the swirl of wine in her glass. Momentary guilt washed over her as she remembered Ellen Henderson's instructions, now disregarded. But then, she smiled to herself with satisfaction, sleep would not be a problem this night. Her love-warmed gaze lifted to meet that of Alex, who sat by her side at the beautiful dinner table, mirroring her thoughts exactly and betraying them with a depth of desire in his eyes that brought a blush of embarrassment to Alanna's cheeks. His thigh seemed suddenly that much closer to hers; his hand moved beneath the table to sear through her dress to her leg. His lips moved, silently but clearly outlining the words "I love you."

Of necessity their outward attention turned back to the others, yet a special awareness filtered through the air between them, charging it with the force of the attraction that always existed for them. Though in company they were removed, secure in their own world within a world with the knowledge of a passion that would surely follow later.

What followed more immediately were after-dinner drinks, again in the living room, and a few moments of conversation alone with Alex's mother and sister while the men saw to some personal matter in the den.

For a fleeting instant, as the men disappeared, Alanna felt a return of trepidation, particularly when Adele Knight brought up the one topic that had nagged at the back of Alanna's consciousness all evening.

"I thought you handled that article very well," the older woman said softly, obviously feeling a need to say something on the subject. "Your statement was a strong one. I'm glad you decided to answer her."

Alanna regarded Alex's mother with respect and

shrugged. "I have to confess that I might have tried to ignore her had Alex not prodded me. He wanted me to do something even *more* vocal."

"*I* would have called a press conference," Amanda exclaimed with the same feistiness that seemed so much a part of Alex's character, as well.

Alanna couldn't help but laugh. "That's precisely what Alex said! You must all think alike!"

"We're fighters." Amanda returned the grin as her thought was promptly seconded by her mother.

"Each in our own way. Alex certainly is." Was there a hidden meaning in what she said? "When he sets his heart on something he rarely lets it get away from him."

Later, as Alanna and Alex drove back toward the city, Alanna recalled the very first day she had met him. He had announced then that he would marry her. Would he? He'd actually gotten her to the point of declaring her love for him. Would an agreement of marriage be next? Despite all her lingering doubts the thought held none of the instant horror it might have such a short time ago. Particularly since seeing Alex's family. . . .

"Penny for your thoughts?" The deep voice broke into her reflection. His hand touched hers; his fingers closed around hers. His self-assuredness flowed through to her. She had no way of knowing of the strength he derived from *her* presence.

"I was thinking of your family. They're lovely, Alex."

"You had doubts?" In the dark of night, with only the intermittent flare of oncoming headlights to illumine his face, she could only hear his smile. There was nothing smug in it.

"I'm afraid," she blushed, grateful that her color would be hidden in the darkness, "that I had formed a picture of them even before I knew I was to meet them."

"Tell me," he coaxed softly.

"They were to be worldly and attractive, attended by a bevy of servants, concerned principally with money matters and very distrustful of, even condescending toward, me."

"And now . . . ?"

"As I said, they *are* lovely. They brought me right into their world, discussing things that, even if I wasn't informed, I'd find interesting. I think your mother, perhaps your sister, too, wasn't quite sure at first about this woman you'd brought home, but they both turned out to be perfectly delightful."

Alanna caught Alex's nod as a car passed. His features mesmerized her for that moment—the chiseled power of his lips, his nose, his forehead. When he smiled the white of his teeth gleamed in the dark. "They liked you."

"How could you tell?" She felt suddenly anxious, realizing that she did want them to like her.

"In the first place," there was undeniable humor in his tone, "my father left you alone with my mother. He doesn't always do that."

"Come on, Alex. Your mother strikes me as a very lovely lady."

"Not where her oldest son is concerned, love. She's known to be very possessive, sometimes too tough. My father quickly sensed both that you could hold your own with my mother *and* that she could easily warm to you."

If what he'd said was true he'd given her quite a compliment. "And in the second place?"

"In the second place," he cleared his throat, "he invited you for a return visit."

Alanna cocked her head in puzzlement. "But that was simply out of courtesy. Any host would have said the same!"

"Not Benjamin Knight. He's reached the stage in life where he only says what he means. Oh, he's never been crude, never insulting. He simply omits the courtesy if it's an empty one. In this case he truly wants you to come again." He paused for a moment, then went on more softly. "Will you?"

There was that hint of insecurity again, but from Alanna's viewpoint it was easily assuaged. "Of course, I will. That's a foolish thing to ask. I'd love to spend more time with them.

"Have you found any solution to that problem of your father's frustration?" she asked. "He seemed fine tonight."

"He was," Alex agreed, "with *you* as a diversion. I've tried your tactic, but it's going to take some working on." He sighed. "That's another reason for you to come back another time. *You* can work on him!"

Once before, Alex had suggested the same. Then Alanna had promptly and unconditionally ruled out the possibility. Now she did not. How things had changed!

Unfortunately, things had *not* changed when Alanna arrived at work Monday morning. The weekend with Alex had provided lots of bolstering, rest, relaxation and loving. If Alanna was puzzled by Alex's failure to pressure her on the issue of marriage she said nothing, grateful only that, given the continued tension at WallMar, he should be so understanding. There was no doubt in her mind that the visit with his parents on Saturday evening had been a subtle push in the direction of marriage. Oh, yes, his approach had grown more subtle, but it was as potent as ever.

By midweek Alanna had grown more, not less, sensitive to the undercurrent of suspicion aimed at her by the WallMar employees. By week's end she felt near defeat. Regardless of how hard she worked, how strongly she projected the image of professionalism that should have countermanded any other image, there was always that distance, that aloofness on the part of the men with whom she had to deal on an everyday basis. It seemed suddenly much harder to get ideas across, to inspire the support of these people whose help was mandatory to the success of her projects.

"I don't know," she sighed in halfhearted resignation when she and Alex were having dinner Friday night at what had become their favorite spot, a small seafood restaurant on the waterfront. "Maybe I *should* resign. . . ."

His gaze narrowed. "You don't really mean that."

"I do. I'm not sure it's worth the turmoil it's caused."

"Come on, love. That's foolish—"

"But I can't get things done the way I could before. It's gotten to the point of being counterproductive."

"Then *do* something about it!" Alex was suddenly vehement; the shooting sparks of silver in his charcoal eyes told her so, as did the fierce set of his jaw.

"Like . . . ?" She readily sought out his opinion. His suggestions were usually good, particularly when she tempered them with her own instinct. She had, indeed, come to rely on hashing things out with him at night.

"Like stepping things up. Taking the offensive. Confronting the men head-on. Demanding *more* of them. Exerting that power you were given as Executive Vice-President. You have no need to be afraid of them. They're trying to see where their silent form of intimidation will take them. Show them, love. Show them that it won't get them anywhere!"

Dubious, Alanna considered his gentle command for several moments before shifting the subject to something less explosive. Her tension remained intact, however. Sensing it, Alex drove to his apartment, rather than hers, when the meal was over.

"You'd rather stay here tonight?" she asked in surprise. It had become their habit to stay together at Alanna's apartment, where Alex had gradually left a collection of personal items. Perhaps he had felt she would be more comfortable at her own place; for her part, she easily accepted the arrangement, pleased simply to be with him.

"I think," he drawled as he parked and led her from the car, "that you could use the pampering tonight. I have a treat upstairs." Cocking his head in that direction, he seemed suddenly filled with mischief.

"A treat?" Alanna's tone was one of skepticism, then caution. "I'm not so sure about you. Your treats . . . a little pampering . . . so solicitous . . . what is it you want?"

Alex's dark brows drew together as he feigned indignance. "Have I ever bribed you?" When she simply stared at him, trying to camouflage her own humor, he repeated his question. "Have I?"

"Well," she hesitated, "not in so many words." There was bribery and then there was bribery. The lure of his body and the fear of its absence were a form of bribery leading toward marriage, as was a personal involvement with his family. Even the promise of a good night's sleep had its power. "OK, so what's the treat?"

He kept her on tenterhooks as they entered his building, took the elevator to the top floor, walked down the long hall to his door and then stood while he fumbled with deliberate leisure for his keys.

"Alex . . ." she warned teasingly. "What *is* the treat?"

But this time it was Alex who was saved by the bell, Even before the door was opened the muffled ring of the telephone penetrated its hard wood thickness. And Alex savored the suspense.

"Now who could that be?" he drawled, lazily guiding Alanna over the threshold and ambling toward the phone. She stood not far from him, hands on hips, watching the firm curve of his manly lips as he spoke deeply into the receiver. Then, abruptly, his smile faded.

Instinct told Alanna that something was wrong—something big. Alex was deeply disturbed. His gray gaze shot toward her, then away. He spoke softly, asking questions she couldn't quite follow. With his body angled away from her he seemed to be shielding her from whatever it was that he said. There was a long silence when he finally replaced the receiver. At last he turned toward her, placing his hands on her shoulders, his expression softening slightly.

"What is it?" Alanna asked, eyes wide with worry.

"It's Jake. He's had a heart attack."

10

A heart attack?" Alanna's hoarse whisper was barely audible, though the tremor of fear that passed through her could not have escaped the awareness of the man who had a strong hold on her shoulders. When disbelief yielded to the look of sorrow on Alex's face she leaned full against him and moaned her anguish. He held her quietly, undemandingly, offering the sheer comfort of his presence until she felt able to learn more.

"When?" She looked up at Alex.

"About two hours ago."

"But I saw him at the office at five."

"It happened shortly after he got home."

Alanna gasped. "Elaine . . . ?"

"Elaine is at the hospital. That was Jake's secretary who called. When there was no answer at your place Elaine suggested she try here."

Alanna's voice was choked for a moment, during which time she could only appreciate the fact that Alex was here with her, offering his silent strength. Finally she spoke falteringly. "Is it bad?"

"He's holding his own, but it was a major attack. The next two or three days will be critical."

Slowly Alanna stepped back from Alex and looked

aimlessly around the room, seeming to search for direction in the inanimate objects before her. When that failed her she dug within to find her reserve of levelheadedness. Turning back to Alex, she spoke softly. "I'd like to go to the hospital. Elaine may need some company."

Alex's voice was sympathetic. "I was going to suggest as much. Come on, I'll drive you right over. You'll feel better once you're with Elaine and can see Jake's condition for yourself."

The drive to the hospital seemed endless to Alanna. What would she find when she got there? Jake and Elaine had come to mean so much to her. If something happened to Jake . . .

"Try to relax." Alex urged her gently from her somber preoccupation, giving her hand a squeeze. "Modern medicine can do wonders."

"But he isn't even sixty! There's so much more living for him to do. I don't understand it. . . . He's had no trouble with his heart before! Oh, Alex . . . Elaine needs him so badly!" It was a moment of true weakness for Alanna. Somehow the luxury of having Alex's sturdy figure beside her allowed her to show the feelings, to express the thoughts, that she might otherwise have bottled up. Absurd as it was to argue with him about the improbability of Jake's falling victim to heart disease, she felt the need to voice her frustration and helplessness. Alex recognized that need, as he always seemed able to do.

"Until we hear otherwise, Alanna," he soothed her, "let's try to think positive. Chances for recovery from heart attacks nowadays are excellent. There are new medicines, with more approved every year, to greatly reduce the chances of follow-up attacks."

She pondered his words, clinging desperately to them. "I only hope you're right," she sighed in prayer.

He was. By the end of the weekend Jake's condition

had stabilized so much that the prognosis for full recovery was good. Though still in the intensive care unit, he had spoken several times with Alanna, assuring her that he felt better and expressing his concern over Elaine, who stayed with him in the hospital. Alex was a comfort to both women. Alanna, for one, didn't know what she would have done without his ever-present moral support.

On Sunday night, when Alex returned with her to her apartment, where they had spent both previous nights, Alanna was particularly quiet. Jake had spoken of other things shortly before she'd left his room, things she didn't want to face until the morning. As always, Alex sensed her wish, coaxing her into several hours worth of chess before leading her to bed. If he had been troubled that night she was too engrossed in her own thoughts to notice. Yet there was a tenderness to his lovemaking that touched her.

It was as though he spent longer looking, tasting, touching her than ever before, as though some deep need had to be satisfied by a slow reacquaintance. Alanna let herself fall under his spell, gladly seeking out the escape from the world of reality that his impassioned virility demanded. There was something poignant in their coming together that night, something that she would not understand until the following morning, when Alex woke her earlier than usual.

"I have to run now, love." He sounded strangely tired.

Blinking away her own fatigue, she struggled to sit up. He was dressed already. "Why so early, Alex? Is something wrong?"

His smile was sad. "Not really. Well, perhaps. I'm not quite sure."

Startled into alarm by his uncharacteristic waffling, she awoke fully. "What is it?"

"I'm going now." He repeated his first words, but there was a new finality about them. "You've got a very busy day ahead of you."

So, he had guessed what Jake's request had been. She had known he would. "I don't really have a choice, do I?" she whispered. "He's been so good to me. He gave me that very first chance. Now that he's down I've got to fill in for him."

Alex stared intently at her. "Acting President of Wall-Mar Enterprises is nothing to apologize for, love. You'll do just fine." Again there was an uncomfortable hint of farewell in his words, upsetting Alanna far more than the prospect of what faced her at work.

Mustering a steadiness of voice, she asked the question that seemed inevitable. "Will I see you tonight?" And the answer, too, seemed inevitable. It had only been a matter of time.

"Not tonight, Alanna," he said gently, reaching up to trace the gentle line of her cheek.

Her breath caught, making speech difficult. Still she forced herself. "Why not? What is it, Alex? Do you have other plans?"

His charcoal gaze speared her reproachfully. "You know I don't."

"Then why?" She felt as though the rug were being pulled out from under her and she struggled for balance. Yes, she had suspected that the time would come when she would have to make a choice. Wasn't that what she had always feared—the choice between career and love? Alex had told her once that there need not be a choice. Was he changing his stance? But why now, when she needed his support so badly?

As though reading her thoughts once more, Alex sighed, looked straight at her and spoke softly. "I want you to listen to me carefully, love, and don't interrupt. I'm not sure I can repeat this. It's taken me a good part of the night to formulate these thoughts—"

"Then it really is over." She struggled for calm, interrupting him against his orders. "Come the time that you can't *sleep* with me . . ." What might have been humorous once was not so now.

"Listen, Alanna!" he fairly shouted, his own tension written clearly on his beloved features as she scanned them, one by one. "You have a very important period ahead of you. You're right; you really don't have a choice. Jake needs you to take over his job for a month or two until he gets back on his feet." Alanna listened to his words, feeling a chill seep deeper into her with each one. Her protective hand drew the covers up more tightly about her as she leaned against the headboard.

"I think that, during this period, it might be best if we took a break from one another. It's been an intensive few weeks . . ."

"Don't you love me?" Her words were choked off as he interrupted her.

"Of course I love you, Alanna. Nothing can change that." The fierceness of his tone convinced her, yet she couldn't assimilate what he was trying to tell her.

"Then *why?*"

"Because you need time and I've run out of patience. Don't you see, Alanna? I want to marry you. I want you to be my wife, career and all." When she would have jumped to accept out of panic he went determinedly on. "But I *know* you. This is the apex, love. This is the high point, at least one of them, of your career. You need to be able to give it your all, the way you would have a month ago, before you met me. You need to work through this yourself."

Alanna lay frozen, feeling the receding of a world of

warmth and beauty, sunshine and sharing that had become a very important part of her. Alex sat by the side of the bed, looking as handsome as ever despite the invisible burden that seemed to weigh him down. Her instinct was to comfort him, to throw herself into his arms in search of that same comfort. Her heart screamed for him, urging her to agree to be his wife, clamoring that she do something, *anything*, to keep him by her side.

Her mind, however, knew Alanna Evans. Her mind knew, likewise, that Alex was right. This was a battle she had to fight on her own if she was ever to come to him with a free heart. It was an awesome challenge. Could she meet it and survive?

The pain of their impending separation edged her voice with a thin, barely wavering timber. "When will I see you?" Her gaze was luminous as it savored every last minute of him.

This, too, he had thought out. "That's up to you, Alanna. Once you get to WallMar today and take over at Jake's desk you're going to be suddenly immersed in corporate business that will demand every bit of your inner resources. I know you can do it; I think you know it, too. But I can't begin to predict when you'll be able to emerge." He paused, studying her with an intensity that spoke of his own immersion in the emotional abyss they shared. "You know where I'll be . . . when you're ready. . . ."

With that he stood and headed for the door. "Alex . . . !" Panic threatened to crumble every defense Alanna thought she'd possessed. Only a last-minute shred of reason held her back. When the tall dark figure turned on the threshold for a final look back she forced a weak smile and an even weaker whisper. "You never did tell me what that treat was. . . ."

He had been several steps behind her, totally lost in the act of leaving. Then confusion gentled to indulgence as he shook his head, sighed, then gazed at her a final time. "A sauna. I had a small sauna installed at the apartment. You would have enjoyed it. . . ."

This time when he turned his step did not falter. Alanna's hand flew to her mouth to smother the cry that hovered in her throat. Gone. He was gone. The carpet muffled his footsteps, yet the gentle closing of the front door was as definitive as a gunshot. Gone. *Gone!*

She didn't know how long she sat without moving. On the heels of silence came an acceptance of what had happened. Then came an outpouring of emotion—of trembling, of chills, of utter dejection, of near terror—and a gradual calming as she finally, inevitably, pulled herself together.

He was right. A challenge stood before her which she had to face, once and for all. But Alex had only mentioned half of what was ahead. Yes, there was the challenge of heading WallMar Enterprises and knowing herself to be at the top, the very top, of the ladder. There was also, however, the test of her future. Having sampled life with Alex Knight, now she would relive life alone. *You know where I'll be . . . when you're ready*, he had said. What he hadn't said was that she should come to him only when *she* was ready for that total commitment. Should she find, in the next few weeks, that life at the top held everything she wanted—*without him*—she would be on her own. The implication was clear. He would bother her no more.

A pervasive sense of loneliness maintained a hold on her as she quietly moved from the bed, showered and dressed for the day. She felt strangely numb, as though the same emotions Alex had unleashed with his entrance into her life had now been temporarily erased. Reason alone remained. As she neared the WallMar complex it was reason that took charge, reason that gave her courage, reason that outlined her plan of attack. *Take the offensive*, he had said. *Confront them head-on. Demand more of them. Don't be afraid.*

Chin cocked at an angle of self-assurance, Alanna Evans entered WallMar Enterprises, strode down the long corridor to the office of Jake Wallace, spent several precious moments engrossed in thought and took a deep, deep breath before calling in the staff who now worked for her. Hands clenched on the arms of her chair, where no one could see them, she addressed them quietly, deliberately, forcefully.

"There are twelve of us here," she began, looking from one to the other of the sometimes curious, sometimes skeptical, sometimes openly antagonistic faces of the men who were sharing the office with her, some standing, some lounging against windowsills and some sitting in the few scattered chairs. "It's up to the twelve of us to keep Wall-Mar Enterprises moving, and moving *forward*, during Jake's recovery." In a momentary diversion she softened, explaining the latest on Jake Wallace's condition as the hospital had reported it to her shortly before she'd left her apartment. That, however, was the extent of the amenities she offered. When she paused for a breath, then began again, there was a strength, a maturity in her voice that perked up even the most irreverent ears in the room.

"Let me begin by saying," her gaze was steady, "that I am well aware of the skepticism many of you feel, and the resentment. Without stooping to answer the ludicrous charges that have already been made against me in the past I would like to move forward. Standing in Jake's shoes may be the greatest challenge I'll ever face. Here is *your* opportunity *and* mine. I'm prepared to prove that I've earned my right to stand before you. If I fail now you may believe what you want. But if I succeed I will demand your respect." Pausing for a moment, she forced her hands to relax, folding them on the desk before her.

"Unfortunately," her tone was even as she continued, "I can't run WallMar Enterprises on my own. I'll need all your help. You are indispensable to this organization . . . and to me. However," her gaze narrowed behind the tinted lenses, "if I find that any one of you refuses to give his all I will have no compunction whatsoever in dismissing him." An imperceptible stirring passed through the group; they had not expected such a speech. "Are there any questions?"

When there seemed to be no immediate rebellion Alanna felt that she had won a minor victory. Minor . . . but a victory nonetheless. "Fine, then. I'm already familiar with the general workings of each of your departments. Now I need to hear the details as Jake knows them. You will all have somewhat more responsibility than you may have had before because I simply cannot shoulder it all at the start. But I would like to meet with each of you today, starting with you, Craig," she eyed the chief of marketing, "at ten. I want you to tell me exactly what your department is up to right now, what's pending for the week, what problems need immediate attention. There will be some overlap and much of what you say I may be familiar with. But I don't want to miss any bases. Understood?"

Amid the nods and low-murmured words of agreement there were no outward signs of complaint. There were questions from several, suggestions from one or two, but Alanna was able to handle them all with remarkable skill. She had passed the first hurdle; Alex would have been proud. Yes, there was a definite tension existing among this group, but that was inevitable. It would be a time of testing, as she had told them. She would be on trial—in their eyes, in Jake's eyes, in her own eyes. As for Alex, some deep, private instinct told her of his faith in her. It was the knowledge of this faith that had given her the strength to face these men, some of whom might well be hostile beneath the skin. Alex would be with her, she knew, in both mind and heart throughout this trial. His presence in her life had affected her deeply; his physical absence now could not rob her of the memories of richness, warmth and love, all of which stood behind her as she faced this professional challenge.

Time and again as the days passed she asked herself if she was ready to call him. Despite her preoccupation with WallMar Enterprises, he was never far from her mind. Could she agree to his terms? Could she agree to become his wife, to bear his children, to share her career? And time and again she saw the wisdom of Alex's distance. It was simply too easy the other way . . . too easy to go on indefinitely loving and enjoying without further commitment. Painful as it was, he had been right. Until every last doubt was erased from her mind she had to remain alone.

The siege lasted for a month. During that time Alanna learned more about WallMar Enterprises than she had ever dreamed possible. By the end of the first week, she had the cooperation, albeit at times reluctant, of the men she had confronted that first day. By the end of the second week she had their cautious and conditional enthusiasm. By the end of the third week she had their reluctant respect. From there it was free sailing.

The last week, in particular, was painful for Alanna. She had neither heard from nor seen Alex and she missed him terribly. Despite her gruelling schedule she thought of him constantly. There was little time in the twelve hours a day spent at the office for personal considerations, or during the hour or two spent each evening with Jake and Elaine, first at the hospital, then at their home after Jake was discharged. Each night—each long, sleep-disturbed night—was devoted to Alex.

It was a time of soul-searching. Yes, she missed him. But what, exactly, did she miss? She missed his quiet company at the end of each day, his unfailing support, his eager enthusiasm. She missed the sounding board that he had become to her in such a very short time. She missed, to her astonishment, his sense of protectiveness, even the possessiveness she might have minded in the past. She missed his smile, his eyes, his hands and chest and shoulders. And she missed the way he made her feel—complete and satisfied—in his arms.

Sleep was an elusive quality once more. Alex's love-making had exhausted her physically, but there had been far more to it than that. More even than exhaustion, the secret of her deep sleep in Alex's arms was contentment, peace, a sense of safety. It was the knowledge that he loved her, that he needed her, that he wanted to spend the rest of his life with her.

Out of sight he was. Certainly not out of mind. He filled her senses, her thoughts, her heart, her deepest, most secret core. The pain of missing him was invisible, intangible and absolutely excruciating. And it grew daily, a bristly weed among the daisies. It was a thorn in her side, embedding itself deeper and deeper. It was a blotch on an otherwise astounding report card. It was a gaping void craving fulfillment.

By the end of that fourth week, having convinced herself, her co-workers, and Jake of the smooth and forward progress of the business under her direction, the moment of truth was at hand. She had done it, had proven what she had set out to prove. As acting President of WallMar Enterprises she had won the respect of the skeptics. Through action, rather than words, she had disproven the scandalous claims of that now-distant newspaper article. Yet she still faced the moment of truth, the moment when there was no longer any question in her mind.

The nights, long nights of loneliness, had painted dark smudges beneath her eyes. The days, long days of work, had left her satisfied, yet not satisfied. When she found herself with her hand on the phone, as it had been nearly every night that month, she knew she could wait no longer. It was a matter of simple honesty. Honesty to herself. Honesty to Alex. Honesty to the love they shared.

"Hello?" His voice was deep and low, sending an instant bolt of pleasure through her. Yet suddenly emotion choked off all sound. Emotion—that same emotion that, had gone unexpressed, that had kept her up, night after night—now welled with frightening force. "Hello?" Alex repeated the word, challenging her, this last time, to respond.

"Alex . . . ?" she whispered. There was no sound from the other end of the wire. "Alex . . . can I see you?" When there was still no response, she panicked. Had he changed his mind, after all? "Alex?"

"I'm here, love." He spoke thickly, the distancing effect of the telephone disguising the depth of his own emotion. "Are you ready?"

There was the question, the thought connecting past with present, present with future.

Alanna had no doubts. "I'm ready. I'm on my way to your place. Will you . . . will you . . . ?" *Be there* seemed far too maudlin. "Will you . . . heat up the sauna?"

Later they would both laugh at the improbable location for a reunion and the spontaneity with which the thought of it had popped to her mind. For now, emotion ran far too high for humor.

"It's hot and waiting, Alanna," his thick tones beckoned. Without a second thought, Alanna headed home.

It was not the sauna that took first priority upon her arrival at his apartment. Rather, it was the pair of arms that

folded her to him, the voice that whispered words of love
in her ear, the tall, dark man who held her away from him
to drink in her presence as she devoured his.

"Talk to me, Alanna," he ordered softly, leading her to
the sofa and sitting beside her. "Before anything happens
I need you to tell me what's changed in that mind of yours
to bring you here."

But Alanna was too drugged with love to want to talk.
Reaching for him, she locked her arms about him, seeking
his heartbeat, savoring it until he set her back purposefully. "Can't we talk later, Alex?" she whispered, craning
to kiss the rugged line of his jaw.

That old, familiar eyebrow arched. "I dare you to talk
now, love. Let's see what kind of self-control you *really*
have!"

"Alex! That's unfair," she chided in soft frustration.
Every nerve end craved his touch, every sense cried for
his possession. But at the moment Alex's need for the
words he'd waited so long to hear was far greater. The
vulnerability in his expression told her that. He had been
free and open with his feelings from the start; it was only
fair that, now that she finally understood her own more
clearly, she share them.

"I love you," she whispered, though she dropped her
arms in acquiescence.

"What else is new?" There was a barbed resignation in
his tone.

For a moment she pondered it. "I deserved that. I *have*
been . . . stubborn, haven't I?"

"Uh-huh." The smiled that toyed with the corners of
his lips was genuine. Glorying in it, she found herself
spurred on.

"I'm ready, Alex, ready to make that commitment."

"Why?"

"Because I love you."

When he shook his dark head she was taken aback. "Not good enough," he announced firmly. "You've loved me for some time now. What makes you suddenly want marriage?"

As she looked into his eyes she saw those silver sparkles, held in abeyance, waiting to burst forth. On impulse, and quite inappropriately, she grinned. "You know, when I was a little girl I had a game that worked with wires and batteries. It was a quiz game, question-and-answer type thing. If you made the right connection the red light went on." Mischief sparkled in her own eyes as slowly, slowly she felt the chill that had occupied her body since the morning Alex had left begin to dissipate.

"What on earth does that have to do with anything?" the cause of the thaw growled deeply.

"It means that your eyes will be my reward when I give the correct answer. Your silver sparkles . . . they're waiting. . . ."

"*I'm* waiting," he reminded her in warning.

At that instant, abruptly sobering, Alanna knew that it was time to end the waiting. For them both. Forever. "These four weeks have been an experience I needed, Alex. They've opened my eyes in many ways." When she reached for his hand he allowed her to take it, yet he sat silent, waiting. "You were right when you insisted I do it alone. I've lived my whole adult life that way. If I hadn't done it alone now I might always have wondered, wondered whether I had it in me, whether I might have made it, whether I would have been sufficient to the task and whether it would have been enough for me."

"And?" His features finally began to relax. Suddenly Alanna found her hand covered by his in a subtle but meaningful turnaround.

"No, it wasn't. I've seen the top of the ladder, reached the heights I'd hoped, in my wildest dreams, to reach.

And no, it wasn't enough. I've learned that I can make it, that I can be *president* if I want. But I don't." She sighed, nearing the end of her control. "These past four weeks have been the busiest I've ever lived through. But I've never been as lonely in my entire life." His image blurred before her as her eyes suddenly filled with tears. "I need you, Alex. I need to be with you, to know that you're here when I come home, to be here for you. That world out there has no meaning unless you're in it with me."

A solitary tear trickled down her pale cheek as Alex drew her against him, ending their separation for all time. "I've missed you, owl-eyes," he groaned, hugging her tightly, absorbing her memories of pain and loneliness and unfulfilled desire, exorcising his own in the process. "These have been the worst days I ever hope to spend."

Alanna turned her luminous cocoa gaze to his features. Now she saw them clearly—the exhaustion, the strain, the drawn look that must have mirrored her own.

"You did wait," she whispered in awe, daring to voice that one most devastating fear for the time spent apart.

"Of course I waited! Did you think I wouldn't?"

"I tried *not* to think of that possibility. You do have the patience of a saint."

"Patience, love, had nothing to do with it. I damn near lost my mind wondering when you'd come to your senses."

"You were that sure?" she asked skeptically.

His response held no skepticism at all. "I was." Then he smiled. "It's been very hard for a man like me, a person who sees what he wants and goes after it, to sit back and wait for what he wants to come after him."

"Why did you?"

A month of asking himself the same question provided the ready answer. "I did it because the prize was worth it.

You've come to me now with that much *more* inside you. And I love you all the more for it."

His words brought a reappearance of the tears that had temporarily dried. Gently he lifted the oversized glasses from the bridge of her nose, then kissed the teardrop from each eye in turn. Her forehead, her cheeks, her nose . . . all received the blessing of his kiss. But her lips, warm and open, eager and inviting, waited. . . .

"Alex!" Exasperated, she took matters into her hands, thrusting her fingers through his hair to the fine-trimmed thatch at the nape of his neck, drawing his face toward hers until, at last, in a moment of mind-shattering triumph, he kissed her.

Alanna had never felt as complete as when those lips slanted hungrily across hers, opening and mastering her mouth with a power that thrilled her. When the tip of his tongue strayed deeper she felt charged with an energy she had lacked since that last, poignant night a month ago.

Suddenly anything, *everything*, in life was possible. The world was hers. Happiness soared through her as a dove before the sun, pure and fresh and sparkling. She felt fully alive and keenly aware, sizzling from head to toe with the force of a love that would be restrained no longer.

How it all burst forth as it did she would never know. But there was suddenly a frenzy of activity, a melange of hands and arms, of fingers fumbling with buttons. With unrestrained abandon they left a trail of clothing strewn behind, a trail of shirts, of skirt and trousers, bra, slip, briefs, panties . . . all leading toward the bathroom, where they moved, as one, toward the sauna.

The sauna . . . a breath of heat from the desert, instantly slowing life to a more languorous pace, toasting all within its reach. As Alex sat on the lone wood bench

Alanna stood before him, reaching unhurriedly to touch his face, to smooth the dark hair back from his brow. Theirs was a world in isolation, a golden world lit by a warm and glowing sun.

He spread his knees and drew her between them, resting his head against the gentle harbor of her breasts. His hands stroked her from shoulder to hip, drawing lazy circles to call forth tremors from deep within her. Overflowing with an emotional ecstasy, she trembled at the physical bounty offered by this man's body, the sinewed strength beneath her tapered fingertips.

"Aaaaah," she moaned, a hoarse sound from deep in her throat as she tipped her head back in delight allowing long, blond tangles to cascade over his fingers. "I've missed you, too, Alex. How I've missed you!"

Her hands clasped against the corded mass of his shoulders, her head dipped forward once more, this time to meet the lips that waited to return the message of love and elaborate on it. In one fluid stroke Alex's hands slid behind her, lifting her, drawing her close until she felt the strength of him that was her power as well. Yet he prolonged the moment, adoring her features with his gaze, then his hands. His man-rough fingers slid easily and with fiery touch around her shoulders to her chest and her breasts, pausing only briefly to tantalize buds that were taut with desire before searing a path lower.

Breath came in ragged gasps for them both as they struggled to express all the thoughts bubbling forth from the heady cauldron of passion.

"I love you, Alanna. . . ."

"I love you, too. . . ."

A flurry of kisses momentarily put a stop to conversation.

"Have you been able to sleep?" he asked, nibbling at her earlobe, his chest rising and falling rapidly.

"No. Have you?"

His fingers delved deeper and she moaned, but he ignored her cry. "Not once . . . through the night. . . ."

The tide of passion carried them higher. Alanna strained closer. "I never knew what I was missing . . . until you came along. . . ." she whispered. This time it was Alex who moaned.

For Alanna that moment was the true pinnacle of her dream of success and happiness. The body that glistened beneath her, before her, was only the start. She stroked it lovingly, mesmerized by the play of rippling muscles and the beaded moisture over its dark, hair-roughened skin.

As Alex shifted her, lifted her, then possessed her in one rapturous motion she cried out her love, then cried no more. For it was a time of living and loving, of sharing and creating. Alex was her equal, her friend. He was her helpmate, her partner. He was her lover; he would be her husband. Through his vision she had glimpsed a future more rich in meaning than anything she had ever conceived of. With him, and only him, she might have that future.

It would be filled with a fine blend of career and family, with Alex beside her all the way. It would have the same ups and downs, the same highs and lows as all of existence had. But it was special, unique, the challenge of a lifetime. Alanna accepted it eagerly.

sweet serenity

1

Humming softly, Serena Strickland gave a final tug to the ribbon she'd just tied, cocked her head in appraisal of her work, then grinned. It was perfect! Mint chocolate peas and carrots in a clear canning jar ringed and crowned with a lavish orange polka-dot bow—the effect was gay enough to make even the most skeptical Minneapolitan believe that spring was around the corner.

Shifting on the high stool behind the counter, she looked up past rows of goody-filled canisters to the front of the shop and beyond, where the sun splashed teasingly through the Crystal Court. Serena couldn't restrain a knowing smile as the crisp rays bounced from column to column, storefront to storefront in the plaza, darting in and around in a game of hide and seek all too appropriate, she thought, for this April Fool's Day.

It had been a long winter, true to Minnesota legend. The snow still lay in mounds at the far ends of parking lots and driveways or beneath trees against which it had drifted and whose shade now shielded it from the melting power of the sun. And, yes, she mused with a note of realism, it would probably snow again before the muck underfoot dried into memory. Five years' living in this most northern of the central states cautioned her against unqualified optimism. But spring would come; she felt it in her freckles. Scattered from cheek to cheek over the bridge of her nose, they were faded now, ready to pop into vivid life with the first of the springtime sun. In anticipation, she flipped the calendar to April 1.

The gentle jangle of the front doorbell called her from her daydreams to the world at hand. Approaching without hesitation was a man she'd never seen before. He wore a three-piece suit, an open khaki trench coat, and a decidedly desperate expression.

"May I help you?" She stood quickly, but had no time to move from behind the counter before the man reached her. At closer range he seemed less sure of himself, almost embarrassed.

He took a deep breath. "Have you got something called . . . Pretzel Joys?" he finally blurted out. "My wife is expecting a baby any day now and says she's got to have some. She's a regular customer of yours."

"Joan! You must be Joan Miller's husband!" Serena's hazel eyes widened as she broke into an open smile of recognition, then grew suddenly apprehensive. "How *is* she? It's been awhile since I've seen her. I wondered whether she'd had the baby yet."

Jonathan Miller grimaced. "She's a week overdue and very uncomfortable. I only wish there was more that *I* could do. So if my picking up Pretzel Joys will make her happy, Pretzel Joys she'll have." He paused in a moment of doubt. "You *do* have them, don't you?"

"Of course!" Serena laughed, rounding the counter and reaching for a glass canister. "And if I didn't have them here, I'd have had some sent special delivery from the manufacturer in Chicago. How much would you like?"

The father-to-be frowned. "I don't know—a pound, maybe two. What would you recommend? *You* know Joan."

Nodding through her laughter, Serena began to weigh scoops of the individually wrapped candies into a brightly patterned bag that matched the walls of the store with its lime-green and fresh pink bamboo design. "I think that two pounds should hold her for a while. If she needs more she can call and I'll have them delivered." Out of habit, she handed a sample to her customer. "Would you like to try one?"

"Oh no," he laughed. "I've got enough bad habits without looking for any new ones." But he picked one up and scrutinized it closely. "What *are* they made of, anyway?"

Serena shoveled in the last of the two pounds, then went to the ribbon rack to tie a cheerful bow on the handle of the pint-sized shopping bag. "They're crushed pretzels rolled into a ball of creamy white chocolate. Do you mean to say that Joan's been hoarding them all this time?"

His low-grumbled "'Fraid so" was offered jokingly. "I never knew how much they meant to her until last night—uh, make that one o'clock this morning. I can assure you that she'll be pleased to see this bag!" After paying for his purchase he swept up the item and headed for the door.

"My best to Joan, and good luck to you both!" Serena called after him before turning to help a customer who had entered at his departure.

For an April Fool's Day the morning passed without shock. Customers came and went, many of them familiar faces stocking up on one or another of their favorite confections. Nancy Wadsworth, Serena's good friend and assistant, arrived at eleven to help sort through the deliveries in the back room while Serena held down the fort out front. With a pickup in activity during the noon hour, when workers from the office buildings surrounding the mall wandered in and out, both women worked side by side, dispensing and wrapping selections of imported suckers, novelty chocolates, and various and sundry jelly beans with the flair which had made the shop known throughout the sweet-circles of Minneapolis. By the time Serena grabbed her purse at one-thirty, she had earned her luncheon break.

"I'm off now, Nance," she stage-whispered to the other woman as the latter put a wide beribboned stopper on an oversized milk bottle filled with malted milk balls. "I'll be back in an hour or so."

"Say," Nancy asked her as the customer left, "did you see the new 'fun jars' that came in this morning? They're adorable—some have frogs on them, others have pigs or ladybugs. You'll have a grand time filling them!"

Serena beamed at the thought. The "interior decorating," as she liked to call the selection and arrangement of candies or nuts in each fancy container, was always a challenge. "Great! I'll take a look this afternoon. I've got to run now, though. I'm meeting André upstairs."

"André?" Nancy feigned a shiver. "Is this business or pleasure? There's something about him that makes me uneasy. Of all your men, I like *him* the least."

"*All my men?* Nancy, you make me sound positively wicked!"

"You're *not*, Serena. That's the trouble. You *should* let loose and have a fling every once in a while."

"Nancy!" Serena chided good-naturedly. "I'm surprised at you . . . a mother and all. . . ."

"My *daughter* happens to be twelve," her friend countered. "You're twenty-nine. There's a difference. You should even be thinking of settling down—"

"Nancy—"

"—but *not* with André. Perhaps with Ken or Rod or Gregory . . . but *not* with André."

Serena laughed. "I think you've made your point. Don't worry. André may come on a little strong, but he's really harmless." At Nancy's look of doubt, she added, "And he is my investment counselor. I've got to keep him on his toes."

"You can have him," her friend snorted softly, then raised her voice as Serena headed for the door, "but have a good lunch. He *owes* it to you!"

Throwing her head back in a half-laugh, Serena left the shop behind. Confident steps took her past neighboring windows, the broad panes of which reflected her slender form, a floating vision with a touch of sophistication. She wore a long-sleeved blouse of Burgundy silk, whose wide cuffs and collar were of a contrasting cream hue that matched the ivory of her lightly flared wool skirt. Her high-heeled pumps and the plush leather shoulder bag that hung by her hip matched the Burgundy of the blouse. If eyes turned at her passing she was too self-contained to notice. Within minutes André Phillips greeted her in the lobby of the restaurant, dashingly bestowing a kiss on each of her cheeks.

"And how's my favorite sweet lady today?" he exclaimed as he held her back to admire the heart-shaped face framed by thick auburn hair that swirled in waves to her shoulders.

"Sweet as ever," Serena quipped lightly. "And you must be having trouble readjusting to the U.S. of A."

"How could you tell?" With an arm thrown possessively over her shoulders, André led her to where the hostess stood awaiting his nod.

"*Both* cheeks, André?" Her gaze narrowed teasingly. "Very European," As the hostess beckoned for them to follow, Serena took advantage of the restaurant's closely set tables to pull from beneath his grasp and move out in front of him. Far from being blinded by his charm, she knew of the high style of life he treasured and, though it wasn't what she wanted, she indulged him in his excitement. Accepting the seat he held for her, she listened patiently as he recounted his Parisian adventures, and took each with a grain of salt.

It had been a month since she'd seen him. As he talked she watched him, acknowledging his good looks even as she stood by her conviction that his dark hair was a bit too neatly combed, his natty clothes a bit too carefully worn, his facial expressions a bit too deliberate for her total comfort. When she'd first sought investment advice several years ago the bank had recommended André as someone in the know. Indeed, his connections reached to the upper echelons of the Twin Cities' power elite. His life was, in his mind, at least, an exciting one.

Though she had dated him on occasion, Serena successfully kept him at arm's length. Thrice-married and thrice-divorced, André held no lure for her other than as the provider of a few entertaining hours of friendship and a large dose of investment advice. If the financial statements she received at regular intervals were to be believed, he had done well for her.

"So, tell me"—he broke off his dissertation to draw her into the conversation—"how goes *Sweet Serenity?*"

Serena pushed a thick lock of hair behind one ear. "The shop is doing just fine, André. I keep waiting for the slow spell that never seems to come. Not that I'm complaining, mind you. . . ." She smiled. "Here it is, the first of April. We've got Easter, May Day, Mother's Day, Memorial Day—you name it and it spells business."

André eyed her askance. "Do you mean to say that you have specials for April Fool's Day?"

"Sure." She was unfazed. "I sold several boxes of white chocolate golf balls this morning. They look like the real thing. Of course, they'll melt in the golfer's hand if he happens to hold onto one long enough. Then"—she grinned—"there are sets of toffee golf tees, tins of red licorice paper clips, bottles of marshmallow aspirin, hanging marzipan peperomia plants—"

"All right, all right! Sorry I asked!" He stemmed the onslaught with a chuckle. "But I'm glad to hear things are buzzing." Then, in the amount of time it took him to cut a piece of his pork chop, he sobered. Serena was always amazed at these sudden switches from lightness to intensity, but she'd long ago attributed them to nothing more than André's high-strung nature and quick mind. "Have you given any more thought to investing in the money fund we discussed before I left?"

Nibbling at her egg-and-avocado salad, Serena chose her words with care. "I've given it some thought, but . . . I'm also beginning to think along . . . other lines."

"Oh?"

"Uh-huh." With a deep breath she broached the topic she'd been toying with for months. "I'm considering opening a branch of *Sweet Serenity* in one of the suburban areas."

An odd silence preceded his "Oh?" No longer eating, he gave her his undivided attention. Serena met it in earnest.

"Downtown Minneapolis has been a fantastic market. But many of my clients come from the same areas that have made the large gourmet markets, Devlin's, for example, such a phenomenal success. People flock there from all over. It has an elegance, a sense of quality about it, that the population is both literally and figuratively eating up." She snickered at the pun, but felt a pang of discomfort when André obviously missed her humor. "You think it's a bad idea?"

He hesitated. "Don't you think it may be a little premature?"

Serena bit at her full lower lip before answering. She respected André's opinions and it bothered her that, even speaking as a friend, he wasn't as enthusiastic as she about the prospect of expansion. "*Sweet Serenity* has been a viable concern now for five years." She repeated the reasoning that had worked so well on herself. "I've been able to reinvest profits—you've done that for me—and we should have *no* trouble setting up a second shop."

"*In* Devlin's?"

"That would be nice," she drawled with a chuckle, "but I doubt we'd get the space in Saint Louis Park. Perhaps in one of the newer stores. Actually, I was hoping to find a spot in Edina or Wayzata."

André pursed his lips as he studied his plate. "I don't know, Serena. I think you should give it more thought." He shook his head, though not a hair budged from its designated spot. "With the instability of the economy and all . . ."

"Oh, it's still at the thinking stage," she was quick to reassure him, "but I wanted to explain why I'm skeptical about investing heavily in anything that might tie up my money for a long period. If I do decide to go ahead with this I may need to get my hands on some of my funds."

As quickly as he had sobered, André smiled. "You may put me out of business, you know."

And Serena then understood part of his hesitancy. After all, he earned his living making investments for businesspeople such as herself. Investments took capital; the more capital she sank into a new shop, the less there would be left to invest. "André," she chided, "would I do that to you? If I open a second store and it's even half as successful as the first I'll have twice as much money for you to play with. And, besides, my interests must be *peanuts* compared to most of your clients!"

He reached down and brought her hand to his lips, kissing its back in chivalrous fashion. "Very tasty peanuts, Serena. But . . . enough of business." He brightened.

"Listen, I'm going out to L.A. next month. Why don't you join me?"

"Join you? André, I have a shop to run! I can't just take off and jet around the country!"

He quirked a brow. "Would you, if it weren't for the shop?"

It was actually a very simple question. For one thing, she had spent her early childhood in southern California. It had been the scene of her father's financial and emotional ruin. She had only painful memories of the area. For another, she had not been, nor ever would be, André's lover. And *that* was the crux of his present proposition.

When she spoke it was quietly and with just enough of an apology in her tone to offset the finality of her words. "No, André. You know that I wouldn't."

"Then I'm destined to bang my head against a brick wall?"

Serena deftly turned the tables on his teasing. "You've been through three awful marriages! You don't need another woman hanging on to you!"

But he was quick on the rebound. "Come on, Serena. When was the last time *you* ever hung on a man?" Her sheepish shrug spoke of her independence. "And you're not about to try it with me, are you?"

She shook her head slowly, her pout one of affection but far from anything more. "No. I'm afraid it's not in the cards for us." As the waiter appeared with their coffee a movement near André caught her eye. At the adjacent table a couple was in the process of being seated. The woman's back was to Serena. The man stood graciously by to hold her chair, then took the seat opposite, offering Serena a clear view of his face.

It held her instantly as a galvanic force ripped through her subconscious. She knew that face! Beyond a doubt, she knew that face! Yet she couldn't place it.

Details were lost in the overall image, whose familiarity rippled through her in repeating waves that stirred her pulse. This was no visage from recent experience. Instinct told her that. Rather, his face whisked her back over time as she sought a memory that was stubbornly elusive. With a taut swallow she dragged her gaze away. Grasping at the nearest diversion, her coffee, she nearly scalded her mouth as she drank it too quickly.

André talked on. She smiled and nodded, participating only distractedly in his chatter. But the puzzle remained. Her attention was drawn back time and again to the man at the next table. She was so certain she'd seen him before. . . .

"What do you think, Serena?" André's question caught her off guard.

"Hmmm? I'm sorry." She shook her head clear of cobwebs. "I was hung up on something else. What were you saying?"

His patience was commendable. "I wondered," he stated slowly, "what you thought of the prospect of Minneapolis replacing Washington as the nation's capital."

"What?" Her laugh had a definite edge to it that had nothing to do with André's thought. "Are you serious?"

"I certainly am," he deadpanned. "There's been a rumor to that effect, you know."

"I didn't!"

"It's true. It's even been put into print that by the end of the century we may house the government workings out here."

The concept was preposterous enough to drive that nameless face from her mind and spark Serena to life. "Heaven forbid! Minneapolis is just fine the way it is. The *last* thing we need is an invasion from Washington—or any other area!"

"And how long did you say you'd been living here?" he teased. "You sound like a die-hard Minnesotan."

"Almost." She grinned, then lapsed into relative silence as her counselor delved into the business prospects of a governmental move, delighted with the fantasy. Serena interjected the appropriate uh-huhs and reallys, but again her mind had begun to wander.

She glanced once more at the next table. The man was engrossed in discussion with his companion, though he was listening more than speaking. With the first shock yielding to frustration, Serena studied his features in search of a clue.

His hair was dark brown, rich and full, the sprinkles of gray in his well-tapered sideburns putting him around the forty-year mark. His nose was straight, his lips firm, his eyes hazel, like her own. He wore a shirt and tie, blazer and slacks, presenting a dignified though sporty appearance that was far from riveting but totally masculine. That he was attractive was unquestionable, and, at the moment, irrelevant. There was something beyond his outward appearance that nagged at her. She stared helplessly at him as the spark of familiarity shot through her again. It settled in her gut in an inexplicable response that shook her complacency and rattled her self-confidence. *Who was he?*

As though in response to her silent plea he looked up. In a moment of inner cataclysm for Serena he caught her eye. *She* caught her breath. As placid as he appeared on the surface, the force of his gaze spoke of a deep inner fire. That was what seemed most familiar to her. Mouth dry, she stared, unable to look away as long as his gaze held hers. His expression held a question, perhaps even faint amusement. Strangely, though, he mirrored none of the recognition she so strongly felt. Could she be mistaken? . . .

When he finally returned his attention to his companion Serena felt drained. Facing André once more, she was too preoccupied to miss his fleeting uncertainty, but he talked on and quickly forgot her diversion. Slowly she finished her coffee. Once more she looked toward the next table; once more her gaze was met. André recaptured her attention with a witty review of the improvisational theater troupe he had seen the night before in Cedar-Riverside. But he lost her a final time to the nameless memory whose eyes shone brightly toward hers.

For Serena it was a disconcerting experience. She'd always been good with names and faces. It was necessary in her business, a small touch that her customers appreciated. But here was someone whose identity mystified her. Moreover, something kept her from alerting André to the man's presence, though he knew almost every distinguished face in the Minneapolis–Saint Paul area.

And this face *was*, in its unpretentious way, distinguished, even aside from the quiet ring of authority in his gaze. Serena devoted a few final moments, as André studied the bill, to solving her mystery. Much as she tried, she could pin neither a name nor a place to this man whose interest was now mercifully centered on his woman-friend, granting Serena as free a perusal as convention would allow.

Then, quite unwittingly, he threw another wrench in the works by smiling. It was devastating in its intensity and totally unique. Had she ever seen that smile before Serena would have recalled it. No, she hadn't seen *it*, but she had seen *him*, of that she was certain.

"I'd watch out for him, Serena." André's warning was soft and spoken with a note of earnestness that stunned her.

"Wh–what?" Had she been that obvious?

"That man behind me—"

"You know him?" she interrupted on impulse.

"No. He must be new, perhaps passing through."

She frowned. "Then why the warning?"

André rose smoothly and came to stand behind her. Bending low in a proprietary attitude, one hand on either of her shoulders, he put his mouth close by her ear. Though Serena couldn't get herself to look up, she sensed his eyes on the next table.

"I have feelings about people. That one strikes me as an agitator."

"An agitator?" she murmured out of the corner of her mouth. "He looks harmless enough to me."

"Is that why you've been staring?"

She couldn't move without André's say-so; she was cornered in every sense. "He . . . looks familiar. That's all. I'm sure I've seen him somewhere, but I can't place him."

André straightened, deftly pulling out her chair and drawing her up in one fluid move. "A mystery man from your lurid past?" he teased her lightly, but she cringed as she draped the strap of her bag over her shoulder, opting for sarcasm as a cover.

"No doubt." Her drawl wafted into the air as the hand at her back guided her from the restaurant. She hadn't had to look at the man again to have his face imprinted in her mind.

There it stayed, in living color, to torment her through the afternoon. Each idle moment brought forth the vision with renewed force. *Where had she seen him?*

Running *Sweet Serenity* provided some respite, deflecting her attention to her customers. However, with the help of Nancy, who left to fetch her teenagers at three, and Monica, a teenager who arrived soon after from school, much of Serena's time was free for "decorating." Her hands were kept busy, carrying out the directives of her mind, while the latter was free to wander.

Inch by inch and working backward from the present, she scoured the years in an attempt to locate that empty slot crying out to be filled. Her past five years had been spent here in Minneapolis, building *Sweet Serenity* from scratch with the money she had unexpectedly inherited from her maternal grandfather. Even now, as she looked around the shop with pride, she recalled the surprise with which she'd received the bequest. Following her father's disgrace, her mother's family had been less than supportive. The fact that a grandfather she'd barely known had entrusted her with such a substantial sum after her father had squandered both dollars and trust had been an added incentive for making a success of the shop.

Five years in Minneapolis. The occasional trip to Seattle to visit her mother and younger brother, Steve, with whom the older, sadly defeated woman lived. Periodic trips to Chicago to attend gift shows or negotiate directly with her suppliers. Had there been, during this time, any man such as the one whose presence had struck such a jarring inner chord today? To her knowledge—no.

Traveling further back, she reviewed the two years she'd spent in Boston managing the Quincy Market boutique that had been the original inspiration for *Sweet Serenity*. During this period she had found herself, gaining self-confidence as a creative and capable woman, self-supporting for the first time and slowly beginning to rebuild her dreams. They were dreams different from those of the naive young girl she had been so long ago, but they were lovely in their own way.

Two years in Boston. Customers coming and going. The occasional date for dinner, a concert, or a show. Many familiar faces, mostly friendly. A landlord, several interesting tenants. A doctor, a dentist, and, of course, the members of the racquetball club. Were there any faces among the lot that resembled this April Fool's Day apparition? No.

The four years she had spent in North Carolina as an undergraduate student at Duke were even harder to examine in detail. Not only was the time more distant, but she had been thrown into the passing company of many, many more people. Students, teachers, house mothers, administrators. Closing her eyes tightly against the peace of *Sweet Serenity* she envisioned her college life, scanning the crowd of faces in her memory for the one whose hidden fire had seared her consciousness today. Nothing. The age was wrong. The face was wrong. Nothing!

In an uncharacteristic fit of frustration Serena crushed the bow she'd been attempting to shape for a crystal martini shaker filled with liquor-stuffed mint olives. *Who was he?*

Intuitively she knew his was no face seen merely in passing at some random point in her life. His gaze had affected her too deeply for that. He had been *someone*—someone important. In retrospect she felt a strange defensiveness, a need to protect herself—though from what she simply didn't know. Perhaps she had to go further back. But each year's regression was more painful.

Seeking escape, she tossed the ruined ribbon into the wastebasket, left the countertop at which she'd been working and rescued Monica from the clutches of long-winded Mrs. McDermott, a regular fan of cognac cordials. After Mrs. McDermott came several clusters of adolescents intent on splurging on one of the exotic flavors of jelly beans or—the current rage among them—gummy bears. Personally, Serena couldn't stand the things. For that matter, she rarely ate any of her wares, sampling them only for the purpose of describing them to customers. Mrs. McDermott, for instance, a sprightly senior citizen, would not have been terribly pleased when the gummy bears stuck to teeth that Serena suspected were removable. On the other hand, it was the mature patrons who could appreciate the rich milk chocolate of the imported candies as youngsters could not. So much of Serena's service involved learning and respecting the tastes of her clientele. It was for this reason that so many had become habitual indulgers since she'd opened her doors.

"Mrs. French!" She burst into a smile as a favorite customer entered the shop. "How are you?"

"Just fine, Serena," the attractive woman replied. "But I need your help."

"What's the problem?" Over the years June French had had "problems" ranging from office parties to Little League banquets to numerous get-well gifts and other more conventional items.

"How about a sweet sixteen sleepover? I need party favors for seven teenaged girls, *all* of them fighting acne, baby fat, and eleven o'clock curfews!"

"I remember too well," Serena quipped. In truth she had never been to a sleepover, much less a sweet sixteen party. At that particular point in her life she had been a loner. But acne, baby fat, and curfews—those she could relate to. "Let me think. . . ."

Slowly she looked around the shop. Along the left-hand wall ran the stacks of oversized canisters whose transparent glass faces displayed goods on sale by the pound. Along the right were shelves of decorative boxes and containers, a sampling of which were filled and wrapped for instant sale.

Tapping a tapered forefinger against her lips, she deliberated. "Of course! The obvious." Several short strides brought her to a shelf that held small, hand-painted tins! Kneeling on the low-pile green carpet, she gathered a selection of tins together. Then she turned to the opposite wall. "Lo-cal suckers. They're fun. Here"—she plucked one of the wrapped candies from its canister and offered it to her customer—"try this. It's tangerine. There are also licorice, raspberry, butterscotch, lime and rum. We can fill each tin with a mixed sampling and tie a different colored bow around each. When the candy is gone the tin can be used for earrings, pins, you name it."

The nod that accompanied Mrs. French's grin vouched for her delight. "You've done it again, Serena. I only wish all my problems were so easily solved."

So did Serena . . . with respect to her own. For as the hours passed and memory persisted in failing her she grew more agitated.

Returning to work behind the counter, she let her mind drift further back to those years she'd spent with her aunt and uncle in New York. Those had been her high school years, right after her father's fall from grace. There had been anonymity in New York, something she had craved after the harrowing experience of stigmatization left her bruised and sensitive. She had spent those years quietly, her peers indifferent to her past. Only one, Michael Lowry, had used it against her, and the memory still hurt.

To hell with this strange man's identity. It wasn't worth the effort of rehashing those years. If she was ever to learn his name it would be destiny that chose the time and place. She'd done everything she could to ferret it out from the annals of her memory, with no success whatsoever. Enough! She had *Sweet Serenity*, today and tomorrow. The past was done!

Buoyed by her newfound determination, she lent Monica a hand with the steady flow of customers during the predictably busy late afternoon hours. Then, when the rush had finally eased, she started packaging the telephone orders they had received in the course of the day. There were several orders to be sent to area hospitals, several to be delivered to private homes. These would be handled with care by the local delivery service she retained.

There were also several orders to be shipped long distance. Each required careful and extensive padding with the bright lime tissue she always used when wrapping or cushioning sales. In those cases where more glass than usual was involved she dug into the stack of newspapers in the back room to supplement the gayer tissue as padding.

Standing behind the counter, she could absently supervise the activity in the shop as she worked. Nonchalantly she reached toward the newspaper, which she crumpled loosely and eased into one of the boxes before her. Three, four, five times she repeated the process until the package was closed, sealed, and its shipping label affixed. Then she began on the next box. She reached for a piece of newspaper, crumpled it—

Reynolds. The name leapt up from the half-crumpled newsprint, slamming her with the force of a truck, freezing her hand in midair, halting the flow of air in her lungs as her heart beat furiously. *Reynolds*. With unsteady fingers she straightened the paper, pressing the creases out with her palms, nervously spreading the sheet atop the counter. The name had been there, buried deep in the recesses of her mind. It took a minute of searching for her to locate the article and she was filled with trepidation as she read it.

MINNEAPOLIS, March 20. The *Tribune* has learned that its major competitor, the *Twin City Bulletin*, has been bought by Thomas Harrison Reynolds of the Harrison Publishing Group. Originally from Los Angeles, Mr. Reynolds takes the helm after months of negotiations, during which he bid heavily against two eastern corporations for ownership of the *Bulletin* and its subsidiary press. Initial reports filtering from *Bulletin* executive offices indicate that the staff will temporarily remain intact as Mr. Reynolds studies its effectiveness. The new publisher has vowed to improve the quality of reporting and . . .

Reynolds. Thomas Harrison Reynolds. A name for the face. And a place. Los Angeles. A time. Sixteen years ago. Tom Reynolds, the cub reporter who had first broken the story that eventually led to her father's indictment on charges of embezzlement.

It had to be a hoax. Serena reread the small article and moaned. Knees weak, she slouched against a high stool for support. Why here? *Why here?* Minneapolis was *her* home now. Here there was nothing to haunt her. She had a happy present and an optimistic future. Of all the places into which Tom Reynolds might have dug his journalistic claws, *why here?*

Tom Reynolds. It certainly explained the gut response she'd had earlier. Even now his name stormed through her, leaving tension in its wake. The last time she had seen him had been in court. Thirteen at the time, she had been vulnerable and impressionable. And Tom Reynolds had impressed her as being hard, ambitious, and . . . wrong.

As she struggled to assimilate the fact of his presence in Minneapolis, her eye fell on the calendar she'd changed just this morning. April 1. April Fool's Day. Was this all an ugly gag?

In her heart she knew it wasn't, even before she looked toward the front of the shop when she heard the bell. There at her door stood none other than the man in question, Thomas Harrison Reynolds.

2

For a fleeting moment Serena was back in that Los Angeles County courtroom, with Thomas Harrison Reynolds standing boldly among the throng of press personnel covering the trial. He had been sixteen years younger then and his appearance had reflected it, from the shaggy fall of hair across his brow to the faded corduroys and worn loafers above which a blazer, patched at the elbows, seemed a begrudging concession to courtroom convention.

Now the corduroys had been replaced by gray wool slacks, the loafers by polished cordovans. Today's blazer was navy, immaculately cut, well-fitted. Sixteen years had handsomely matured his skin and dashed the silver wisps she'd noticed earlier through his hair. But his eyes and the depth of his expression hadn't changed a bit. On their power she was hauled forward over the years.

Tom stood at the door, Serena behind the waist-high counter. Twenty feet separated them, twenty feet charged with waves of electricity. Caught in the middle was Monica, looking from one face to the other, instantly sensing something unusual astir.

Serena would never know why the shop had suddenly grown quiet. Where had the customers who had been milling around moments before disappeared to?

As though to further the developing nightmare Monica, seventeen and infinitely perceptive, slipped softly past her. "I'll unload those late deliveries, Serena," she said, then was gone.

For the first time in recent memory Serena didn't know what to do. One part of her felt like that frightened thirteen-year-old back in Los Angeles; the other part was a poised and successful twenty-nine-year-old businesswoman. Somewhere in the middle of the two she waffled. Why was he here? What did he want now?

Paralysis seized her; she was helpless to function. In the span of what seemed hours, yet could have been no more than a minute or two, she felt raked over the coals for a crime in which she'd had no part. Tom's gaze grilled her with the persistence of an inquisitor. Beneath its force the knot in her stomach spread slowly through her system.

Then, as though in partial answer to the prayer she hadn't had the presence to offer, the door opened and another customer entered the shop. Tom moved easily to the side, stopping to lean casually against the wall by the door.

A flicker of annoyance passed through Serena that he should post himself so confidently on her terrain. The thought was enough to stiffen her backbone. If it was a demonstration he wanted, a demonstration he'd get. This *was* her turf. Satisfying customers *was* her specialty. That Thomas Reynolds should presume to intimidate her in her own shop galled her.

Only he could see the fire in her eyes as she left the safe haven of her counter to approach the newcomer. In her determination to ignore him Serena missed the hint of a smile that both curved his lips slightly and sparkled in his eyes.

As much in defiance as in deference to the customer,

she put a purposeful smile on her face. "May I help you?" she asked the middle-aged woman who, from the moment she'd entered the shop, had been entranced so by the cheery array of goodies around her that Serena's approach startled her.

"Oh! Uh, yes!" She looked up quickly, then was drawn helplessly back to a dainty, hand-sewn pocketbook, child-sized and filled with individually wrapped suckers. "This is adorable. I want to pick up something for my granddaughter. This might be just the thing. Today's her birthday."

"How old is she?" Serena asked, noting out of the corner of her eye that Tom had straightened and begun to look around the shop himself.

The older woman grinned. "Just seven, God bless her!"

Tom moved slowly in their direction, idling nonchalantly before various items, but moving onward nonetheless. Serena grasped at the escape hatch opened by her customer. "Seven. How wonderful! May I make a suggestion?"

"By all means."

"I could fill *that* bag," she pointed to the small pocketbook that had charmed the woman, "with Jelly Bean Hash." Without waiting for approval she retreated toward the rear of the shop, as far as possible from where Tom had paused to pick up and study an oriental lacquered box, to the crystal cookie jar set prominently on a corner of her work counter. It was filled to the brim with Jelly Bean Hash.

"Jelly Bean Hash?" the woman echoed Serena, her question echoed in its turn by Tom's dark brows, which rose as he looked Serena's way in wry amusement.

Serena concentrated on the sale. Lifting the lid of the cookie jar, she removed one of the cookie-shaped candies with the scoop left nearby for the purpose. "Assorted jelly beans dropped into a white chocolate 'batter.' Kids adore them. The purse will hold perhaps half a dozen. I could wrap them in colored plastic wrap to match the fabric of the bag, if you like."

Beaming, the woman nodded. "I would like that. Thank you. It sounds perfect."

To Serena's temporary relief Tom had gone back to his studies. She set to work wrapping the hash in deep red plastic to match the bag her customer had chosen, then tied a vibrant yellow bow around the whole. "There!" She held up the finished product for inspection before sinking it in a bag. "How's that?"

As the woman expressed her pleasure and paid for her purchase Tom silently nodded his approval, too. Even this peripheral participation in the exchange rattled Serena, who seemed to spend longer fumbling for the correct change of the twenty-dollar bill the woman offered than she'd spent recommending and wrapping the item.

With each step the woman took toward the front door Tom moved closer to Serena, who grew increasingly uneasy. She had never felt so awkward. Could she treat this man as simply another customer? Could she pretend, after the intensity of their exchanged glances that she had never seen him before?

The shop was quiet, with only the intermittent rustle of Monica working in the back room to break the silence. Despite the absurdity of the situation Serena couldn't quite find any words with which to break the ice. As she lifted her eyes from her clenched hands, her own fear and resentment clashed in silent battle with the curiosity and confusion in his gaze. *Why didn't he say something? What was he up to?* If only Monica were out here with her to serve as a buffer. But that was the cowardly approach, she chided herself. Then, once more, she was saved by the bell.

"Serena!" A tall bundle of knee-length rabbit fur and shimmering red-gold tresses surged through the front door, crossing the room before the jangle of the bell had died. "I need Red Hots! You've got some, haven't you? Oh, excuse me—" Cynthia Wayne came to an abrupt stop beside Tom, her striking blue eyes wide. "I can wait, if you're busy." Her gaze didn't budge.

"No, no, that's fine," said Serena, enthusiastically recovering the use of her tongue. "It's good to see you, Cynthia." *She would never know how good!* For the first time in the four years that she and Cynthia had been weekly racquetball partners Serena actually welcomed Cynthia's very blatant sensuality. Anything to sidetrack Thomas Harrison Reynolds from his enigmatic quest. "You sound desperate," she teased her friend. "Any problem?"

Cynthia faced her and grinned mischievously. "Nothing a pound of your spicy little Cinnamon Red Hots can't solve." Narrowing her gaze at the assortment of Chinese-style takeout containers on a shelf behind the counter, she pointed to one. "I think that blue-and-white-checked job over there should blend just beautifully with his office."

Though Serena was uncomfortably aware of Tom following the conversation closely, she couldn't resist a soft-spoken jab at her friend's humor. "Now, now, Cynthia. Who is it you're trying to burn?" Behind Cynthia, Tom smirked.

"My boss, as it happens." She tilted her chin up in revolt "He's been really short with all of us today. I'd like to see him take a handful of these and stuff them in his mouth with his usual greed. *Then* he'll have something to bark at!"

"He'll be breathing fire," Serena warned her lightly.

"He deserves it," the other woman shot back. Full lips curved into a seductive pout, Cynthia tossed a sidelong glance at Tom. His eyes, however, were firmly trained on Serena.

If Monica had been perceptive beyond her years, Cynthia's insight was a product of hers. Had she not been in a rush to get back to the office she might have been tempted to stay and chat with her friend. Had this man, whom Serena had notably failed to introduce to her, not been standing by waiting patiently for an unknown something from Serena, Cynthia would have lingered even in spite of her boss's decree. She was a born flirt; but she also knew when a man was irrevocably indifferent to her charm. And this man *was*. Her provocative appearance hadn't sparked him in the least. With a sigh she took her purchase from Serena's outstretched hand.

"Thanks, love," she murmured in answer to her friend's feeble excuse for a smile. Both women walked to the front door.

"Go easy on him, Cyn," Serena quipped when she knew they were out of Tom's earshot. She was unprepared for her friend's retort.

"On him? What about you?" Her whisper stopped as she glanced back over her shoulder at Tom. "What's going on with *him?*"

"Nothing."

"He's gorgeous."

"I really hadn't noticed." They stood now at the opened door, Serena with her back purposefully to the inside of the shop.

"Come on, Serena. I know you're not a wild dater, but he's not here for gumdrops." In the face of Serena's helpless expression, Cynthia knew she would get no information beyond what she had observed herself. There was definitely something going on between her friend and the dark-haired man in her shop. Perhaps Serena would tell her more when they played. "I'll see you at the club tomorrow night, love."

"Sure, Cyn."

"Take care!"

Despite the unmistakably naughty drawl in the redhead's voice, Serena watched her departure with reluctance. The furred form flew on down the stairs toward the street level of the plaza, then disappeared through a doorway to the outside world.

Serena sighed. Then, with a deep breath and a longer sigh, she turned.

The soft carpet had silenced Tom's footsteps as he had approached. A gasp of fright escaped her when she found herself face to face with him. Face to face? It was more a case of face to throat! Standing at such close proximity with no buffer between them, Serena was appalled at the discrepancy in their height. The intensity of his expression, laced heavily now with amusement at her discomfort, was intimidating enough without this added leverage he seemed suddenly to have gained.

Lips dry, she bit her tongue to keep from wetting them in a gesture she knew would be misleading. Her heart beat double-time; her legs were momentarily shaky. Clearing her throat, she took a breath to begin—then stopped. Something . . . something in his expression brought back to mind the bizarre thought that had raced quickly through it earlier in the restaurant. Was there a possibility that he had *not* recognized her? Could some other unfathomable purpose have brought him into *Sweet Serenity?* For an instant she was aghast at the realization of how rude she had been, if that was the case. Then she reminded herself that it was Thomas Harrison Reynolds who stood before her. Straightening, she steeled herself to confront the enemy.

For lack of a better opening she slipped into the role of

shopkeeper. "May I help you?" Her tone was as even as she could produce under the circumstances, but it was far from completely self-confident. Chin up, body taut, she was mindful of the thudding in her chest.

Tom drew his brows together, then frowned more deeply. As he peered down his face held a mixture of varied and fleeting emotions. Many were the same she had sensed in him earlier—confusion, curiosity, skepticism, boldness, determination. There was still that noticeable absence of recognition—but there was also the presence of that fire, burning through the flickering hazel of his gaze. And there was something else deep within . . . working its way to the surface. . . .

To Serena's consternation, he put his head back and laughed. Only after he caught his breath did she hear his voice for the first time in sixteen years. It was smooth and steady, not as deep or gruff as she would have imagined, and it carried a gentleness totally at odds with her expectations.

"You *are* a character!" he marveled, confounding her further.

"Wh-what?"

"You're very unusual."

"Oh?"

"Uh-huh."

She paused. Would he declare his purpose? "Well . . . ?"

"Well, what?"

"Is there something I can do for you?" Her voice had risen in pitch along with her body heat.

"I hope so," he drawled, butter smooth. This was not at all what she had expected.

"Are you looking for something?"

"Could be."

The conversation was going nowhere. Only her heart

tripped recklessly forward, sending blood through her veins at breakneck speed. She sighed. "You're staring." *Where was Monica?*

"So are you," he rejoined, undaunted.

So she had been, though not of her own volition. It was as though that fire in his eyes drew her; she had no choice. Mustering the fragments of her self-possession, she tore her gaze from his and walked quickly behind the counter to finish the packing that had been so abruptly interrupted by her discovery of this man's identity.

In a move she might later question she thrust the single condemning sheet of newsprint to the side for safekeeping and completed the chore. Though her fingers fumbled busily, her mind couldn't escape the absurdity of the situation. Did he recognize her or not? In either case, what did he want?

"Are you buying a gift for someone?" She tried again, looking at him over the counter. He had come to stand flush against it, his forearm resting on its raised rim. His hand was long, strong, relaxed, clean—much as its owner who, for the first time, seemed to grow impatient.

"Of course not. I'm here to see *you*."

"About what?" she came back too quickly, apprehensive once more.

Her fear puzzled him nearly as much as his motive alarmed her. Before either of them could say another word the jangle of the bell offered a respite. With a meaningful nod in the direction of the oncoming customer Tom stood to the side as Serena moved forward. Five minutes later, having sold one wire chick filled with oversized coconut jelly beans, she was back at ringside. Tom picked up where they had left off.

"What about? I was hoping *you* could tell me that. It's not every day that a woman in a restaurant eyes me the way you did today."

"Oh?" What else could she say without tipping her hand. If he truly didn't remember her *she* had the upper hand. While one half of her ached to cry out its bitterness toward him, the other half exerted good sense and stifled the words.

"I still can't figure it out." He continued to scrutinize her closely.

"What?"

"Those very pointed daggers you threw at me during lunch."

Had she been more obvious than she'd thought? Or had she simply been unaware of the strength of her mysterious resentment? "Daggers? I . . . you . . . you just looked . . . familiar. . . ."

"Hmm." He offered a crooked smile that lacked any humor. "You must have some enemy!"

How right he was, she mused sadly. If only he'd never moved to Minneapolis! If only she'd never had cause to remember him and the past he had helped to warp!

"How did you find me?" she asked softly.

Tom was pleased by her curiosity, a definite improvement on curtness. The warmth of his gaze was suddenly contagious, spreading over his features, threatening to extend to her own. She fought it by looking away.

"After you left I asked the hostess about you. She suggested I try *Sweet Serenity*. She also said"—there was humor in his tone—"that I'd have to wait in line."

Serena laughed innocently. "That might be true just before Christmas, Valentine's Day or Mother's Day. But, as you can see, on normal days we keep things moving."

"I don't think that was quite what she meant." One dark brow arched chidingly.

"Oh?" It took her a minute to catch on.

"Will you have dinner with me tonight?"

His invitation was so guileless that it made the situation

that much worse. "*What?* How can you even suggest such a thing?"

He shrugged. "It's really not so unusual. Men and women do it all the time. I seem to recall that you had a very attentive luncheon partner."

"So did you," she lashed back, then blushed.

"Ah, you noticed. You see," he grinned playfully, "it is fairly common. How about it?"

Serena shook her head in amazement. How had she found herself in this situation? "This is ridiculous," she whispered, half to herself.

But he was fast to call her on it. "How so?"

Slowly she tipped her head back to face him. He was very attractive and, in all probability, very interesting. Had things been different she might have been tempted. As things stood, however, it was out of the question. She could never betray her father's memory by socializing with Tom Reynolds.

"You don't even know me," she hedged.

"That can be remedied," he countered.

"I could be married."

"To your lunch date?"

"He's my investment counselor."

"Ahh," he sighed softly. "But you did go to lunch with him. Why not dinner with me?"

"I had a good reason to have lunch with André. I don't have *any* reason to have dinner with you."

When he grinned the echo of his smile tingled strangely through her. "You just might enjoy yourself."

"I just might *not!*"

He frowned, perplexed. "Do you have a reason *not* to have dinner with me?"

"Yes."

"You *are* attached?"

"No. . . ."

"Then why not dinner?" he persisted.

Serena enjoyed a momentary feeling of power. "You look surprised, Mr. Reynolds. What's wrong—not used to being turned down?"

Tom grew alert. Straightening his shoulders, he took control once more. "You *know* me." His gaze narrowed with the flat statement. "I had that impression. How is that?"

"I . . . I read about you in the newspaper."

Her stammer fell victim to his slow headshake. "No good. The papers carried no photographs. I've been insistent about that."

"Insistent?" She was temporarily sidetracked by curiosity.

"Anonymity is something I prize," he stated simply.

"Hah! This must be a recent twist!" she scoffed in spontaneous sarcasm. Sixteen years ago Tom Reynolds had come brashly forward to denounce her father, first in print, then in court. She could almost hear the bang of the judge's gavel, then she realized it was the birth of a headache.

Every bit the investigator, Tom prodded further, which did nothing to discourage her headache. "You didn't learn my identity from the paper, Serena," he called her by name. *Thank you, Cynthia*, she mused wryly, then trembled. It was only a matter of time before he knew the truth. "You've known me in the past. Why don't I know you?" His features formed a deeper frown.

Her patience began to wane. "Could be that you've known so many women in your life you can't keep them straight. A dime a dozen?" She had sputtered at him in pure anger, heedless that her words were inappropriate. She was quickly sorry.

Retribution took the form not of anger but of smooth seduction. Tom's gaze fell from her eyes to the soft and vulnerable curve of her lips, lingering long enough to send a new and unwelcome tremor through her. "I've never dated you," he said huskily as his eyes made a slow exploration of her pale cheeks, the lazy auburn curls that fell there, the path of faded freckles across her nose. "I'd certainly remember you if I had. You're different. . . ."

Once more Serena was stunned into momentary sympathy by the innocence that surmounted even seduction. His inner struggle was obvious as he tried in vain to place her, much as she had wrestled with her own memory for the bulk of the afternoon. After all, she scowled grudgingly, what cause would he have to remember each of the stories he had covered, the subjects he had made or broken with the casual power of his pen? What cause would he have to consider the hapless families which his journalistic fervor had destroyed? Different, he had called her.

"I should hope so," she said with fiery indignation.

"Then, where . . . ?" His head jerked toward the door in irritation when the front bell rang again. Lips thinned into a grimace, he stepped aside more reluctantly now.

Serena, however, was grateful for the interruption. With an outward calm belying both the jitters in her stomach and the ache behind her forehead she dished up a pound-and-a-half order of Ice Cordials, wrapped them, bagged them, received payment for them—all the while drawing out each step as though she were headed for the gallows when she was through. By the time her customer left the ache had developed into a dull throb and she felt as pale and iced as the candies she'd just sold. Distressed, she cast a glance toward Tom, whose impatience was obvious, but under control.

"As I was asking"—he straightened and stalked her— "before we were so rudely interrupt—"

"Serena?" Monica's loud call from the back room, followed by her ruffled appearance, was as reassuring to

Serena as it was irksome to Tom. The fire in his gaze seemed ready to escape its confines; Serena escaped first.

"Yes, Monica?" She turned to her young employee.

"I'm sorry to bother you." Monica looked timidly toward Tom, then lowered her voice for Serena's ears, "but I've got a problem with the new shipment of trail mix. It looks weird." She crinkled her nose. "There's pink stuff sprinkled in it!"

"Here, let me see." Without a word to Tom, Serena disappeared into the back room. She recognized the problem instantly and returned to the front of the store to phone the distributor and report a spill of strawberry confetti chips.

"All set?" Tom asked when she finally replaced the receiver in its cradle. Like an old friend, he leaned casually against the counter.

"Yes. We'll get a new shipment tomorrow."

"What is this . . . trail mix, anyway?"

She smiled wanly. "It's a mixture of nuts and dried fruits—cashews, walnuts, raisins, dried apricots, pineapple, banana. We sell a lot of it for—"

"—the trail?" The glint of humor in his eyes brought a helpless grin to her lips.

"For the trail. I only hope we won't have many trailgoers in for it between now and tomorrow afternoon."

"Does this kind of thing happen often?"

Serena grimaced. "Not very, thank goodness. I mean, there are always small problems here and there,"—she rubbed her temple absently—"but it's unusual when an entire shipment is bad." Her head shot up. "This isn't an investigation, is it? Are you looking for corruption in the candy business?" What had started as a quip developed into an indictment. "You aren't hoping to find someone worthy of assassination *here*, are you?"

His eyes flared, but he remained calm. "No, Serena. I

don't do investigative reporting any more. And even if I did, this would be an unlikely spot for me to start searching."

"You'd be surprised." Her eyes narrowed angrily. "It's the most unlikely spots that often get hit!" Her thoughts were of her father, who had always been an upstanding member of the community. Why had Tom gone after him?

Tom sensed her anguish. "Look, is there somewhere we can talk uninterrupted?"

"I'm a working woman. My day isn't over until well after six."

"But you've refused to have dinner with me—"

"Then I guess you're out of luck." She put her fingers to her temples to still the thudding that had settled there. "Besides, there's nothing to talk about. You looked familiar to me today in the restaurant. I stared at you. That's all. *Fini*."

"Not quite. You still haven't told me how you know me. And you haven't given me a good reason why you won't go out with me."

Serena wanted to scream, but she internalized the urge along with the need to pound something. The gremlins within her head were doing that on their own. "Let's just say I don't like you," she mumbled.

"I know that. But I'd like to know why. What have I ever done to you? What have I ever done to deserve your disdain?"

"You really don't remember." Her statement reflected her disgust that what had meant so much to her family had meant nothing to him.

"No, I really don't remember. Why don't you make things easy for me?"

"Are you kidding? You'd like *me* to make things easy for *you*?" Furious, she went on. "Since when do *you* need

help? Aren't you the all-powerful? All you have to do
is to put your pen to paper and"—she snapped her
fingers—"you've got what you want."

"Now, just a minute—"

"No. I think you should leave."

"I'm not going anywhere until I find out what you have
against me!"

"Then I'll just call the police. You're trespassing . . .
and causing a . . . disturbance. . . ."

They stood facing one another with only the counter
between them. Tom's body was taut with anger; Serena
trembled with the same. Both of their voices had been
low, with the force of fire held in check. Now he spoke
with the conviction she recalled so well.

"You won't call the police, Serena, because you really
don't want to dredge up the past . . . whatever it is. . . ."
His words trailed off lethally, leaving her a fragile mass
of agony.

"You wouldn't. . . ." Her eyes widened; her head
throbbed.

"I would."

Serena looked away, then swallowed hard. She believed him. He would have no qualms about destroying
her life to find out what he wanted to know. Her whitened
fingers curved around the edge of the counter as she
slumped against a stool. Tom's voice jolted her, yet she
couldn't look up.

"Monica!" he called toward the back. "Monica? Could
you come out here, please?"

Within seconds Monica answered his summons. But it
wasn't to Tom that her attention turned; rather, she stared
at Serena's face, downcast and deathly pale.

Tom rounded the counter. "Monica, would you take
care of things out here for a few minutes? I'm taking Serena out back. She's not feeling well." At Monica's look of

alarm he reassured her quickly. "It's just a headache. But she could use a breather. Can you handle this?" His hand had already closed on Serena's arm; she felt too threatened to fight him.

"Sure. I'll take care of everything. Serena, are you sure you're all right? Can I call someone?"

"She'll be fine," Tom answered before Serena could answer for herself. "She's got me."

Feeling suddenly sick to her stomach, Serena yanked her arm from his grasp and fled to the back room, where she rested against a tall carton, propping up her elbows and cradling her face on her fingertips. In her bid to escape she had missed the smile and accompanying wink Tom had sent toward Monica by way of mollification before he stepped confidently past her and followed Serena.

Assuming that she was witness to a lovers' spat, Monica was only too happy to respect their need to be alone. It was what she had sensed earlier, when she had diplomatically excused herself. Now they wanted more privacy. She could understand that. Cheeks flushed, she grew more starry-eyed. Mr. whoever-he-was was very, very sexy!

Serena, however, was at the moment oblivious of any such charm. Head bowed, she struggled to regain control of the weakness in her stomach and the ache in her head. Breathing deeply, she feared she might even cry.

"Are you all right?" Tom's voice came more gently as his long fingers drew her hair back from her face.

She flinched and jerked away, unwittingly backing herself into a corner. The only positive aspect of the situation was the waist-high stepladder against which she was able to lean. Given the jelly-weakness of her knees, it was a minor blessing.

Tom stood over her, close enough for intimidation even as he spoke softly. His hands were thrust in the pockets of his slacks, his stance casual. Only the intensity in his eyes and the stubbornness underlying his quiet tone betrayed his tension.

"Now," he began, "you can start by reminding me of the first time we met." Serena wrapped both arms around her middle, looked down and said nothing. "Serena," he warned her.

"I'm not playing your games, Reynolds!" she whispered at last, not trusting her voice to remain steady if she spoke any louder. "You seem to know everything, despite that look of innocence you put on from time to time."

At the edge of her downcast field of vision his legs shifted. "Since you know so much about me, you also know that I'll carry out my threat. Would you like me to start searching through your past?"

She looked up slowly. "That's blackmail."

"You're *that* frightened of what you have to hide?"

"I have *nothing* to hide. You've got nothing on *me*. But I won't have you destroying my life now for something my father did years ago. He paid—we all paid!" Once more she dropped her eyes, closing them, lifting a hand to shade them from Tom's keen scrutiny.

His voice was lower, his words carefully chosen. "Tell me, in your own words, what your father did, Serena."

"You know. Why should I humiliate myself further?"

"Because"—his fingers took her chin and firmly raised it—"I want to hear you say it."

Serena tried to twist her head away, but the pounding got worse with the movement. "You must be sick!" she seethed.

"Say it. . . ." he warned again.

"What kind of pleasure can you get from this?"

"Serena, tell me about your father!"

She gritted her teeth. "I'll tell you as soon as you take your hand off me." For several moments they stared at one another. Then for the first time Tom yielded, dropping his hand, freeing her chin. It was an empty victory for Serena, for he took no more than a half step back, crossed his arms over his chest, and waited.

"Go on."

She took a shaky breath, propped herself once more against the ladder, and looked up defiantly. "My father was a good man. He loved his family and worked hard as an accountant. But he looked around and saw wealth on every side. And he was human. He made a mistake. You seized on that mistake as your stepping stone to success, capitalized on it, and made a public spectacle of my father." Her entire body trembled.

"What is your last name?" he asked softly.

"What?"

"Your last name—what is it?"

"My God!" she cried. "You don't even remember the name! Just how heartless are you, anyway?"

"The name, Serena. Tell me."

"Strickland! Strickland! My father was John Strickland. *Was.* He had a stroke several months after the conviction, while his lawyer was in the midst of the appeal process. It never went on. My father was paralyzed, spent weeks in the hospital, then three years in a nursing home before he died. Needless to say, life was just lovely for all of us during that period." Her note of sarcasm at the end did nothing to blunt the pure venom of her attack. But it left *her* writhing, rather than Tom.

To her dismay he stared at her as though she had risen from the dead. He seemed stunned. "Strickland," he said in an amazed whisper as his eyes covered every inch of her face. "Serena Strickland." Still he stared. "I remember your father so clearly, and your mother. There were two children, a boy and a girl. The boy was very young—"

"He was eight."

"And the girl wasn't much more than—"

"I was thirteen."

Tom continued as though in a daze, his brows drawn together with his frown. "She was kind of awkward, a little pudgy and very . . . very . . ."

"Vulnerable." Serena's breathing was uneven as she clung to her remaining self-control.

Astonished, he shook his dark head. "I can't believe you're the same girl!"

"I'm not," she snapped, shaking again. "And the hell I went through during those years had nothing to do with adolescence. Do you know what it's like to have friends whispering behind your back or suddenly avoiding you? It was as if I had the plague. I was 'daughter-of-the-thief'! Do you have *any idea* what that was like?" She paused for a breath, oblivious of the pained look spreading slowly across Tom's face. "No. Of course you don't. *You* never lived through anything like that. *You* are Thomas Harrison Reynolds of the illustrious Harrison publishing family. You never had to face the kind of disgrace you caused my father—"

"Serena," he cut in on a very quiet note, "I didn't tell him to steal."

"But you told everyone else *about it!*"

"I was a journalist. It was my job."

She tipped her head up in anger. "Now tell me you were only acting on orders."

"You know who I am." He threw her argument back in her face. "I don't follow orders."

"You were a young reporter then. It was your chance to hit it big on your own, is that it?"

"No."

"Then . . . what?" she cried more softly, feeling drained, tired, dizzy. Her headache had reached migraine proportions. "Why did you go after my father like that? Why . . . like that?"

Her voice died on a tremor that matched the shimmer of tears in her eyes. Tom's face blurred before her, his features blending in a dark cloud. Closing her eyes against further humiliation, she dropped her chin to her chest. Her shoulders rose and fell in her agitated attempt to stop short of an outright crying jag. Everything hurt so very badly.

"Let me get you something for that headache." Tom's voice was close above her and very gentle.

"It's all right," she whispered, knowing it wasn't.

"Have you got any aspirin?" She merely rocked back and forth, trying to comfort herself. "Serena, don't you have a bottle of aspirin around?"

"Marshmallow," she croaked feebly, clamping her eyes more firmly shut against the nearness of this man who, by rights, was her enemy. Strangely, though, she couldn't fight any longer. Her fiery reaction to Tom had been out of character and she was too miserable now to persist.

Though he couldn't see her defeat, he sensed it clearly. Quite spontaneously he reached out, put his hands on her shoulders, then slid them around her back as he drew her to him. Serena went without a fight, too weary to reject his gesture of comfort. His identity was as unimportant as the fact that it was his presence that had caused her to get upset. The only reality was the pair of arms that steadied her and the warm body that absorbed her trembling.

Breathing deeply, Serena felt the slow return of strength to her limbs, but, reluctant to launch herself back into the fray, she made no attempt to move. Her cheek lay against his chest, her hands splayed on either side. Beneath her right hand his heart beat strongly, making him seem infinitely more human than he had in the heat of the fight.

Then, strangely, he was all too human. Suddenly she

grew sharply aware of the strong length of his body, its strength barely concealed by the trappings of civilization. His clean, manly scent teased her with each breath she took. His chin rested on the crown of her head, threatening to hold her forever in this deceptively tranquil pose. He was a man to rest against . . . a man to lie against. . . .

With a gasp she pushed herself away, finding her legs as she fought the flush that threatened to betray her thoughts. "I–I think you should leave now," she whispered, pressing two fingers against the hammer behind her eyes.

"*I* think you should take something for that headache."

"It's a migraine. I used to get them all the time. It's been years since I've had one, though." She looked up at him. "You brought it on; perhaps if you leave it will go right along with you." The chances of that were slim, as past experience reminded her. It would, undoubtedly, be a bad night.

"Let me see you home."

"Is that the offer of a guilty conscience?"

"Not guilty. Perhaps pricked, but mostly sympathetic. You look as though you're in pain."

"An apt analysis," she muttered beneath her breath. "Perceptive."

"Come on." He ignored her sarcasm. "Get your things. I'll take you home."

"No, thank you. I can't leave until the shop closes. And that isn't for a while yet." As she recalled *Sweet Serenity* and what she'd made of it pride bolstered her. "I'll do just fine."

Tom stared at her a moment longer, his gaze expressing his obvious skepticism. Finally he turned and left without a further word, at which point Serena became the skeptic. The next ninety minutes were excruciating. As she tried to function she pushed all thoughts of Tom

Reynolds to a far corner of her mind. But from that corner he pounded at her head, growing more and more impatient, if the strength of her migraine was any indication.

Monica earned her pay three times over during that short space of time. She asked no questions, simply took over the handling of customers with the tact and self-assurance of a pro. And her boss was eternally grateful.

"Thanks, Monica." Serena forced a smile through her discomfort as they were closing up. "You've been terrific this afternoon. I'm not quite sure what I'd have done without you."

"I'll be back tomorrow." The teenager smiled. "If you feel like, you know, taking off for a while I'd be glad to cover."

"You're a dream"—Serena gave a genuine smile—"but I'll be here. This is my baby. There's nowhere I'd rather be."

The declaration referred to tomorrow. Right now, the only place she wanted to be was in bed under the weight of two quilts with the night cushioning her from the world. Senses dulled beneath the force of her headache, she stumbled through the last of the chores necessary after closing each day, threw her smart wool jacket on over her shoulders, grabbed her purse, knit hat and mittens, and made for the door. Blind to just about everything but her determination to get home in one piece, she turned her back on the plaza to lock and double-lock the door of *Sweet Serenity*. It was only when she turned back that, through the pain centered just above her eyes, she saw Tom.

3

He pushed off from his casual stance against the balustrade opposite her shop and stood no more than an arm's length away; she couldn't miss him.

"Oh, no," she murmured softly, taking a quick look at his face before averting her own.

"All ready to go?" he asked nonchalantly.

Bent on willing him out of existence, Serena stepped forward without a word, mechanically following the path she'd taken to and from work for the past five years. Beyond the blinders of her headache she was marginally aware of Tom keeping pace with her, but she was too miserable to argue. She paused only once, when she left the enclosure of the plaza and stepped into the cold night air, to button her coat to the throat, pull the thick wool hat over her ears and bury her shaking hands in the depths of her mittens.

"Cold night, isn't it?" Tom said with annoying light-heartedness, having stopped beside her to don and button the thigh-length, sheepskin-lined jacket that had been thrown over his arm.

Serena's grunt was as much at his company as his comment. But if she'd hoped he would take the hint that his presence wasn't wanted, she was disappointed. And she couldn't do anything to shake him, given the precarious state of her own health. It was enough to concentrate on putting one foot before the other, to combat the raging hammer in her head and the churning in her stomach. If the lights of the buildings on either side were excruciating to her vision, those of the oncoming cars were worse. When she pressed one mittened hand to her temple Tom grasped her other arm to steady her. Again she was too overwrought to protest.

What was in actuality no more than a ten-minute walk seemed a marathon to Serena. She thought she had never been as happy to see anything as she was when her apartment building came into view—then amended that at the relief she felt on finding herself on the fifteenth floor, at her own front door. She groped for the keys at the bottom of her bag, then fumbled with the lock until Tom took over the chore without a word. At that moment she could not care that he was on the threshold of her apartment. Her only thought was on getting to bed.

She was through the door and halfway across the living room without a backward glance when Tom switched on a light. Wincing, she shielded her eyes from its blinding glare, then reached the hall and finally her bedroom by sheer force of the momentum she'd established.

When she closed the bedroom door the noise reverberated through her. Stumbling forward, she pulled the curtains shut to blot out the lights of the city spread below her.

Darkness was a welcome friend. Slowly she shed her coat, hat and mittens, stepped out of her shoes, then one by one stripped the clothes from her body, draping the skirt and blouse on a chair, letting the rest fall haphazardly on the thick pile carpet underfoot.

A pair of slim bikini panties were all that was left as she stumbled to her bed, pulled back the covers and crawled beneath the heavy layers with a soft moan. The sheets soothed her; the dark enveloped her. With the quilts pulled to her ears she buried the worst of her migraine against the pillow. Her mind was a jumble of discomfort, with nausea coming and going in waves. As seconds passed into minutes and on toward an hour she sought nothing but the release of sleep.

Every so often she turned and burrowed more deeply into the bed, then moaned softly at the pain that persisted. The quiet sounds from her apartment—someone rummaging in the bathroom, the kitchen; a low voice on the telephone, at the door—failed to penetrate her door. Even if they had, she would have been deaf to them . . . or indifferent. The events of the afternoon had faded into a haze of pain. Nothing mattered to her but getting to sleep.

A widening sliver of light fell across the bed when the door opened. Serena was sufficiently buried beneath the covers to be undisturbed by the intrusion. When she was turned onto her back and bundled, covers and all, into a half-seated position, she squeezed her eyes shut.

"Go away," she whispered.

"Here, Serena. Take this."

"Aspirin won't help."

"It's your prescription."

"No! It's too old—"

"I know. I've just had a refill delivered."

"Oh—"

He handed her a small white pill and a glass of water, holding her steady as she took the medicine.

"OK?" he asked, taking the glass from her lips and putting it down on the night table by her bed.

Her echoed "OK" was barely audible.

Easing her gently back on the bed, Tom sat for a minute, then stood and left, drawing the door tightly closed, leaving her alone once more in her cocoon of darkness.

Almost instantly she began to feel better, though the medication could not possibly have worked so quickly. Later, somewhere in her mind, came the soothing vision of a warm hand on the bare skin of her back, a strong arm supporting her, long fingers stroking wayward strands of hair from her cheeks. The sensations were very real, their pleasantness lingering to bring her relief until the time when the medicine entered her bloodstream and went to work. Then she fell into a deep and restorative sleep, awakening once very much later to walk to the bathroom for another pill and set her alarm before falling quickly asleep again. When she awoke the second time it was morning.

Despite the deep sleep induced by the medication, her alarm had not yet rung. Groggy, she sat up, blinked, stretched, pushed the hair back out of her eyes. She felt decidedly better. The residual ghost of her headache would ease now with a dose of aspirin. The nausea was already long gone.

Slipping from bed, she donned a robe and stepped into slippers, took fresh underwear from the drawer, and headed for a hot shower. It felt divine. Turning slowly, she soaped herself, applied a generous helping of shampoo to her wet hair, rinsed off the lot, then stood. And stood. Turning occasionally. Letting the water cascade over her gentle curves. Repositioning herself to let the steaming spray hit her neck, her back, her chest, her shoulders. It was only when she began to feel immoral at her lavish use of hot water that she reluctantly stemmed the flow.

The heat of the shower had warmed the fluffy towel that lay in waiting across its rack. With a definite sense of pampering herself she reached for it and patted the water from her body before treating it to a helping of scented moisturizing lotion. She wrapped the towel around herself, then vigorously rubbed her hair with a smaller towel before brushing through the tangles. It was only then, as she stared into the mirror at the reflection of her pale though recuperating self, that she allowed herself to think of Tom.

Tom Reynolds. The devil of her memory. The uninvited visitor to her shop yesterday. The inquisitor. The cause of her migraine headache. Then . . . the self-appointed guardian who had seen her safely home. The silent protector. The gentle caretaker. All in all, a potpourri of conflicting characteristics. Who *was* Tom Reynolds?

Her gaze grew puzzled as she noticed the new bottle of medicine that he had had the presence of mind to order. Why had he waited outside *Sweet Serenity* last night? Why his insistence on walking her home? Why had he bothered to see to the medicine and make sure she was sound asleep before leaving? It made no sense.

Shaking off the last of her fogginess, she faced the future. It was a new day. She felt vastly improved. And she would *not*, she vowed, be driven to another headache by Thomas Harrison Reynolds. Seeing him yesterday had been a shock which she was now over, although there remained the matter of her past, which he had recalled. Intuitively she sensed that he wouldn't betray her, though she knew that, for her own peace of mind, she would eventually have to confront him about it. She'd have to know for certain that her life in Minneapolis would be safe from the taint of the past. But that would be for another time, should their paths cross again. For now, there was the day to welcome.

It was a relatively steady hand that applied her makeup, working more carefully with color around eyes dulled by last night's headache, adding a bit more blush than usual to still-pale cheeks. She stroked through her hair with a natural bristle brush, bringing up a fine luster, pushing willful curls this way and that until she was satisfied with the results. Then, encouraged by the normality of her appearance, she set out for a cup of hot, strong coffee.

Her apartment was small but well-planned. Its single bedroom and bath opened off a hallway from the living room. The kitchen had two open archways, one opposite the bedroom, the other leading directly into the living room. It was through the first that she entered, humming softly to herself. The fresh, dark brew was dripping into the pot within minutes. Its aroma never failed to please her. Smiling, she savored its richness, then headed for the living room and the *Tribune* that would be on the mat outside her front door.

She managed to set only one slippered foot into the living room. Then she gasped. For rising slowly to a sitting position on the sofa, his back to her, was the figure of a man. She had no idea that he'd spent the night; the thought hadn't entered her mind. Yet there before her was a sleep-disheveled, very groggy Tom Reynolds.

His back was a broad expanse of white shirt; his dark head was bent forward. Serena stared, fascinated, as he put a hand to his neck to massage away the cricks that her sofa had undoubtedly planted. His fingers worked at his taut muscles and he stretched to relieve the stiffness.

Her eye followed the manly ritual, yet she was touched by something totally non-physical. Unobserved as he thought he was, he seemed utterly human and very vulnerable. Despite his great status, he was prone to the same aches and pains as the next man. And he was here, in her apartment . . . still. Why?

She emerged slowly from the doorway to walk hesitantly around the sofa, pausing in front of it when Tom looked up, sending a momentary quiver through her. Yesterday he had been immaculate in his appearance and handsome; now he was tired, his chin shadowed by a beard, seemingly at a disadvantage. Seemingly, yet not. For he was still more attractive, crumpled shirt, heavy eyes and all, than any other man she had ever known.

"Good morning," she heard herself announce softly and quite civilly.

Tom looked dubious and sounded even more so. "Umm. Is that smell what I think it is?" He raked his fingers through his hair as he shot a glance toward the kitchen.

"Uh-huh. Would you like a cup?"

" 'Like' has little to do with it. 'Need' is more the issue." In one surprisingly fluid movement he was off the sofa and headed toward the kitchen. "If you'll excuse me . . ."

Serena quirked an auburn brow at his grumpiness, smiled, then followed through on her original intention. When she returned to the kitchen with the paper in hand she paused on the threshold, this time with a note of trepidation. After all, she wasn't sure why Tom was still here. And nothing was worth another headache.

Reading her thoughts, he looked up from the coffee cup he'd found and filled. "How are you feeling?"

"Better."

"You slept well?"

"Yes."

"The pills helped?"

"Uh-huh. And . . . thank you." She looked down, unsure for a moment. "I'm not sure I could have done *anything* last night, let alone think about getting a refill on my prescription."

He shrugged, standing up to lean against the counter by the sink. "It was the least I could do." His eyes were unreadable.

Standing awkwardly by the door, Serena wasn't quite

sure what to do. It seemed to be a recurrent ailment when Tom was around. Finally her own need drove her toward the cabinet, a cup, and some coffee. "I'll repay you for whatever you spent on the pills," she offered without looking up.

"That won't be necessary."

"I'd prefer it."

"I said it won't be necessary." Draining his coffee, he helped himself to more.

But if his insistence was due to early morning testiness, Serena's was based on principle. Despite the fact that Tom had been the instigating factor behind her migraine, she wanted to owe him nothing. "If you'll just tell me what it came to I'll pay you. I don't like being indebted to anyone."

"Especially me?"

Her direct gaze held a challenge. "To *anyone*."

Tom studied her through less hazy eyes. "A legacy?"

"If you will."

"It's not necessary in this case, you know." He spoke more gently in response to her vehemence. "We're only talking about a couple of dollars. And since I was responsible for upsetting you it makes me feel better knowing that I've been able to aid in your recovery." His hazel eyes flicked quickly over her. "You do look better. Is the headache gone?"

"Pretty much. I'll take some aspirin before I leave for work. It'll be fine."

But he was skeptical. "Considering how sick you were last night, I would have thought you'd stay in bed, at least for the morning."

"I can't do that," she answered softly. "*Sweet Serenity* is *my* responsibility. If I don't get there to open it up it doesn't open."

"What about your help—that young girl I saw yesterday?"

"Monica comes in after school. I do have another woman who works mornings for me, but she has a family and can't get away in time to open the shop."

"What if you were *really* sick? Isn't there anyone who can take over for you?"

Serena answered him calmly. "Fortunately I've never *been* really sick, so the matter hasn't been put to the test." She looked away more pensively. "And even if I was unable to open for a day, the world would survive."

Her philosophical quip wafted into a small eternity of silence. Neither said a word. As the seconds ticked away she thought of the man who stood with her in her kitchen. Never would she have imagined him here. Indeed, one part of her wanted to be angry at him, to denounce him scathingly, to oust him from her apartment, from her life. Yet she somehow couldn't seem to translate the thought into action. Instead she simply stared at his rangy form as he lounged against the counter.

He stared back. His features were deceptively calm, masking the thoughts that swirled within. But the fire was there in his gaze, tempered, but refusing to be overlooked. By instinct Serena knew that she was his focal point. She grew suddenly and uncomfortably aware of the simple wrap robe she was wearing and tugged it more tightly around her.

"Would you—would you like some breakfast?" she finally stammered when she could stand the silence no longer.

His brow arched. "You'd really cook me breakfast?"

"Of course." She frowned, pausing. "You seem . . . surprised. I *do* know how to cook."

A snort of amusement preceded his explanation.

"That's not the point, Serena. You weren't exactly thrilled to see me yesterday. And I'm sure you never planned on having me spend the night in your apartment. I am, after all," he drawled facetiously, "the enemy. Am I not?"

Intentionally or otherwise, he had summarized her quandary. "I suppose so. . . ." But she was unable to hide her puzzlement.

Tom noted it and went on. "So it's natural for me to be surprised that you're offering me breakfast."

"Perhaps I feel that I owe it to you. For the pills and the care, and all," she rationalized off the top of her head.

"And all." He smiled sadly. "I really didn't do very much."

"You were here," she blurted out unthinkingly, then swallowed the revealing words that might have followed.

Their eyes met as they recalled the same moments. A hand on her back. Fingers stroking her hair. Arms supporting her. The solace of a human presence. Serena was overwhelmed by confusion, trying desperately to remember who he was, all the while feeling herself drawn to him.

"Look—" she began, only to be interrupted.

"Tom. The name's Tom."

"Tom." It fell softly, for the first time, from her tongue. "What would you like?"

Straightening, he took several steps toward her, then stopped. His gaze grew more sensual, falling to her lips in a visual caress that shimmered through her newly awakening body. Suspended in time and unreality, she couldn't move.

Tom opened his mouth to speak, then thought better of it and clamped his lips together, only to take a breath and begin again seconds later. "I'd like to clean up a little, if you don't mind. Then some eggs, toast, whatever, will do."

"Sunny-side up?"

"Over easy."

"Butter on the toast?"

"Jam, please."

"Orange juice?"

"Tomato will be fine."

"Wow! You really *did* go through my refrigerator last night. It's not everyone who keeps a full stock of tomato juice." She looked at him askance. "What kind of jam?"

Though he feigned timidity there was no hesitation in his response. "Wild plum? . . ."

She mocked disgust. "Hmph. You'd even ask for my prize possession."

"There's plenty in the jar—"

"You've already looked *inside?*"

"Well"—he threw his head back—"I *was* here all evening. I was hungry." He smiled.

Serena flew to the refrigerator, extracted the decorative jam jar, and analyzed its contents. "You didn't make a meal of wild plum jam, did you?"

"Actually," he drawled on his way toward the bathroom, "it was dessert—atop a couple of crackers."

"And the main course?" she called after him.

"That jar of herring in wine sauce did the trick."

"My herring in wine sauce?" she cried, aghast. She'd been saving it for a special occasion, some night when she felt the need for a treat. Now Tom had devoured it whole. "You didn't!" She followed him to the hall, only to find herself face to face with the bathroom door.

Slowly it opened. "I did." Smiling pleasantly, Tom stood before her, leisurely unbuttoning his shirt, then pulling it out of his pants. Serena momentarily forgot the point of her chase. The sight of him standing there, tall and straight, at her bathroom door, his face shadowed in sensuality, his chest firm and manly, drove prudence from her mind. He was the enemy, yet from the start he had embodied a fire that captivated her. In the restaurant yesterday it had been a fire from the past; here and now it held no memory. It was new and unsullied, a spark of wonder that flared from him with breathtaking intensity. Its heat consumed her antagonism even as it inspired cravings Serena would have refused to believe had she not felt the warmth that suddenly flowed through her veins.

Enthralled by his nearness and the effect of his virility, she felt a tug from deep within, willing her forward, urging her fingers to touch what he had so knowingly laid bare. Unsure of everything but the force of the attraction she tore her gaze from the matted richness sprawled beneath his shirt and sought his eyes.

In an instant he closed the short distance between them and stood no more than a breath away. Serena's breath caught in her throat. The push she had felt moments before from within was now a summons from Tom, a call from his manliness to her womanhood, a primal note she had never in her wildest dreams expected and against which she had no defense.

Tom lifted his hand to her face, gently threading his fingers through the damp tendrils of her auburn hair, softly caressing the creamy smoothness of her cheek, planting new images and fresh sensations with every stroke. On instinct she tipped her head to his palm, all the while unable to take her eyes from his. He seemed as mesmerized as she by the moment; all was irrelevant save the two of them. He searched the depths of her gaze as she explored his. And then, slowly and inevitably, he lowered his head by fractions of inches until his lips very lightly touched hers.

Serena was entranced, having lost all touch with reality under the onslaught of this man's sensuality. She felt his mouth as it sampled the soft curve of her lips, whispering a kiss at each corner. The musky scent of his skin drugged her further, sending her reeling into a world of sensation. Had his free arm not surrounded her and drawn her close against him she would have fallen. Her limbs trembled beneath the unexpected attack, and a sweet attack it was.

From the start her defenses had been down. She was a woman with a core of passion that had long lain dormant. Tom Reynolds had struck the match and now warmed her with it. His lips were firm, yet gentle, coaxing hers to open to his repeated forays. As for Serena, she was beyond rational decision. When her lips finally parted in longing there was nothing rational about it. She was driven by desire, strong and pure.

Tom welcomed her kiss with a joy transmitted by the tremor of his body when he clutched her more closely. He held her head to explore her lips, running the tip of his tongue along her teeth before plunging further. Serena could only quiver at the heady invasion and respond in kind, opening her mouth further in invitation, freeing her own tongue to exact passionate retribution.

Somewhere along the line her arms found their way beneath his shirt to his back. En route her fingers savored the firmness of his flesh, its rough man-texture so much in contrast to her own silken skin. She was delirious at the difference, gasping into his mouth at the feel of his body as he pressed her to him. He was warm, strong and hard, his friction kindling tiny fires at every touch point. And they were both still dressed. . . .

As though reading her thoughts and sensing their direction Tom drew back to frame her face with his hands. Slowly she opened her eyes.

"You'd only hate me more." He spoke thickly, his breath coming in uneven gasps that matched hers. It took Serena longer to recover from the trance of arousal he'd inspired. At her puzzled frown he explained, laboring as he struggled to contain his own primitive heat.

"You hate me for the past, Serena." His eyes circled her face, pausing to appreciate each feature. "But there's a flame between us that isn't just destructive. I only know I want you. I've wanted you since I first saw you yesterday afternoon, when I had no idea who you were, only sensed that you felt very strongly about me." His thumbs caressed the back of her neck, his fingers crept across her cheeks toward her mouth in helpless wandering. "You're very lovely," he rasped, dipping his head to touch her lips a final time. Serena was all too eager to return, if only for the instant, to that mindless state of sensual excitement. But it was too brief. And Tom was determined to remind her of who she was, of who *he* was.

He was more strongly in control when he spoke again. "I couldn't sleep last night, having held you in my arms like that. Do you know what it does to a man to find the woman he wants in bed, naked?"

For the first time it dawned on Serena that her action might easily have been interpreted as a lure. "I'm sorry." She shook her head. "I didn't realize. I always sleep like that and I was sure you would leave."

"I didn't. I couldn't."

She had no answer for him. What could she say? There was so much to be considered, so much to be worked out in her mind, before she could try to explain her emotions. To make matters worse, with each passing moment the enormity of what she'd craved just now crowded in on her. Tom tuned in to her dilemma.

"You see?" He set her back just out of reach, dropping his arms limply to his sides. "We could have made love. . . ." As his words trailed off he stared once more, long and hard, at her expression of slow-growing horror, then turned and shut himself in the bathroom again.

As though rooted to the hardwood floor Serena stood, stunned, appalled, confused. It was only the gentle reminder at her temple, the soft throbbing echo of yesterday's headache, that finally freed her from the spot and turned her toward the kitchen. When Tom emerged from the bathroom ten minutes later she had regained a semblance of composure. Nothing had been resolved; the situation hadn't changed. But for the moment she was unable to do anything about it, and making breakfast seemed the only plausible course of action.

"You showered and shaved?" She looked up in surprise at his well-groomed visage as he entered.

Tom grinned. "I hope you don't mind, I helped myself to your things. There's nothing worse than feeling grubby."

"You had enough hot water?" She thought of the indecently long shower she'd taken not terribly long ago.

"*Hot* water wasn't what I wanted. Except for the shave. And the last of the shower. *After* the cold water had done its thing." The mischief in his eye did its thing, stirring Serena afresh. "But, yes, I had enough hot water for my needs. Thank you."

Serena shrugged, then turned silently to put the eggs and toast on a plate, which she handed to him. Then she reached for the coffee. She kept her eyes averted, refusing to let his physical appeal blow her mind again. It was only after she'd slid onto the chair opposite his that she dared to look at him again.

"Mmmm, these eggs are just right," he said, ignoring the tension between them.

"You really didn't remember me, did you?" Serena refused to evade the issue.

"Any salt?"

"Tom . . ."

"The salt?"

She sighed in defeat and reached for the shaker. She watched him sprinkle the salt on his eggs, then start eating again. After several mouthfuls he looked up in surprise.

"You're not eating?" he asked innocently.

"I have toast," she said with a glance to her plate, "and coffee. That's all I ever have."

"Not healthy."

"Neither is salt."

"Touché." He returned to the serious business of eating, undaunted by her claim.

"I didn't even call your bluff." She took a different tack, shaking her head in self-disgust. "You were just fishing for information and I gave it to you."

"You were upset. I'm sure that you're usually much sharper."

"Oh? Now why would you be so sure?" she prodded.

"I looked at you. Your shop. Your apartment. Your life. You must be a very efficient—and sharp—lady to manage everything on your own."

"A person does certain things because she has no other choice."

"You didn't have to open a shop of your own. You could have chosen to go through life without that responsibility."

She held his gaze more confidently. "*Sweet Serenity* means a lot to me. I need it."

"And you've made a success of it, which makes my point. If you had nothing on the ball"—he tapped his head—"the shop would have folded long ago."

Serena nibbled absently on her toast. "Tom, why *did* you come to the store yesterday? If you honestly didn't make the connection between the past and me, why did you come?"

"I told you that yesterday. You intrigued me. I wanted to find out who you were."

"And now that you know," she said uneasily, "what do you intend to . . . to do with that information?"

"With what information?" He seemed genuinely puzzled.

"The Strickland connection."

He looked at her as though she were warped. "Absolutely nothing! Is there something I *should* be doing with it?" When Serena didn't reply but merely looked away, he put down his fork. "Serena, that's ancient history. It's a closed book. You seem to be the only one aware of any 'Strickland connection.'"

Her gaze shot back to his. "Not exactly."

"What do you mean?"

"I mean," she spoke quietly, tempering the hurt that still lingered, "that some information has a way of finding itself in the wrong people's hands. It's happened before and it could happen again."

"Explain." He rested his chin in the crook between his thumb and forefinger, stroking his jaw thoughtfully.

Suddenly realizing that she had opened up much more than she'd wanted to, she demurred. "Never mind; you were right. It's past history."

But Tom wouldn't let her off the hook. "Finish what you've begun, Serena. What happened?"

Strangely, Tom was the first person to know enough about her past for her to speak freely about the pain of it. Even more strangely, she heard herself telling him about Michael Lowry.

"When I was a senior in high school—I was living with an aunt and uncle in New York at the time—I became involved with a fellow." Her voice lowered with her eyes. "He was in college. Older. More worldly. From a prominent family."

"That mattered to you?"

"No! I couldn't have cared less! But it mattered to *him*.

He let me know in no uncertain terms just how prominent his family was."

"What happened?"

She hesitated, feeling awkward. It was only the compassion on Tom's face that gave her the courage to continue. "As I said, we became involved. It went on for
several months. I had been accepted at Duke University,
but I wasn't sure I wanted to leave him. So . . . I confronted him about it."

"You wanted him to marry you?"

"No, not really. I just wanted him to give me some indication of his feelings. If he had felt that we might marry
one day I would have gone to school in New York."

"And . . . ?"

Again she paused, frowning at her clenched hands,
swallowing convulsively. This time it was the sight of
Tom's hand and its warmth enveloping hers that buoyed
her. "He made it very clear that he could . . . *never* marry
me. After all," she mimicked Michael's long-ago statement of what he saw as the obvious, "what with my family history, his parents would never have even considered
the match."

Tom's body stiffened as his hand tightened over hers.
"He was using you all that time?"

"No, I can't really say that." Her gaze was sad but
sincere. "We both enjoyed the relationship. He never
made any promises. It was me—me who needed the
reassurance—me who needed the . . ."

". . . love?"

Her soft-whispered "perhaps" was another beginning.
"It had been a very lonely time for me. Once I left California I needed someone to take the place of my family.
Oh, I had my aunt and uncle, but there was something
strange about their attitude toward me. I've never been
able to figure them out—they seemed torn between duty

and conscience. They were warm and caring enough, but I can't go so far as to say that they loved me." She shrugged off that particular hurt. "At any rate, Michael filled a need. I thought he loved me. I guess I was simply imagining much more than there was."

For a time there was silence. Tom stood to pour them each more coffee, put the pot back on its warmer, walked to the window, then returned to where Serena sat. "That has to be over ten years ago. Were there any other incidents?"

Serena's laugh held a wealth of bitterness. "You can be sure I never put myself in that position again."

"You haven't been with a man since?"

She ignored the implication. "I haven't looked for anything more than an evening's fun."

"A *night*'s fun?"

"An evening's fun." She sighed. "No, Tom, I sleep alone. That avoids a lot of pain."

"It also rules out fulfillment."

Threatened anew, she looked away. "I fill my life with . . . other things."

"Is that why you responded to me the way you did a little while ago?"

"Tom . . ." she protested.

"No, Serena, don't stop me. You opened up to me as a very passionate woman. Can you really keep all that stopped up inside?"

"I don't."

"But you just implied . . ."

"No, I don't sleep around. But I don't suffer from pent-up frustration, either. Much as you men would like to believe that every single woman could have all her problems cured by a man, it just isn't so."

"I should hope not." He sipped his coffee slowly, absently. "But the passion's there, Serena. In you. Maybe not for just any man. But it's there for me."

"No," she lied, unwilling to face that fact herself.

Tom didn't push her on it. "Let me ask you something." He hesitated for a moment to gather his thoughts. "Why have you told me all this—about that guy in New York and all?"

Lashing out in self-defense, Serena grew more tense. "Perhaps I wanted you to know some of what I went through as a result of what you did."

"So we're back to that?"

"Always! When I see your face," she lied again, "I see the man who was responsible for all the torment my family suffered. Oh, I know it was my father who committed the crime. You don't have to remind me of that. But you were the one who exposed him so cruelly. You were the one who put him on the front page. You were the one who publicized his error. You were the one who magnified the humiliation for *all* of us!" In her anguish she bolted from the chair and stormed into her bedroom, slamming the door behind her much as she had done last night, though this time not seeking darkness. On the contrary, it was the light she sought. Reality. Awareness. It was all too easy to forget what Tom Reynolds had done to her family. In his arms it was all too easy to forget everything.

"Serena?"

Whirling around, she found him in her room, not an arm's length away. "Please, Tom. Enough's been said. I've got to get dressed and get to the shop. Please leave."

"All right, Serena. I don't want to upset you. Believe me, it gave me no pleasure to see what I'd done to you last night. But I want you to know that I'm not giving up." Suddenly his quiet air took on an edge.

Her eyes widened fearfully. "What are you talking about?"

"You and me. I didn't spend the whole of last night on

your sofa just to wake up this morning, say good-bye, and walk out of your life."

"You have to."

"I don't have to do anything. And"—his gaze narrowed—"I don't think you really want me to vanish."

"Yes I do!"

"Do you?" He tipped his head in skepticism. "Can you deny what happened before? Wouldn't you like to follow it through, to see where it will lead?"

"No!" she whispered on the fragment of a breath.

His hands came down firmly on her shoulders, holding her still when she might have run from him. "Listen to me, Serena." He spoke more softly. "I've been burned, too. My life hasn't been the song and dance you'd like to believe. I've had my share of heartache. And, to be perfectly honest, I don't know what the hell I'm doing telling all this to you. But I spent last night fighting the frustration of wanting you and not knowing why. And if there's one thing I've learned in my business it's that when a hot tip comes in I owe it to myself to follow it. I'm going to follow this one, Serena. It may be a dead end. But somewhere in my gut I have a feeling . . ."

"No!" she murmured in a half-cry, slowly shaking her head.

"Yes. I'll see it through."

Serena tried to pull away from him, but his grip merely tightened. "No . . . no . . ." He was close and alluring; the battle was now within herself.

"Serena," he moaned with an agony that stilled her. Again she felt herself falling under his spell. "Serena . . ."

He caught her lips quickly, as though afraid she'd fight. But the devil within her had taken temporary advantage, stirring up her need to the exclusion of reason. His clean scent pervaded her being; his body offered its protection;

his lips consumed hers with a hunger that surmounted the purely physical. Serena fought to stay above the tide of passion, but its force quickly overpowered her and, with a soft cry from the back of her throat, she yielded to its drive and was lost.

Or was she? Was this surrender, or victory? Defeat, or discovery? Once more Tom's seductive prowess flooded her with delight, drowning any resistance she might have intended to make. Was she weak in capitulation, or strong in the height of the passion he evoked so easily? It was raw pleasure she felt at his touch, and she thrilled to it.

Eager to explore the glory of her womanhood, she wound her arms over his shoulders and around his neck, thrusting her fingers through the fullness of his hair as she urged him closer. Tom sensed the change and his fierceness eased, calming to a more seductive exploration of her mouth, her eyes, her cheeks. His tongue found her ear and traced its intricacies, sending ripples of excitement from one cell to the other.

Serena glowed, blooming beneath the nourishment of his affection. She reveled in his care, savored his appreciation, all the while seeking more and more from him. Her lips explored the rougher texture of his skin, kissing, nipping, tasting his unique flavor while her hands discovered his manly shape.

The sounds of the morning were gentle ones, soft sighs and breathy moans of delight. When Tom swung around and sat on the edge of her bed she was drawn to him still, held between the strength of his thighs with her arms draped over his shoulders.

"Mmm, Serena," he rasped, trailing the fire of his tongue from her ear to her neck and into the hollow of her throat. She pressed the flush of her cheek against his hair, holding him against her, wanting this joy to continue. Long ago, in another's arms, she had known the pleasures of love, but there was something different now. There was maturity behind it all, a finer realization of the pinnacle of ecstasy to be shared between a man and a woman. Suddenly she wanted to see it through. Suddenly she needed to assuage the taut yearning at her core.

"Yes, Tom," she whispered in a haze of passion as she arched instinctively toward him. She framed his face and tipped it up, lowering her own to kiss him with the heat of the fire that flamed from within. As his mouth covered hers his fingers found the tie to her robe, easily releasing it, pushing the soft fabric aside, trembling as he spanned the flesh of her waist then moved upward.

"Ahhh," Serena whimpered, acutely aware of the throbbing knot inside. "Oh, Tom . . ."

Her breasts swelled beneath his touch, filling the hand that covered the delicate lace of her bra. The finger that slid within had the gentle roughness of a cat's tongue, driving her to distraction as it worked its way to a pebbled crest tipped with rose. Again she called his name, wanting him, needing him, aching for more than the demands of the morning would allow.

Her impassioned trance was so thick that she wasn't aware of his tension until his hoarse-muttered "Damn it" tore through her. "Damn it," he growled a second time, more vehemently now and with the intent of distracting himself from the love-play that was nearly out of hand.

Gasping for breath, Serena allowed herself to be pushed away. "Tom?"

"Damn it! I don't want this!" he fairly screamed. *"I won't do this!"*

His face was a sudden mask of anger, terrifying Serena. "What is it?" she asked, frantic. But he wouldn't say anything more. Instead he pushed himself from the bed, headed for the door and disappeared toward the living room, leaving her a shaky melange of desire, frustration, and outright perplexity. "Tom?" she called a final time, but quietly, because something held her back. When she finally dared to venture from her room and searched the apartment he was gone.

Dazed, she returned to her room and sank into her Bentwood rocker, moving absently back and forth to the rhythm of defeat. As it slowly circled the room her eye fell on the clothes she'd discarded so carelessly last night, the bed still mussed from her drugged sleep, the family photo atop her dresser. Despite what he had done to her in the past, and whatever his motives for leaving had been just now, Serena was grateful to Tom for his exit. He'd been only partly right earlier, she mused sadly. For not only would she have hated him had he taken her, as she had all but begged him to do, she would have hated herself forever. And *that* would have been, by far, the worst.

As it was Tom could—and would, if his parting words meant what she thought they had—disappear from her life for good. And she had somehow to cope with the self-disgust she felt at having totally surrendered to the charm of him, her sworn enemy. But had the farce been seen through—*that* would have been tragic.

With an initial stop in the bathroom for the aspirin she had promised herself earlier Serena forced all thoughts of Tom from her mind as she cleaned the apartment, dressed, and headed for the shop. She opened on time, with no one to know what had happened during those nighttime hours. Only Serena knew. Only Serena remembered . . . against her wishes. Only Serena trembled in hindsight. And only Serena understood when, shortly after noon, the florist delivered a small bouquet of delicate baby roses, a spray of pert pink petals in a bed of bright greenery. The brilliant white of its message card reached out to her; driven by an emotion she refused to analyze she reached for it almost with eagerness.

"To sweet Serena," she read. *"Perhaps one day you'll forgive me. Tom."*

The script was firm and bold, much as the man behind it. Was this a farewell he'd sent? she wondered through the afternoon as her gaze brushed the fragrant bouquet time and time again. If so, it was surely for the best. She had her life, her friends, and *Sweet Serenity.* Tom had his papers and the power they gave him. Their lives ran in opposite directions, their backgrounds even more so. She liked her eggs sunny-side up; he preferred his over easy.

She frowned. But what about wild plum jam? And herring in wine sauce? And the heat of passion unleashed?

Then, that very evening, she learned of another shared love when she arrived at the racquetball club to find none other than Thomas Harrison Reynolds, devastatingly masculine in shorts and a jersey, ready to serve his partner from the far end of Court One.

4

To Serena's chagrin she and Cynthia were slotted for Court Five, directly across the way and within clear sight of the match just beginning on Court One.

"Pretty clever." Cynthia smiled, coming from behind to startle her from her trance. "Did you arrange to meet here? Have plans for dinner later?"

"No!" Serena exclaimed. "I had no idea he'd be here."

"You two did work things out though, didn't you?"

"Uh . . . not exactly."

Serena's vagueness captured her friend's curiosity. "What does that mean, 'not exactly'? This is very mysterious. I love it!"

"Don't." Serena frowned. "There's nothing mysterious about it. Actually, there's nothing about it at all."

"You mean that you haven't made your play yet?"

"I mean that I don't intend to make a play."

"Serena! I'm crushed. How can you let such a prime sample of masculinity slip right through your fingers?"

"Very easily."

Serena let it go at that as the two women stood watching the progress on Tom's court. She noticed that he was a skilled player. In fact, she would give her right hand to play with him.

"Who is he, anyway?" Cynthia broke into her thoughts once more.

"His name is Tom Reynolds."

"Tom Reynolds." The redhead tapped her lips with the lacquered tip of one tapered fingernail. "Tom Reynolds . . . where have I heard that name before?"

Serena saw no point in secrecy. After all, Tom's identity was public information. "He's the new owner of the *Bulletin*."

"You're kidding! *That* owns the newspaper?"

"*That* does."

"And you'd blow a chance to be with him?"

"I'm not blowing anything, Cynthia," Serena calmed her friend. "We just have our differences."

"Racquetball isn't one of them."

"Umm."

"Did you know he played here?"

"I didn't know he played, period. That should tell you something about our relationship."

"I'm all ears." Her friend smiled coaxingly.

But Serena had never been one to confide deeply in others, particularly about such personal matters. "I'll bet." She smiled back, but shut her mouth firmly by way of delivering her message. She never knew whether Cynthia received it, for the other woman's attention was glued to the action opposite them.

"He's good," Cynthia murmured with a touch of awe.

A deep voice responded, drawing both women's attention momentarily away from the game. "He *should* be! He was the fifth ranked player in the country a while back. He was instrumental in establishing racquetball as a going sport."

Cynthia was the first to recover. "And how do you know so much about him, Willie?"

"I work here, doll. He's been in several times a week

for the past month. Just moved to the area. I'd say we're pretty lucky. Could be that he'll spice things up around here!"

Serena's laugh erupted spontaneously and held its share of sarcasm. "Could be," she echoed tartly. "He's a born agitator." The instant she spoke she caught her breath. That was what André had said just yesterday, when they had seen Tom in the restaurant, when neither of them had known who he was. Sixteen years ago he had earned the label. Did it still apply? What he had done to her yesterday and that morning added up to a more private form of agitation. What *was* he like as a person?

"He's good!" Cynthia repeated her earlier exclamation, to be echoed by Willie once again.

"I'll say! He doesn't compete anymore, but he sure could beat the pants—pardon me, ladies—off anybody here!"

At that point, bidden by some unknown force, Tom looked up and focused on them. Cynthia nudged Serena, whose pulse tripped dangerously even without the reminder that Tom had seen her. When he finally turned back to play, all eyes were on him. His opponent served, he returned a ceiling ball; his opponent slammed a kill shot to the corner—and Tom missed.

Serena turned on her heel, having seen enough. The image was all too fresh in her mind—long, muscled arms and legs, a natural grace amid the speed of the game, an undeniable mastery of the sport itself—and did even less for her concentration than her presence had done for Tom's. Had it not been for his obvious skill and the information Willie had freely offered, she might have wondered if his presence was something short of coincidence. But he was a pro—and he had been as stunned to see her as she was to see him.

Serena felt no satisfaction at having distracted Tom. When Cynthia teased her, she came to his defense.

"Wow! You sure shake *him* up!"

"Not quite, Cyn. He was just surprised, that's all. Willie was right; I'm sure he'll beat the pants off that guy!"

She didn't linger to watch the outcome of the game, but dragged her friend toward their own court. Her play was far below par, though. And Cynthia noted that, as well, commenting on it when the hour was up.

"Boy, you two better get it together or you'll both be kicked out of the club," she teased. "Better still, we'll put you on a court together and you can stand there looking at each other. If nobody serves the ball, nobody misses."

"Cynthia, have pity on me," Serena gasped, collapsing on the sidelines while the redhead collected her things.

"He's gone, at any rate."

"Oh?"

"As if you didn't know."

Serena *did* know. She knew at precisely what point he had finished, precisely how long he had followed the activity on Court Five, and precisely which men he'd spoken to as he headed for the locker room. It was no wonder her own game was shot, she'd barely been aware of what she was doing!

Moments later the two women headed for their own locker room. "Listen, Serena, if you're not interested in him, I'll be glad—"

"Thanks, but I'll let you know," Serena interrupted, not sure what she was talking about, though her words sounded full of confidence. In fact, she was sure of nothing, except the fact that she could *not* turn Cynthia loose on Tom. Not that she had any claim on him herself, or *wished* to have any, nor that *he* had serious designs on her, but she was simply not ready to make any definitive judgment where Tom Reynolds was concerned. There was still that spark he lit in her, a spark no other man in recent years had ignited. Granted, she'd let no man get as

close as Michael Lowry had been—for the very reason
for which he'd scorned her. But Tom knew about that
past; he'd said it didn't matter. Could she ever see eye to
eye with him on that score?

As the days passed Serena wondered often about Tom.
He was a link to her past, a potentially devastating one,
yet she didn't feel threatened as she had at first. She
trusted him in some strange way, though the "why" of it
eluded her. Much as she felt guilty at the aggressive behavior she'd shown that morning in her apartment, she
couldn't squelch the curiosity she felt—any more than
she could the remembered tingle that came to her often in
the night when her thoughts returned with agonizing pre-
cision to the body that went with the man.

But life went on. April saw more snow, as she'd expected.
It also saw continued prosperity for *Sweet Serenity*. It saw
Serena at her gourmet cooking class every Tuesday night
and at the racquetball club with Cynthia every Thursday
night. It saw her out on the weekends with Gregory Wolff,
a lawyer she dated occasionally, and with Rodney Hen-
dricks, a psychology professor from the university. Both
men knew better than to expect commitment from Serena; with each, she kept her private world off limits. Only
Tom had penetrated that world—and there was neither
sight nor sound of him.

The bouquet he'd sent had long since died, its small
basket now a poignant fixture on her dresser, holding the
decorative combs and hair clips she wore for the occasional added touch of sophistication. It was an exquisite
tortoiseshell fan of a comb that she fished out to wear on
the evening of André's party. Pulling her curls straight
back into a severe knot, she replayed in her mind the discussion she'd had with André just two days before.

"I don't know," she had hedged. "You know how I hate parties, André."

"But this is *my* party, Serena." His voice had been firm over the phone. "It won't be anything all that big—just a few of my friends. You already know some of them. And there will be several aldermen here. Since you're so bullish on Minneapolis you'll love talking with them."

"I'm sure it will be lovely, André, but I really think I ought to pass it up."

He'd been persistent. "Nonsense. I haven't seen you since I returned from the coast. The party will be quiet and interesting. I'll pick you up myself—say about eight?"

Serena took a stab at an alternative. "Listen, I have an even better idea. I've been taking this gourmet cooking course. Why don't you come over and let me practice the art on you one evening after work next week?"

"Uh-uh, you can't get out of this one so easily. In the first place, between that course and your racquetball and the other gents who follow you around, not to mention my own schedule, we'd never be able to agree on a night. In the second place, an evening alone with you might be more than my wounded heart can take—"

"André," she chided, "so melodramatic . . ."

"Could it be," he struck a hopeful, though teasing, note "that you've changed your mind about *us?* Has absence made the heart grow fonder?"

She sighed at his resort to cliché, smiling patiently. "No, André."

"Then humor me and come to my party," he pressed. "As a friend? Please?"

Serena had had no choice. She didn't want to hurt André; she was, after all, fond of him. And then there was the matter of *Sweet Serenity*. She'd been hesitant about raising the issue of expansion again. If she yielded on the party André might be more approachable.

It was nonetheless with mixed feelings that she found herself dressed in a green silk tunic and pants, with high-heeled gold sandals on her feet, a ghost of lavender on her lids, a touch of mascara on her lashes and a blush of pink on her cheeks. Small pearl buttons graced her ears, a delicate drop to match lay softly on her throat. She was the image of sophistication, with only the shadow of her freckles to betray the lighter spirit within.

The buzzer rang promptly at eight. Within minutes she was downstairs in the lobby greeting her host, sliding into his car, being driven to his spacious home in Kenwood, a section outside downtown Minneapolis. The house was a legacy of the last of his marriage, his ex-wife having happily deserted him to return to New York.

As Serena had often noticed, André's lifestyle was one of lavish consumption. With three ex-wives and a mansion to support, not to mention natty clothes, a late-model sports car and the traveling style of a jet-setter, his financial obligations must have been staggering. Since he never spoke of hardship, she assumed that his work supported him well. *Very well*, she amended the judgment, admiring the artful landscaping, well-lit by floodlights, that surrounded the circular drive leading to his door. *Astoundingly well*, she modified it further, surrendering her light wrap to the uniformed man on duty at the door, taking a glass of champagne from the tray borne by another, and sampling the array of hors d'oeuvres offered to her by a third.

André beamed by her side as he motioned that he wanted to introduce her to several guests whose arrival had preceded theirs. Serena held him back for a minute, putting her hand gently on the sleeve of his black evening jacket.

"I thought you said this was a *small* party," she accused him in a chiding whisper. "You've got at least four or five people in to help here."

André shrugged, smiling without guilt at the deception. "It's really nothing, Serena. Don't worry about it. Clients. Friends. Politicians. Relax, you'll have a good time. Oh, there's Ted Franck from the brokerage firm. Come on, he's anxious to meet you."

Uncomfortably aware that, having arrived on André's arm, she would be considered "with" him, Serena acquiesced for the moment, graciously crossing the room beside him, being her most poised and charming self through the introductions and subsequent conversation. In actuality, it wasn't as bad as she had anticipated. As the guests arrived and the room grew more crowded there was less and less of an opportunity for intimate discussion with anyone. And *that* pleased Serena to no end. She strove to keep a low profile, which was why she generally avoided parties. Constantly shuttling from one cluster to the next, she avoided any involvment to speak of—until a firm hand took her elbow just after André had excused himself to attend to business and guided her toward a corner of the large living room.

"How are you, Serena?"

Her head snapped around in instant recognition of the voice. Stunned, she could only stare for several seconds. When she finally spoke she was shakier than she had been all evening. "Tom! What are you doing here?"

"The same thing you are, no doubt." He grinned, spreading a quick fire through her.

"I'm simply obliging André," she went out of her way to explain. "He begged me to come. It seemed to mean so much to him. Now I find that not only are there at least a hundred people here—when he promised me something quiet—but he's disappeared to talk politics with the men."

She frowned, still unable to assimilate Tom's presence. "What's *your* excuse? I didn't know that you and André knew each other."

"We don't." Tom looked uneasily around the room. "I was brought by a mutual friend of ours—in fact, I believe he's closeted with her right now."

Serena shook her head. "Uh-uh. He's discussing some earthshaking matter with the aldermen. There are several here tonight."

His dark head lowered as he stifled a smile. "He didn't tell you then, the sly fox. Your friend André is with the aldermen, all right. One of them, though, is a *she*."

"Ahh."

"You're not angry?"

"At losing André? Not in the least. He's a friend, nothing more." Her lips thinned in mock chagrin. "But I *am* slightly annoyed at having to put up with this"—she gestured widely toward the crowd milling about the room—"all night."

"Come on." His hand was gentle at the back of her waist. "Let's find a quieter spot."

Had it not been for her irritation at being misled by André, Serena might have thought twice about going anywhere with Tom. After all, the last time she had seen him had been at the racquetball club over a month ago, when they had exchanged nothing more than potent stares. And since then they had exchanged absolutely nothing. Going back a step further, she clearly recalled the morning she had all but thrown herself at him in her apartment. What must he think of her? Then, of course, there was the past. . . .

After ushering her into a small den Tom pulled two easy chairs around to face each other. Serena sank willingly into one, slipping out of her shoes impulsively and curling her legs up under her.

"Comfortable?" he mocked with a smile.

She blushed, aware that her pose wasn't at all in keeping with her sophisticated appearance. "Uh-huh. Finally. My shoes were killing me."

"Famous last words." His eyes caught hers and held them with an intensity that rendered talk superfluous. It seemed forever that they looked at one another, lost in memories, neither wishing to break the spell. To Serena's surprise her thoughts were all positive. Once again she had banished Tom's treachery from mind, aware only of the strength she found so appealing.

"You aren't terribly surprised to find me here," she observed when curiosity finally propelled her on.

Tom smiled in understanding. "I had this funny feeling when Ann mentioned André's name that he was your friend. I don't suppose there are too many investment counselors named André in this area."

"No," she answered softly, admiring the dashing appearance Tom made in his dark European-cut suit. André might have worn the same cut, but it was Tom who carried it off with style, holding himself with just the right air to express self-confidence, rather than arrogance.

"Are you his date?"

Serena grimaced. "He picked me up and brought me here. But I'm certainly not his 'date,' at least not in my mind. Anyway, look where his attentiveness has left me—uh, excuse me, that sounded all wrong." Her cheeks burned. "I meant he deserted me quickly enough, and he's really more interested—"

"I know what you mean, Serena. Believe me, I'm not at all offended. Actually, this couldn't have worked out better," he declared smugly.

Not knowing what to say, Serena looked down awkwardly. The rebuff Tom had dealt her that last morning in her apartment was fresh enough to add to her confusion.

Even the recollection of the flowers he had sent was small solace for that embarrassment.

"You look beautiful tonight," he began. The gentleness of his voice added to her consternation. "Green becomes you. It picks up the color of your eyes."

"They're hazel." She shrugged. "Nothing spectacular."

"Oh, they're spectacular enough when they get going. Those sparks were the first thing I noticed about you."

The feeling was mutual, but she chose not to enlighten him on that score. Instead she frowned, concentrating on the soft folds of her tunic across her thighs. "You have a knack for inspiring that type of thing."

"Do I still upset you as much?"

"No," she answered half-honestly. "It was the initial shock of seeing you and the memories it dredged up that were so bad. At least I've gotten over the shock." She was certainly not about to mention the new wave of feelings he'd created, many of which were as disturbing in their way as the old, painful memories.

Tom leaned forward to rest his elbows on his knees. He studied her self-consciousness, looked down at his own hands, then spoke his thoughts aloud. "You're a puzzle to me, Serena." That, too, was a mutual sentiment. "On the one hand, you are what you do. You couldn't have chosen a better name. *Sweet Serenity*. It's you." Unsure, she looked up, to be met by a beckoning warmth. "You *are* sweet—I saw you in action in your shop. You genuinely want to please, and you do. Those customers obviously love you as much as your candy. I honestly don't think you'd hurt a soul, unless you were pushed to an absolute extreme."

"I enjoy pleasing people. Perhaps that's why I enjoy *Sweet Serenity* the way I do. But what is it that puzzles you?" she asked.

He amended his choice of word. "Perhaps 'puzzle' is

the wrong word. 'Intrigue' may be better." At her baffled look he explained. "It's the part about serenity that's only half true. At the shop, in public places—like that restaurant, this party—you *are* serene. Perhaps it's that you're always serene on the surface—smooth, calm, even—"

"How can you say that, Tom?" she interrupted. "*You've* seen me in a fury. *You've* seen me at my worst. That night, the next morning . . ." Moaning, she looked away. "I'm not particularly proud of the way I acted."

"Don't hold *that* against yourself. We all have our bad moments. And yours wasn't even all that bad, compared to some."

If he was trying to tell her something she was too enveloped in remorse to hear. "To *me* it was terrible! I've never thrown myself at a man before."

"It wasn't one-sided, Serena," he chided. Again, she barely heard.

"It was horrible! I don't *do* that!"

His whispered "I know" was strangely soothing. She let the silent magic work away some of her tension, aware of the hum of talk from the other room, the strong presence of Tom leaning close to her. When he took her hand in his she didn't pull away. His grip was filled with a reassurance she needed.

"You've made my point beautifully, Serena. You're a very controlled woman, very calm and, yes, serene. But you keep everything bottled up inside. My appearance shocked you enough to punch a tiny hole in that veneer, but I also stirred up enough anger in you to give you a whopper of a headache." He paused, his thumb passing across the back of her hand. "Have you had another since?"

"I haven't seen you since," she quipped in retaliation.

His answering look held a determination she hadn't expected. "Well, you *will* be seeing me and I won't have you getting constant migraines. I guess I'll have to teach you to scream and yell rather than lock that tension inside when we're together."

"You must be my self-appointed analyst." Still awkward, she put a hand up out of habit to smooth back her hair.

"You look fine." He caught her at it. "By the way, you looked pretty good on the court."

"So did you. Is that how you let off steam? You were playing pretty hard."

"When I wasn't distracted."

"Sorry about that." She smiled shyly. "We didn't mean to stand there staring but, well, I didn't expect to see you there and then Willie explained that you're a pro, and we amateurs can always use a few pointers."

The light in his eyes was suddenly hotter. "For you, Serena, any time."

Serena stifled the gasp his innate sensuality evoked. Her eyes were bright, held tightly by his. As always, he had that power; now he used it to its fullest. She wanted to protest, but no sound came out. Her mind cried out against the time, the place, the man, but her body stirred toward him as he reached to touch her face.

"I missed you," he whispered, tracing a path of heat from one to the other of her features. "I wanted to call."

"Why didn't you?" she startled herself by asking.

"I didn't want to hurt you. I still don't."

Her own voice was no more than a raw murmur. "Then, why are you here, doing this to me?"

"I'm only touching your face. That's all. It's so smooth and soft and open. . . ."

"Oh, Tom," she cried in soft desperation, "you do so much more to me. Can't you see that?"

He gazed at her with something akin to pain in the depths of his eyes. "Let me kiss you."

"No, don't. . . ."

His head moved closer—or was hers moving to meet it in denial of her protest? "Just once, Serena." His husky murmur warmed her lips, teasing them open with a tenderness that spread excitement through her body. She wanted to resist, but her need for him was greater. Her sensual sigh told him all he wanted to know.

His lips touched hers lightly, caressing them gently, responding to her with controlled fervor. As though fearful of frightening her off, he held the reins of emotion tightly, savoring the sweet opening she offered. He kissed her, then pulled back. Then kissed her again, and pulled back again. Far from using each withdrawal to muster her protests, Serena found herself craving more.

"You taste so good, Serena," he moaned, shifting lithely to perch on the arm of her chair.

She tipped her head back as his lips descended again, welcoming his kiss with the warmth of her mouth and the reciprocal play of her tongue against his. She felt pleasure at the depths she offered him and took pleasure in the feel of his thorough exploration. His fingers splayed across her neck, inching their way toward her throat. Driven by the rippling excitement surging wildly through her, she arched closer. Tom sensed her rising desire and trembled under the strain of restraint. His thumb propped her chin up; his fingertips inched down beneath the silk of her collar, pointing heatedly toward her breast yet unable to move further.

"Let's get out of here," he rasped hoarsely, tearing his lips away to breathe heavily against her temple.

"I can't leave," she gasped, unaware that she clutched his wrist tightly. "André will be looking for me—"

"To hell with André!"

"Tom, he brought me here."

"And I brought Ann. But the two of them are busy

enough discussing something. . . ." His words trailed into unexpected silence, arousing Serena's curiosity.

She leaned back in the chair and let her hand fall to her lap. "Who is Ann, anyway?"

"No one important." Gradually his breathing grew steadier.

"She's an alderwoman. She *has* to be someone."

"Not to me."

"You brought her," she pointed out softly.

Tom was momentarily distracted, straightening, standing, walking slowly to the window. His reflection showed a scowl, but when he turned he was under control. "She's an acquaintance. She needed an escort."

Moving quickly, Tom leaned over Serena, his arms on either arm of her chair. "Come on, honey. Let's go somewhere."

"No, I can't."

"To talk?"

"Tom, I can't hurt André like that."

He threw up his hands in frustration. "Sweet Serena! What did I tell you? Always thinking of others. Well, what about *me?*"

The two stared at each other silently, then, with a sigh, Tom lifted a hand to massage his neck, thrust the other in his pants pocket for safekeeping, glared darkly, then stalked from the den to become lost in the crowd.

Serena sat without moving, recalling his final words. "What about *me?*" he had asked, as if he were a child who feared he'd been cheated of some treasure. Was this merely the privileged aristocrat pouting at being thwarted, or was it possible that she'd struck a very private and raw note in Tom? There had been nothing put on about his plea; it had seemed to come from the heart. What should she make of it?

"There you are, Serena. I've been looking all over for

you." André advanced with a sure step, his conference evidently finished and matters settled to his satisfaction. "Come on out. There's someone I want you to meet."

She felt no surprise when he led her to a group dominated by a petite, dark-haired firebrand of a woman. Mercifully, Tom was nowhere in sight. "André"—the woman turned at their approach—"this has to be Serena." A cool hand was perfunctorily extended. Serena met it with a matching sense of duty, no more, as André completed the introduction.

"Serena Strickland . . . Ann Carruthers. Ann is one of our esteemed alderpersons, Serena. We're in fine company tonight."

Considering the fact that her mind was on a missing person, Serena managed a cordial exchange that gave proof once more of Tom's insightful analysis. She was sweet and serene, all the while troubled within by the question he had posed. But there were other questions, too, and they nagged at her mercilessly. Where was he now? What was it he wanted? And why did it all matter so much to her, anyway?

It was a definite relief when, after several moments of small talk, Ann was approached and whisked off by another of the guests. Unfortunately, though, André hung on to Serena to guide her through the ever-revolving sea of faces whose names flew past her within seconds of their introduction. Neither Serena's mind nor her heart were on the party.

By pure accident André singled out Tom for attention. "Excuse me," he spoke more formally than usual and with an edge Serena couldn't quite identify. "I don't believe we've met. I'm André Phillips."

To Serena's dismay Tom straightened from the doorjamb against which he'd been leaning, shifted his drink, and met André's outstretched hand. "Tom Reynolds here."

André hesitated for one awkward moment. "Tom Reynolds of the *Bulletin?*"

"The same."

"Then I'm certainly pleased to meet you. Ann did say something about dragging you here." What was intended as humor missed its mark, but neither man seemed to notice.

Serena stood suffering quietly beside André, her eyes glued to Tom's face. She felt the wariness that verged on hostility between the two men and couldn't begin to understand it. André had been the perfect host all evening and Serena knew how adept he was at hiding his feelings, yet here was a dagger nearly unsheathed. Was André interested in Ann? Was *Tom?* As though hearing her silent mention of his name Tom's gaze slid to her face, softening instantly and setting a wholly new set of vibrations astir in the air.

André reacted quickly, again out of habit. "I'm sorry. Serena Strickland . . . Tom Reynolds." He paused, studying each in turn. "But you two know each other, don't you?" he asked, fitting the first piece into the puzzle. He clearly recalled the incident at the restaurant over a month ago. Then Serena had denied knowing Tom; now the expression on her face made a mockery of that denial.

It was Tom who came to Serena's aid, a knight in shining armor. "We met earlier," he answered noncommittally, avoiding a direct lie, but very clearly protecting her secret. Serena's eyes transmitted their thanks as she nodded in ostensible greeting.

André, however, was less concerned with the connection than he was in gleaning information. "I understand you've begun to make some changes at the *Bulletin.*"

"A few." Tom kept his distance. "I've only been there a very short time. I'll need a while longer to have any kind of impact."

André's smile lacked its usual perfection. "So you are planning to stir things up? I'd heard rumors to that extent."

"I'm planning to turn the *Bulletin* into a first-rate newspaper. If that takes stirring up, as you put it, then I'll be stirring things up."

"It must be a difficult business," André went on pointedly. "There seems to be a backlash against newspapers and the power they wield." Serena stiffened at his latent hostility, but neither man noticed. "I read about more and more lawsuits, for libel. You folks have to be very careful."

While Serena's stomach twisted at the direction the conversation was taking Tom seemed utterly calm. "We always have been and still are. That's not to say that the occasional irresponsible reporter can't do some damage. But it's up to the editorial staff to prevent wanton mudslinging." He tipped his head in a self-assured manner. "I'm not worried about the *Bulletin*. We'll have our facts straight."

"Excuse me," Serena broke in, unable to bear the discussion any longer. "I'm going to freshen up." She spoke softly to André, nodding to Tom as she turned and walked with forced steadiness through the crowd, into the foyer, down the hall, and into the peace of the bathroom. When she emerged her direction was even more sure. Retracing her steps, she stood at the entrance to the living room, located the tall figure she wanted and approached him without hesitation.

"Could we leave, Tom?" she whispered, not fully understanding her action, only knowing that she wanted to go . . . with Tom.

"André?"

"I'll leave a message with . . . the butler." She smirked, then sobered in a silent plea, slipping her hand into Tom's, seeking his strength. His fingers tightened as he drew her beside him. She began to breathe freely only once she'd been comfortably settled in the front seat of his two-seater Mercedes. Leaning her head back, she closed her eyes and listened to the sounds as he slid behind the wheel, turned the key in the ignition, shifted into gear, and accelerated, leaving behind the bright-lit mansion and its crowd of partygoers, including, she thought quite happily, André. He had offended her with his subtle attack on Tom, though he had done nothing more than express sentiments with which she agreed wholeheartedly. Had she grown that protective of Tom that she took *his* side on such an issue? Impossible! She was simply tired.

Eyes still shut, she felt the gentle touch of Tom's fingers on her cheek. "Headache?" he asked softly.

"No. I'd just had enough."

The steady hum of the well-tuned engine was soothing. Serena felt strangely calm and totally trusting of her driver.

"Not a party girl?"

She chuckled. "Not by a long shot." Then she quickly opened her eyes. "Oh, Tom, if you wanted to stay—"

"No, no." He held out a hand to stop her. "I prefer my evenings quieter. I only went at Ann's urging, but she really didn't need an escort. I'm sure she won't miss me."

"Will she be expecting you to take her home?"

His smile was barely visible in the darkness. "I left my message with the butler, too. It's good to know he's served some practical purpose for the money he's being paid."

"Do you like Ann?"

"Sure I like her. But if I wanted to be with her I wouldn't be driving you home right now."

For the first time Serena glanced out the front windshield. "Tom, you're going in the wrong direction. We have to head back toward the city to get to my apartment."

"We're not going there."

"But you said—"

"Home. *My* home."

With the tension of the party gone a new wave of emotion swept over her. "Oh, Tom. I don't know." She remembered his kiss, her kiss, earlier that evening. "I think you should turn around."

"No way."

"Tom . . ."

But he had no intention of altering course, despite her soft plea. Rather, he grew more adamant. "We're going to my place to talk, Serena. There's an awful lot I want to say, and even more I want to hear."

"Tom, I don't know if I'm up for this."

"You've had a month!" With the force of his exclamation he swerved to the side of the road and stepped firmly on the brakes, his arm shooting out to hold her in place. When the car had come to a complete stop he turned to her, leaving only the memory of his strength where his arm had been a moment before.

"Listen, Serena. There's something we have to hash out. Until we do we'll both be in limbo."

"No."

"Yes! Don't try to deny your response to me. I felt it back in that den tonight. I felt it back in your apartment that morning. Damn it, I felt it in that restaurant that very first day!"

"You're confusing the issue, Tom," she argued softly. "That first day I was stunned to see you—"

"Could it be that there was something more, even then? It happens sometimes, you know. Instant response. Biological attraction. Chemical communication."

"No."

"You're *that* sure?" Darkness hid his expression, but his profile was uncompromising.

Serena shivered as she stared at him, simultaneously trying to consider and dismiss his claim. In the end she had to be honest, with him and with herself. "No," she admitted wretchedly.

Tom started the engine. "Then let's go. We'll work this all out, one way or the other. I've got to know what's going on in that head of yours or I'm apt to go right off the deep end myself."

"Hmph . . . true justice . . ."

He ignored her sally. "Justice is your giving me an hour of your time in return for my rescuing you from André's party."

Serena's eyes glittered in the passing headlights. "From the frying pan into the fire?" she quipped dryly, quietly, but not quietly enough.

"There's always been a fire with us, Serena. That's what this is all about. Fire can be either destructive or purifying. Either we douse it for good, or we let it flame."

His point was well-taken, expressing much of Serena's own sentiment. Tom had been on her mind enough in the past month to merit this time spent together. He was right; it *had* to be. For her own peace of mind as much as for his, they had to talk things out. Talk was good for the soul. But the body, what would answer its needs?

"I'll take you home later, if that's what you want." Tom spoke gently, reading her mind, in total understanding of her fear. It was this very understanding that reassured her, and the fact that she did trust him. "OK?" he asked.

She hesitated for just a moment before giving the only answer conscience would allow. "OK," she murmured and he purposefully stepped on the gas.

5

For a Saturday night the traffic was negligible, reducing what might have been a drive of forty minutes to a simple twenty-minute trip.

"I didn't realize that you lived in Wayzata," Serena commented, easily recognizing her surroundings.

Tom's eyes remained fixed on the road. "There's a lot about me you don't know. Which will be changed soon enough."

She shot him a slanted look. "Why does that sound ominous?"

"Does it?" he asked innocently. "I hadn't meant it to be ominous. Perhaps . . . enticing?"

"Oh, yes, enticing." Her echo held enough amusement to cover the trepidation she felt. What had she let herself in for?

"Having second thoughts?"

"Naturally."

"I wouldn't do anything to hurt you. You know that, don't you?"

Serena answered impulsively. "I wish you had made that promise years ago. My family might still be in one piece."

"No, Serena. If it hadn't been me it would have been

someone else—reporter, detective, district attorney, take your pick. Your father broke the law. He had no one to blame but himself."

"You didn't know him," she argued softly, lowering her gaze while images of her childhood passed before her. "He was a good man. . . ."

Tom considered her words and, more important, the heartfelt belief behind them. Serena had adored her father; even now, though she might acknowledge that he'd done wrong, she could not think of him as a criminal. In her dreams she often imagined him vindicated through the process of appeal. In reality he hadn't lived long enough.

"Here we are." With a turn of the wheel Tom turned from the main road onto a private drive that wound around for a short distance and ended in a graceful arc.

"Tom, this is beautiful!" Serena exclaimed, captivated at once by the moonlit manor before her. In the total absence of artificial light its profile was impressive—tall in the eaves, broad in the wings, and strong in the sturdy brick of which it was molded. "It's you!"

Scrambling from the car, she was aware of Tom's instant materialization by her side. "It will be one day. Come on"—he took her hand—"we go over this way."

Bemused, she followed his lead, away from the larger house toward a small cottage on its far side. She heard the gentle sounds of her high heels tapping on the flagstone walk, the wind playing through branches just shy of their spring buds, and a softer, more rhythmic lilt from the lake nearby. But the hand of night was reluctant to reveal more than one bit of beauty at a time. Serena clutched Tom's long fingers as he headed toward the single lighted lamppost.

"Tom?"

"Uh-huh?" He fished in his pocket for a key.

"I'm not sure I understand."

"What?" Amusement lacing his tone, he opened the door, reached within to switch on a light, and stood to the side for Serena to pass.

"The house . . . *that* house, is *it* yours or is *this?*"

"Would it matter?" he drawled tartly.

She shrugged. "Only to satisfy my curiosity, or if I needed an address to send a quart-sized carton of Cinnamon Red Hots to."

"You'd be that cruel?"

"You wouldn't *have* to eat them," she said sweetly over her shoulder as she stepped across the threshold of the quaint brick structure and found herself in a surprisingly open single room, contemporary both in design and furnishing. "This is amazing, Tom! This is like a modern mountain hideaway."

The soft click of the door as it closed added to the intimacy of the surroundings. As she admired the long, plush-cushioned velour sofa and matching armchairs, the low coffee table, the freestanding television and stereo unit with its sectioned desk and inevitable typewriter, she felt a surge of warmth.

"You like it?" he asked.

Her hazel eyes sparkled her approval. "It's delightful. Do you really live here, rather than at that house?"

"For now."

"And what does that mean?"

"It means," he sighed, "that I can't be bothered by the worries of running a large house. This is just my size."

Surprised, Serena turned to stare at him. "You do own the house?"

His firm lips rose at the corners. "I had to buy it to get this."

"Tom"—she frowned through a skeptical smile—"that's ludicrous. People don't buy huge estates simply to live in small cabins."

"You may have a point," he rejoined tongue in cheek. "To be more precise, what I really wanted was a small place on the lake. I had to buy the whole parcel of land, with the woods surrounding it, to get the privacy I wanted. The house was thrown in as a bonus."

Serena chuckled. "Some bonus!" But she grew more serious. "You really do want privacy?"

"Yes."

"But why? From what I can imagine, given the fact that your family is a prominent one, you must have been raised in the public eye. I'd think you'd be used to it."

He gestured toward the sofa, watched as she sank into it, then eased his long frame onto its far end. Appreciative of the distance he'd deliberately put between them, Serena relaxed.

"I may be well used to the limelight, but that doesn't mean I have to like it. From the start I preferred a more private life."

"Could've fooled me." She looked away.

"Even then. What you saw of me was my job. There was—there is—a private man behind the notebook."

It was his vehemence that coaxed her eyes back to him. She might have been dubious still, but she wanted to know more. "So you bought this place. You've done it over?" Again she perused the decor, admiring the palette of browns and creams, accessorized in gray to emphasize the masculine tone.

Tom nodded. "Privacy doesn't rule out convenience. I bought the estate when I first arrived here, then lived in a hotel while the interior of the cottage was completely torn out and redone. It needed wiring, plumbing, plastering—everything." Tipping his head back, he smiled. "Not bad, if I do say so myself. I enjoy it here."

"Where do you *live?*" she burst out, qualifying her question at his frown. "I mean, this seems to be the only room. I assume that's the kitchen"—she pointed—"and that's the bath, but . . . ?"

Tom leaned forward, his voice a hair lower. "If you're asking about the sleeping arrangements, you're sitting on them."

"The couch? You don't sleep on the couch every night, do you?"

"Now, now, don't knock what you haven't seen. It just so happens that this couch is no ordinary couch. It opens into the most comfortable king-sized bed you've ever seen."

"That's not saying much, since I haven't seen many." Her quip was as pointed as she dared make it without inspiring Tom to revenge. As it was, she was at a disadvantage, here in this cozy cabin with him. Granted, his tall and muscled frame lounged several feet away, but her pulse fluttered strangely every time she looked at him. And it certainly didn't help to know that they were sitting on his bed. It was like sipping champagne from a loving cup.

As if he had caught her thought Tom unfolded his limbs and rose in one smooth motion. "Would you like some wine?"

Feeling in sudden need of fortification, she nodded. "That would be nice." But her mind was still on the king-sized bed. "Tell me, Tom. Once before you said you'd been 'burned.' What did you mean by that?"

"You *are* curious."

"*You* were the one who suggested we talk. And you were the one who pointed out how little I know about you."

Tom remained silent for a time, bent in concentration over a conveniently stubborn cork. With its climactic pop he seemed to reach a decision.

"I was married once. It was a long time ago. I was—we

both were—very young." Returning to the sofa, he handed her an empty glass, skillfully filled it halfway, then retreated to his end of the couch to fill his own glass and sink back in a posture of brooding. "She had an image in her mind of what she wanted from life, with riches and glamour ranking high on her list. I guess I was a disappointment."

"A disappointment?" she asked, incredulous. "How can that be? Certainly you could have given her all that."

"To Eleanor, wealth was a goal in itself. To me, it's simply the means to an end that may be totally different, such as the modesty of this cabin. I realize that to you my attitude may sound callous. In my life money has never been a problem and most likely never will. In that respect I *am* arrogant, I suppose." His brow furrowed beneath the swath of dark hair that the evening breeze had ruffled. "I enjoy the finer things in life, but in a very private, very personal way."

There was something comforting in what he said, for Serena was, herself, a private soul. "But your wife couldn't agree?"

"Hah! She couldn't *stand* it. I put up with the parties and the globe-trotting as much as I could, but there's a limit for every man beyond which he simply can't go. When it became clear that we were headed in different directions in life we called it quits."

"A mutual decision?" Serena asked softly, touched by his willingness to share this intimacy, sensing that he rarely did so.

At last he looked at her. "Yes. Fortunately there were no children. It was difficult enough."

"You loved her."

"Yes." He took a deep breath. "In my way I did love her."

"Do you ever see her?"

He shook his head and studied the smooth swirl of wine as he moved his glass. "She's married again. He's a European hotelier. From what I hear they have several kids already."

Serena was aware of the vulnerability in him, of the hurt he must have suffered. Much as she wanted to attribute only the harshest qualities to him she couldn't ignore the more human element that never failed to touch her deeply.

"Do you want them? Kids?" she prodded gently.

"Sure." He smiled impulsively, then again more sadly. "That's what the big house is for. Someday . . . perhaps . . ."

Serena ached with the dying off of his voice. She actually wanted to slide across the distance and hold him, comfort him, even promise him those things he wished. *It was absurd!* This was Thomas Harrison Reynolds! How could she sympathize with *him?*

"That's a strange expression you're wearing," Tom observed, suddenly more humorous, as though freed of a burden. "It's a combination of compassion and anger." He paused. "What are you thinking, Serena?"

"I'm thinking that you totally confuse me. You're not at all what I expected to find."

Tom stared at her in silence. His features grew more gentle with each passing second. When he finally spoke it was very softly. "That has to be a compliment. I can imagine what it took for you to offer it."

She burst from the couch, nearly spilling her wine, and paced to the low-silled window on the far side of the room. "It's the truth. Unfortunately."

"Unfortunately?"

Her hazel-eyed gaze locked with his as she turned. "It would have been so much easier to hate you. With everything that happened back in L.A., I *should* hate you!"

He rose from the sofa with an animal grace that evoked a similarly primitive response in Serena. "But you don't," he stated quietly. Again she was perplexed, for where there might have been triumph on his face there was only a look of gratitude.

"No," she whispered, mesmerized once more by the manly strength of his features, now hovering dangerously close.

"Do you hate yourself for that?"

"I don't know. I can't think when you're around."

"Oh, Serena," he murmured, kissing her with the same gentleness that puzzled her so. Responding to the longing within she returned the kiss in kind, expressing that irrational desire to protect and comfort through the warmth of her lips as they moved against his. But there was still so much to be said, and Serena was not up for rejection just yet. It was she who broke the tender embrace.

"Tom, we have to talk. You said so yourself." The words ran into each other with the speed of her racing heart. "This is the problem. It's so easy to become lost in . . . in . . ."

"Desire?"

She looked down, nervously fingering a button of his shirt, barely aware of her action. "Yes. Desire."

"It's a beautiful thing, isn't it?"

The warmth of his body reached out to her fingertips, counteracting her desperate attempt at self-control. A frown tugged at her brows, marring the face he had earlier called serene.

"I'm—I'm not sure."

"Now, what's *that* supposed to mean?" He closed his large palms around her shoulders but held her at arm's reach, demanding an explanation.

"Just that," she insisted unhappily. "I'm not sure."

"Come on, Serena. You've been honest so far. Don't

stop now. It's one of the things I admire about you. Why can't you admit to the pleasure you feel in my arms?"

Embarrassed, she tried to pull away, but his grip tightened. "I *do* admit to that pleasure. But desire, and its end . . ." She looked down again. "It's been a very long time. . . ."

"Ahh," he crooned, drawing her against the solid wall of his chest and cradling her there. "So you *are* thinking of the future. That's a good sign."

"I don't know about that either," she moaned, fighting the havoc wreaked by the mingling scent of wine and man that permeated her senses and clouded her brain. "If anything I feel more guilty thinking about it now than I did then."

Tom grew still, let his chin fall to the crown of her head for a pensive moment, then released her. "You're right," he sighed. "We have to talk." Again he gestured toward the sofa. Again she sat. This time, however, he stood more warily before her. "OK, Serena, let's have it out. First of all, I'm going to tell you what's on *my* mind." With a brief pause, his gaze grew darker, if possible, even more intense. By intuition alone Serena read his thoughts. But he spoke clearly, boldly.

"I want you, Serena. It's as simple as that. I want you. I want to be with you, to get to know you. Right now I want to take you to bed and make love to you. There! Are you shocked?"

"I'm twenty-nine years old, Tom. Shocked? No. Frightened? Very."

"You've got nothing to fear from me, honey. I've told you as much before."

"It's not you, Tom." Her lips thinned in frustration. Sighing, she shook her head in disgust. "It's me. Things may happen between the two of us that I can't control. I'll want them while they're happening, but how do I live with myself afterward?"

Even now, she craved the protective solace of his arms. Yet he stood alone before her, legs planted firmly in a wide stance, hands on his ruggedly narrow hips. "Then we're back to the issue of guilt. And I *know* that the guilt would have little to do with the actual act of making love, would it?"

She shook her head, missing the bouncing shelter of the hair which usually fell so freely but which was still anchored firmly at the nape of her neck. "We're living in modern times—"

"And you've lived the life of a nun for the past ten years."

"What is this, Tom? Would you rather I slept my way through life, consorting with every man who crossed my path? It just so happens that *that* doesn't appeal to me!" Scowling, she burrowed deeper into the cushions. "Sex has to mean something. It's not something I'd do for desire alone."

"You thought you loved this—what was his name—Lowry?"

"I did, at the time."

"And do you love me?"

"Love has nothing to do with this."

"But you'd go to bed with me."

"No!" She jumped up, then stormed out of his reach. "I haven't said that either."

"You implied it."

"You twist everything I say!"

"But you want me?"

"I want you out of my life!"

"Let's try desire. You desire me?"

She whirled around, eyes flashing with anger. "Damn it, yes! I desire you—if we're down to playing word games. I'm human. I have natural cravings. I'm a woman! And yes, I *desire* you!" She spat out the word with scorn.

"You've made your point." He sighed in defeat, astonishing her with his blunt capitulation. She watched warily as he retrieved his wineglass, filled it again, and strode to the window to stare into the night.

Serena was more confused than ever. She'd told him the things he wanted to hear, yet he seemed more lost than before. Drawn by the same enigmatic force that confounded her, she found herself approaching the window, putting her hand on his arm.

"I'm sorry. That sounded so angry."

"You *are* angry, honey. That's the point." He glanced sidelong down at her.

"The point," she confessed, "is that when you look at me like that and call me 'honey' the anger I feel vanishes. It's *that* that terrifies me."

Tom turned slowly, cradling her face in his rough palms. "What if I said that I was just as frightened? Would you believe me?"

"You? Frightened?"

"Yes."

"Of what?"

"Involvement." His gaze traced electrifying circles around her face.

"With me?" With the strength of a reflex built up over years she stiffened. "Because of me? My family?"

"No! No! Serena, how can you say something like that?"

Her eyes glistened. "It happened once before, Tom. I can't forget it."

"I know," he whispered, caressing her cheeks with his thumbs. "I know." The tenderness of his tone sent shivers of arousal through her body. He was close and warm and understanding of her every emotion. "Oh, Serena," he gasped. "It's happening again. It's the same with me, Serena, something I can't seem to control." His lips lowered to brush against her forehead in agony. "I want you so."

Serena felt the tremor that shook him shudder through her own limbs. She closed her eyes as sanity receded, then opened them quickly to grasp common sense.

"We can't, Tom," she moaned softly. "This is wrong. It's not good for either of us." But her hands itched to touch him and she did, reaching out to circle his waist with her arms and move against his manhood with a tormented sigh. "Oh, Tom . . ." Her words echoed in the far depths of his mouth, his lips seizing hers with the same fierceness that inflamed her entire body. What had begun at the party that night—what had begun a month ago in the restaurant—seemed destined for completion. Serena wanted Tom more than anything she could have imagined. Her body ached for his vibrant pulse, for the possession that would bring her to fruition as a woman, complete and loved if only for the evening.

"What if we were to pretend," Tom began, breathing raggedly by her ear, "that we had no past? That we were two different people? That we were in love?"

Serena put her arms up over his sinewy shoulders and clung tightly, burying her face against the warm, beating pulse in his neck. "We're adults, Tom," she whispered, tasting the heady tang of him as she acted the devil's advocate. "We can't play games."

He stroked her back, pressing her closer as his fingers drew erotic designs on the clinging silk of her tunic top. "We have to do *something*. I've tried staying away for a month, a whole month, and look where it's left me. I feel more out of control than ever." His teeth settled on the lobe of her ear, nipping it, grating against the gleaming pearl of her earring. "You look beautiful tonight. I could have taken you there in that den of André's."

Serena measured the strength of his back with her palms splayed over its muscular breadth. "Oh, Tom," she sighed wistfully. "Why did you ever show up there tonight?"

His fine shiver of tension passed easily as an extension of passion. "Let's call it fate, Serena," he murmured, crushing her more fiercely to his taut frame. "It's the same thing that brought us eye to eye in the restaurant that first day."

"But I would never have stared if I hadn't recognized you." Even as she offered the feeble protest she knew it to be a dubious point. Tom himself had planted the seeds of doubt in her mind. Would she have sought him out regardless? Was there indeed an unfathomable attraction surpassing all else that brought them together?

"We'll never know for sure," he argued softly. "What if . . . what if we'd never seen each other before that day? Would you be wanting me now?"

"Yes. Oh, yes." Her body rippled with swelling excitement at the seductive timbre of his voice. Her hands found their way to his waist, granting eager fingers the free exploration of his firm, hard body. She could only repeat his name, over and over again, as though hypnotized.

"Pretend?" he begged with an urgency that thrilled her as much as the iron-strong hands that worked their way almost timidly across her body to the side bow that held her tunic wrapped about her waist. A single tug released it and Serena knew she had reached the moment of decision. Even amid the thick sensual fog settling heavily over them she could still see her way clear to escape, if she wanted to.

"Serena, what *do* you want?" Without doubt he wavered at his own point of no return. She could feel it in the thrust of his body.

"Heaven help me, Tom. *I want you!*" she cried in the agony of responding for the sake of raw pleasure. "I'll pretend. I'll pretend. I need you, Tom." The last was without pretense.

His answering groan was an excruciating one. "Oh, Serena. Come here, love."

"I'm here. I'm yours." She gloried in the game, reaching in wonder to touch his face, exploring each manly feature with her fingertips. The depth of his eyes, his brows, the strong line of his nose and lean planes of his cheeks, the faint rasp of the beard that had been shaved hours before, the jaw that spoke of the character she was just beginning to know. With an imperceptible movement of his head he captured a wandering finger and sucked on it deeply. "Tom!" she gasped, quavering his name mindlessly.

"Pretend." He murmured the watchword again, drawing her into the safe harbor of his arms, pressing his lips to hers and parting them easily with the moistened tip of his tongue.

Serena melted like ice from a wintry mountaintop flowing surely to warm lower pastures. When he held her back to slip open her blouse the chill was a momentary thing. His hands, male-textured against the smoothness of her flesh, quickly replaced the discarded fabric, covering her with the searing heat of desire.

"Beautiful Serena," he breathed against her neck when his hands moved upward to cup the gentle fullness of her lace-covered breasts. She arched toward his palms instinctively, feeling the explosive need to be his at once.

But he was the master, prolonging every bit of his heaven and hers, as though they'd never make it there again. Slowly he reached to release the catch of her bra and peeled off the wisp of material to let spill the ivory wealth of her. She was naked from the waist up and at his mercy. His eyes devoured the twin swells before he loosed his questing fingers to her flesh.

"How can you be so cruel?" she whimpered at his tantalizing play, crying out when he took each nipple between thumb and forefinger and rubbed sweet pain round and about them.

"It's all in the game," he gritted back, the pain his own as well.

"Then I'm playing too." Deliberately Serena tugged loose the knot of his tie, released each button of his shirt and pushed the fine fabric from his shoulders to join her silk tunic on the floor. Leaning forward, she put her lips to his chest and kissed her way across its matted plain. The path she left was moist and heady. She thrilled to the success of her revenge, evident in the intermittent groans he gave.

And Serena pretended. On Tom's prescription she pretended that there had never been a scandal sixteen years ago. She pretended that she'd seen Tom that day in the restaurant for the first time in her life, that there was nothing, *nothing* to keep them apart. She offered herself up to the fantasy of womanhood, believing Tom's words as he finished undressing her. "So lovely . . ."

The sofa was their bed, though neither thought to unfold it or seek the sheets that would be inside. The plushness of velour was a regal mattress, the narrowness every bit wide enough for one body atop another.

She lay where he had eased her back, naked, watching as he quickly matched her in that state. Bare-chested, his body had been intimidating in its virile pull. Now, totally nude, it instilled a mindless frenzy that tremored continually through her. She reached for him when he approached, then cried aloud when he came down to her. His flesh was hot against hers, sending a now-familiar fire raging to each of her nerve endings in turn.

Her hands grasped the smoother flesh of his hips and

urged him closer. But he was not to be rushed in the illusion of love. His gaze smoldered as he lingered, savoring the touch of his lines on hers. With a leisure that heightened her cravings even more he took her hands, kissing them both, holding them to his lips as he looked with slow thoroughness over her body.

"Tell me again," she pleaded with a shudder at the last shadow of doubt.

"Pretend. Pretend. We're two people with no past. Only each other. Now." He paused. "I love you." Softly: "I love you." With more conviction.

Her heart stopped, then burst with need. "And I love you," she whispered. Again. And again.

Having said the words that made it all possible, the fantasy was nearly complete. A hoarse and primitive sound reverberated from Tom's throat to be muffled against her breasts as he lowered his head. His mouth found the crest it sought, surrounding and sucking the rosy peak, sending an urgent message to the heart of Serena's femininity.

"Don't keep me waiting, Tom," she moaned, writhing beneath him. "I need you. Please . . . now . . ." In an instinctive surge toward ecstasy she arched her hips against the boldness of his. "Now!" she cried a final time before he seized her lips and his body covered her.

His muscled thigh parted her legs and Serena gasped loudly as he filled her both physically and spiritually. She was part of him and he of her; the joy of that knowledge lavished sensual satisfaction through her entire being.

Tom kissed her as he set the pace, slow at first, then with driven speed as he, too, fell victim to the ancient and primal force that brought them together. Serena answered his heat with the fervor of a woman possessed, meeting his passion equally, relinquishing herself totally to the soaring unreality. Her hands measured the strain of his muscles, then lost all awareness when her own senses blinded her to everything but his body—on her, in her.

Together they built, then peaked, then toppled, drenched in each other's sweat, limbs intertwined. Fighting the return to reality Tom stayed inside her, clasping her body to his only until his ardor returned. Then, in a miraculous repeat, they loved once again.

It was a long, long time before Serena's breathing steadied and her quivering body stilled. She lay against Tom, her head on his damp chest, her leg thrown intimately over and between his. Neither said a word for fear of shattering the illusion that had brought such pleasure, such utter fulfillment.

Tom spoke at last, but only after he had brought his free arm around to lock tight the circle in which he held her. "I knew it would be like that, Serena. I knew it from the first." Eyes shut against the cushioning hair of his chest, she savored his words through the lingering haze of her passion. "It's the fire inside you, love. The same fire that pits us against one another has the power to let you love me the way you did." She felt the warmth of his breath as he tucked his chin in to look down at her. "I've never seen such passion, Serena. It's innocent at the same time as it's worldly and wild. How can that be?"

"I don't know." She smiled, shifting more snugly against him. Even the slow return of reality could do nothing to dampen the contentment she felt by his side. "You seem to bring out the basest instincts in me!"

He chuckled. "You can say that again."

"No need," she murmured, brushing her lips against a taut male nipple, then smiling at his response.

"Come here," he growled, surprising her when he pulled her over him and went to work at the back of her neck. "I should have done this earlier. Your hair is too lovely to tie back, even if it *did* look gorgeous tonight."

Within seconds he'd freed her auburn tresses and spread them gently over her shoulders. "There," he breathed in deep satisfaction. "That's better." He surveyed his handiwork for a moment longer before easing her down beside him again.

"How do you feel?" he asked, pausing. "I didn't hurt you, did I?"

Serena smiled. "That's a dumb question. Did I seem like I was hurting?"

"I'm not sure. At one point there I thought I felt nails digging into my back."

"You're wicked."

"I'm serious." Again he paused, this time quite meaningfully. "Are you all right?"

Her soft-whispered "yes" was poignant.

"Are you sorry?"

"No."

"Do you feel guilty?"

"Not now."

"But you will?"

"Probably."

"I won't," he declared. "Not ever. It was beautiful, what we just shared."

"Beautiful, but dangerous." She thought of the future, of the taste of Tom that lingered in her mouth, her veins, her heart. Could one become addicted so easily? Or had she simply chosen to ignore the earlier signs, the thoughts of him during the last month, the memories of his hands and kisses and care?

He cupped her chin and lifted it, forcing her eyes to meet his. "Dangerous as in pregnancy?"

Serena was stunned. "I hadn't even thought of that." When Tom exhaled loudly and shook his head she misinterpreted his gesture. "I'm sorry. Don't worry, I would never hold you respon—"

"Serena!" He squeezed her into silence. "That's not what I meant at all."

"Then what?"

"I just marvel at you. Your purity and honesty. I've never met anyone like you."

"And if I *did* become pregnant? Would you be marveling then?"

"Yes." There was no doubt in his voice.

But Serena's held enough for them both. "You wouldn't mind my bearing your child?"

"Of course not."

"Even knowing what you know?" At his frown she elaborated. "Even knowing that the truth would come out one day?"

Taken off guard, Tom let her go when Serena scrambled over him suddenly. Heading for the bathroom, she stopped short, hung her head, and waited. She knew what it was that had just driven her from Tom's arms, but she wasn't ready for it.

"Don't do this to yourself," he groaned from directly behind, turning her into his arms to rescue her again. "I've told you once that the past doesn't matter to me. If I could do it all over again I'd do things differently. But it's done. I can't change what happened then. And it has no bearing on what's happening now." Cupping her face in the power of his hands, he tilted it up. "Don't you see, when I look at you I see none of the past. I only see now, and tomorrow."

Serena was unprepared for this softness, just as she'd been unprepared for all the very positive things she'd discovered about Tom. She was drawn to him, excited by him beyond belief. The thought of never seeing him after this night was as painful as the thought of living with this ghost from the past. Her eyes brimmed in anguish as she returned the intensity of his gaze with her own.

"Oh, Tom, what am I going to do?"

6

Tom kissed her tenderly. "What you're going to do, Serena, is to stand right here for just a minute." He touched her lips lightly with his, then proceeded to convert the sofa into the king-sized bed he'd touted earlier that evening.

Serena watched him as he worked. She tried desperately to be as nonchalant about his nakedness as he appeared to be, yet she found herself entranced, unable to look away. His body was spectacular, that of an athlete, well-toned and muscular, with the coordination to match.

"Do you play tennis, too?" she asked impulsively.

Pausing in his work, Tom straightened and grinned. "How could you tell?"

In answer her eye fell to trace the faded lines of his tan, the faint ring on his upper arms, his calves, his thighs.

"Are you disappointed?" he smiled crookedly, standing boldly still.

"That you play tennis?" She groped for reason, far too aware of her own nudity as she studied his.

"That I'm forty, with the body to prove it."

"Tom, it never *occurred* to me to think of your age." But she grinned. "You must be searching for compliments. You know you're in your prime."

The gleam in his eye teased her further, though he

bent to finish his work. "There! Now, you, Serene Highness, go here." Leading her lightly by the hand, he sat her in bed. "I'll be your backrest." Climbing agilely in beside her he propped pillows high beneath his head and drew her down against his chest.

"Now what?" she whispered, unsure once more.

"Now we talk."

Serena exploded into giddy laughter. "Talk? You make me feel like a very naked queen and expect me to talk?"

"Would you rather make love again?"

"Shame on you, Tom." She fought fire with fire. "You're forty years old. Are you really up to it again?"

Without warning he slithered over her, trapping her in his web of masculinity. "That will definitely cost you," he growled half-playfully, pinning her hands to either side. "Kiss me."

"We'll talk."

"Kiss me!"

"Tom, this won't solve anything—"

"Kiss me!" The fire in his eyes was the same that she identified so strongly with the cub reporter of her memory.

"Please," she pleaded. "You frighten me when you look at me like that."

He softened instantly but held her still. "I'm sorry, love. It's what you do to me. I could make love to you all night. But we *do* have to talk. Now,"—he grinned—"just a little kiss."

Telling herself that she acted only to please him, Serena raised her lips to his and delivered what she intended to be a "little kiss." Somewhere between "little" and "kiss," though, she found herself partner in a volatile venture that threatened an imminent explosion. He let go of her hands and she used her freedom to start a foray of her own that left him shuddering with reawakening excitement.

"What was that you were saying about my age?"

Through the pleasure of what she felt she couldn't be angry. "I was saying that you are very definitely in your prime. And that we should talk."

"Serena."

"Yes?"

"Uh . . . that's enough . . ."

"Something wrong?"

"Serena!"

"What is it, Tom? Speak up."

"Damn it, Serena. I can't think rationally, let alone talk, unless you stop what you're doing!"

"You started it."

"*You* stop it!"

Feeling eminently powerful, Serena tormented him for a moment longer before leisurely trailing her fingertips up his body to the throbbing pulse point at his neck. "Better?" she crooned sweetly.

Her humor eluded Tom. "Give me a minute," he rasped, taking several deep and steadying breaths. Finally he gave an exaggerated sigh. "All right. We talk."

"Tell me about your work."

He opened one lazy eye to look at her. "*I* should talk?"

"Yes."

"What do you want to know?"

"What you do."

He sighed patiently. "I publish newspapers."

"*Every day*, Tom. What do you actually *do?*"

When his answer was slow in coming she looked up at him, resting her chin on his chest. He was studying her closely. "Why are you asking me this, Serena? I would have thought it was just what you wouldn't want to hear. As a matter of fact, I'm amazed at your calmness."

His line of thought was easy to follow. "So am I," she whispered almost to herself, lying back on the sheet and staring at the ceiling. "I'm not quite sure I understand *myself*."

"And that's what *I* want to discuss. You. Your feelings. About what just happened. About what happened sixteen years ago." Tom rolled to his side and propped himself up on an elbow. Serena turned her head sideways to look at him.

"This is all so strange," she began, struggling to piece together the puzzle. "I mean, here I am . . . lying here . . . with you."

"And you seem very complacent about it all. Very serene."

For an instant her hazel gaze flared. "What would you prefer? That I rant and rave? Scream that you made me do it? I'm not that way, Tom. You should know that by now!"

"But, I didn't—"

"*I know that!* That's just the point. Nothing has happened here that I didn't want to happen. I enjoyed every minute of your lovemaking." She was about to mention the game, then thought better of it. What had begun as an illusion had burgeoned into the real thing. The thought hit her with stunning force. Looking away, she fought the abrupt awareness of her emotions. When she turned her head toward him once more there was sadness in her eyes. "It's odd, what's happened. When I'm with you, looking at you, touching you, wanting you to do the same to me, I can't remember who you are. I only *feel* things now. You blot out all thoughts of what I should be remembering." Her voice rose in agitation. "And the worst of it is that, even right now, I'm not sorry. I don't *want* to remember anything. I know it's there, but I can very happily push it out of my mind—at least until tomorrow."

"It *is* tomorrow, love," Tom spoke on a sober note. "And we've got to work this out. You've created a dichotomy in your mind. On the one hand, there's the

Tom Reynolds whom you hate on sight. On the other, there's me."

She grimaced. "Very well put."

"The question is, how do we bring the two together?"

For the first time since she'd sought the solace of Tom's arms Serena felt truly disturbed. "I'm not sure that's possible. It'll always be there, Tom. I'll always know that you were the one who broke my father."

Tom's heated glance had nothing to do with passion. "That's the crux of it, isn't it? You refuse to face the truth."

"The truth? *Whose* truth?"

He ignored her barb. "Your father broke himself, Serena. I didn't do it. Oh"—he held up a hand to ward off her protest—"I know what I did. I confess to being impulsive and arrogant. I saw my soapbox and climbed on it with the eagerness typical of a kid. I was young and brash. But though I might have been guilty of zeal, my sense of conviction was intact. I did what I thought was right."

Clutching the sheet to her breasts, Serena rose to a sitting position. "Ruining a man and his family?"

"Standing up for honesty."

"You were ambitious! You were looking for headlines!" Her eyes grew misty. "You didn't care what happened, only that your paper got the story under *your* byline!"

"No, Serena." Tom, too, sat forward, the sheet falling to his navel. "That was a minor point. You didn't know me then. It was idealism as much as anything else that drove me. I was disgusted with what I'd found in that spotlight series of white-collar crime. Your father wasn't the only one exposed."

"He was the only one who mattered to me!"

"I know, I know," he said softly. Lifting a hand, he reached to brush a wisp of hair back from her face.

Serena flinched, her eyes full and luminous. "It's things like *this* that confuse me. How can you be so gentle? . . ." Her words died at the tightening of her throat. How could she be in love? It wasn't right. It wasn't fair. It wasn't possible. Or was it? Tormented, she swayed toward Tom.

"Hold me," she cried in agony. "Make me forget it all, Tom. You can do that." Seeking his strength, she reached tentatively for him.

"Serena, I don't know. . . ."

"Please, Tom." The need was born and swelling fast. "Love me again. Help me."

With a shuddering groan he gathered her to him. "Oh, Serena, Serena. What am I going to do with you? You're as much a split personality as you believe me to be. There's the Strickland side of you that refuses to forgive me for what happened so very long ago. And then there's . . . Serena. Beautiful, sweet Serena. Tranquil to the world, a flame of passion in my arms."

"Tom," she whispered his name against the warm hair of his chest. "Love me . . ."

Knowing he had no choice, his own emotions rising to meet hers, Tom loved her long and hard. This time there were no words of pretense and illusion. There was no slow seduction, no masterful torment. Rather there was the richness of love, raw and new, all-encompassing in its frenzy, and totally beyond control.

The silence of the night was broken only by moans and sighs, by cries of need and gasps of satisfaction. Again and again they sought each other, finding glory in the loss of separate identities, joy in becoming one. There were no attempts at explanation when they fell to the bed a final time, exhausted and weak, yet content. It was as though neither wished to disturb the tentative peace. The light of morning would do that on its own.

* * *

Serena awoke to the smell of fresh-brewed coffee and the sight of Tom sitting beside her. He wore nothing but a pair of hip-hugging jeans and an expression that was decidedly troubled.

"I'm sorry." She pushed herself up against the pillows, holding the sheet to her breasts. "You should have woken me sooner. What time is it?"

Returning from the private world of his thoughts, Tom blinked. "It's just after ten. You were tired."

"What about you? Been up long?" She took the mug he had been using when he offered it and sipped the coffee. Its warming effect was secondary to that of the intimacy of sharing.

"Not long. How do you feel?"

She stretched, then blushed. "A little stiff."

"How about a hot shower?"

"Mmm, that sounds good."

"Serena . . ."

"Yes?"

He seemed strangely unsure. "You're free today, aren't you?"

"It's Sunday. The shop's closed."

"No, I mean other things. Can you spend the day with me?"

Looking away, she frowned. "On one condition."

"What's that?"

Her gaze retraced its path to his with deliberateness. "I don't want to rehash that whole thing. Not today." Not after the heavenly night they'd spent in each other's arms.

"Wouldn't it be wise to try to work something out?"

"Not today."

"What good will waiting do?"

Sighing, she closed her eyes and laid her head back against the pillows. "I'm not sure. Put things in perspective? I don't know. It's all bound to hit me when I get back to work tomorrow. I just don't want to rush it."

"You're postponing the inevitable, Serena," he chided, but gently.

"You're right." She grinned, finding strength from some unknown source. "Would you rather take me home now?" The twinkle in her eye was deceptive. Tom saw through it.

"You stay."

"On my terms?"

"On your terms."

"Are you always this agreeable?" she queried in an attempt at lightness. But she hit a raw nerve.

"I'm really not the ogre you try to make me out to be, Serena. I *can* be a nice guy."

Momentarily taken back by the force of his words, she grew sober. "I know that only too well, Tom. And what I'm saying is that I don't want to talk about the ogre today. It's the 'nice guy' I'd like to spend the day with."

As quickly as she'd sparked him she brought a return of pleasure to his morning-fresh features. "The 'nice guy' you've got," he promised, popping a kiss on the tip of her nose before bounding from the bed. "Now, I'd suggest you get yourself into the bathroom while I see to breakfast. Unless," he peered mischievously at her, "you'd rather trade chores."

"No, no. I need the shower." Sitting up, she stopped short, looked around, then down. "Uh . . . Tom?"

"Uh-huh?" Hands on hips, he smiled wickedly.

"I've got one small problem."

"I'll say." The suggestive grin he sent her way spoke of his complete comprehension.

"Well what should I do? I don't really feel like putting that dressy silk thing on again."

Taking pity on her, Tom crossed the room and opened

a closet door, promptly disappearing into an interior Serena hadn't known existed. Leaning forward, she caught sight of shelves and drawers in addition to the standard hanger-laden bar.

"Not bad," she said at Tom's return from the cedar-lined cubicle. "A walk-in closet."

"It holds a world of goodies. Here." Tossing her a large plaid flannel shirt, he continued through to the kitchen. Serena accepted the donation gratefully. Moments later she disappeared into the bathroom.

It was odd, she mused, taking in every detail of the newly refinished room, that the tables seemed to be turned. That first morning, over a month ago, following the more innocent night Tom had spent at her place, he had been the one to make himself very much at home; now she helped herself to towels and shampoo with similar ease. The heat of the shower did wonders for her muscles. The sharp spray drove away the last of the grogginess left by a meager night's sleep. Wrapped tightly in a dark chocolate towel, she stood in delight beneath the overhead heat lamp, combing a semblance of order into her auburn tresses with the gentleness of her slender fingers.

There was a natural beauty about her when she emerged from the bathroom and walked barefoot to the kitchen. Tom was struck instantly.

"Is–is something wrong?" she asked hesitantly.

"Oh, no. Nothing's wrong." His very obvious appreciation underscored that claim. "You look great."

Serena looked self-consciously down at the shirt that fell softly to mid-thigh. She had rolled the sleeves to the elbow and left the collar button undone. As it happened, the second button was sufficiently low to create a decidedly seductive slash from her throat to the swells of her unconfined breasts.

"Maybe I should put the tunic on after all."

"Don't be silly! That's perfect!" In actuality his appreciation was as much for the freckle-studded face, heart-shaped and free of all makeup, with its reckless clusters of auburn waves all about, as it was for the lure of her attire. "Here"—he cleared his throat of its sudden rasp—"have a seat. Brunch is just about ready."

Feeling more confident, she sat before one of the settings he had so carefully placed. "What's on the menu?"

"Nothing exotic—French toast."

"Great! Can I do something to help?"

"No, I'm all set. You just sit and relax. You had a tough workout last night."

Serena propped an elbow on the table, smothered a grimace against her palm and shook her head sheepishly. "That was a cheap shot, but I'll forgive you this once."

Tom's back was to her as he finished at the stove, so she missed his suddenly pensive expression. She did notice that he'd put on a jersey and wondered whether it had been for the sake of warmth or sanity. Either way, she was grateful. The shower had done nothing to purge her of the carnal cravings that his magnificent physique could so quickly stir. It would do well to talk, though. They had both agreed to that.

"I'm sorry I don't have confectionery sugar," he apologized as he put a filled plate before her.

"That's OK. I certainly don't need any. Maple syrup will do just fine." Reaching for the dark brown bottle, she watched Tom settle gracefully opposite her. His eyes studied his own plate.

"It looks prettier with white sprinkles," he commented softly, lost in memories of a favorite childhood meal.

Serena burst into a gay laugh. "You sound so disappointed." Her hand covered his consolingly. "Look at it this way. At *our* age, *neither* of us needs the extra calories.

As it is"—she looked helplessly down—"this is loaded!"
She took a new tack. "Besides, I see enough sugar coating
every day to go without on Sunday."

The smile Tom sent her was devastating. It sent rays of
pleasure echoing through her and left a telltale flush on
her cheeks.

"Your smile threw me," she confessed on impulse.

"What do you mean?"

"That day in the restaurant when I first recognized
you. It was your eyes, their intensity, that seemed so familiar. I knew you from somewhere, but I couldn't place
you. Then, at one point, you smiled at your . . . date."

"She's an editor," he corrected her firmly.

"Whatever." It really was irrelevant at the moment.
"Your smile is unique, you know."

"So I've been told," he drawled. *That* bothered her
more than the thought of the editor she'd seen in person.

"Women must tell you that all the time."

"No. But I have been told so before." He paused. "It's
nicer coming from you." He smiled openly at her.

"Ahh . . . you did it again. There it goes. It's very distracting. But I was positive I'd never seen it before. I
would have remembered if I had."

Tom grew serious. "You mean that I didn't smile brilliantly in triumph on the day your father was sentenced?"
His voice was thick with sarcasm.

Unfortunately, he wasn't far off the mark. She lowered
her eyes. "I meant that you never smiled at all during the
proceedings. I'm sure you took it all very seriously."

"Thank you."

The silence between them was like a knife cutting into
Serena's heart. "Tom, I meant no offense. It was an obser-
vation."

Nodding, he concentrated on eating. She studied his
bent head. His hair was still mussed from sleep, its gray

flecks suddenly more prominent. An odd protectiveness shot through her, making her want to reach out and comb through his hair with soothing fingers.

Needing a diversion, she jumped up. "I think I'll help myself to some coffee. Can I refill your cup?"

"Please." He remained distracted.

By the time she sat down again she felt discouraged. "I don't think this is going to work, Tom." Was bed the only place they could find true compatibility?

"Tell me about *Sweet Serenity*."

She stared in surprise. "I will, if you stop gritting your teeth."

Her pertness brought a merciful softening to his features. "Am I doing that?" he asked more gently.

"Uh-huh."

"OK, no gritting," he vowed, deliberately relaxing his jaw. "Now, tell me. How did *Sweet Serenity* get started?"

Between juice and coffee and French toast smothered in maple syrup, Serena told the simple story. Engrossed in a subject close to her heart, she felt thoroughly comfortable. Her enthusiasm was hard to ignore.

"It sounds as though Minneapolis has developed a taste for sweets."

She grinned. "It took awhile, but I think we've caused a few addictions. The dental association must love us!"

Tom's answering smile was as fresh and bright as any dentist would have wished. "Dentists may be your biggest fans. For all you know there are a slew of them eating Munch-N-Crunch on the sly."

"Munch-N-Crunch? You remembered! You must have been really observant that day." She recalled her own distraction during the time Tom had been in the shop and wasn't sure whether or not to be offended that his mind had been so free to wander. Reluctant to begrudge him anything at the moment, she chose to for-give him that, too.

"Your stock is original. Very easy to remember. Catchy names. Bright packaging. Personal service. I think you've found the formula for success."

Serena blushed under the praise. "I can't take credit for total originality. Most things come to us with those names. As for the rest"—she shrugged—"it's caught on." Then she paused, suddenly wanting to bounce her idea off Tom. "I'm even thinking of expanding."

"Are you?" he exclaimed, genuinely enthusiastic. "That's great!"

Serena nodded. "*I* thought so. Unfortunately, André didn't quite agree. We were discussing it that day in the restaurant, as a matter of fact."

"What does André have to do with your expanding?"

"He's my investment counselor. For the past few years I've handed over as much of my profits as possible for re-investment. *If* I decide to go ahead with a branch of *Sweet Serenity* I'll have to withdraw a good sum of the money that André has placed for me."

"He didn't like the idea?"

"Of expansion? No."

"What exactly did he say?"

"He feels that it's premature. That, with the economy and all, I'd be taking too great a risk." She waited for Tom to rebut André's claim. When he didn't, simply continu-ing to frown deeply, she asked him point blank, "What do you think?"

He seemed to grapple with a dilemma. "I don't really know all the facts, Serena. I haven't seen your books."

"But you do know something about the economy. And I'm sure, what with all the investigative reporting you've done over the years, that you've got some kind of a feel for business. Is it stupid to consider expanding into one of the suburbs?"

"Business has been that good in the downtown store?" He eyed her over his coffee, then sipped pensively.

"It's been better than I ever dreamed. In addition, I've gotten into offering services that I never planned on, precisely *because* there's a need. You'd be amazed at the amount of color-coordinated catering I do."

"What the devil is *that?*" Tom looked at her skeptically.

"*That* is when people come in with dishes, bowls, flowerpots, decanters, soft sculpture, decorative crystal, you name it, and I fill it with goodies that are color-coordinated with the room in which the piece is to sit. Most people come in before parties. Some come in weekly for standard refills." With Tom now lounging back in his chair, apparently amused by her eager sales pitch, Serena ran helplessly on.

"I never expected to get into corporate work, either, but you wouldn't believe the number of businesses that order custom-made chocolate bars with their logo raised on the front."

"You don't do the actual candy-making, do you?" he mocked in horror. "Somehow I can't picture you standing over a bubbling cauldron with a puffy chef's cap on your head."

The improbable image brought a smug grin to Serena's lips. "Not quite. I've never gotten into candy-making. We have a specialist who takes care of orders like that. As a matter of fact, most of our things are shipped fresh from Chicago."

"You go there often?"

"Not as much as I did at first. It took awhile to get orders straight and pick, by trial and error, the distributors whose goods met the standards I set. Things work pretty smoothly now." She grew more alert. "Which brings me back to the question of expansion. What do you think?"

Tom inhaled deeply, then cast a troubled gaze out the window. "What other capital do you have to work with?"

"Other capital?" she echoed him meekly.

"Don't tell me André's got everything?"

"Just about. I mean, I have some money in the bank for emergencies. But I never had cause to stash any under the mattress, if that's what you're asking. I'm a single woman without dependents. I saw no reason not to let André take care of things for me. He came highly recommended."

Tom scowled unexpectedly. "I'm sure."

"What's that supposed to mean?" Did Tom know something she didn't?

"Oh, nothing. I just don't trust the guy."

"I thought you didn't know him. Wasn't last night the first time you two met?" Then she recalled the brief conversation between the two men that had sent her scurrying off to the powder room. "Hmm, he *was* a little offensive there, wasn't he?"

"*You* were more offended than I was." Tom cocked his head and looked closely at her. "Why *did* you get upset like that? Not that I'm sorry, mind you. It was right after that that you asked me to take you away. It seems that André unwittingly did both of us a favor."

Serena wasn't sure enough of the answer to his question even to take a stab. She remembered a feeling of anger, a sense of irritation that André was somehow threatening Tom. Was protectiveness an extension of love? Yet André's caveat had related to the power of the press, its misuse, and subsequent libel actions. Theoretically, given her family's experience, Serena should have sided with André. But she hadn't. Therein lay a poignant message.

"He's not a bad sort." She smiled sadly. "He enjoys a

very fast lifestyle and is perhaps a bit too fastidious, but he's a nice guy."

"Then why is he against your expansion?"

With a shrug she offered her own rationalization. "Perhaps he's reluctant to let go of the money I'd need to start the new shop."

"Come on, Serena. I mean, to be honest, he must have plenty of clients who invest far greater sums of money than you do."

"That's what *I* told him."

"And what did he say?"

She recalled how quickly he had changed the subject. "Oh, he kind of made a clever answer and let the matter drop." Her pout fell far short of the indifference she'd intended. It occurred to her that now Tom was overreacting. Was *his* motive protectiveness? Or was he simply emphasizing her questionable judgment in trusting André so explicitly?

"Hmph!" Tom's grunt and its implied disgust would have bothered her far more had it not been for the telephone—it rang, startling them both. "Who the hell could that be? This phone number is unlisted. They know I don't like to get phone calls on Sundays. . . . Hello!" His voice was gruff as he tilted his chair back, the receiver against his ear. Serena was disturbed even before his gaze shot to her. "Yes. This is Reynolds. . . . André?" His tone grew more even, with the barest edge of ice that could only have been detected in contrast to the heat moment before. "How did you get this number? . . . Ah, I might have suspected. . . . Serena? Yes, she's here. . . . Hold on. I'll see if she can come to the phone." The last was drawled on a facetious note and was paired with a gaze tinged with wry humor.

"Are you available?" he asked loudly, making a mockery of his burial of the receiver against the fabric of his jersey. Without hesitating, Serena was beside him, reaching for the phone. But he held it out of reach, forcing her nearer, relinquishing it only when she passed the gates of his knees and stood imprisoned between the iron bars of his thighs. With his ankles crossed behind her she was locked in. A reflexive hand clutched at his shoulder for balance while an impatient one grabbed the phone.

"André!"

She looked down at Tom, he up at her. "Yes, I'm fine."

"Why on earth did you leave like that?"

"Oh, I don't know, André. The party was big and noisy. I just got tired, I guess." She squirmed, aware that Tom's gaze had left her face to study the flesh between the lapels of the flannel shirt. "You got my message, didn't you?"

"Sure, but I was worried."

"There was no need. I'm a big girl."

As though in response to her conversation Tom brought his hands to her shoulders, measuring their slenderness, then seeking other curves. Serena tightened her own hand on his shoulder, but he refused to get the message.

"What are you doing there?" André asked, obviously tempering his agitation.

"Here?" she gulped. "Ah . . . ah . . . Tom was good enough to . . . take me home."

"To *his* home?"

Normally Serena would have had no trouble parrying André's inquiry. It was very difficult, however, with Tom's nearness, the feel of his fingers now dancing at her throat and working their way steadily downward, and the incipient tingling that weakened her knees so that she was grateful for the support of his. Even now she wondered how she could react so quickly to him.

"I was at your house last night," she mustered an argument. "Today I'm here."

"Serena, I've been trying you all night. You haven't

been home at all. I finally began calling other people until I found someone who saw the two of you leave together. Very cozy."

Serena closed her eyes and swayed toward Tom, who had very deliberately undone the first of the buttons of her shirt and was working on the next, well aware of the debilitating effect he had on her lucidity.

"André"—she sighed in helpless pleasure at Tom's ministration—"is there something in particular you want?"

"I want to know what you're up to."

"That sounds an awful lot like jealousy, André. It doesn't become you. You *know* that there's nothing at all between us." She tried to make her voice as gentle as possible, but it was impossible to hide the shadow of impatience that was caused in large part by Tom's tormenting fingers, wandering now inside her shirt, touching her flesh, creeping along her rib cage to ambush her breasts with devastating accuracy. Arching closer, she moaned a whisper for Tom's ears alone, having the merciful presence of mind to turn the phone away.

"What I really want to do"—André was wrapped up tightly enough in his own world to miss the state of Serena's mind—"is warn you about that fellow."

"Who?" she murmured.

"Reynolds. He's dangerous, Serena. He's a newspaperman."

"I know that." But right now it didn't matter.

"I don't trust him."

"That sounds familiar."

"What?"

"Nothing, André."

"Look, Serena. How about if we meet for lunch. Tomorrow."

Tom had cradled the firmness of a breast in his palm

and lifted it to meet his mouth, which enveloped its rosy nub with a heat and moisture that sent her to the far reaches of agonized desire.

"Tomorrow?" Her voice was a weak tremble. "Ah . . . I can't make it."

"Tuesday?" he prodded, while Tom did some prodding of his own, darting his tongue against her other nipple. Sucking deeply, he extracted a sweet sigh from Serena, who held the phone convulsively against her hip.

"Tom," she whispered frantically. "Stop it! I can't think."

"That's the point." He grinned sadistically. "If you can't think, get him off the phone."

In desperation she returned to André. "How about Wednesday? I'll be able to get away then."

He sighed with distinct annoyance. "If that's the earliest you can make it I'll have to settle for it. Wednesday. One-thirty. The usual place. All right?"

She sucked in her breath as Tom's hands scalded the skin of her hips and thighs. "Fine. See you then." She held her breath, praying that André would settle for the date and hang up. Fortunately for her distracted state, he did. It was only when she heard the click on his end and the subsequent dial tone that she collapsed against Tom and let the receiver fall to the floor.

"How *could* you, Tom?" she cried, burying her face in the thickness of his hair. "That was unfair."

"What's unfair"—he tore his mouth from her breasts long enough to argue—"is the softness of your skin beneath my fingers." The digits in question curved around the supple swell of her bottom, coaxing her even closer. "You're so sweet. . . ." His tongue tasted her, leaving hot spots everywhere it touched. She wound her fingers through his hair and forced his head back to stop the torment, but in moments his kiss fanned a red-hot fire against her lips.

Serena had no thought of protest. Tom's every move pleased her beyond imagination. The pain of desire only served to enhance her satisfaction when it came in the form of each deeper foray. They were engaged in an age-less enterprise, though there was nothing of the game in it now. It was for real. And she loved him. Yet she bit her lip to keep from crying it out. The time for confession had yet to come. There was too much to be understood, about him and herself, before those heart's words would be spoken.

A soulful sigh escaped her lips at the willful roaming of Tom's hands. Her entire body was his to explore and he left no niche neglected. "Tom, Tom," she gasped. "What you do to me." Her head fell back to give him access to the sensitive cord of her neck. He gently pushed aside the soft curls of auburn to nibble at her shoulder blade. Cup-ping his head, Serena pressed him closer, caressing his neck, kissing the crown of his head while his fingers worked hot magic around her navel and across her lower abdomen, down to her thighs and between, intuitively seeking the dark warmth that opened only to him.

Caught once more in the abyss of sensuality, she lost sight of everything except Tom and his body and the driv-ing power of love he inspired. His soft words of pleasure thrilled her in accompaniment to the bold fingers that touched her so tenderly. Crazed with desire, she was barely aware when he shifted her weight to remove the final barriers between them. She knew nothing until sec-onds later when a hand slid behind each of her thighs to part them and raise them, then positioned her correctly. Slowly, slowly, he guided her down, arching himself to her, moving smoothly as she gasped throatily, her cries bearing the resonance of passion.

"Tom." She panted while he grinned his pleasure at her surprise.

"Didn't expect that, did you?" he murmured.

"No! Oh, Tom . . ."

"Tell me what you want, love." He held himself still, but Serena felt his trembling need of her.

"You. I want you."

His breath came hot against her breasts as his hands stroked the length of her legs curved about his hips. "You've got me, Serena. You've got me."

His lips sought hers in an escape from words. His hands moved to guide her hips. With a heat intense from the start, their momentum picked up with astonishing speed, sending them quickly to the star of fulfillment which sparkled brilliantly, blindingly, before sputtering to a bright shadow, then, finally, a memory.

Arms and legs still wrapped tightly around him, Serena let Tom lift her and carry her back to bed, where they lay spent beside each other in silent awe of what had taken place. They dozed, then awoke and spent the afternoon in easy conversation about a wide range of irrelevant topics. It was only when Serena dressed again in her green silk for the return to her apartment that the name of André Phillips came up.

7

You're going to meet André for lunch on Wednesday?"
Tom asked, deep in thought as he absently unlocked her
apartment door, pushed it open and held out her keys.

"I think I'd better."

"He was that annoyed?"

A puzzled frown marred the smooth serenity of her
features. "Strangely, yes. Though I can't for the life of me
understand why." She turned and sank deeply into a chair,
leaving Tom still standing. He closed the door, but remained leaning against its frame, all business.

"Perhaps he was miffed that you left without him.
After all, he *was* your escort."

"No, it couldn't be that. He knows how I feel—and
don't feel—about him. And he was busy enough as host
not to miss me." Her auburn waves bobbed gently. "It
doesn't make sense."

"Perhaps he was miffed that you left with *me*."

Serena met Tom's gaze head-on. "*That* makes sense.
He's very wary of you." She grinned. "He specifically
warned me about you."

Tom's "And rightly he should have!" was growled as
he crossed the room to bend over her. "I have an insatiable appetite for sweets." Their lips met in a tasting kiss.

All too soon he drew back and straightened. "Tell me, Serena, you're a busy lady. Who the devil are you lunching with on Monday and Tuesday?"

It was the image of innocence that looked up at him. "You," she whispered in a half-question to which Tom chuckled a satisfied reply.

"*That* deserves another kiss." He promptly delivered. It, too, ended too soon to appease Serena's own appetite. "Pick you up at the shop at one?"

"I could meet you somewhere if it would be more convenient," she began, only to be soundly chastened.

"Serena, the next thing I know you'll be insisting we go dutch. Forget it. I'm fetching you at *Sweet Serenity* and treating you to lunch." His good-humored fierceness faded to an endearing plea. "Let me be gallant. OK?"

"OK," she whispered, loving him all the more.

Just as Serena had worried it would, Tom's absence allowed for an invasion of unpleasant and remorseful thoughts. The power of his presence had blinded her blissfully, but without him she was unprotected. His company made her a creature of the present. On her own she was a product of her past, a past in which Tom was a very definite demon.

She was as unable to deny her love for him as she was to foresee any future commitment. Even if Tom loved her he'd been badly hurt once in marriage. Serena questioned whether he would be game to try again.

Game. How satisfying it had been to hear him say that he loved her. Her eyes brimmed in the glow of recollection. But it had all been make-believe. She had to remember that.

Then, of course, there were the Strickland ghosts. In her mind Tom would always be the villain of that debacle. She would forever doubt his actions, perhaps even his motivations. And the weekly Sunday evening call she made to her mother was a further complication. How could she ever, *ever* explain a relationship with Tom to that sad-hearted woman?

Riding on the tail of an uncomfortable sixteen-hour stretch of soul-searching, Serena was wary of what she was doing when Tom entered *Sweet Serenity* Monday promptly at one. She looked sharply up from the customer she was helping, sent him a smile that held its share of tension, and tried to ignore the conflicting thrill of excitement that shot through her at the sight of him.

Tom sensed her tension as though he had expected it. He stood waiting patiently, much as he had done that very first afternoon, until the customer had been satisfied and Serena was free.

"Nancy, I'd like you to meet Tom Reynolds. Tom, this is Nancy Wadsworth." Having made the proper introduction she escaped to the back room to claim her purse, assuming that Nancy would keep Tom entertained for the moment.

Her heart beat quickly, working double-time to integrate doubt and delight. Breathing deeply, she looked down at the hands that clutched the soft leather of her bag. What was she doing? Where was she headed?

"Serena?"

Twirling, she looked shamefacedly up at Tom. "I'm—I'm coming."

The sadness in his eyes spoke of his complete understanding of her plight. "Oh, Serena," he sighed, drawing her gently against the strength of his chest. "I knew this would happen as soon as I left you alone. I bet you didn't sleep at all last night."

"I did. Finally. After all, exhaustion has to take over *some*time."

"Ever the witty one, aren't you?" He stroked her hair

for a moment, then held her back to search her face. "You've been agonizing over it all, haven't you?" After a long, regretful pause she nodded. "I'm sorry, Serena. The last thing I want to do is hurt you."

"I'm all right."

The pad of his thumb caressed her cheek, magnetized by the curve of her lips. "You will be. You're a survivor."

"I try." She spoke softly.

He studied her vulnerable expression and breathed in unsteadily. "I should never have taken you home with me Saturday night. It was wrong of me. I knew what would happen. It's only caused you grief."

Serena smiled her love, aware of Tom's own uncertainty. "I wouldn't say that."

But he needed further reassurance. "Should I stay away? Is our seeing each other just stupid?"

"No!" No matter what doubts she had, the thought of not seeing him was excruciating.

"Then"—he grinned half-jokingly—"I ought to keep you with me all the time. Maybe we should marry—"

"No!" She stumbled at his surprise. "You're no more . . . no more ready for that than I am." It was much too soon for any such thought.

He smiled knowingly, ruefully. "Then what *do* you suggest?"

"Lunch?"

Tom acknowledged her coup with a glance of admiration, then captured her chin with his fingers. "First, a kiss." It was warm and moist, reawakening worlds of pleasure with its simplicity. His lips worshiped hers, moving soulfully against, then with, them. She opened herself to his opiate, let his heady nectar chase away those nagging doubts. When Tom finally and reluctantly released her she was his once more. He sensed his triumph and smiled in victory, but it was a victory they shared. Serena happily took the hand he held out to her and they headed for the plaza.

Having passed that initial hurdle, Serena was as relaxed with Tom as she had been on the day before in the never-never land of his cottage. He charmed her to the exclusion of all hesitancy; she held nothing back. Over huge deli sandwiches in a tiny restaurant in Cedar-Riverside, where they were afforded the privacy they sought, she regaled him with tales of the occasional business blunders she'd made, most notably the day an irate wife appeared to complain about the order of passion-fruit-flavored jelly beans that had been inadvertently delivered to her house rather than to that of her husband's mistress.

"It was a simple mix-up in addresses," Serena explained with a guilty grin, "but you can be sure I've been more careful since. The husband, my customer, thought he was being terribly clever. He insisted I write the name of the flavor in bold letters on the package. Unfortunately, his wife didn't appreciate it."

"I should think not," Tom chided gently. "That could be very embarrassing for a fellow."

Serena reacted too quickly to catch the humor in his eyes. "It would serve him right! Any husband who blatantly cheats on his wife deserves to be caught. I'd just rather not be the one who's responsible for spilling the beans—no pun intended."

Tom steered the talk toward something that had evidently been on his mind. "Which reminds me, tell me about the men in your life. I got the impression there were quite a few."

Her laughter was light and generous. "You're thinking of that hostess's comment about having to 'wait in line'?" At his look of surprise, she teased him. "I caught it, all right I may have been distracted that day, but I'm not *totally* thick."

He squirmed in an almost boyish way. "Well?"

"What?"

"Your dates. *Is* there a string of them?"

She lowered her voice. "Jealous?"

"You bet."

"Well, you needn't be."

"Elaborate."

When she feigned distraction and glanced lazily off toward another table Tom reacted with a quick growl. "Serena, tell me about them."

Turning back, she wore a pert smile. "Let me see. First off, there's Greg. He's a lawyer. Kind of like Chocolate Sesame Crunch."

Tom raised both brows speculatively. "Chocolate Sesame Crunch?"

"Uh-huh. Smooth outside, crunchy inside. Pleasant to be with as long as nothing pricks the surface. His inner self is weird."

"That's nice." He smirked.

"Then there's Rod. He teaches psychology at the university." Her hazel eyes hit the ceiling in thought. "He's like gummy bears. Fun and chewy. Too much, though, sticks to the teeth." She looked directly at Tom again. "I'm not wild about gummy bears."

"Thank heaven for that," he muttered under his breath. Serena went on undaunted, thoroughly enjoying her analyses.

"Kenny works at the racquetball club. You may even have met him. I like to compare him to very pretty mint lentils. They're great to pop for quick enjoyment," she informed him in a conspiratorial tone. "Don't look for anything deep in them, though."

"I won't," he drawled, relaxing further. Then he hesitated. "What about me? Have you made a snap comparison?"

Serena stared thoughtfully. "Apricot Brandy Cordials," she announced at last. "Initial judgment, of course. Rich. Sophisticated. With a tang of liquor that can be slightly intoxicating. And sweet. Pleasantly sweet."

"And André? Where does he fit in?"

Though she had never stopped to categorize André before her response was instantaneous. "He's a lo-cal piña colada sucker. He's smooth and cool and tasty. But," she said, seeming almost puzzled, "you get nothing for nothing. He leaves you with a very strange aftertaste."

"You may be right," was all Tom said before changing the subject again, apparently satisfied that his competition was no competition at all. And though the matter of André Phillips and the role he played in Serena's life was on both their minds, Tom didn't refer to it again until the next day, when they caught a quick dinner before he dropped her off for her cooking class. Even then, they spent the bulk of the discussion on other, more agreeable topics.

"You never did tell me about your everyday work, Tom," she said, buoyed by the warmth of the embrace he'd given her in the privacy of the small Mercedes before entering the restaurant.

"You're up to it?"

To her own surprise she felt that she was. "I think so. I have to face the reality of what you do sooner or later. And I *am* curious. You don't seem harried like the stereotypical newspaperman."

"I'm not. I *own* the paper. I may write editorials and set policy, but I pay others to meet the deadlines. I make sure they've got the necessary tools and provide them with overall direction, but as for the everyday sweat, it's theirs."

Something melancholy caught her ear. "Do you miss it?"

"The running around—no. I spent over twelve years running. To be blunt, I'm tired. I want to catch my breath, to think, to begin to enjoy the fruits of my labors, so to speak. I paid my dues in the city room; now I've moved on."

"Up," she corrected gently.

He shrugged, as though it didn't matter. "Whatever. I have to admit"—he eyed her with a hint of regret—"that I do miss the excitement of investigation. That's why I—"

When he broke off at mid-sentence Serena prodded. "You what?"

"I like to supervise what the *Bulletin* reporters are doing." He went quickly on. "It's like putting together a puzzle. You fit the border pieces together first, then move carefully and deliberately in toward the heart."

"You sound as much like a detective as a reporter," she said with a shiver as she studied his engrossing hazel eyes and the sense of commitment etched into his features. "I've always wondered at the similarities. Why, for example," she heard herself blurt out, "did you get the story about my father before the police did?"

As though afraid of losing her, he took her hand and held it firmly. "There are several reasons, Serena. One is political. Traditionally the authorities have been more hesitant in searching out the white-collar criminal, who may very well have contributed to the campaign chest of the favorite son." He sighed. "Another is practical. The police are bound much more stringently by rules regarding what is admissible in court. If they're doubtful whether they have sufficient evidence to prosecute they may drop the whole investigation, even though they're convinced of a subject's guilt. And then, of course, there's the economic reason. Money. Police departments work within very tight budgets. Newspapers can splurge more often." He held her gaze with an intensity that dared her to turn away from him. "If they hit it big, what they gain in prestige or sales more than compensates for the outlay. Besides"—a grin split his features—"the average investigative reporter doesn't charge time and a half for overtime. Let me tell you, there's plenty of *that* involved. Over the years I came to know intimately the insides of many a library, city hall, and records department."

Serena nodded silently. Why was it that, on Tom's tongue, it all sounded so fair and upright? How could he so easily rationalize what often resulted in such pain for others?

Reading her mind, he answered her question softly. "You have to look at the other side, Serena. The victim. Regardless of what the crime is, there is always a victim. In your father's case the victim was a corporation. In other cases the victims are individuals. In every case someone is hurt, either directly or indirectly." When she still seemed skeptical he ventured further.

"How would you feel, Serena, if you were the victim? Supposing, for the sake of argument, that you were ordered to donate $10,000 in cash to the office of a senator or risk losing *Sweet Serenity?*"

"That wouldn't happen."

"It shouldn't, but it could. Schemes like that have been known to take place. If someone threatened to hike your rent so that you couldn't possibly afford to keep the store—unless you made the contribution—how would you feel?"

"Furious!"

"You bet you would. And you'd be justified. Then how would you feel if you went to the police with your story and they refused to do anything? What if they were looking out for their *own* hides? How would you feel then?"

"Furious. Frustrated. Helpless."

"What if *I* then came to you and offered to expose the corruption in my paper. Would you go along with it?"

He'd made his point quite cleverly. It didn't take her long to agree. "Yes, I would."

Tom sensed that he'd given Serena something to consider, but that he'd said enough on that topic for the moment. Not wishing to dwell on it, yet having good reason, he broached the subject of André. "You're meeting Phillips Wednesday?"

She took a breath to relax. "Yes."

"I wish you wouldn't."

She looked at him askance, nervously mooring her hair behind her ear. "Why not?"

"He may still be angry."

"André? No, he'll have calmed down. If I were to walk into the restaurant with you he'd be furious. But by myself I don't threaten him." Tom seemed to contemplate her every word with care. "And anyway, I have to speak to him."

"About the branch store?"

"Yes. If I'm going to go ahead with it I'll need money."

"*Are* you going ahead with it?"

Serena turned the tables, answering a question with a question. "What do you think I should do? You never did give me a definite opinion the other day. We seemed to have gotten sidetracked." The flush that accompanied her shy smile brought the memory vividly back into Tom's mind. Beneath the table his hand slid upward on her thigh. Serena felt the instant pounding of blood through her veins. Her only solace was that, if the smoldering fire of Tom's gaze was any indication, her effect on his senses was no less.

"From my very unbiased standpoint," he drawled facetiously, "I think it sounds like a great idea." He sobered fractionally. "If Phillips gives you any guff about handing over the money, let *me* know."

"You'll tie him to the rack on the front page, is that it?" She grinned, delighted at having received Tom's blessing.

"Something like that," he teased, growing bolder.

"Tom!" she cried softly. "This is a public restaurant." Her hand covered his to prevent further mischief, yet she made no move to push it away. Rather, she savored the intimacy of his touch, and let it compensate for the brief chill brought in on the tails of their discussion. *Would* André still be angry? Would he persist in trying to dissuade her from expanding?

At first her worries seemed to have been for naught. When André came forward to meet her Wednesday afternoon he was as warm and chipper as ever. After greeting her with a kiss on the cheek he launched into a dissertation on the glory of the May sunshine and other such pleasantries. Serena indulged him as long as she could. By the time they were well into their luncheon crêpes, however, she felt compelled to touch base on business.

Paving the way for the matter of *Sweet Serenity* and its expansion, she sought to patch up any old wounds. "You're not still angry with me, are you?"

"Angry? With you? No," he drawled with deceptive calm. "I was never angry. I was just worried. Especially when I found out you'd left with him."

"What have you got against Tom?"

"I don't like your spending time with him."

"Why not?"

"He makes me nervous. I don't trust him. If it were me, I'd steer clear of him."

Serena couldn't stifle a chuckle. "The two of you sound like little boys in an argument. It's like listening to a recording." Puzzled, she frowned. "And I really can't understand it. Why are you both so wary of each other?"

André shrugged innocently. "He's got no reason to distrust me. But *I* know what he is. He's a reporter."

"*Used* to be."

"He snoops into other people's business."

"Now *that* sounds like you have something to hide," she commented lightly.

"Me? Of course not! But reporters have been known to ruin people. They tend to foam at the mouth when they catch sight of what may be a story. It doesn't matter whether their facts are straight—"

"It does!" she exclaimed with a force she hadn't expected. Quickly she softened her tone. "At least, to Tom it does." André gave her no time to ponder the crux of her admission.

"You've known him for a long time, haven't you?" he took her off guard.

"In a way. Yes and no."

"He came from the L.A. area, just like you did. Were you involved with him then?"

"I was a child then, André. I left the West Coast when I was thirteen."

André nodded, taking in her sudden apprehension. "And what is he to you now?"

The pointed nature of his questions had quickly become offensive. "That's between Tom and me. I don't think it's at all relevant to *us*." She paused, trying to bring up the subject of expanding as smoothly as possible. "What *is* relevant to us is whether or not I have the money I need to open a branch of *Sweet Serenity*. According to the statements I've received I should have plenty to cover whatever I'll need to get going."

Serena was more disconcerted by the hardening of André's features than she was by his subsequent retort.

"You're not still thinking about that, are you? I thought we had agreed to forget about it."

"Not at all," she argued. "I've spent a good deal of time thinking about it and I happen to think the time is right."

"The economy is all wrong, Serena. I told you that before."

"The economy may be shaky, but *I* think *Sweet Serenity* can handle it. Regardless of how tight money is, orders are still pouring in. I know that the rent will be high at whatever location I decide on, but I'm convinced that in the long run the store will turn the same kind of profit that the downtown store does."

André was firm, his face set in a mask of civility that belied his inner irritation. "Is Reynolds pushing you into this?"

"Tom has nothing to do with it."

"But he's in favor of it?"

"He agrees with me that it's a good idea. But that's really not the point. *I've* made the decision to go for a second shop. *I* take the responsibility for it."

"Even if it's against my advice?"

Serena was astounded by the vehemence of his warning. She had expected some resistance from him, but not this. "You're my investment counselor, André, not my business manager *or* the chairman of the board. I wish I had your approval; after all, we *are* friends. But it was *my* decision to open *Sweet Serenity* five years ago and it's now my decision to expand."

"It's final then?" he asked, momentarily more sympathetic.

Serena smiled. "Nothing's final until there's a signature on the bottom line. *You're* the one who always tells me that," she teased gently, coaxing him back into a better mood. "I'm going to begin actively looking for locations and figuring out costs from my end. What I'd like is for you to do the same."

"The same?"

"Could you tally up the amount of money I have to work with? My latest statements haven't arrived yet and I have no idea what the dividends will show." When André simply stared silently at her she grew worried. "Is there a problem?"

"No problem." He shrugged too quickly. "When do you want all this?"

"Next week? Same time? Same place?" She tried to make it sound casual in a vain attempt to stem a vague feeling of unease. Mercifully André rose to the occasion, doing one of his characteristic flip-flops, growing instantly charming again. But Serena gave his grave doubts more thought later that afternoon. Much as she tried, she could find no justification for them.

Indeed, she was more determined than ever to go ahead with her plans. The irony of it was that her involvement with Tom, totally aside from the approval he'd given, pushed her on. She had no idea where the relationship was headed, she knew only that the love she felt for him grew by the day. There was still so much to face and work out, though. In that respect, *Sweet Serenity* was her designated diversion. The planning of the new shop would take hours of her time, hours that, should Tom suddenly vanish from her life, would be her key to survival. *Sweet Serenity*, both parent and child-to-be, was her insurance policy for sanity. Through it she had found identity once; if necessary she would cling to it for her life.

"Someone's in love!"

"Excuse me?"

"You heard me, Serena." Cynthia tossed her fire-bright curls back from her cheeks and laughed gaily. "If you could only see your face. You look like a kid caught with her hand in the cookie jar."

Serena's blush approached crimson. "Not quite," she hedged.

"Not quite what? In love? Or caught at it?"

"Not quite either."

"Serena," her friend began as though scolding a child, "you're wearing the evidence, for Pete's sake. It's written all over your face, and you haven't stopped looking around for him since you got here."

"That's not true, Cynthia! He won't be here for at least another hour."

"Ah-hah! So you *are* meeting him here?"

"He's picking me up afterward."

"He's not playing himself?"

"Not tonight. He's got a meeting to attend." Serena bent to lace her sneakers as she recalled Tom's preoccupation when he'd picked her up at work. They had eaten at her apartment before he had dropped her at the racquetball club. His warmth toward her had encouraged her. As always, the doubts that burgeoned with his absence were quickly chased away. But he *had* been distracted; she had sensed something afoot. When she questioned him about it he stilled her with his kiss and the powerful intoxicant of his embrace. She happily pushed aside all worry.

"You *are* in love with him, aren't you?" This time, Cynthia was more serious.

Wrenched abruptly from thoughts of Tom, Serena jerked her head up at her partner, then looked down again to fiddle idly with her laces. She made light of it. "Who knows? Love can blow this way and that. Only time will tell."

Later that evening she feared that time was her enemy. Tom had emerged from his meeting in a shroud of tension that enveloped Serena the instant she set foot in his car.

Their conversation during the short drive to her apartment went no deeper than small talk. He was deeply bothered by something, and much as Serena tried to get at its source she could make no headway.

With the panic of a woman in love she concluded that Tom had greater problems with their relationship than she had anticipated. Perhaps there was something more than his failed marriage that tormented him; perhaps there was still a side of him she didn't know. Yet for the first time in her apartment he made love to her and her fears fell victim to the fierceness of his passion. In his arms she knew him well, understanding him and satisfying him with the same fervor he showed her. For those few thoughtless moments they were in harmony. Soon after it was shattered.

8

I've done some thinking about your plans for *Sweet Serenity*," Tom began as they lay in bed together, her head nestled on his shoulder. "Maybe you ought to wait before opening a second store."

"What?" Serena bobbed up in surprise, but he pressed her back with a determined hand and held her there.

"The branch store. Why don't you wait a few months?"

"What difference would a few months make?"

She felt his shrug beneath her head. "Rents may have leveled off by then, money may be that much freer."

"Do you really believe that, Tom? Do you really think a few months will reflect a turn in the economy?" She offered soft skepticism.

"Never can tell." His nonchalance was more than she could bear, particularly given her doubts of earlier that evening.

"I don't understand," she argued in a hurt whisper. "You were in favor of the idea when we discussed it the other day. Why have you suddenly changed your mind?"

"I haven't changed my mind about expanding per se. I'm simply suggesting that you may want to wait before taking such a large step. It may be premature."

"I can't stand it!" she exploded, overpowering him and sitting up. "Now you sound like André! What is it with you two?" Her gaze narrowed. "Who *was* your meeting with tonight, anyway? You were pretty vague about it before."

Tom stroked her arm slowly. "It was a matter relating to the paper, Serena. I can assure you, I've had no meetings with André. The incident at his party was enough to persuade me to keep him at arm's length. I only wish you would."

"He controls my money, Tom. I can't very well avoid him. And besides, I still don't see what you have against him."

Tom said nothing, simply reached up to twist an auburn wave through his fingers. His eyes—those fire-laden eyes—held an enigmatic blend of gentleness and anger. Serena was totally confused.

"This is absurd!" She finally cried out her frustration. "The two of you seesaw and I'm stuck in the middle sliding first one way, then the other."

"It's not that way. At least, I had hoped that I had the greater weight of emotion on my end."

With a sigh of helplessness at the beseeching look in his eyes she let her arms rest on his chest, then slowly settled down on its solid expanse. She breathed in the musky scent of his skin. "Oh, Tom, you know you do. It's just that, well, *Sweet Serenity* is my passport to security. It means the world to me. Expansion is something I've been considering for a while now. Perhaps I'm worried that if I put off the move I may get cold feet myself."

He held her quietly, ingesting her words, his arm circling her ivory-sheened back. "You're a very stubborn lady," he admitted at last, "but I suppose it's one of the things I like about you. You're committed to this, aren't you?" She nodded, rubbing her cheek against the dark mat of hair just below his throat. "Just promise me one thing?"

"Hmm?"

"If Phillips gives you trouble, let me know?"

Startled, she looked up again, only to be beset with perplexity when her memory dredged up a similar warning that Tom had given her last weekend. It was as though he actually expected André to present a problem, and that was the last thing she anticipated. Wary, and feeling as if she had missed a vital clue, she sought to reassure Tom once more.

"I'm sure there won't be any trouble, Tom. André was hesitant at first, but that was only natural. He expressed the same doubts you just did. But I seem to have convinced him. We're meeting next week to discuss specifics. He'll have the figures with him, plus papers for me to sign. I have to say that he was a gracious loser." She paused and studied Tom's frown for a minute longer before a saucy smile toyed with her lips. Drawing her leg up along the man-roughened length of his she lowered her voice to a whisper. "What about you?"

To her delight the frown evaporated into the late May night as Tom's lips found hers in a final impassioned seal of affection before he reluctantly hauled himself from the bed and dressed. It was amid promises of a weekend together that Serena mustered the strength to let him go, her spirits high in anticipation.

They dined in elegance Friday night following a performance at the Guthrie Theater. For Serena, however, the highlight of the evening was the return to Tom's cottage and a night of bliss spent in his arms. When she impishly told him so he grinned and kissed her before urging her to sleep.

He drove her to *Sweet Serenity* on Saturday morning, then brought in roast beef sandwiches for three at noon, automatically including a noticeably starstruck Monica in the trio, putting her gently at ease. For the first time since opening the shop Serena would have liked to have taken the whole day off to be with Tom. But his acceptance of her obligation and his very evident admiration of her dedication compensated for his absence, temporarily appeasing the addiction she now freely admitted to herself. When he reappeared at six to pick her up she felt the familiar surge of excitement.

Even the brief stop at her apartment for a change of clothes was more than Serena would have wished. She breathed a sigh of relief when the sturdy oak door of the small brick cottage closed behind them, excluding the world and its worries from their utter intimacy. Here she felt free of all care. Here she blossomed as a woman in Tom's hands, letting the love she felt be contained only by fear of confession. For though his behavior and the very way he looked at her bore all the warmth she might have hoped, he spoke no words of love.

In her way, despite the strength of her own emotions and the love she felt for Tom, Serena was grateful. There were still those fleeting gremlins of doubt flickering through her mind at idle, solitary moments. Until the last of these was banished she was no more ready for commitment than was he.

The first part of the week flew by with hardly a moment's breather. Not only was there the routine functioning of *Sweet Serenity* to oversee, but Serena's sights were set on the future. Leaving Nancy to man the store for several hours each day, she made a whirlwind tour of available rental spots in the communities surrounding Minneapolis, communities she had previously targeted for potential branch stores. In the end there were three viable possibilities, any one of which would have pleased her.

Armed with a folder of facts, figures, and statistics, she met André as arranged. It was with mixed emotions that she submitted to his warm hug in the foyer of the restaurant, then let him rest his arm on her shoulder as they walked to their table. Much as the open, and shallow, display of affection bothered her, she felt she was in no position to offend André by making an issue of it. She was grateful enough for his good mood to overlook the indiscretion.

Over the course of the meal they discussed the details of Serena's plans. She produced sheet after sheet of projected expenses, relying on André's friendship more than his occupation, under which such duties did not traditionally fall, to guide her. He listened to her presentation with a positive concentration that encouraged her so much that when, at last, he withdrew a sheaf of papers from his own pocket she readily signed her name to the consent form allowing André to retrieve her money on her behalf without stopping to read carefully through it. When he promptly pocketed the form and leaned forward to excuse himself from the table for a moment she sat back with a decidedly satisfied air.

As the seconds ticked away, however, her satisfaction thinned. It had been too easy; André had been too agreeable. Considering the force of his opposition at the start of their discussion last week, his unquestioning cooperation seemed odd. Or, she asked herself in an attempt to be fair, had Tom merely planted the seeds of doubt in her mind? Perhaps all was well. But where was André?

Rather than abating, her apprehension grew at the sight of him walking confidently toward her. For in contrast to the benign smiles he had bestowed on her earlier, his expression now held the same hardness she had seen last week. Then he had persisted in fighting her intent; what now? It had all been decided; she had given him her instructions to see about withdrawing her capital. Then it suddenly occurred to her that André had not yet shown her the full figures on her accounts. As he sat down she stiffened slightly.

She picked up where they had left off before André had smoothly pocketed the release form. She struggled to keep her voice nonchalant. "Is everything all right?"

There was an insidious tilt to his smile. "Everything is fine," he reported, downing the last of his wine and facing her boldly. She felt instinctively that they were talking about totally different things.

"When will I have access to my money?" she asked, barely concealing her timidity behind a skillfully smooth facade.

"It will be a while."

"A while? Is that days . . . weeks?"

"It's hard to tell, Serena. I'll let you know as soon as I learn anything."

"André, I don't understand. I thought that I would be able to get my funds within days, no *more* than a week."

"Times are tight."

"It's *my* money." She frowned, tempering her growing irritation. "By the way, have you got some figures for me? I haven't seen the tally you were going to make. I'm not even sure exactly how much we're talking about."

He didn't blink. "I'm still working on putting the figures together. I'll get back to you on it." A smile that was intended to pacify her missed its mark entirely.

"You're putting me off, André," she accused softly.

"Of course not, Serena. Everything will be taken care of in due time." He patted her hand as though she were a pet, angering her all the more. "Just be patient."

"But I'm ready to go. There doesn't seem to be a point in delaying, unless you have some other reason . . . ?"

"Patience."

Taking a different approach, Serena withdrew her hand from the tablecloth, tucked it tensely inside the other on her lap and took a deep breath. "André, what's going on? Something is very strange here. You remind me of the salesperson who's full of smiles when a sale is made, and all but cursing you when you bring the item back because it doesn't fit properly. We're friends. I don't quite understand your attitude."

Neither did she understand the glitter of power that his eyes held, nor his seeming indifference to her concern. "Don't push it, Serena," was all he said through a brightly pasted smile.

"André . . ."

"Don't push!" He grew abruptly sober, as though she had, with her gentle prodding, offended his pride and cornered him.

Serena was totally confused. What puzzled her most was the sense of inevitability in what was happening. "André, you *do* have the money I gave you to invest, don't you?" She spoke on impulse as the terror of suspicion entered her mind. Was it possible that something *had* happened to her nest egg, and that he was afraid to tell her for fear of upsetting her? But she was upset enough as it was. Now she wanted the truth. She was stunned into silence by what André had to say.

"I know about you and Reynolds, Serena."

"Wh-what?"

The venal narrowing of his gaze sent a shudder of fear through her. "I went way back to the time you lived in California. You left with quite a bang, didn't you?"

Serena blanched, staring at him with every bit of the disbelief she felt. Forgotten was the lovely atmosphere, the hum of chatter all about them, the many pleasant times they'd shared as friends. She could only focus on his words and their vicious implication.

"What are you talking about, André?"

"Your father." He stared hard. "I know about your past."

She held her breath for the half-minute it took her to recover from the first of the shock. "Yes, well . . . what does that mean? What difference does it make?" Hadn't Tom told her that *she* was the only one to whom that long-ago trauma was meaningful? Evidently he was wrong.

The gleam in André's eye spoke of the pleasure he received from her vulnerability. "I knew there was something odd in the way you looked at him that day." His voice was low, his mind raging in its own direction. "Reynolds was the one who exposed your father. The newspaper files had it all, right there in black and white."

She could only swallow hard and repeat her earlier question. "But what does that mean? I know what's there. But I don't see that it has any relevance to what you and I are talking about. All that happened sixteen years ago. My father paid for what he did. It has nothing to do with my plans for *Sweet Serenity.*"

"I hope it won't have to."

The hollow in her stomach gaped with the lethal calm of his voice. "André!" she cried, exasperated and confused. At his warning glance around, a reminder of the public nature of their surroundings, she dropped her voice to a more cautious pitch. "I can't believe this! I must have missed something somewhere along the line. Why don't you explain it to me?" Her appeal was to the friendship they had shared once, but it fell on ears to which that friendship apparently meant nothing.

He sat forward, smiling for appearance's sake. His tone held neither humor nor sympathy. "All right, Serena, though I had thought you were quicker. Let me spell it out. I can't give you your money now and I won't be pressured. If need be I can easily spread word about your family's history. That might make it more difficult for you to find a landlord willing to rent to you."

Horrified, she could only take one thing at a time. "Wait a minute. Let's backtrack here. You say you *can't give me my money now?* Why not? I thought that every investment you made for me had a clause concerning withdrawals—"

"They may have."

"Then, why . . . ?" With understanding came even greater dismay. "It's gone . . . you've done something with it . . . how *could* you?"

"I've done things I thought would work out. I just need more time. You'll have your money, Serena."

"When? This isn't fair! I need that money if I hope to open—"

"I've already advised you against expansion at the present."

"And I can see why!" Furious, she had to lower her voice again. "How could you do this to me? How could you do it to *any* client?"

The slightest flicker of remorse appeared in André's eyes, then vanished with a return of his rock-hard expression. "I have my own pressures, Serena. It's not easy to support my ex-wives, the children, the house in Kenwood, and my other expenses. I've simply used your money—"

"—only mine?"

"Yours and *others*' money, to make different kinds of investments. They've been slightly more speculative. I'm waiting for them to pay off. Then I can return your money to you." A fine line of sweat just above his lip belied the calm tone of his voice.

"And you honestly think you'll hit it big?"

He tilted his head in a cocky manner. "I don't see why not. It's just taking longer than I had expected. Actually,

I hadn't thought you would want to use that money so soon."

Serena's gaze leveled in anger. "It's theft, André. You know that, don't you?"

"I like to call it borrowing."

"Call it what you will, it's a crime—"

"—about which you will do absolutely nothing!"

"How can you be so sure?" she asked. "Do you know what that money meant to me, André? Even aside from the matter of a second store, it was the bulk of my savings. I'm on my own. I don't have anyone looking out for me. I don't have an inheritance coming to me. That's my future you're playing with, and I don't like it! What I've given you over these past few years may be less than what some of your other clients have, but to me it's a large sum. I can't believe you'd do this to me, André! I can't believe it!"

André seemed indifferent to the hurt in her eyes. "I'm sorry, Serena," he offered impassively. "All I can say is that you *will* get your money. Sooner or later."

She drew herself up stiffly in her chair. "You bet I will!" Though she had no particular plan in mind she knew she had to do something. As the victim of such a cold-blooded scheme she was incensed.

André, however, anticipated her. "Don't do anything, Serena. Remember, I know everything."

Her breath caught and hung in her throat. He did know and the determined set of his features said that he would indeed use anything and everything against her. "You really would hurt me, wouldn't you?" she finally choked out, struggling to think straight.

"Reluctantly, Serena." He reached out to take her hand, but she snatched it away quickly. André was undaunted. "You know how I feel about you—"

"It won't work!" she lashed out. "You can't hurt me with your stories."

"They're not just stories, Serena. You know that. The papers were quite specific about both the charges and the conviction."

"That's history. I have my own life now."

"You're right." He smiled smugly. "You've got that very sweet little shop of yours. Your customers adore you. They think you're the very image of innocence. It would be a shame if they discovered that your father was a convicted felon."

The knot in her stomach had spread, leaving her pale and taut. "You really would try to destroy me, wouldn't you?"

"Only if you force me to. Actually, there's no reason why we can't make an agreement."

"What kind of agreement?"

"It's very simple. You bide your time on the second store until I cash in on my profits. I'll even give you an added bonus. Call it interest."

"That's disgusting! I don't want any of your money, I only want mine."

He shrugged. "I'm sorry."

In that instant Serena made a decision. Where she found the strength she would later wonder, but there was no hesitation in her voice when she called André's bluff. "I'll expose you, André. This isn't fair. I trusted you, gave you practically every extra cent I made on the shop. What you've done is criminal."

"You won't expose me."

She shook her head. "Don't threaten me again. It won't work. You can go ahead and spread any story you want. My family paid years ago for what my father did. I refuse to pay again now. I've worked too hard in the past five years. The reputation of *Sweet Serenity* can stand on its own."

It had been her hope that André would back down under the threat of his own exposure, even offer to retrieve whatever funds he could for her. When he simply reached into his pocket, put before her the same sheet of paper she had signed earlier and leaned complacently back in his chair she froze.

"What's this?"

"Read it."

"It's the paper I just signed. A release for you to withdraw my funds."

"Read it."

Trepidation shot through her as she lowered her eyes to the paper. At once she knew it was different. Whereas the piece of paper she had signed had been set in the standard form of a release, this was a letter. The only thing that was the same was her name, signed in her own hand, at the bottom.

She was overwhelmed with confusion, then disbelief, then fear as her eye moved from line to line, slowly down the page. Blood thundered through her veins, reverberating throughout her body, amplified in her head. When at last she put the letter down and looked up she was dazed.

"I don't believe this," she whispered. All the color had drained from her face. Her hazel eyes were suddenly hollow.

André could as easily have been telling her about his plans for the weekend for all the nonchalance of his declaration. "You'd better believe it, Serena. What you have before you is a letter that implicates you in everything I've done."

Her voice wavered. "It does more than that and you know it."

He smiled. "So you did get the gist."

"It not only proclaims my involvement, but implicates *me* as the mastermind!" Appalled, she looked down again. "But this is false! I never signed anything like this!"

"That's your signature," he said, enjoying his feat.

"Yes, I know. But I didn't put it here . . . on this piece of . . . trash. . . ." Taking the paper, she waved it in the air.

"I'd warn you to be careful, but that's only a copy. I have another safely tucked away." He patted his breast pocket.

Serena was still stunned. "How did you . . . my signature . . ."

"Very simple." He grinned, leaning forward with pride. "The *top* paper, which you signed, was the standard release you thought it was. *Underneath* was the letter you're holding."

"Then this is a carbon . . . ?"

"Can't tell the difference, can you?"

Peering closely, she studied her signature. To her chagrin she couldn't see any difference. It looked exactly like the original. "No one would believe this . . . this nonsense."

"Anyone who knows of your past would believe it in a minute."

"How could you!"

"Now, now." He squeezed her hand. She was too dismayed to move it "Keep your voice down. We've got lots of witnesses. Witnesses to our frequent luncheon dates. Same time. Same place. Witnesses to a hug here, a kiss on the cheek there. For all outward purposes we could be lovers."

"Heaven forbid!" she spat out with the thrust of the horror she felt. "This won't work!"

"Are you going to put it to the test?"

He had very deliberately hit on the crux of the matter. *This* was his bluff; did she dare call it? On the one hand, if his threat held up, she would face the loss of her shop, perhaps worse. On the other, she would simply have to postpone plans for expansion. He might even come through with her money eventually. Otherwise she would have to accept its loss.

Either way, her choice was a poor one. And, in the state of emotional upset to which his well-plotted scheme had reduced her, she couldn't make the decision. Without another word she clutched her bag, rose from her seat, and headed for the door. André, however, caught her hand as she passed and stopped her short. In the same fluid movement he rose to stand beside her. The pressure of his fingers ensnaring hers contrasted sharply with his outward show of control, which in turn masked the venom of his low warning.

"I'd think about it carefully, Serena. You have everything to lose." He bent toward her ear. The faint tug of his arm held her in place. "And I wouldn't go to Reynolds with this, if I were you. He'll blurt your admission all over page one. And, after all"—he straightened—"I have my reputation to consider."

Serena's body felt suddenly chilled. "Tom wouldn't do anything to hurt me."

"For your sake, I hope not. But his business is newspapers, Serena. He gave you a good example of his power back in Los Angeles. I wouldn't trust him, but then, I've told you that before, haven't I?"

His taunting leer revived her anger. "You're a snake, André. A snake. And you *will pay* for this, so help me."

"Don't make threats you can't keep."

In a burst of fury-driven strength Serena tore her hand from his and made for the exit, refusing to look back, holding her body steady, her head high. She was unaware of the beauty of the fine spring day, oblivious of the gay flowers that had materialized by the trees far below in the plaza. She looked nowhere but forward until she reached *Sweet Serenity*; only then did the enormity of André's threat hit her. It was nothing short of blackmail, but, for

the life of her, she didn't know how to fight it. She had
worked so hard to make a success of her life. Now because of a tragic misplacement of trust, she risked losing
it all. She retreated into the back room to consider her
alternatives.

"Another headache, Serena?"

"Oh, Monica!" Serena twirled around to face the
young girl. "Yes, I do have one. It's not too bad, though.
Perhaps you could cover for me up front?"

"Sure. Is there anything I can do?"

"No." Serena shook her head sadly. "I think I'll just
take care of some of these things." Her gaze blindly
skimmed the throng of sacks and cartons. "You go on out
there. I'll be fine."

Monica promptly disappeared, leaving Serena alone
with her fears. It seemed an insurmountable problem.
Could her past really have come to haunt her this way?

Her eyes suddenly filled with tears. Had Tom been
wrong, after all? Was she destined to be forever tormented by what her father had done so long ago? But, no,
Tom had *not* been wrong on those other things. *He* had
been wary of André all along. He had questioned her putting all of her eggs in one basket. *He* had justified his own
actions as a reporter by forcing her to picture the anguish
of victimization. Now it was no picture. It was real. Fact.
And she finally understood the pain of the true innocent,
for it was hers.

"Serena?"

Startled from her fog, she glanced up at Monica.
"Yes?"

"There's a phone call for you—Mr. Reynolds."

Throat choked with anguish, Serena simply shook her
head and waved a hand to indicate that she couldn't talk.
Whatever could she say? One part of her—the part that
was filled with fury—wanted Tom to do just what André

had suggested he *would* do, to splash headlines over page one of the *Bulletin*, decrying a crime in the process. But such a headline would surely incriminate *her*, rather than André. *He* had covered his steps quite nicely.

Monica reappeared through a mist at the door. "He'd like you to call him back when you're free."

Serena nodded, then immediately ruled out that possibility. This was not Tom's battle; it was hers. She could not face the hypocrisy of running to him for help after she had accused him of using his paper for gain. What was the alternative? Could she go to the police? But what if they believed André? What if the police decided that she *had* been the mastermind of the entire scheme? *What if Tom believed it as well?*

It was this last thought that shook her the most. When he called a second, then a third, time she refused to take his calls. Knowing that she'd taken the route of the coward, she also knew that she needed some time to think. She still had the option of going along with André's directive, of remaining silent and simply waiting for her money. But what about her hopes? Her plans? Her dreams of security and self-sufficiency if the money was lost?

She steadied herself, fighting to control rising panic, struggling to contain the headache that throbbed loudly. Time. She needed time. But when Tom stormed into the shop shortly after five she knew that time had run out.

9

"Where is she?" His voice resounded from the front of *Sweet Serenity* to its back, where Serena stood carefully unwrapping a delivery of delicate crystal decanters. Her hands trembled as she placed the one she held back into its box; then she hung her head in defeat. "Serena?" His voice was closer, louder, filled with an anger that was miraculously mixed with concern. "Serena!"

She didn't look up to admire the way his manly frame filled the door or how handsome he looked in his customary blazer and slacks. All that was inscribed on her mind's eye; her own would merely blur the image.

"Serena?"

Had he yelled in anger she might have been able to put him off. But the exquisite tenderness in his tone was her undoing. Covering her face with her hands, she began to cry softly.

"Oh, Serena." He was beside her in an instant, pulling her toward him, into the sanctuary of his embrace. "What is it, Serena? Please tell me." But she couldn't speak, and simply clung to him. And he held her tightly, waiting patiently for her to regain her composure.

"You shouldn't have come," she finally gasped against his shirt, fingering the moisture left by her tears.

"Like hell I shouldn't have! When you refused to take or return my calls I got concerned. And it's a good thing I did!"

"No, you don't understand." Pushing from his grasp, she looked up, unaware that her fingers pressed her eye to still the throbbing just above it.

He took one look at her. "Damn! Come on, we're leaving." He looked around for her bag at the same time that he curved his fingers firmly about her arm.

"I can't leave now, Tom! There's still another hour before closing time!" Her whisper held the ragged remnants of weeping.

Tom's voice was softer, more understanding. His eyes held incredible warmth as he brushed at her tears with his free hand. "Monica can take care of things here. She can close up for once. You've got a headache, and your medicine is at home. Right?"

Through her misery she nodded. "But Monica's never closed up before."

"There's a first time for everything. She'll do fine. If there are any problems she can call me and I'll come back here to help. Now, do you need anything besides this?" He had somehow found her pocketbook in the array of goods surrounding them.

Serena shook her head. "Really, Tom . . ." But she felt worse than ever and broke off her own protest. It seemed that history repeated itself. Such a short time ago Tom had invaded her world, coming to the shop that afternoon, taking her home that evening, caring for her in a way that had sown the seeds of love. Now she understood the fullness of her love, *and* the awesome mess she was in. Somehow a dose of medicine sounded very much like a makeshift solution. Evidently Tom agreed.

"I'll take you home; you can take a pill and lie down.

After an hour or so, when you're feeling better, I want you to tell me what's bothering you." His order was given only after he'd helped her into the Mercedes. By that time she had acclimated herself to the idea of leaving *Sweet Serenity* for the day. Spilling all her problems to Tom was another matter, but one she couldn't contemplate through the incapacitating thud in her head.

By car her apartment was two minutes from the shop. Before she was even able to suggest that Tom leave her and come back another time he had taken her hand and led her inside, guiding her into the elevator and up, opening the door for her and ushering her in. Through it all she kept her eyes downcast, to ward off the pain.

Last time she had staggered alone to her bedroom; this time Tom was by her side the whole way, leaving her only to get her pill and some water, returning to help her undress and get into bed. This time he stayed in her room, keeping guard in the darkness, waiting for her revival. As before, she buried her head against the pillow, dozing as the medicine went to work. When she awoke, however, her hand was in Tom's and he sat close beside her, stroking her hair with infinite tenderness. To her chagrin she started to cry once more.

"You—you should go," she stuttered in muffled misery.

"I'm going nowhere." To emphasize his determination he bodily lifted her and set her against him as he leaned back against the headboard. "Now, cry if you want, but get it out of your system. I want to hear what happened today to upset you like this."

"Oh, Tom, it's such a mess. You don't want to hear . . ."

"Would you rather I rushed out of here and took my fury out on André Phillips?"

Her whisper was weak. "André?"

"Yes, André! I know you had lunch with him today.

And, according to Monica, you were upset from the minute you returned. Now, will you tell me what happened—or do I go to *him?*"

Much as she needed the comfort of his nearness, Serena pushed herself away and sat up. "I'd like to wash my face. I feel terrible." Without waiting for his approval she threw on her robe and fled to the bathroom, emerging after a short time feeling no better for the cold water she had thrown on her burning cheeks. She walked to the refrigerator, where she helped herself to a tumbler of iced water, then looked up to find Tom following her every move.

"Would you like to wash the floor and clean the oven before we get down to this?" he drawled facetiously. "Or do you think we can finally talk?"

Serena escaped past him to the living room. "There's really nothing to say." She hugged her middle with one hand, her chilled glass with the other.

"I can't imagine that anything's happened between us to upset you; you were happy enough last night."

"It's nothing to do with you."

Tom had advanced and now stood tall behind her. "Then it has to do with our friend, the money man. Are you going to tell me what he said when you met with him today?"

"It's not important."

"Like hell it isn't! It was enough to keep you from speaking to me this afternoon. Tell me, Serena!" She simply shook her head and looked down. "Then, I'll call him."

"No!" She whirled around, oblivious of the water sloshing on the rug.

"Then you tell me."

"I can't!" Her voice was higher with each protest.

"Serena . . ."

"No!" she screamed, then again, "No! I can't take any more threats. Don't push me into a corner, Tom! I don't think I can bear it!"

With deliberate calm Tom took the glass of water from her hand and put it safely on the mantel. His fingers cupped her chin and tipped it up until she had no choice but to look at him. What she saw stirred every bit of the love she felt and she trembled anew.

"If there's something wrong, Serena," he spoke slowly, softly, "I want to know."

"It's *my* problem," she began in a whisper, only to be jolted by the quiet vehemence of Tom's correction.

"It's *our* problem. Haven't you learned that yet? It's *our* problem, Serena."

Still her protesting whisper persisted. "I can't run to you with my burdens, Tom. I can't just dump them on you. It's not fair!"

He hesitated for a split second before voicing thoughts that had been held off for too long. "Is it fair that I love you?" he murmured achingly, bringing both hands up to frame her face. "Is it fair that, after everything I did to your family years ago, I expect that you might love me back? Is it fair that I've finally found what I've searched for all these years, only to have it kept away by a ghost from the past?"

Serena couldn't believe the words Tom spoke, but they were reinforced by the gentleness of his touch and the devotion in his eyes. They were words she had wanted so badly to hear; she should have been ecstatic. Why, then, did she feel an overwhelming sense of fear? Was the greatest hurdle still ahead?

Her hazel eyes widened as she stared at him. Her words were choked when she forced herself to speak. "I don't know what to do."

For what seemed an eternity of silent communication

Tom read in her eyes the message of her heart. "Do you love me?" he whispered at last. When she nodded, his hands tightened by her ears. "Then trust me. Please. That's the only way we can see through this. Trust me. Trust me to be able to help you, to do what's right. If you can't do that we have no hope."

"I want to trust you, Tom. You have no idea how much. And I do. It's just that . . . I feel so . . . helpless."

Leading her gently toward the sofa, he sat her down, then knelt before her. "All right, honey. Now, I want you to start from the beginning. It's got to do with Phillips, doesn't it?"

She nodded, then slowly gathered the strength to tell him everything. She held nothing back, counting on the force of his love and the trust she felt to overcome any doubts either of them had. When she had finished relating the course of her meeting with André she hesitated, noting Tom's deep concentration. "You must think I'm a fool for getting into this mess."

Her vulnerability snapped him from his preoccupation. He moved to sit beside her and drew her against him. "I think you're a fool for not having called me the minute you got back to the shop after lunch. What ever possessed you to keep this to yourself?"

Her words were muffled against his chest, but she answered him anyway, suddenly needing for him to know everything. He was right; if there was to be any hope for their love only the complete truth would do.

"I felt ashamed, for one thing."

"Ashamed? Honey, he's a scoundrel. If it wasn't you it would have been someone else. And from what you say, there *are* others whose funds he's used."

"But you warned me. And I didn't listen."

"It was just a hunch on my part then. This is the first piece of concrete evidence we've got against him."

There was a greater meaning to his announcement than Serena was able to assimilate at that moment, so intent was she on telling him all. "But it would have been hypocritical for me to run to you and expect you to publicly expose him after I'd held you at fault all those years for exposing my father like that."

"Serena," he murmured against the warmth of her hair, "I was overzealous way back then. I've never regretted exposing a crime, though I have agonized over my methods. I've mellowed, I suppose. We'll deal with André in a different way."

"You do believe *me* then?"

"What?" He held her back to study her fear. "Did you honestly think I might not?"

"Well, after all, I am the daughter of a convicted felon."

"Serena! When are you going to be able to forget that? I'm in love with you because you're sweet and sincere, innocent and warm, brimming with bundles and bundles of love. I don't give a damn who or what your father may have been. It's you I love! You!" Short of taking her by the arms and shaking her he couldn't have made his point more forcefully. The fire she knew so well was in his eyes. It was the fire of love.

His kiss held the promise of a future filled with that same fire. She returned it eagerly, gaining faith with each caress and hope with each soft-whispered vow of love. All too soon he held her back to look at her. Satisfied that the worst of her torment was behind, he set about working to eliminate the rest.

"I'd like to see the paper André gave you. Have you got it?"

"I certainly do." Without hesitating she retrieved it from her purse and handed it over to Tom.

He studied it closely, turning to catch the light at

different angles. When he looked up, there was taut-held fury in his gaze. "That swine. He thought he could blackmail you with *this*?"

Serena frowned, then brightened at his implication. "You mean it *won't* pass as an original?"

"To the naked and untrained eye, perhaps. To an expert, no way. Unless André produced an original he'd never have a case."

"The original *was* a standard release form. He told me that. And I'd bet that he tore it up and flushed it down the pipes when he went to the men's room. He was in an un-natural rush. But, Tom, the only way we can prove any-thing is if we go to court! I don't want it to come to that!"

Seeing her distress, he took her hand. "It's not going to go that far. André is bluffing; you know that. And, inno-cent that you are, you didn't call him on it and make it stick any more than you called me on my bluff that first day when I really didn't remember who you were." Lean-ing forward, he pressed a gentle kiss to her lips. "I do love you." He smiled, shaking his head at the wonder of it. "And I do want to protect you. Do you know that that was the very first thing I felt that day in the restaurant? There was such hurt in your eyes when you looked at me. I didn't know who you were, only that I somehow wanted to protect you. Little did I know that your fear was of *me!*"

Entranced by his fierce tenderness, Serena wove her fingers through the hair by his temples and brought him forward for another kiss. Her lips were a warm breath of femininity on the male-firm contours of his, speaking of her own adoration with startling aggressiveness. Needing to know of her love, Tom held up his response, forcing from her a most glorious statement, written by her lips, underscored by her tongue, and backed by the way she opened completely to him. With a low moan he yielded to her power, succumbing to the golden glow she cast over him.

"Serena," he groaned, "we've got to stop this. There's so much to figure out." Panting, he sat back. "I could make love to you all night, but that won't do anything to solve this problem with André. Let me think." Knowing his withdrawal to be in her own best interests, Serena moved further back on the sofa and tucked her feet under her. The dilemma with André hadn't eased in the least, yet knowing that Tom would share in the solution brought her great reassurance. She believed in him. She trusted him. Together they would work something out.

Together they did work something out. Or, rather, Tom did, for Serena remained confused, largely in the dark, following his directives without quite understanding the power of the punch line.

She had some doubts when she put through a call to André that evening, claiming that she wanted to talk again, even offering to cook him breakfast the next morning. Made complacent both by the note of fear in her voice and the state of his overblown ego, he accepted her invitation.

She had further doubts when Tom left her for a short time that night, returning under cover of darkness with armloads of recording equipment and one plainclothes detective who quite casually spent the night on the sofa while Tom shared Serena's bed.

She had even greater doubts when, early the next morning, she calmly greeted André at her door, showed a properly civil front to offset his arrogance, and served him eggs Benedict on her good china, for old time's sake. Once again she prodded him on the matter of her money, confronting him with the falsified letter, engaging him in an argument perfectly designed to reveal every last detail of his devious scheme.

Her most grave doubts came, however, when the detective emerged from the bedroom and read André his rights. For an instant she was stirred by the stunned expression on his face, but when a mask of sheer ice replaced it she, too, hardened.

"None of this will stand up in a court of law," André seethed, coldly watching Tom, who had come to stand beside Serena.

It was the detective who answered. "Perhaps not the letter. Any expert will discredit it. Now, as for these tapes, and a star witness . . ." All eyes turned toward Serena; at that moment she was terrified.

Tom, however, recognized her fear. Taking her hand he intertwined his fingers with hers and tucked her elbow through his as he stepped forward. "I don't think Serena will ever get to court." His gaze flicked warmly toward her before moving chillingly back to André. "My guess is that you'll make a plea."

André seemed unfazed. "I have nothing to confess."

"You may sing a different tune before long," Tom continued. "Larceny under false pretenses is one thing. Conspiracy to commit bribery on top of that is quite something else."

Serena wasn't the only one to stare at Tom. André paled. "What are you talking about?" he asked more quietly.

"Ann Carruthers. Edward Grant. I believe they're friends of yours. And I believe your schemes involve them, as well." André's concerned glance shot from Tom to the detective, then back. But Tom hadn't finished. "I know the Attorney General will appreciate your cooperation in bringing those aldermen to trial. If you do turn state's witness I'm sure we can settle this smaller matter quietly."

"*Smaller* matter?" Serena miraculously came to life.

"What about my money, Tom? Have I lost it all? What about the satisfaction of seeing André pay for the agony he put me through? Where's the justice there?"

Turning, Tom put a forefinger against her lips. "Shhh." Then, glancing above her toward the detective, he snapped his head toward the door. Within a minute they were alone. "Listen, Serena, I'd like to go downtown with them. Just to make sure our interests are protected."

"When will you explain all this to me?" she asked, still bewildered and unable to accept that it was, in all probability, over.

"I'll be done later. You go to work. I'll stop by there on my way from the police station."

"Work? How can I think of work today . . . after this?"

"There's *Sweet Serenity*," he reminded her with a teasing smile. "It's your baby."

"But, Tom—"

"Shhh." Again he quieted her. This time, however, he reached for a folder that lay atop the recording equipment. "Here, take this with you. If you get a minute look at it. OK?" Before she was able to examine its contents Tom had kissed her and left.

10

This particular morning Serena's heart was no more in *Sweet Serenity* than her mind was on it. She opened the shop as usual, tending to the early dribble of customers only until Nancy arrived, when she took refuge in the back and opened the folder Tom had given her.

Anticipation of its contents made them no easier to examine. Even after sixteen years the pain of her father's downfall was intense. Yet what lay before her was no rehash of the newspaper clippings that had cut her so sharply once. Rather, Tom had offered his own file, his notes, his comments, his strategy, his raw data, and his personal log for her study.

For the first time Serena looked at the case from the standpoint of a less partial observer. For the first time she saw it through Tom's eyes. And, in the period of time it took her to go over each bit of information he'd gathered, each personal notation that had gone into the presentation of *his* case, she came to the conclusion that what he had maintained from the start of their reacquaintance had been true. She might fault him for overenthusiasm, for making headlines of something that, given other circumstances, might have been buried on page forty-eight, but

he had not been wrong in his indictment any more than
the court had been wrong in its conviction. Her father had
been guilty of embezzlement. For the first time she could
truly accept that.

Closing the file at last, she came to a realization that
had even more relevance to the present. Not only had
Tom's findings been correct, but he had gone about reaching them in a faultless manner. His investigation had been
a painstaking one, much slower and more cautious than
she had previously imagined. His personal jottings revealed his own hesitation to print a word without what
he felt was sufficient corroboration. Through it all came a
very clear sense of conscience. With dawning respect for
his commitment she wiped away the last of her doubts.

Suddenly it became imperative to speak with him. Her
watch read eleven-thirty. The bustle of the lunch hour
was approaching, but she couldn't wait. For everything
that *Sweet Serenity* meant to her, Tom meant more. Leaving Nancy at the helm, she charged from the shop and
took a cab to the police station.

The sergeant on duty was less than sympathetic.
"Look, miss," he cajoled her, "*all* our business is urgent.
Relax. Take it easy. We'll find him for you." With an in-
dolence that made Serena want to scream the officer
picked up the phone and made several calls before directing her down one corridor, up a set of stairs, to the left,
then the right, then straight on ahead.

The miracle was that she found her way without a
hitch. It helped that, on the last straightaway, Tom came
running out to meet her. "What is it, Serena?" he cried in
alarm, his hazel eyes as wide in fright as hers were in
determination. "They said it was urgent. Is something
wrong?"

"Can we talk somewhere?" she gasped, panting from

the exertion of racing to find him. "Some office, a closet—somewhere?"

Relieved to find her neither crying nor in the throes of a monumental headache Tom calmed down a bit. "Here, let's see." One by one he opened doors along the corridor, excusing his intrusion until at last he found a small cubicle with a table, two chairs, and total privacy. "This should do," he declared, following her in and closing the door behind them. "Now, what's this all about? What's happened?" He leaned back against the door, braced for a complication that was never to come.

For Serena faced him, smiled brightly, and rushed to wind her arms about his neck. "I love you. I just wanted to tell you that."

Incredulous, Tom studied the upturned face just inches below his. "What?"

"I love you."

The corners of his lips twitched in delight. "You ran all the way down here to tell me?"

"Yes. I love you."

"Say it again."

"I love you."

"You're sure?"

"Yes. I love you."

His arms grazed her hips as he raised them to lock about her waist. "No more doubts?"

"No."

"Go on." He waited for the chorus.

"I love you."

With a moan, he tightened his embrace, crushing her against him for a moment before lowering his head to kiss her. His lips parted hers; his tongue touched hers. And they both gasped at the shock that sent a burst of fire through them.

"Ahh . . . why here? Why here?" he rasped, trailing his fingers down her spine to the small of her back. His subsequent pressing of her hips to his spoke of his instant arousal.

Serena's eyes held a hint of mischief. "Because I couldn't wait any longer. To tell you that. *And* to find out what's happening. Tell me about André's scheme."

He grinned. "You're a witch. Do you know that?"

She backed away from him and led him to the table, leaning against him when he perched on its edge. Her arms were still around his neck. She had no intention of letting go. "Tell me," she ordered in an urgent whisper.

Tom sighed. "André's theft of your money is only the tip of the iceberg. In the company of Alderpersons Carruthers and Grant the plan was to use municipal funds, supposedly invested in bonds, for reinvestment in the speculative deals he mentioned to you. In exchange for his use of the money André was giving healthy kickbacks to the other two, over and above his own killing."

"But he got nothing, or so he said."

"That was the catch. Had his speculation panned out he would easily have been able to replace not only your money, but the city's, without anyone being the wiser. Unfortunately, he's lost almost everything."

Serena had somehow been prepared for that. Her more immediate concern was elsewhere. "You knew about this before he talked, didn't you?" She eyed him askance.

"Yes, Serena. I did."

"That meeting that upset you so?"

"That was part of it, yes. I guess you want the whole story?"

"Well . . . ?"

"The Mayor contacted me shortly after I arrived in this area. He knew of my reputation as an investigative reporter and asked if I would keep an eye on something. He already suspected what was going on, but he needed evidence. This was one of those situations I mentioned hypothetically, where people in politics were involved and there was a question as to how deep the corruption ran. I was an outsider, a newcomer. It seemed a logical move."

"Have you gotten much?"

"Dribs and drabs. He was shrewd, for the most part. He slipped up when it came to you. He totally underestimated you." Tom smiled. "*He* didn't know about the fire in you."

"But he suspected you." She ignored his bait to rush on.

"I'm afraid my reputation preceded me, even though I retired from most investigative reporting several years ago. He was wary of me based on that reputation, but *our* relationship certainly didn't add to his peace of mind. And my knowing of your business involvement with him did nothing for *my* peace of mind. I feared you'd be put right in the middle and you were. Fortunately it's turned out for the best."

Serena nuzzled the firm skin of his neck. "You know, I was appalled at the insane desire for vengeance I felt before. That was an awakening! You were right about that, too—the sense of being victimized and having no faith that justice will be done. What will happen to André?"

"That's for the judge to decide. He's in the process of confessing everything, at his lawyer's recommendation, no less. The case against him is strong enough that, considering the public furor there will be when it all gets out, he'll be lucky to get away without serving hard time."

"He's ruined. It's a shame."

"It always is."

Their thoughts converged not on André, but on Serena's father. At last they were in agreement and the matter was closed. With its closing, however, came the opening of a new, more immediate, yet far-reaching consideration.

"You'll marry me, won't you?" Tom asked softly.

"Is that what you want?" Her eyes glowed even through her concern.

"More than anything."

"But you've been through this once."

"No. It was totally different then. We were too young. We were totally ill-equipped to understand each other's needs, to fulfill them, and then, when it started to fall apart, to do anything about it."

"You said once that you feared involvement," she reminded him gently, wanting no stone left unturned.

"I was wrong then as you were wrong to let the ghost of the past haunt you, though I'm sure as hell glad it did. Otherwise you would have been long since snatched up before *I* arrived on the scene. I need you, Serena. I want you with me always." As she basked in the aura of his love he paused, waiting. "Well . . . will you . . . ?"

Her acceptance was whispered against his parted lips and was sealed with a kiss that stirred their depths to fan the smoldering fires. At that moment Serena knew that their love would conquer any obstacle that might fall in the path of their happiness. With Tom by her side she would find the strength to convince even her mother of its rightness. Once she was Tom's wife one *Sweet Serenity* would be more than enough to occupy any idle time he might leave her. And, when the time was right, her "new baby" would be a human one, with the promise of hazel eyes, good health and a smile that radiated from ear to ear.

"Let's get out of here," he growled, echoing her sentiments exactly. Totally wrapped up in each other, they headed home.

* * *

Her loose auburn waves brushed against his thigh as she made her way slowly over his body, savoring the taste of his flesh, exploring every last inch.

"Serena . . . Serena!" Reaching down Tom grasped her upper arms and hauled her abruptly along his length until she lay on top of him, eye to eye. "What do you think you're doing?" he asked half in fun, half in frustration. In truth he was driven nearly as wild now by the crush of her full breasts as he'd been by the sweet torment of her lips.

"I've changed my mind," she announced pertly.

"You've *what?*"

"Changed my mind."

Her smile and the sensuous way she slithered over him precluded true alarm. "About what?"

"You. You're no Apricot Brandy Cordial." She touched the tip of her tongue to his lips, then traced their manly line.

"Then what *am* I?" he murmured with the mingling of their breath.

She sighed happily. "A pure chocolate heart. Solid. Rich. Sweet. And endless."

Like our love, she thought, and nibbled some more.

Leo Cole was doing something different. The sound Charlotte heard as she approached was a sporadic clattering, like he was hurling something against metal. She couldn't tell what it was until she rounded the Cole curve and saw the floodlit slope of his roof. Two ladders stood there; near the top, a board stretched between them. Boots on the board, Leo was prying up shingles, tossing one after another into the Dumpster below.

She looked for the dog, didn't see it, walked slowly forward. When she was close enough, she linked her hands behind her and watched for a while. Oh yeah, she had told him that his shingles were lifting. Watching him, though, she guessed he had known it. The way he went at the task spoke of experience. His movements were methodical and sure. From time to time, he grunted with the effort of removing a stubborn piece, but for the most part, he seemed untaxed.

In time, he stopped, pushed a forearm up his brow, hitched the claw tool to the next shingle in line, and reached for a bottle of water. That was when he spotted Charlotte, though if she hadn't been looking closely, she wouldn't have known. He didn't jump, didn't even fully turn, simply looked sideways as he drank. When he was done, he wiped his mouth with the back of his hand.

"Why am I not surprised?" he muttered just loud enough for her to hear, then reached for the claw and continued his work.

She heard derision. But anger? Not really. "You knew about the roof problem."

"Yup. I ordered shingles a month ago."

"Why do you do this at night?"

He was silent. Then, "Why do you want to know?"

"Human interest." She shrugged. "Boredom."

He pried up several more shingles and tossed them back before saying, "Sun's down. Wind's down."

"When do you sleep?"

Another shingle fell. "When I'm tired."

"Studies show that the less sleep you get, the greater your chance of stroke."

"Studies get it backwards," he countered. "Insomnia is caused by stress, which causes high blood pressure, which causes stroke. I'm not stressed."

She might have argued for the sake of argument, if he hadn't made total sense. So maybe he worked all night and slept all day. "You don't have a nine-to-five job?"

He worked on, finally said, "Nope."

"How do you pay for the shingles?"

He glanced down, sounding annoyed. "What's it to you?"

"Nothing. I'm just curious." Looking around, she spotted the toolbox. "If you have another roof ripper, I could help."

He snorted. "Dressed like that?"

"I'm not dressed any different from you." A tank top and shorts. His tank was chopped unevenly at the waist, the shorts as dark and drapey as always.

"You don't have boots."

No, but her sneakers were designed for traction. She turned one to show him the sole. When he simply went at another shingle, she said, "Seriously. I can help."

"You've done this, too?"

"I have."

He worked on for a bit. Then, "Nah. Only one claw." Moving to the right to reach a new spot, he said, "Want to make yourself useful, pick up the shingles that missed the Dumpster."

With the floodlight aimed at the roof, the ground was dark. Only when her eyes adjusted did she see what he meant.

But she didn't move. Climbing a ladder was one thing; groveling around on the ground with her arms and legs exposed was another. "Where's the dog?" she asked.

"In the bushes."

"Will he attack?"

"Not if you pick up the shingles and leave."

Trusting that he could control his dog, she collected an armful of shingles and dropped them in the Dumpster. After a second, then a third, she was done. Brushing off her hands, she called up, "What else can I do?"

"Get away from the Dumpster. Stay there, and you're gonna be hit."

"You wouldn't aim at me."

He barked out what might have been a laugh. "If my aim was perfect, you wouldn't'a had anything to pick up just now."

He had a point. Moving away from the Dumpster, she folded her arms on her chest and watched him work. He must have been trying harder, because every shingle went into the Dumpster, so there was nothing to do. After a bit, she sat.

"You said you'd leave," he charged.

"You said that. Not me." Her curiosity was far from

satisfied, and the dog hadn't appeared. "What's it like being in jail?"

He shot her a look. But he didn't call the dog. "That's a dumb question. It *sucks*." He pried up several more shingles, tossed them down with greater force. One hit the ground, but he didn't seem to notice. "How'd you know I was in jail?"

"People talked about it back then," she said, standing, waiting. As soon as he tossed down the next shingle, she darted in for the one on the ground and tipped it into the Dumpster.

"You were here before?"

"Well, now you've hurt my feelings. I spent seventeen summers here. So I didn't make any impression?"

He stretched to reach higher shingles. "I don't remember much."

"High on Cecily's cures?"

Bracing the claw against the roof, he scowled down at her. "One of the reasons I work at night is because it's quiet. If you're gonna stay here, you have to shut up."

At least he wasn't harping on her leaving. This was progress. "I can shut up."

"Do it. Please." He moved farther right to work on a final swath of shingles. "And you're wrong. I wasn't high all the time. I was angry."

"Seriously," Charlotte mused. That scowl was what she remembered, but she didn't hear anger. "What did Cecily die of?"

He worked for a bit. She guessed he was ignoring her, but she had interviewed reluctant subjects before. She was about to lob up an easier question, when he said, "Pneumonia."

Pneumonia. That surprised Charlotte. Cecily would have known how to treat pneumonia. "I was thinking it had to be cancer."

"It was. She went to the hospital for that. While she was there, she got pneumonia."

Charlotte had heard similar stories, but it suddenly made Leo more human. "That's bad. I'm sorry."

"Not as sorry as I am," he said, grimacing against a stubborn shingle. "I was the one who dragged her to the hospital."

Since Quinnipeague had no hospital, that would have been on the mainland, and what Charlotte heard went beyond regret to guilt. Gently, she asked, "Is that why you hang around here, to keep up her house and garden?"

"Among other reasons."

"Like what?"

He looked down, annoyed again. "Don't you need to be somewhere?"

"Actually, no," though, sitting still, she was feeling a chill, so she unwound the sweatshirt from her waist. "Nicole's in New York. It's just me at the house." She looped the sweatshirt around her shoulders.

"Should you be telling me this?" he asked.

"Why not?"

"I'm dangerous."

"So they say," she remarked, because she was still alive now after, what, four visits?

"You know different?"

She smiled. "I know karate."

The movement of his cheek might have been a smile or a wince, though it was lost when he hung his head. After a minute, he straightened and took another drink of water. Then he climbed down the ladder.

Not trusting him, Charlotte stood. "Another few minutes, and you'll be done," she said, studying the small strip of remaining shingles. "What's next?"

He stood an arm's length away, seeming taller than he had the night before, when she'd passed him on the drive.

"If you've done a roof, you know," he warned. The slightest pat of his thigh caused a rustle in the bushes.

Tar paper was next. But the dog was at his side now, so she put a smile on her face, turned, and sauntered off.

Karate might protect her from the man, but the dog? She didn't know which was more dangerous—or whether either was, certainly a thought there.

Look for these classic romances—now available as
e-books—from beloved bestselling author

BARBARA DELINSKY

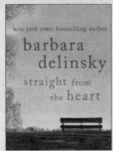

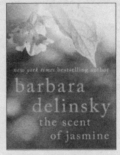

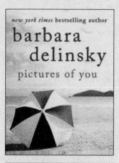

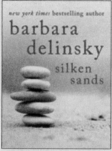

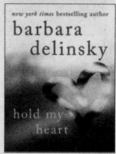

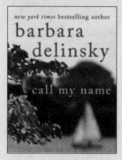

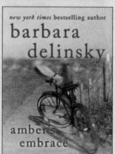

From St. Martin's Press